# THE INFERIORS

*Jessica K. McKendry*

*For my dad, who thought I'd never finish this one, but supported me anyway.*

# PROLOGUE

Raval Tazrin raced through the halls of the royal palace. His black combat boots thudded against the shimmering jade floor as his heart drummed out a similar rhythm in his chest. Raval had always been a fit man, but there weren't many occasions now in which he, one of the most powerful men in the galaxy, had to run.

Yet this was no ordinary occasion.

And he had very little time.

He knocked on the large, silvery doors decorated with jewels and the royal crest. No answer came, so he pounded harder. Sweat drenched his body, and a few curls of his dark brown hair clung to his forehead. Although he hated to admit it, he was afraid.

So horribly afraid.

He didn't dare to think what would become of her if he were too late.

"Your Highness!" Tazrin cried, pounding on the door, gasping for air.

The large doors finally opened, and a guard with green-blue eyes peered through the crack. There seemed to be only darkness behind the man.

"General." The guard bowed his head slightly. "How may I be of service?"

"I demand an audience with the Emperor," Tazrin shot back.

"My Lord has asked not to be disturbed."

"I have urgent news for him. Open the damn doors before I demote you."

Fear crept into the guard's eyes. He hesitated a moment then nodded. "Y-yes, sir. Of course, General." The guard stepped back into the darkness behind him, opening the door for Raval.

The palace guards never put up much resistance. They knew not to question his orders.

Tazrin rushed into the crystal emerald room. He had only been to the Emperor's private chambers twice, and both occasions were before High Prince Savran was coronated. When the old Emperor still held power, weapons from all over the Alliance neatly lined the spacious walls; ancient spears and swords, gold-tipped executioners axes, and helmets of renowned warriors throughout history.

Almost everything had changed now. Some of the old weapons remained, like the gold-tipped axes, but the walls were cluttered, with several expensive landscape paintings and looked overdone. Even the little cracks in the emerald walls had been filled with gold.

A portrait of Emperor Savran's mother, who had been killed seventeen years ago was the largest painting of all. Next to her portrait was an empty space, as if another picture used to hang there but had been torn down. A capped, white stone urn rested on a pedestal beneath the empty space.

The Emperor stood alone in the light of the large window overlooking the Crystal City at the back of the room. Tazrin knelt before him. The Emperor of the Imperial Alliance was twenty-six, a little over half Tazrin's age, merely a child. The slender boy ran his fingers through his shiny black hair then turned to face his guest. Although he was a bit shorter than Tazrin, the coldness in his gray blue eyes demanded respect. His silver and red silk robes fell heavily around him, dragging on the floor.

A few guards stood at attention in the shadows of the room, their eyes resting on the floor. Out of fear or admiration, Tazrin couldn't know.

"My Lord," Tazrin muttered, more out of habit than respect. It had been almost ten years since Tazrin, the appointed regent, turned over the throne to the new Emperor, but he still felt the young man was unfit to rule. Emperor Savran hadn't been in his right mind since his mother was assassinated in a bombing aboard a star cruiser.

The Emperor lifted his gaze to the guard who had let Tazrin in, and made a simple two finger gesture toward the door. The seven royal guards stationed around the room moved along the walls and silently filed out of the room, closing the large door softly behind them.

Finally the Emperor nodded, his gray blue eyes clouded as ever. "General Tazrin, you may rise."

Tazrin stood and took a deep breath. "Have you heard word from the Trials?"

"Yes, Raval, if you must know, I have." The Emperor smirked.

Tazrin fumbled with the silver ring on his left hand. He twisted it gently, the inscription on the inside brushing against his finger, a gesture he always found comforting. "Did you see the list?"

The Emperor's eyes narrowed, his gaze on Tazrin's ring. "Virana won, the rest is irrelevant." He sneered and turned away, facing the giant window overlooking the center of the Crystal City. "You never fail to try my patience, Raval. You enter my private chambers when I ask not to be disturbed, you rudely *demand* my audience...and you wear that *obscenity* in my presence." He laughed mockingly and gestured to the ring. "Is there anything else I can offer you?"

Tazrin started to speak.

The Emperor raised his hand. "I don't answer to you anymore, General."

Tazrin gritted his teeth. "Forgive me," he said darkly.

"Ah?" The Emperor raised an eyebrow.

Tazrin's eyes burned with rage. He could kill him if it came to a physical battle between them, but he held back. There was too much at risk.

"Forgive me, *my lord,*" Tazrin corrected himself as he bowed again. His hand trembled slightly, but he clenched his fist and tried to hide it. During his regency, the boy showed him respect. They had spent time together, talked politics and philosophy. Power destroyed the boy. He had long since stopped caring for anyone else, and he knew nothing of ruling. The Emperor would never understand what Tazrin had sacrificed for the Alliance. What Tazrin had to live with.

The Emperor nodded as he poured himself a short glass of Myrym, the galaxy's finest whiskey, and gulped it down in a single sip. "Now that you've mentioned it," he said in a very soft, unnervingly calm voice, "I do recall seeing the list."

Tazrin swallowed hard. "And...?"

"And what?" the Emperor demanded. Then he grinned. "Oh. Right. I'll take care of it."

"Your father promised me she'd be safe." Tazrin tried to keep his voice steady, but his blood turned cold.

"My father..." The Emperor chuckled softly and shook his head. "My father made many empty promises."

"You know what happens if you don't protect her," Tazrin reminded him. "They'll come back."

"This is why my father was a fool," the Emperor spat. He poured himself another glass of Myrym but only kept it in his hand. "You don't make deals with outlaws."

"If you don't protect her, I will find someone else to do the job," Tazrin replied. "Such as the Prince of Earth."

The Emperor laughed and took a step back. He stretched out his arms as if asking Tazrin to hit him. "You'd trust Prince Melohem to keep her safe?" He lowered his arms and then moved almost playfully closer to Tazrin. Emperor Savran took a sip of Myrym. "You really are a desperate man. You realize how much that man has going against him. He could very easily be... *removed* from the picture." The powerful, intoxicating beverage made his voice raspy.

The Emperor's amused, sly grin unsettled him, but Tazrin held his ground. "Not if I ask my men to protect him."

The Emperor's lip twitched. He gulped down the remaining contents of his glass then forcefully set it down, making tiny cracks appear in the bottom. "Your men answer to me, General. You often forget that you do as well."

"And you forget which one of us has lead them into battle," Tazrin shot back. The moment he spoke, he knew he'd made a mistake. That was his weapon, the one he'd use if it came to it, but that was a scenario neither of them wanted to address.

The Emperor's eyes turned cold and unforgiving. "Your intel brought down the resistance fifteen years ago. Your success is inspiring, I'll give you that, but you're no hero to them. I have given them a legend."

"Your assassin," Tazrin guessed.

The Emperor grinned. "The Shadow Hunter, yes. The men think he's invincible. I'm starting to believe it, myself."

Tazrin took a very cautious, slow breath. "What are your intentions, then?" His voice was low and soft.

"I'll tell you what I would love to do." The Emperor paced slowly toward the wall with the portrait of his mother. "I'd love to order her public execution." He reached the white urn and gently touched the sides, staring at it almost curiously with a deep, enraged fascination. "And I'd love to bring Amara here and make her watch before returning her to prison. What I'd really love is to see her face when the light leaves her child's eyes."

Tazrin was frozen; he couldn't move, rendered powerless by the Emperor's horrific words. He tried to speak, but the words caught in his throat.

The Emperor released the urn and turned to Tazrin. "You should see yourself, General. You look terrible." He sighed and shook his head. "I'll protect her, at least for now, as long as they don't try anything foolish."

Tazrin couldn't help but feel relieved. He took a deep breath, and his muscles started to relax. "How do we protect her from them, then?"

The Emperor took a seat, leaned against the glass table where he had left his cup, and placed his forehead in his hand. "Alert your men in the area to look out for suspicious activity, especially in her district. Pick someone she trusts and screen him. Make sure he keeps an eye on her. Arrange for her to be married."

He nodded, but still felt uneasy. "The law states that marriage can only be recognized when both parties are over eighteen. The rules can be bent, but the algorithm doesn't select anyone underage."

The Emperor shook his head. "We can't wait. By the time she's old enough, they'll have her. Find a way around it. Because if and when they find her, I can't protect her anymore, even if I want to."

"Thank you, my lord." Tazrin bowed graciously, though he felt nothing close to gratitude.

The Emperor sighed and closed his eyes, pinching the bridge of his nose. "Wait until she's seventeen. Not a week later, do you understand? We must tie her down to the City."

It was a generous offer. Young and inexperienced as he might be, the Emperor was smart, and twice as ruthless as his father.

As much as Tazrin hated to admit it, he would not likely receive a better agreement. He headed for the door and opened it.

"General," the Emperor called.

Tazrin halted and faced him.

The Emperor's expression hardened. "Should you fail to keep her contained, I will send the Hunter after her."

Tazrin swallowed hard and nodded. "I understand."

He stepped out of the room, and the royal doors slammed shut behind him.

# CHAPTER ONE

FOUR MONTHS LATER
I stare blankly at the silverscreen, but the words don't make sense. There must have been a mistake. Maybe they have the wrong name.
Maybe this isn't intended for me.
It can't be for me.
Yet as my gaze follows the strokes of each letter, and the letters that form each word, no amount of lying to myself will blind me from the truth.

*Jaina Indera,*
*You have been selected as a genetic match for Sean Maralo, 22 standard years of age. You shall report to building 21147, room 1217 at 8:00 tomorrow*

1

*night for the physical compatibility test. Proceed about
normalities until you receive further instruction.*

I run my fingers through my hair. By the stars, what do
I do? I feel lightheaded and I realize how quickly I'm
breathing. *Genetic match.* I feel sick.

This can't be happening to me.

Not this soon.

Not yet.

Everything comes rushing back to me. I close my
eyes, and I relive it all. We were home, oblivious to
the pain we'd come to endure. I remember when
they called our names. When the eight of us, Dragon,
Liam, Xana, Kavi, Luci, Seth, Avan and I were all selected to represent Virana in the Trials. I feel so vividly
my complete shock when I discovered Dragon was my
long lost Altair.

When we entered the Trials, everything changed.
Everything I'd been taught couldn't have prepared me
for those seemingly eternal days. I will never forget
the first person I killed. The boy with midnight skin
and even darker eyes, I remember the sound. The soft
shush as my blade entered his chest, the splatter of
blood across my face, the warm trickle that flowed
into my hands, the shock on his face, the light leaving
his eyes, how could I forget?

Azad.

As much as I try, I know I will never erase his
memory from my mind. I remember the night we met,

the night he captured me and took me away from my team. How he tried to get me to betray the only family I would ever really have, and how he tortured me with fear. His angry eyes are burned into my memory.

I remember how he returned in the last few days. Xana and I were his prisoners, and any escape attempt was in vain. I remember how he carved his own initials into my skin. I still feel the pain, I feel the fear, I watch in horror as the glimmering blade glides across her throat. Again, I hear a sound. Different this time.

I hear her choking. I see her eyes rolling back as she topples onto the ground.

Then I killed him.

Azad was dead, and we won.

Yes.

I remember it all so clearly.

The last few months are blurry. Each day lasts both a minute and year. Sometimes I wonder what would've happened if I had never entered. If I had listened to Kavi's advice so long ago, how different would things be? Would Xana be alive? The first person I killed? Would any of us be in the Crystal City? What would've become of Dragon?

Dragon. It's been four months on the day since I last saw him.

It feels like a lifetime.

Tears fill my eyes. I'm so confused. For so long, I thought I knew what I wanted. I had it all planned out.

I miss home.

I never used to think of that quiet island as home until now. The word never made sense to me before. I miss the quiet swishing of the palm trees, the way the sand felt between my toes. The innocence of life before the Trials. How did I imagine that a place more perfect could exist?

It's all my fault.

I wanted to enter the Trials. The weeks of competition, the battle of strength and wit that could get people killed, that's what I wanted to be a part of. The Masters encouraged it. They needed us to fight, to be Superior. For what?

For the glorious title?

I'm clenching my teeth so tightly my jaw hurts. I take a deep breath and try to relax.

I don't feel any glory.

I am so afraid.

# CHAPTER TWO

Kavi's face isn't naturally pale, so when her face goes completely white, reality starts to sink in, and the gravity of the situation holds my throat in a death grip. Even in the dim light of the Gava Palace restaurant, her face is ghostly pale.

"*WHAT?*" she shouts.

My body stiffens as I glance around the room, hoping she hasn't attracted anyone's attention. The Gava Palace is dark, with dimly lit, yellowy lights. There aren't many customers yet, which is fine by me. The bar at the front of the restaurant can't fit more than ten people. Afternoon light shines brightly through the small windows, illuminating little specs of dust floating in the air.

"Jaina." Kavi leans over the table, the muscles in her face are tight. "Are you sure?"

I place my elbows on the glass table and rub my eyes. "Of course I'm sure."

Kavi drops her fork into her salad.

"I have a match." The words feel foreign in my mouth.

"In the name of the galaxy..." she mutters. "Who's the guy?"

A soft wind blows into the open windows of the restaurant and a few napkins go flying. Kavi watches a few of them float past before snapping her attention back to me.

"His name is Sean Maralo," I manage feebly. "He's twenty-two."

"But you just turned seventeen yesterday!" Kavi furrows her brow. "I thought they only matched people over eighteen."

"Apparently not."

"Oh, wonderful. *Happy birthday.*" She rolls her eyes and stabs a leaf with her fork. "Have you met him yet? I guess it's not such a bad thing if he's hot."

I shake my head, and grimace. "Ew, Kavi. No. I'm supposed to meet him tonight in some sort of test."

"I've heard about that," she says. "They make people take a bunch of strange compatibility tests to make sure they're a good match."

I feel trapped in my own skin, and I shift in my seat. Her words certainly don't make me feel any better. "What kind of tests?"

"I don't know." She takes a deep breath then smiles a bit and leans in closer. "You know, I'm on this secret dating site. If you don't like the guy you could always sign up."

I pull back, and can't help feeling a bit shocked. "Isn't that illegal? You should seriously think about deleting your account." I keep my voice down.

She nods quickly. "It's illegal, but everyone uses it."

"Thank you, but I think I'll be fine."

She looks down at her salad as if it suddenly spoiled. "I'm sorry."

"Don't be," I breathe. "This day has to come for all of us. It just happened early for me."

A glimmer of pain appears in her sparkly brown eyes, like a sliver of wood. "Don't pretend like I've forgotten."

"Forgotten what?" I shoot back.

She shifts uncomfortably in her chair then leans in toward me. "Jaina, I know you still have feelings for Dragon, okay?"

"I'm over him, Kavi." The words hurt but not more than admitting to the truth–I'm afraid I'll never be over him. "I've told you. In the Trials, yes, I had feelings for him, but now...it doesn't matter."

"You have to stop saying that. Lying to yourself won't make things better. I know–" she cuts herself off as an Alliance Guard in black and red armor walks by.

The guard nods at us. "Good day, ladies."

"And you," she replies kindly.

He smiles at us and passes on.

Kavi's grin fades, and she rolls her eyes.

"I'm not lying to myself," I whisper, "but there's nothing I can do. I can't refuse."

"I know." She shakes her head and takes a disinterested bite of her food. "It just isn't fair."

"No one ever said it would be." I feel my body wilt back into the chair and I gaze out the window.

"Did you tell Dragon yet?"

My eyes involuntarily meet hers. "Um…"

She raises an eyebrow. "You're going to tell him, aren't you? I mean you *love* him. He should know."

"Stop. I do not love him," I reply darkly.

"You're such a horrible liar. I can see right through you."

I pick at my dark purple half-polished nails to avoid looking at her, slowly chipping off the color. "Kavi, I couldn't."

"You *could*," she snaps back. "You're just choosing not to."

A horrible thought creeps into my mind. "What if…" I take a deep breath. "What if he doesn't care anymore?"

"Now, don't start that–"

"I haven't seen him since we got here, and not caring would be better for him anyway."

Her face is shadowed with defeat, and she lowers her eyes to the table. "He misses you."

My chest tightens.

"He asks about you."

My mouth opens in slight surprise. "And you tell me this *now?*"

She doesn't meet my eyes, and turns a bit red. "I thought it would only make you sad."

"Why the *shaav* hasn't he contacted me? Why hasn't he even tried?" I ask angrily. I feel so childish asking, but I can't help it.

Kavi sighs. "The job the Alliance chose for him is… demanding."

"What does he do?"

She shrugs. "I don't know. It's confidential."

"Will you tell him for me?" I murmur.

"Come on, Jaina, why can't you just–"

"Because it hurts." Thinking of him only brings me pain. The aching need for his presence burns within me, and the pain grows worse knowing that I *shouldn't* be wishing for him. "It hurts too much, Kavi."

Her face tenses. "Alright. Fine. I'll tell him."

The weight on my shoulders seems to lessen slightly, but I'm not sure if it makes me feel better or worse.

By the stars, I miss his voice. "I have to get back to work."

"Are you going to be okay?"

"Maybe." Not really.

"I'm worried about you. Do you want me to send Liam over? I'm sure he wouldn't mind taking care of you for a few days. Besides, he lives near you, doesn't he?"

Of all of my teammates, Liam was the only one chosen to live near me. In the apartment complex right across from mine. "He's different, now," I whisper. "He hasn't been the same since..."

Kavi swallows hard.

A deep-pitted empty feeling buries itself into my stomach.

The pictures of that night bubble near the surface of my mind, but I push them away before they take their poisonous effect.

Kavi stares down at the table, yet her eyes look past it, like it's not even there. "He's still trying to get over it."

"We all are."

She pushes her salad away from her, and toward me. "He needs your help, and you need his."

"I'll be fine," I insist.

Kavi shakes her head slightly, and I see the disappointment in her eyes. "I'll see you here next week?"

"Count on it."

The walk from lunch to my workplace isn't far, and work in the City is mechanical. When we first arrived, it took a while to get used to. The caste system in the City is based on the time we've lived here and the efficiency in which we complete our given assignments. All the newcomers are stuck with the jobs at the bottom. And until I've lived here for a year, or proven to be above the menial tasks of "the bottom," here at the bottom is where I'll remain.

The work we're assigned seems random. Some days I'm working at a bakery; others I'm a secretary. All in all, we get around to doing everything in our community.

This week, I'm a secretary.

I hate my secretary job.

When I reach the office, I take the stairs instead of the lift to the twenty-second floor. It's so easy to get out of shape here since there's really no need to stay fit. I open the door and walk into the cold air-conditioned space. The change from the outdoor weather makes me shiver. I should've brought a jacket.

Between the walls and the purplish-gray, shiny silk carpet, the floor shows through to be Tarnoshian marble, the most expensive marble in the galaxy, which happens to be used in many buildings on Virana. By the stars, it reminds me of home.

Someone taps me on the shoulder. "Jaina, where were you?" Mavanie whispers in her accent.

"Lunch," I reply.

"The boss was upset that you weren't here," she breathes. "Hurry, you must act like you've been working. He left for coffee twenty minutes ago. Pretend you've been here."

Mechanically, I take a seat at my desk and she sits beside me at her computer. I turn on my computer, log on to the system and start organizing files. The job requires very little.

"Ms. Indera!" calls a soft, sickly voice.

I look up to see my boss. He's some sort of alien with gray, pasty skin and tiny bumps all over. I'm not sure if it's from a disease or if that's how he's supposed to look, but he always has some cough that he can't get rid of. He has four thick fingers on each hand, but his thumb sticks out of his wrist and bends inward, like they were built for climbing trees. It's bad enough that he's always trying to get some alien girl to sleep with him, but I'll say the worst part is his halo of eyes. Not just in the back, all around.

Did I mention he absolutely hates me? I don't blame him; I'm always late for work.

My stomach lurches and I feel like I might be sick. He's the last person I want to see today. "Yes, sir?" I ask.

"When did you decide to show up?"

"I got here twenty minutes ago," I reply carefully. "The waiter was giving me trouble at lunch…"

His face contorts into a disgusting, shriveled up raisin.

"Mavanie," he snaps.

Her bright silvery eyes flicker up to him. "Sir?"

"When did Ms. Indera arrive here?" He asks.

Her gaze finds the ceiling, and her dark purple lips tighten. "Twenty minutes ago?"

He glares at me menacingly and growls, "Don't be late, next time." With that, he stalks off.

Mavanie shoots me a glare and shakes her head. "That was close."

"Tell me about it," I murmur.

She continues to look at me, more kindly now, and I try to ignore her. But in the end, she wins over.

"What?" I ask, finally turning to her.

I've only known her for the past four months, but I've already learned how to read her. Her bright red skin glimmers beautifully under the light. The three sharp horns circling her head make up for her lack of hair.

Mavanie sighs. "Tell me what's wrong."

"Fate," I whisper.

She tilts her head, arching her eyebrows.

I sigh and I bite my lip. "I have a match."

Her face doesn't change much. I can't tell if my news upsets her or if she's happy for me.

"How is that possible?" She asks. "Aren't you seventeen?"

"I am. I don't know. I have no idea how it works, but they found me a match."

Mavanie taps her fingers on her desk. "Don't be afraid. It's a simple process, and it's nothing to worry about. Did you meet him?"

I shake my head. "I will tonight."

She nods. "My friend had to take tests with her match to make sure they were right for each other. Everything turned out fine."

My hands are sweating and my stomach churns just thinking about it. "What kind of tests?"

"You go to the room you're assigned and they have it all set up. For her, they just had to talk together then save each other."

"Save each other?"

She nods. "The doctors felt they would best stay connected if they experienced something terrifying together."

"What happens if you fail?"

Mavanie stares down at her desk. Her face hardens slightly, and she furrows her brow. "I don't know. I've never met anyone who has failed."

I feel sicker than before. What do they do with people who fail? "How many tests are there?"

She leans back in her chair and returns her gaze to me, her lips pursed and her eyes partially squinted. "It depends. They will continue tests until they are sure about your match."

"Do you love him?"

She shrugs, smiling a bit. "Most of the time. Sometimes he's a *katiaj*, but he's a good man."

"Mrs. Delarees!" calls the boss.

Mavanie looks up at him. "Yes, sir?"

"Let Ms. Indera get back to work!" He sneers.

Mavanie rolls her eyes and does as she's told. I pretend to do the same, but I can't focus. Not at all.

"Don't worry, Jaina," she whispers. "It'll be okay."

By the stars, if only I could make myself believe her.

# CHAPTER THREE

Tall, circular, gray, and shiny, Building 21147 is completely uninviting from the outside. Dozens of numbered doors, some open, some closed, are spaced evenly around the building. It doesn't take long to find door 1217.

I take a deep breath and walk into a white room with black marble floors. The door closes behind me, and my throat constricts. I start to panic, but when my eyes adjust to the darkness I realize it's not pitch black. The lights are very dim, but I can see. To my left and right, the walls are made of glass tinted slightly greenish blue. Identical rooms seem to extend along the entire inner wall of the building connected by the blue-green glass.

A woman sits behind a desk with a privcom–private communicator– flashing blue in her ear. I approach her desk. Her bright yellowy eyes flicker up to me. She tosses her shiny orange hair over her shoulders and takes the end of the pen she was chewing on out of her mouth.

"*Namenja*," she says. Her voice comes out surprisingly accented. She must be a native Cora speaker.

"*Namenja*," I reply shakily. "Hello."

She smirks a little. "*Cora val dorvasé byvet?*"

I'm a little stunned by her sudden sentence, and I quickly try to translate in my head, probably looking like an idiot. *Cora val...*Cora your...*dorvasé...*native land...*byvet...*tongue? Cora your native land tongue?

I shake my head. "No," I say gently. "I started learning Cora, but it's not my first language."

"Ah." She nods and looks down at her desk. "Fingerprint please." She takes out a small, flat square, and places it on top of the desk.

I press my finger to it and a light comes on green.

"Jaina Indera?"

"Yes."

She taps the privcom in her ear. "Escort for Jaina Indera."

My palms sweat, yet I feel cold. I close my eyes and try to stay calm. *It's going to be okay.*

A gentle whooshing sound makes my eyes open, and a man in a white coat enters the room from a door to the right of the woman's desk. He has black hair and dark eyes, and his cheekbones are a little too low for his high but not well-defined jawline. He's short, too, probably as short as Avan was when I last saw him.

"This way, Miss Indera," he says without a hint of emotion in his voice.

I trail behind him like I'm on autopilot. My actions are blurred, everything moves fast and slow simultaneously. Too slow, I want this to be over. Too fast, I'm not ready. We're in a long corridor. The man in the white coat snatches a clipboard from a shelf. He glances back at me. "I'm Doctor Roman-Fritz. If you don't know anyone who has been chosen for this, it'll be completely painless."

The corridor opens up into another small room with black obsidian walls and floors. It's dark except for a purplish light that shines down from the center of the cube shaped room. Another glass wall divides the room and the other side has a white ceiling and white floor. An examination table of sorts sits along the back wall of the white room, but Dr. Roman-Fritz stops walking.

"Alright, Miss Indera. I just need you to undress," he says mechanically.

I'm frozen in place, and I'm not sure how to react. "I'm-I'm sorry?"

Dr. Roman-Fritz looks at me without any sort of expression on his face. He's like some sort of statue, chiseled with his placid, almost robotic expression, incapable of expressing any other emotion. "I need you to remove all of your clothing," he says in the same tone, just a bit slower.

My cheeks turn red, and I look down at the floor. "Right here?"

"Yes."

I want to protest, but I it's better to get this over with as fast as I can. Besides, he's a doctor. Quickly, and without taking my gaze off the floor, I undress until I'm completely naked. I pick up my clothes off the floor and hand them to him, along with my shoes. The air is cold, and the unfriendly black obsidian floors are even colder on my bare feet. I cross my arms over my chest. It's the only place I can cover without making it obvious that I'm uncomfortable.

Dr. Roman-Fritz makes his way through a small glass door that leads to the other side of the room and places my small pile of clothes onto the examination table. When he returns, he gently taps a glowing green touch sensor on the wall.

"Now, Jaina, I just need you to spread your arms and take in a nice deep breath."

Standing alone at the center of the room, I shiver. My toes start to turn purple at the tips. The hairs on my legs that I forgot to shave this morning stand on end, and tiny mountain ranges of goosebumps rise up all over my skin. I spread my arms out as he instructed, palms open, and take a deep breath.

A thin, green, laser-like light scans me slowly from bottom to top. As the light rises up my legs, my skin becomes more translucent than it already is, every muscle, every vein suddenly visible. The urge to run nearly overcomes me, and I force myself to close my eyes. After a few more moments, the light warms my cheeks, and I see it through my eyelids.

"You're all done," Dr. Roman-Fritz says gently.

I open my eyes and look down. My skin has returned to it's natural, less-translucent state.

"What was that?" I ask.

Dr. Roman-Fritz motions for me to follow, leads me through the glass door, and gestures to the examination table. "You can put your clothes back on. The scan was to test your blood, check for any diseases, your fertility and such."

I dress as quickly as possible. "How does everything look?"

"You are completely healthy." He hesitates. "Yet the likelihood of you being able to conceive a child is nearly impossible."

For some unknown reason, my hands quiver. I step back and lean against the examination table for support. "Why...?" My voice comes out soft and weak, like a scared child.

The doctor shakes his head. "Sometimes it just isn't meant to be."

I don't know why I'm trembling. I don't know why this all sounds like some inconceivable horror, why hearing those words is so…sad. I don't want kids, not with this man to be my husband. It shouldn't matter at all.

But for some reason, it still hurts.

I stand up straighter, feeling the slightest bit hopeful *and* the slightest bit afraid. "What does this mean? What will happen to me now?"

Dr. Roman-Fritz keeps his placid steady gaze on me. "Well, nothing. Nothing different than what would have happened. You are still to be married if everything works out."

"Am I going to meet him now?"

He nods. "Yes. Come this way."

After walking through a corridor too short to give me time to think, I find myself in a small, comfortable room. I'm not sure if I can even call it that–it's more of a hallway trapped between two doors with a mirror along one wall.

"Wait here." Dr. Roman-Fritz walks through the door at the other end of the hallway-like room after scanning his fingerprint along a small screen next to the door.

It's just the two of us now, just me and my reflection. I'd rather be alone. I know how I look; I don't need reminding of my imperfection.

My hands are still trembling. I am infertile. I should be alright with that, since I don't want children with this unknown man, but I'm not.

By the stars, was this why I wanted to come to the Crystal City? Was it just a self-confidence issue? If the

Crystal City is perfect, then everyone living here is perfect, too. And if I live here, then logically, I'm perfect as well.

We're all pressured to get here, but it was *my* choice...

I run my fingers through my hair, trying to straighten it as much as I can.

*Shaav.* What am I doing? Am I trying to look nicer? It'd be better if Sean Maralo didn't like me much anyway. Our feelings would be mutual, and I wouldn't feel so badly about resenting him.

But for some reason, I do care. Maybe it's because I'm a girl. I try to be tough, try to pretend I don't care about being beautiful or lovable. But maybe deep down, I'm just weak, sensitive, and insecure. I'd never admit that, not to anyone, but in my heart, I know it's probably true.

I'm not beautiful, not pretty or cute either. My eyes are darker than usual, so brown they're almost black, engulfed in the slightly purplish sinkholes of my eye sockets. My lips are just barely pink and my long brown hair isn't straight, but it's not really curly either, like it can't make up its mind.

The white door at the front of the room opens, and Dr. Roman-Fritz gestures me forward. I follow him through the door to find a man standing before me, staring at me, studying me, the way I'm facing him, studying him.

He's tall and built, more so than Dragon. He has close-cropped, stark blond hair, and steady brown eyes. His face is smooth and untroubled, like all is right in the world. His expression is so controlled, so serene and content that for a moment, I almost feel that way myself. He's...stunning.

"Ms. Indera...?" he asks in a deep, kind voice.

My mouth doesn't move. Well, it does, but no sound comes out.

Dr. Roman-Fritz stands to my left and clears his throat. "Jaina Indera, this is Sean Maralo. Sean Maralo, Jaina Indera."

"It's-It's a great pleasure to met you, Jaina," Sean says.

A door behind Sean opens and another man in a white doctor's coat enters the room. The room is rather small with doors on either end, but it's larger than the tiny, hallway-like excuse for a room that I waited in.

"Dr. Roman-Fritz," the second doctor says, his voice harsh and irritated. "You cannot expect this to go through." He turns to Sean. "Mr. Maralo, she is infertile."

The words spark a tiny little flame inside me.

Sean looks at me, his gentle expression hardening a bit. "But she is my match..."

The unnamed doctor glares at Dr. Roman-Fritz and me. "Yes, but I'm sure the IA would gladly make an exception. The point of all this is to create the best chance for your offspring, and this woman, if you can even call her that, cannot guarantee any children at all."

The urge to slap the *shaav* out of this man is nearly overwhelming. "How can you say that about me?" I lash out. "What the *shaav* is your problem, show some *shaavez* respect. How are you allowed to be a doctor?"

Dr. Roman-Fritz raises a hand, his face serene as ever. He doesn't look my way, and keeps his gaze on the other doctor as if I hadn't snapped. "The odds of her being able to conceive are highly unlikely, however it is not entirely impossible, Dr. Harrison. Miracles do happen."

Dr. Harrison scoffs. "Always the optimist." He turns to Sean. "I would strongly advise that we find you another close match if we can."

Sean studies me carefully. "What will happen to her if..." His voice is pleading, kind, and sweet.

"She is not needed. And that is that."

"What if I want to try to make things work?" Sean asks. "As her doctor said, miracles do happen."

Dr. Harrison shakes his head quickly. "Not like this. Not with these odds." He types on his silverscreen in his hand, but then he suddenly stops, and his face goes white. He clears his throat. "Dr. Roman-Fritz," he says, his voice completely different now, almost trembling with...fear? "Come with me. Can we talk?"

The two doctors head out the door I came from and whisper inaudibly.

"I'm-I'm sorry," I say, feeling more than a bit hurt and rather stunned. Tears well in my eyes, but I force them away. *Show no weakness.*

"For what? You did nothing wrong." He blinks those handsome, golden-hazel eyes.

"I just can't believe I'm..." I feel dizzy. This isn't fair. It's not right. "What will they–"

Sean takes my hand. His touch is surprising, gentle, light, and friendly. His hands are soft, his grip tender, so unlike Dragon's rough, worn hands. "Nothing bad will happen to you. I'm sorry about all this, and I apologize for the rudeness of my doctor. Try not to listen to the things he said, please."

My hand trembles within his and I squeeze it. He squeezes back reassuringly, and I feel a little better.

The doctors return and I release Sean's hand. Their faces are both much whiter than before. Dr. Harrison's hands tremble, and my fear and anxiety return. They're afraid.

"I think," Dr. Harrison says, his voice quivering, "it's best for you two to try and work things out."

"Wait, but just a minute ago..." Sean's voice trails off.

"I know what I said," Dr. Harrison snaps. "I changed my mind. It would be...best for us *all* this way."

A chill runs through me and I can't help wondering what he fears enough to reevaluate his decision. I want to ask, but my own uncertainty about all of this makes the words stick in my throat.

"So now what?" I ask instead.

"Now," Dr. Roman-Fritz says, "you kiss."

I feel Sean looking at me and my face burns.

"Right now?" Sean asks.

The doctors nod.

"In front of you?" I ask.

"We need to evaluate how fit you are for each other," Dr. Harrison says.

I glance up at Sean and feel hot all over. This is so unnatural.

He takes an awkward step forward, and I suppress the urge to step back. My hands are trembling and my heart is pounding against my chest. I'm not afraid, but I have never been more uncomfortable in my life.

Sean gently places his hands on my shoulders and clears his throat. "You okay?" he asks, never breaking eye contact.

I nod and take a deep breath. I've never kissed anyone but Dragon.

I can't do this.

Sean leans into me, and I return the gesture. I close my eyes, and his nose brushes against mine. His warm arms embrace me, and I finally feel the soft, gentle pressure of his lips against mine. Shivers run through me but not the cold kind. I feel warm, refreshed. Safe.

What a strange feeling.

His lips are softer than Dragon's.

Dragon.

Altair.

My love.

I feel *his* lips. Dragon's hand gliding across my cheek. His warm breath, his strong, rough, powerful hands.

I open my eyes and pull away from Sean.

"How was that?" I ask coldly.

"You are both free to go. Return in three days for a final evaluation," Dr. Roman-Fritz says.

Turning my back on Sean, I storm out of the room and leave the building as fast as possible.

The fresh air engulfs me when I step outside, but I can't stop panting. Dizziness takes over, and I feel like I can't get enough air into my lungs. I breathe faster and faster until my throat is dry, until I start to feel sick. By the stars, I can't.

This is too much.

How can anyone put him or herself through this? How can anyone live like this?

Fury and rage course through my blood. The fear, the complete hopelessness... How can I do this and live with myself? I need to get home.

My lips feel dirty. Tainted. Impure. I kissed another man, someone I just met, someone I'm supposed to marry.

"Jaina!"

I turn around. Sean's following not too far behind me, but I keep walking. This is the last thing I need right now.

"Jaina, wait!"

I don't want to talk to this man. I don't even want to see him. We'll have plenty of time to get to know each other while we're married. Why can't it *shaavez* wait until then?

But I stop and stand there, my back toward him. He's panting a little behind me, and I whirl around, my arms crossed. My body tenses.

"What do you want?" I snap.

He jerks back. "I just...I wanted to say it was nice to meet you." The sad, pleading look on his face takes me by surprise.

"Save it. See you in three days." I turn and start to walk away.

A couple steps later, there's an intense pressure on my arm, and I gasp, whipping my whole body around. I see his hand on my forearm, his shy eyes flickering from my face to the ground as he lets go. "Sorry," he mutters. "I'm sorry." He sighs. "Can we talk?"

The muscles in my face tighten. "What the hell do you possibly have to say to me? We're spending the rest of eternity together. Why can't it wait until then?"

"I'm sorry."

"You already said that."

"No," he says. "I'm sorry about this. About...having to be with me." His eyes are glassy but serene.

His soft words settle in and I start to relax. I let the cool, evening air fill my lungs. The sun descends behind the giant, domed building, setting fire to the purple evening sky.

His eyes are fixed on the ground, but as he speaks, his gaze meets mine. "What I mean to say is...I know what it looks like when someone is in love."

I clench my jaw, and my muscles tense again. "What is that supposed to mean?"

He looks around, as if he's suspicious of someone listening, and it sends prickles down my spine. "Jaina, I think we should take this conversation somewhere else."

"Conversation?" I raise my voice. "What is there to talk about?"

Sean sighs, and his shoulders slump. He takes a step closer to me, and I'm tempted to back up. "Jaina, I just want a chance to get to know you. That's all. The way people should. If we really are to spend the rest of our lives together, I want to get a head start in knowing you. Is that too much to ask?"

*Yes*, I want to scream.

But I don't.

"Can I just walk you home?" he asks.

By the stars, why? I look down and sigh. "I'm not going to stop you."

I move forward, down the marble pathways through the city, and Sean seems to float at my side. My sweating hands tremble a little. I get this sort of choked feeling in my throat, and I know I'm blushing. I don't look at him. My whole face feels hot. Why the hell is he following me home?

"Alright, Sean. Are you going to walk me home or what?" I keep my eyes locked on the path ahead of me.

"This isn't so bad you know," he says casually.

I shoot him a glare. "Saying that doesn't make me believe it."

But the truth is, I almost do. His gentle tone makes me feel numb and sort of light, like even though everything has already gone wrong, there is no reason to worry or to be afraid. How can he do that? Make me feel nothing?

The new, wonderful sensation nearly overcomes me. I feel absolutely nothing. And it's beautiful.

He looks at me blankly. Then a warm glow grows in his eyes. "Do you like it here?"

I gaze up at the slowly darkening sky. "It's beautiful."

"Where are you from?" he asks, his voice softer than a summer breeze. "Where was your school?"

"My school was on Earth. I went to Virana."

His eyes widen. "Virana? Your parents must be important."

"What do you mean?"

"Oh, you know. You have to be somewhat royal to go there. Either that or you're simply outstanding."

I shake my head and manage a half-hearted grin. "Maybe I'm just outstanding."

"I'm sure you are."

I'm not really sure what to do or say or feel in reply to that, so I remain silent.

"Did you ever know your parents?" he asks.

"No." I can't help thinking of how Azad brought up my mother. "I was taken when I was just a baby."

A sad shadow seems to pass over Sean's face, and his eyebrows crinkle a little. "You don't remember them at all?"

"No." I'm not sure why I'm even bothering with him. I'm feeling tough and stubborn, but his calm demeanor makes me want to tell him the truth. The nothingness, the pure emptiness in me is welcoming. If he can give me that, maybe he deserves some answers. "Well sometimes... I don't know."

"It's okay," he says. "You can tell me."

I truly try to recall the earliest days of my life. "I...I don't think there's anything. I get pictures in my head sometimes, but I don't know if they're from dreams or reality."

"What *might* you remember?"

"Starships," I blurt out. "Fighting. Blue eyes. Bright, icy blue eyes filled with so much kindness."

"Your mother's?"

"Maybe. And there's this silver ring…but that's really all." I'm surprised with all the words that come out of my mouth, surprised myself with how much I remember. Those icy blue eyes. Not quite like Dragon's sea-blue eyes. Could they be my mother's?

To think that this whole time, in my whole existence, I've never thought much about my parents. About before. It surprises me. Maybe it's because the truth bothers me; that I still don't know who I am. I don't know where I came from.

Sean smiles. "Maybe you'll find them, someday."

"I don't know if I want to. Maybe the less you remember the better," I breathe.

"I guess."

The sky becomes noticeably dark. The city lights prevent the stars from peering through, and a sense of loneliness envelops me. There's no real darkness in the sky.

The Crystal City has replaced the the stars with lights of their own that spill from skyscrapers, and transports, towers, and gardens. Even the marble pathways are broken here and there with a shard of golden luminescent stones embedded into the ground. The City is perfect, it really is, yet in it's perfection, it has managed to destroy everything beautiful. It suffocates the stars, drowning out their gentle music with its own mechanical tones. It has destroyed the random beauty of a forest, of life, of love.

"What did you mean when you said you know what it looks like when someone is in love?" My voice trembles slightly as I say it, but I do my best to stay strong.

He studies me for a moment. "There's someone else for you, isn't there."

It's not a question.

"Well…?" He asks, raising his eyebrow.

I look down. "It doesn't matter at this point."

He smiles sadly, yet there's a hint of amusement lingering in his eyes. "Was he on your team?"

"You don't want to hear about it."

Sean shrugs. "Secrets aren't good for relationships."

"We aren't in a relationship, Sean." I let out a sigh and stop in my tracks. "This isn't real. Whatever I'm supposed to pretend to feel, I can't. Now can you stop being so smiley and acting so cocky like everything is going to be okay?"

His smile disappears, and his golden-hazel eyes flicker with something that might be pain. The muscles in his face tense up.

I can tell he's about to speak and I'm ready to cut him off, to walk away faster and just get home, but the calmness in his voice stops me.

"She was on my team," he says as he takes a seat on a silvery bench near us. He keeps his eyes fixed on the ground. "Our team lost, and I was chosen to move to the Crystal City. She wasn't."

The air feels cold in my lungs. What the hell am I doing. This man that I'm supposed to marry, is telling me everything while I shut him out. My heart sinks a little, and I take a seat next to him on the bench. I stare forward into the marble pathways between the sweet-scented, unnatural gardens. "Did you love her?" I ask.

"I still do."

His words echo in my mind. I look down at the path beneath my feet. "He was on my team. When I was six and he was eight, they took him out of the school. I'd known him my whole life, and they just took him away." I pause, expecting to feel the tears welling in my eyes, but there's nothing. My eyes are empty. My heart is numb. "Years went by, and then he came back."

Sean's nod is visible out of the corner of my eye. "What was he like?"

I laugh. "Frustrating all the time. He never followed the rules, everything had to be *his* way. Dark, with a gentle heart."

"Sounds like someone I knew back in school. What's his name?"

"Altair." I almost flinch at the sound of his name. It hurts to remember, knowing we can never be together. "Altair Kasev."

"Dragon?"

Shivers race throughout my body. "What?"

"Dragon? Did he go by that when he returned to Virana?" Sean asks.

"Yes..." My voice is hardly a whisper. "H-how did you know?"

He shakes his head. "He was friends with a friend of mine. We all were in school in Manincia."

By the stars. My hands are shaking, but I almost don't notice.

"He went to Manincia?" I ask, pretending not to know already.

Sean nods. "He came when he was eleven. His dad would pick him up every summer, and they'd go places or train or something. He was a mysterious kid."

"His *dad*?" I choke out.

"Yeah. You should've seen Dragon, though." He shakes his head. "That kid came to the school so shy and closed off in his own head that it was a miracle he became so popular. If it weren't for Azad, I don't know what would've become of him."

My breath catches in my throat, and I sit up straighter. My body stiffens, and I almost choke on my own saliva. Time hardens into a viscous sort of fluid until it stops altogether, and all I feel is the burning of that blade against my skin.

"By the stars, Jaina, are you alright?"

I try to nod, but I end up shaking my head. "Azad," I mutter. "How did you know him?"

Sean shrugs. "He was a friend. Why do you ask?"

No.

No.

No.

"You were..." My voice catches and cracks a little. "You were friends with him?"

Sean's face darkens, and for the first time since I met him, I feel afraid. He remains calm and composed, but as his gaze meets mine, the worry flickers against the golden nuance of his eyes. "Jaina, did *you* know him?"

I shake my head. "No. Dragon told me about him. A little."

He furrows his brow, and I think he knows I'm lying. "Oh. You sure you're okay?"

I nod. "Yeah. Um, tell me more about Dragon and Azad."

Sean relaxes a little. "When Altair came to the school, he wouldn't talk to anyone. He was so alone, and he seemed to like it that way. Maybe even took pride in it. Azad was the first person he was set to duel, and Altair lost miserably. It was an intense duel. For being suspended from Virana, he was an amazing fighter. Altair hated Azad for a little while after that, but it wasn't long before they were friends. They would train together, and they won so many duels, it made them popular. They were gods." He pauses. "When Altair was thirteen, we started calling him Dragon."

"Why'd you call him that?"

"I think it started off as some inside joke between him and Azad," he replies. "After Altair won this ridiculous fight against three other students, Azad stood up, laughing, and he shouted, 'you fight like a dragon!' And everyone started chanting 'Dragon, Dragon, Dragon!' Ever since then people called him that."

"So they really were friends."

Sean laughs a little. "They were like brothers. And then there was Azad's sister."

I feel even colder. "Sister?"

He nods. "Rasha. Rasha Viraak. She was head over heels for Dragon."

Azad's story of Dragon murdering his sister resurfaces in my mind. "Did he love her back?"

Sean shrugs. "Sometimes he acted like he did, and other times he acted like more of a friend."

My throat feels dry, and my stomach wrenches. What Azad told me is true. At least parts of it.

I stare up above the city, into that void where I know the stars should be. "I need to go home," I whisper.

Sean sighs, stands, and reaches for my hand to help me up. "It's weird that you know him. Dragon, I mean. I didn't like him that much, but I respected him."

My hands feel cold. "I'm glad you knew him, too."

"I...I think I'll stay out here a while longer. Just tell me one thing...is he dead?" His voice is heavy, and deep. "Azad?"

37

I take a deep, shaky breath. "Sean, I—"

"I saw that look in your eyes. When I mentioned his name, you were nervous. Is he dead?"

I finally let my gaze rest on him. I say nothing, but let the answer show on my face.

A sad shadow passes over his face. "Thank you."

I bite my lip and turn away. "I'm sorry."

"It's not your fault."

If only he knew. "Goodbye, Sean," I breathe.

"Goodbye."

# CHAPTER FOUR

B y the time I get to my apartment, it's late. Much too late.

The past never goes away. Maybe eventually it will fade, but thus far, it has remained.

Everyone tells me to let go.

They talk about it like it's easy.

They talk about guilt like they've never killed, like they've never stolen someone's right to live.

They talk about love like they've never truly loved, like they have never had their heart unwillingly stolen.

And maybe they haven't.

Am I weak for not being able to let go? Of guilt? Of love?

When I open the door to my apartment, I start to feel a little better. It's been the closest thing to home for the past few months. I press the touchscreen on the wall to my left and my living room is brought into light.

My apartment isn't big, but it's enough space for just me– and a guest, if anyone ever wanted to visit. My dining table sits in front of the small kitchen to the left, and all the way on the other side of the room, a large balcony overlooks the city.

Collapsing onto the couch next to my silverscreen, I contemplate calling Dragon. Kavi's right. I should tell him. We haven't spoken since we arrived in the Crystal City. A twinge of regret shoots through me. I should have at least *tried* to contact him. Maybe I assumed he'd contact me first. Maybe I assumed that he'd miss me enough to seek me out.

Maybe I was wrong.

I pick up the phonicom with shaking hands and dial his number before I have time to change my mind. Kavi gave it to me about a week after we arrived here. I honestly didn't *mean* to memorize it. I just remembered because…well…it's Dragon.

My stomach churns with nervous sparks. An electronic ringtone sounds in my ear. The moments drag on as I wait for him to answer. Part of me hopes he's not there. Another ring. Maybe he's not home.

A beep sounds in my ear, and I jump when a mechanical voice answers the phone. "Altair Kasev unavailable. Please try again another time. Thank you."

Unable to take the raging torment of my thoughts any longer, I hang up, half annoyed and half despairing about the misery of my life.

I snap my fingers twice and turn on the holoprojector. A science fiction show pops up, and I'm immediately annoyed. I swipe my finger across my silversceen to change channels. Science-fiction bores me.

Finally, I hit the news channel. The newscaster– a pale, turquoise colored creature with sharp, needle-like teeth and an elongated face– laughs heartily at a joke I missed. I let myself sink into the couch and grab a blanket that I folded neatly on the couch this morning. Wrapping myself up in it, I lean back and try to relax.

"Now, for some important updates. IA officials have reported outbreaks of the deadly disease, Dramaska, in outer-rim systems. Luckily, these have been short and losses have been minimal. On another note, I am required to inform everyone of the recent outburst of organized crime. Calling themselves 'freedom fighters,' these terrorists have bombed IA bases in multiple systems. Though there have been no casualties, men, women and children in surrounding villages and cities have been taken by the terrorists and sold into slavery in exchange for ammunition. This is being broadcast to every system in the Imperial Alliance. If you are aware of any suspicious activity, please report to an official immediately. Also–" He stops and taps the phonicom in the hole on the side of his head, the equivalent of an ear to his species. He nods, looking down at his desk then glances back up at the camera, with a blank, stunned sort of expression. "I–I'm sorry, I've just received terrible news..." The newscaster clears his throat, a solemn expression on his scaly face. "Prince Shirez Melohem of Earth is dead."

I hold my breath. My throat constricts at his words, and I grip the armrest of the couch, doing my best to process it all. No. No, that's not right. That can't be right.

"...was found in his home, lying on the kitchen floor. Though his body held no trace of physical wounds, investigators claim he was poisoned. Whether there was foul play or he committed the act himself remains unknown. Now, a few words from Raval Tazrin, General of the Imperial Alliance Army and royal advisor to his Majesty the Emperor."

The screen changes to reveal General Tazrin standing behind a silver podium. His face is familiar, even though I've never had the misfortune of meeting him. His hair is dark, and his eyes range from a striking hazel to a pale brown. Something about him makes me uneasy. He looks so sad, not just today, but every time he appears on the holovision.

General Tazrin clears his throat. "People of the Imperial Alliance, people of Earth." His voice echoes across the jade floors of the Crystal Palace. "Today, the IA mourns the loss of a great man, the son of Javan Melohem and the last Prince of Earth. Shirez was born a leader. He was a stubborn man, but well respected by his peers, and loved by his people." The general looks down and sighs like he has something else on his mind. "It is my obligation to inform you that the new prince will not be the son of Shirez Melohem. The Prince of Earth shall now be Maron Dymetree. The inauguration shall be held on the 340th Earth day of the year."

He continues to speak, but I don't hear him. Shirez is dead...the great Prince of Earth is dead...

I snap my fingers again, and the holoprojecter shuts off. Numbness tightens its tingly fingers around me.

First Xana.

Now Shirez.

Who's next?

A knock at the door jolts me from my thoughts, but I don't bother moving. If I wait long enough, I'm sure they'll leave. The urge to do anything is gone.

The knock comes again.

What if it's an IA guard? I moan softly to myself as I stand. The soft, purple blanket around my shoulders drags on the ground behind me, like the train of a wedding dress. The thought puts a bitter taste in my mouth.

I lazily make my way to the door and open it. Who could possibly–

"Liam," I cry, dropping my blanket onto the floor. "What are you doing here?"

Dark circles ring his eyes, and his hair is ruffled like he just came back from the dead. His eyes radiate the complete numbness he's fallen into, but as he looks at me, his face becomes more relaxed, more emotional. He's wearing all black, like a combat suit. No, it *is* a combat suit.

"Kavi told me to make sure you were okay." His voice is soft, but slightly forced, as if it takes effort to get the words out.

I stare back blankly. "Oh...well, I'm fine." I try to close the door on him.

He holds it open with his boot. "Jaina, I heard what happened."

I clench my jaw and try to stop the tears from welling in my eyes. "About me or Shirez?"

"Both."

I back away from the door and turn around so I don't have to face him. The city lights from outside shine through the window. *Shaav you, Kavi.* I told her not to send him. What was she thinking?

I hear the door close and his gentle footsteps behind me.

"I'm not trying to upset you," he says. "I'm trying to help."

"You're miserably failing." I whip around and glare at him.

He's closer than I expect him to be, and for just a moment it makes me forget my anger. He places the purple blanket neatly on the couch. "Stop it. Please." Liam takes my hand gently, but holds me tight enough so I can't pull away. "Jaina, after everything that's happened...after all we've been through, we're all worried about you."

The seriousness in his voice startles me. Sure, in the Trials he had moments of seriousness, but it wasn't like this. He's changed so much.

I pull away from him and take a seat on the couch. The soft fabric engulfs me. "Why?"

Liam's lips smile, yet the rest of him remains solemn. He stands awkwardly in front of me. "Because we're your friends."

I attempt a smile.

Liam nods then wanders into the kitchen. Things shift around, cupboards open and close, glasses bump against glass or the stone countertops.

After about a minute, I call, "What in the name of the galaxy are you doing?"

He continues sifting through my cupboards. "The Myrym."

"The what?"

"You know, Myrym," he says. "Very expensive, very intoxicating..."

I furrow my brow. "Yeah, I don't drink."

"Aha!" He walks back over to the couch and sits down next to me. He has two plastic cups and a large, unopened glass bottle of black liquid. On the front is a label in some language I don't know. Liam raises an eyebrow at me. "You were saying?"

"Where did you get that? I swear I haven't seen that in my life."

Liam smirks. "That's because you weren't looking for it, love. There's a bottle of it in every apartment." He pops open the bottle, and a powerful smell that I can't quite identify floats through the air. "Made from the ginger root of Kerra-16. Each bottle is at least seven hundred years old." He pours the Myrym into both cups, the liquid bursting into color and creating a galaxy-patterned design in the glass. Liam hands the first cup to me.

"Really," I insist. "I don't drink."

"You do now. Cheers." He bumps his cup against mine then gulps his down.

"Cheers to *what*?"

He swallows what's left in his cup, his eyes slightly red. "By the stars that burns," he manages through coughs as he pours himself some more. "Life. Cheers to life."

I sigh with a slight laugh. "Are you joking?"

Liam rolls his eyes. "Just drink."

At this point, what do I have to lose?

I lift the cup to my lips and down every drop. It's surprisingly cold, but it burns all the way down my throat, and it's so strong that I'm tempted to spit it out. The moment I swallow, I break into a coughing fit, and my eyes start to water. I can't see a thing, but I hear Liam laughing.

He puts his hand on my shoulder. "You okay?"

My throat burns, and when I finally manage to breathe a bit, all I can choke out is, "What the hell?"

Liam laughs again and rubs my back. "How do you feel?"

I gulp down a few more breaths and lean back in my seat. My throat still burns, and my eyes still water. "By the stars, that's awful."

"How do you *feel* though?"

I take a moment to analyze. Warm. Pleasantly warm. A little tingly. A little dizzy, and a bit foggy, but relaxed. I smile a little. "Alright, considering everything."

He smiles. "There you go."

"More?"

Liam picks up the bottle and pours a little more into my cup. "If this is your first time drinking, you should probably take this slowly."

"It's not like I care anymore."

"Even more reason for you to be careful. Drink it slow."

Despite myself, I do as he says and take a sip very slowly. It burns, but I'm expecting it this time, and the fit of coughing that follows isn't quite as much of a shock. My body relaxes a bit more as a feeling of warm peacefulness settles in, so powerful it's almost inhibiting. I take another sip. "What's your job here, Liam? Won't the officials wonder where you are?"

"They won't miss me. I got assigned the same job Dragon did." He rolls his eyes and his face hardens as he takes another gulp of Myrym. "As if I didn't see enough of him in the Trials."

I lean back against the couch pillows. My mind grows foggy, and everything in my apartment seems to have a soft, golden haze to it. My fingertips feel tingly, but it doesn't bother me. "The only reason you didn't like him was because of me."

"Reason enough," he mutters.

There's an awkward pause as Liam stares at the wall, but I don't bother breaking it.

"Jaina, everything's going to be okay."

I slowly shake my head. "No, it won't."

Liam sighs. "Did you meet him?"

My stomach drops. "I did, today."

"How did it go?"

I shrug and try to keep a steady expression on my face. "It could've been worse."

He leans forward a bit, and I get the sense that this is turning into an interrogation. "What happened?"

I shake my head. "Nothing."

"Really?"

"It was fine."

"Jaina, you can tell me."

I sneer. "I said it was fine, Liam. Leave it at that."

He looks down at the floor and presses his lips together. "I'm sorry."

I have to change the subject. "How did you hear about Shirez? It just came on the news when you knocked on my door."

"It has to do with my job."

"And what would that be?" I ask.

He takes another sip of Myrym. "It's classified."

I stare at him with a half-hearted glare. "You can't tell me?"

"You especially. You're too dangerous," he jokes, smiling ever so slightly.

I raise an eyebrow.

He groans, dropping his head into his palms and running his fingers through his dark brown hair. "Alright, alright. I'll give you a hint. It has to do with the IAA."

I shoot him a skeptical glare. "Dragon got the same job you did?"

Liam nods.

"Isn't Dragon a little...*smart* for the Imperial Alliance Army?"

His expression darkens, and he tightens his grip on the armrest. "What's that supposed to mean?"

I raise a hand in surrender. "Nothing. Sorry. But it has to do with the IAA? Like guarding or spying?"

"All I can say is it's a very important and *thought-provoking* duty, but our job allows us to break the rules now and then."

"Can you get me out of this marriage?" I laugh in defeat.

Liam's eyes darken a little, and he smiles sadly. "I'd do anything for you."

I look away from him and stare forward, not really at anything in particular. My whole body is relaxed. "It really isn't fair," I whisper.

"It's what we all asked for," he replies after a moment.

I take a deep breath and close my eyes. "I was thinking earlier about how we struggled so much, how we worked so hard to get here. I was thinking about how it's so perfect here...and it's taken the beauty, the joy out of everything." I find the courage to look at him. "And I'm not perfect, Liam."

Liam puts his cup down on the glass coffee table in front of us, and I put mine down too. He takes my hand in his and squeezes gently. "Jaina, you're here. You fought so hard, and you are fully deserving of being a Superior."

Tears well up in my eyes, and I bite my cheek. I shake my head. "But I'm not. Liam, I have no place in this society, I can't..."

He scoots even closer to me, wrapping one arm around my shoulders. "You can't what?"

I clench my teeth, but Dr. Harrison's words still sting in my head. "I shouldn't be upset–"

He shakes his head. "No, no. Tell me, what is it?"

"I…" I take a deep shaky breath. "I can't have kids."

His grip tightens a little around my hand.

"Liam, I can't have kids. I can't ever have a baby. I can't…" My throat tightens, and I look at the floor as a tear glides down my face.

"Shh." Liam massages my hand with his thumb.

"I can't do what every single woman is supposed to be able to do." My body trembles. I wipe my eyes, but the tears keep coming.

"Hey." He brushes my hair to the side. I turn away so he can't see my face, but he leans in closer, touches my chin, and carefully turns my head. "Jaina, it's okay."

My tearful eyes meet his, and I lean into his shoulder. He wraps his arms around me and whispers. I can't make out what he says, but the sound of his voice and the warmth of his embrace comforts me.

"It's okay," I finally hear him say. "You're perfect to me."

His words make me tremble, and my heart sinks. I stay in his arms another moment before I pull away and wipe my eyes again.

"I'm sorry. I want to get out of here."

Liam smiles sadly. "I wish I could give that to you."

I reach for my cup and take another large gulp of Myrym. It sends tingles through my body, and I try to reclaim that numbness Sean helped me find in myself. "It's alright. So what rules *can* you break?"

"Now that is *extremely* confidential." He smirks, but there's still a sad sheen in his eyes. He nods at my cup. "You want more, or are you good?"

I shake my head and feel a bit dizzy. "I'm good."

Liam raises an eyebrow. "I see you don't need much to really affect you."

"I don't," I choke out. "You see how small I am? It shouldn't take much."

He leans back into the couch. "We partied too much, back on Virana. That's how I got used to it. The Myrym."

"I was never invited to those," I say softly.

"Of course you weren't. Someone as smart as you shouldn't have gone to those, anyway."

I roll my eyes. "You make me sound so boring. What was it like?"

"To have fun?"

"Ha. Yeah." My voice cracks a bit. Back on Virana, I really didn't have fun. Why was that?

Liam looks into his cup, takes another sip, and lets out a breath. "They really weren't very fun. All we did was drink and talk and do stupid things. We'd go out on the beach and mess around while the Masters and the rest of the school slept."

"How did you ever find anything to drink? I mean, they had water and juice from the kitchen, but nothing like Myrym."

"Ah." He smiles slyly. "Teaching a bunch of kids is a stressful job, Jaina. Look hard enough through any staff room, and you'll find Myrym."

"Doesn't it make you hallucinate?"

He shakes his head. "Not really. The Masters just said that to scare people. It can make you have weird dreams, though."

"Oh. I had no idea."

"I'm pleased to inform you." His lips contort into an awkward smile. "Also, I need to ask a huge favor of you. It kind of has to do with my, uh, job." His tone of voice suggests he's trying to tiptoe around something.

"What is it?" I ask.

"I've been assigned to your apartment," he blurts out. He looks down at the floor, his cheeks flushing red. "Just for the next twenty standard hours."

"Why?"

"Safety purposes."

"You're supposed to be guarding me?" Somehow, I'm having trouble believing that.

He doesn't meet my eyes and takes a sharp breath before he speaks. "More or less..."

Why would the IAA want me guarded? Am I in danger? Maybe I'm in trouble. Did I do something wrong?

"I guess I don't really have a choice, do I?"

Liam shrugs. "Not really."

I moan with annoyance, but it's really just an act. Him being here *does* make me feel safe. Of course, I can't let him know that, or he'll go completely crazy.

"Alright. I'm going to bed." I stand and start on my way to my bedroom, but everything is hazy, and I feel much lighter than I normally do, so I hang on to the couch for a moment.

Liam smiles just a bit. "You feel floaty? Everything glowing a bit?"

"How'd you know?" I ask sarcastically.

"It'll do that to you. Don't worry." Liam lies down on the couch, sprawled across the cushions like some giant pet. He puts his hands behind his head, all comfy and relaxed like this is his home.

I grab the purple blanket from the side of the couch and I gently place it over him.

"Purple?" he asks, gesturing to the color. "Are you kidding?"

"It's the only one I have." I laugh quietly.

"For galaxies sake, get some new ones. I'm sure you can afford it."

He watches my every movement as I pull the blanket up to his chest. I pretend not to notice. His gaze meets mine when I kneel beside him.

"Anything else you need?" I ask.

Liam's eyes take me in, his breath is deep and unsteady, and I realize he's holding my hand. Quickly, he lets go and looks away. "No. I'll be fine."

I nod and head off into the hallway toward my room.

"Wait," he calls.

I stop and peer around the corner at him. "Yes?"

"Do I get a goodnight kiss?" There's a sudden, mischievous look in his eyes.

"I'm engaged, Liam."

"My job lets me bend the rules. Please?"

I'm surprised he'd dare to ask. "Goodnight, Liam."

"Is that a no?"

"Yes," I reply.

"Wait. So it's a *yes*?"

"Goodnight!" And I head off into my room without another word.

# CHAPTER FIVE

I wake with an odd sense of insecurity, and a burning need to cry. I climb out of bed, and without bothering to change out of my nightclothes, I walk into my living room. Liam is asleep on the couch.

By the stars, that was all real.

I was hoping so desperately that last night wasn't real. That maybe I hadn't met Sean. That maybe Shirez is still alive.

My head swells as reality comes crashing down on me. My body feels cold and hot at the same time, my pulse drums against my throat. I imagine the gray matter of my brain expanding like a balloon in my skull, adding pressure until it can't take any more.

Liam shifts a bit. Maybe he feels my gaze on him or my presence in the room, but he opens his eyes, and looks directly at me with a blank expression on his face. "Good morning," he says, his voice soft and sleepy. "How are you feeling?"

"Still a bit dizzy. I think it's more from shock than the Myrym, though."

He stretches a bit and moves his hands behind his head. "Seems about right. With as much as you drank, the effects should've faded after a few hours."

"I still feel hungover."

"Nah," he laughs. "Not from the Myrym, anyway. Did you know it's almost 11:30?"

I can't help feeling a bit embarrassed for waking up so late, he must think I'm so lazy. "I- I know. I woke up a while ago and read for a few hours," I lie.

He studies me shamelessly and I feel awkward in my slightly-too-revealing pajamas.

I cross my arms over my chest. "I want to take a walk."

"Do you have to work today?"

I shake my head.

Liam looks at me with such pity it almost makes me sick.

In a stern voice, I add, "You can come if you want, but I'm going, regardless."

"Don't you want to rest?" He asks.

I ignore him, walk into my room, and head for my closet. There are a few racks of clothing and a dress I have hanging up, but I haven't really gone out to buy anything. They give everyone 500 Imperial

Ariks upon their arrival to spend on clothes, food, and other things one might need in a home. I still have about 240 left over. There isn't anything else I want.

Despite my scarcity of options, picking out something to wear is such a pain. I end up with silvery leggings, a black one sleeved shirt that's asymmetrical at the bottom. I grab my most comfortable shoes and slip them on.

I'm about to stride into the living room, when I hear Liam whispering. I can't quite make out what he's saying, so I inch closer, lingering in the hall.

"I'm trying, okay?" He's hunched over on the couch, speaking into a phonicom. "Shut up, I'm doing my best. You don't think I know that? Look, if you don't like the way I do things then maybe you should do your own dirty work... Yeah...uh huh...Everything will be ready by tonight. I've got everything under control... No. If things go wrong, you can go *shaav* yourself." At that, he hangs up.

I walk into the room and stand in front of him, and he glances at me a bit nervously. "Who were you talking to?" I ask.

"Oh, um, m-myself..." he manages unconvincingly.

I raise an eyebrow. "You can go *shaav* yourself?"

"Fine." He sighs. "I was talking to my boss."

"So Dragon is your boss." It's not a question.

Liam looks down, defeated.

"How is he?" I ask.

"Do you want to go on that walk now?"

My body tenses, annoyed he didn't answer. But I nod.

Liam slept in his clothes, so it doesn't take him long to get ready.

We take the lift downstairs. When we reach the bottom, I walk through the lobby and out of my apartment complex. He follows close behind as I lead us into the golden light of the late morning.

My apartment is built on the outskirts of the Crystal City Plaza, a large area paved with white Tarnoshian marble. Every few meters or so, gardens line the paths. Strange, unfamiliar birds hop around and bathe in the sun. They're smaller and more colorful than any of the birds I knew on Virana. Their songs are more intricate, like wind chimes.

Things were so different back home.

The air is more stale here, the breeze less...real. There is not a breath of disorder, and it makes everything feel so wrong.

Children toss pebbles and gems in fountains to make a wish. People gather around tables eating, talking, and laughing together, seemingly enjoying the sun or the shade. Buildings encompass the orderly pathways along with restaurants and little shops selling the finest silks, the most exotic teas, and treasures from across the galaxy.

"You look better," Liam murmurs as he walks at my side.

I glance at him, trying to decipher what he means by that.

"The fresh air seems to have done you some good," he finishes.

"Oh. Yeah. It usually helps," I manage. I try not to think of how much I revealed to him last night. I can't believe I cried in front of him. Before he can say anything else, before he can turn this into some deep discussion, I say, "I miss the ocean air, though."

He nods. "Me too. It's funny. We used to spend all our time thinking of life off that island, but it's the only place that's ever felt like home."

"It's sad to think we'll never go back."

"Don't say that. I'm sure we could, someday."

"Not as long as we're here."

He looks around the moment the words leave my lips. His body becomes tense, and he takes a shaky breath. His eyes scan over everything around us. "Careful, Jaina."

I study him, and his eyes meet mine. My heart starts to race, and I can't help feeling momentarily terrified. He works for the IAA. I really do need to be careful about what I say. "I'm sorry. I've started to get bad habits from Dragon."

"I thought you hadn't seen him since we got here."

I avert my gaze. "I haven't."

A few silent moments drag on until Liam steps in front of me and stops me in my tracks. "Jaina, I don't want you to get hurt."

"I can't possibly hurt any more than I do right now," I say in a whisper.

"Jaina," he says very sternly. "Please. You have no idea what they could do to you." His voice is dark and quiet.

I start to feel warm with the smallest sparks of anger. "Are you threatening me?"

"Of course not. I'm sorry, and I know all of this is unfair–"

"Don't pity me." I sneer.

"I don't *pity* you."

"You do. I can see it in your eyes. You know what, Liam? I don't want it. So you can take it all back and shove it up your *nav'ra!*" I shout angrily.

A few passersby shoot us furtive glances, and I can't help blushing.

Liam places a hand on my shoulder and leads me over to a park bench by a fountain.

"What are you doing?" I ask, annoyed.

He takes a seat and gestures for me to do the same. After a moment, I sit next to him, but not too close. I cross my arms over my chest like some unappreciative teenager…which maybe I am.

The Plaza around us is like a small, organized forest. The marble pathways flow around clusters of trees, flowers, and bushes like shiny white rivers, each of the eight trails leading to different parts of the city. A slow trickle of people filter through the garden.

Everyone looks so happy.

They always do.

I wonder if I look happy to them.

Maybe we're all dying on the inside.

Just ahead is the circular center of the garden. Because circles represent perfection.

Trees bearing fruit from every corner of the galaxy grow here. They surround us like attentive servants but are unbending to my will. If I could climb them, if I could be raised to the sky, somewhere far above this sad world, maybe I could leave this pain behind. If only I could rise above these feelings that tie me down.

Finally, I decide to speak. "You were never like this, Liam."

He smiles sadly. "You didn't like me the way I was."

"I loved you."

There's a long, cold silence. When I process the words I said, I too, feel cold. I'm thankful he doesn't look at me, but I can tell he's tense.

"I wish you had told me," he whispers softly into the air.

I shake my head. "You knew, Liam."

"I didn't—"

"You did." My voice is angrier than I mean it to be. "Everyone knew it. Don't pretend you were oblivious. You chose not to believe it."

"I was stupid. I know that."

In his eyes, I see nothing. Nothing of that boy he used to be, none of that playfulness, none of that light that used to shine in his sly eyes. It's as if his soul has been drained by the reality of everything, by the way it has all turned out.

Liam stares back blankly, letting me see into him, pouring out his soul from his eyes.

I feel no contempt, no anger or even regret.

Just sadness.

"Liam, I loved you for who you were. You didn't have to change for me. I loved that fun, stupid, mischievous boy." I laugh softly. "The one who didn't make any sense but made me forget about all that seriousness of Virana."

An inconsolable smile plays at his lips. "I'm sorry."

"When did you change?"

He stares forward, hunched over a bit, with his elbows resting on his knees. "When Xana died."

I nod, a bit sickly.

"You never told me what she said..." he breathes softly. "Her last words."

"You don't want to hear them, Liam," I whisper.

His eyes darken a bit. "I know. But I need to know."

I avoid his gaze, contemplating what to say. "I never told anyone."

"It was about me, wasn't it." It isn't a question.

I hesitate, but he deserves to know. "It was," I breathe. I let there be a short silence, and my body tenses. "We were in a dark cave. We were at the last crystal. The sacrifice was death. He had her on her knees." How have I not started crying? I feel nothing at all. "He...he asked her if she had any last words." I look up at him to see the pain registering on his face, to see those crevices that knowledge and time engrave in the surface of skin.

"What did she say?" he asks.

I open my mouth to speak, but words don't come out.

A sad rage glows in his eyes, and he says again, "*What did she say.*"

It's a demand.

I take a deep breath, and my voice quivers. "She said, 'I should have been kinder. Tell Liam I'm sorry.'"

He exhales deeply and unsteadily, staring forward. His eyes are rimmed with red as he tries to hold back tears.

"I- I didn't know why..." I start.

Liam shakes his head. "But I do."

"Liam, did you..." I sigh. "Did you really like her?"

He swallows hard, and as he runs his fingers through his thick brown hair, I notice a tremor in his hand. "I didn't like her that much." The saddest, most painful and pitiful laugh escapes his throat. "And I didn't know her long enough. Not long at all. But there were moments..." He shakes his head.

I put my hand on his shoulder. "Yes?"

His face goes hard and unreadable. "Never mind."

We spend the rest of the afternoon in the gardens. He buys me lunch, and we talk, but I don't process what he says. I don't think he does, either. The motions are so rehearsed. So typical. He asks how work is. How long my shifts are. About my boss. I tell him.

Afternoon passes, and the sun is on its last hour of light. I tell Liam it's okay if he leaves, but he insists on staying. I don't know if it's because he wants to stay, or if he's been ordered to stay.

At the end of the day, we stop at the fountain. It's funny that the center of the garden is a fountain. Maybe no one thought about it, but water is ever changing. It's imperfect, out of control. How ironic.

"I should go home now." I stare down into the water.

"I should too," Liam replies. "I like this fountain, though."

"It reminds me of home."

"When we were little, Altair and I used to race to the fountain." He smiles gently. "He'd always win."

"He used to protect me," I say. "When the other kids made fun of me or locked me in closets or lockers, he'd always be there."

"Yeah. He was like that annoying older brother in all the stories. He'd always protect me, too, but I hated it. I got picked on because I was weak, but the last thing I wanted was someone protecting me." Liam shakes his head. "Things got a lot worse when he left." The pale orange light of the sunset illuminates his face and he is in every sense, desirable.

"Your eyes are brown," I manage in a very soft voice. He smiles. "I know."

"I thought they were blue. Gray blue."

"No." He laughs. "They're lighter when I get lots of sleep, and spend time on the beach. But never blue."

For some reason, it's an imperative detail. How did I not realize his eyes aren't blue? "I didn't notice. I used to dream about your blue eyes and describe you with blue eyes…"

His face becomes impassive. "You must have been dreaming about Dragon, then."

I don't want him to linger on the subject of Dragon, so I clear my throat. "Will you walk me home?"

He smirks that trademark smirk of his. "Of course, my lady."

I take a quick step back from the fountain to start home and bump into someone behind me with enough force that I'm nearly thrown off balance. An armored hand grabs my left wrist, and images of Azad spark through my head. His grip is so tight that I gasp.

"Watch it there, miss." The guard holding me sneers.

His eyes are blue, really deep, ocean blue. His face is scarred by time and war, or at least I assume it's war because not all of the lines are quite as clean and natural as those that are caused by age. Nothing about him says *kind* or *caring* or even *merciful,* and it sends shivers through me. He's no Azad. There's none of that rage, that red hot inferno of emotions in his eyes. There's only darkness. Not even some sort of human-like emotion. Just cold.

"Do you know who you ran into?" he asks, his voice more threatening than before.

Liam stands directly behind me. "Sir, please forgive me. My friend is not well."

"Shut the hell up." The guard glares at me. "I asked you a question, girl."

My eyes fall on the man in the royal red and black robes, who is looking at me with a bit more intensity than I appreciate. The horror of recognition floods me.

Liam takes my right hand and pulls me away from the guard, relieving my left wrist of his terrifyingly tight grip. I want to make a run for it, and I'm sure, by the look in his eyes, that Liam does too. Instead, he kneels, pulling me down beside him, so I kneel too.

"General Tazrin." Liam bows his head low.

I keep my head down and struggle not to look up and stare at the man, the man who always appears on the holovision, the man with the sad hazel eyes, and dark brown hair peppered with streaks of gray. The same man who brought down the Resistance and saved the IA from chaos. The man is a national hero.

"General Tazrin," I manage bravely. "Please forgive me. I didn't mean it."

"No excuses, miss!" cries the evil-looking guard. "You are going to pay for–"

"Colonel," says a kind voice. "Please. Step aside."

"But, sir–"

"That is an order."

I'm shaking. Liam holds my hand, and I hope he can't feel how afraid I am.

General Raval Tazrin approaches us, yet all I allow myself to look at are his feet. "You may stand." His voice is soft, warm, and inviting. Deep and sad.

Liam stands then kind of pulls me to my feet. Finally, I let myself look at the General. My face burns red; I'm not sure why. He looks younger than he does on the HV, maybe in his mid forties.

He studies me hard, yet it's like he already recognizes me. "Have we met?"

Liam clears his throat. "I don't think so, sir."

He shakes his head. "Not you."

I swallow hard, and shivers run through my whole body. "I don't think we have met." As I speak, the words don't sound right.

He whispers something under his breath, and his lips move to form a word that sounds like, "uh-mar" but I can't quite catch the rest of the sound. "Indera... are you...are you Jaina Indera?"

My heart stops in my chest.

Liam looks from the General to me, then back to the General.

"I am. How do you know me?" I ask.

The guard standing at Tazrin's side shoves me back a bit. "Don't ask questions."

Tazrin bares his teeth at the guard. "Stay out of this, Colonel." He looks at me like he's evaluating some exquisite piece of art.

It should creep me out and make my skin crawl, but for some reason, the longer his kind eyes study me, the better I feel. He doesn't look at me with those dark lustful eyes like Azad. It's like the way Shirez looked at me, kind and understanding. It's unsettling, he is the last person I'd ever expect that sort of empathy from.

"Ms. Indera, are you alright?" Tazrin asks.

I nod slowly.

General Tazrin sighs. "Please excuse my escort, I hope you'll forgive me."

Liam and I exchange glances. General Tazrin is one of the most powerful men in the galaxy; he doesn't need to impress lowly citizens like me or Liam. Maybe he's trying to make a point to his guards?

"I...I'm fine, sir. Thank you, sir," I choke out.

The General looks to Liam then back at me. "This is your...husband?"

I shake my head immediately. "No. Just a friend." I shift uncomfortably then decide to add, "I'm getting married soon."

Liam's gaze is fixed on the ground. He's a bit red.

General Tazrin takes on a sad, even painful look of understanding. "Ah. I see." He glances to his guards. "Colonel, would you please excuse us a moment?"

The Colonel sighs then waves the rest of the guards off. They take up position a bit farther away so they are out of earshot, but they keep a good watchful eye on their General.

My whole body is held in a cold suspense. This man is too kind to be the Commander in Chief of the IAA, the Supreme General and advisor to the Emperor.

Too kind to be the murderer that he is.

"You are good friends, then?" asks the General.

"For most of our lives," Liam says.

The General nods then looks at me. "You're to be married soon?"

"Yes," I reply, my voice weaker than before. "I am."

"You should be heading home then," he says softly.

Something about him makes me want to stay and ask him questions, but I don't even know what I'd say. What is there to say? If the General wants me to leave, then I'll leave.

I bow my head slightly. "Yes, sir."

I begin to make my way back to my apartment building. After a few steps, I glance back. Liam isn't at my side. Glancing back, I see Liam with a gravely serious look on his face, standing next to the General. The General's lips are barely moving, as if he's trying to conceal the fact that he's talking to Liam.

If it were Dragon with that look, I wouldn't worry as much. But this is Liam. For him to be this serious, that is something to worry about.

The General makes a slight gesture with his left hand, signaling his guards to return. Liam turns on his heel and marches away, more like a soldier than himself. He doesn't follow me.

I almost call to him, because I really do enjoy being around him. Because he makes me feel so much less alone. Maybe it's out of pride, or maybe it's out of fear, but whatever the reason, I remain silent and walk home without him.

I close the door and stand in the darkness. The cold wraps its irresistible arms around me. I don't turn on the lights. The dark reminds me of Dragon– the way it holds me, the way it closes my eyes, allowing me to momentarily forget the horrible truths of the world.

My scimitar glows faintly in its place on the wall. The Trials, bloody and terrible as they were, held the best moments of my life. Back then, I had more than I knew. I had Dragon. He's the only person in the universe I wish to see.

I drag myself into my room and put on my light blue tank top and soft black pajama pants. Shivering against the chilly air, I jump into my bed and pull the warm, fuzzy blankets around me. Yet the cold persists without him near. By the stars, I'd give anything to see him.

I miss him, the way that one misses a dream just after waking. A throbbing realization that what you had will not return. Even if you close your eyes.

# CHAPTER SIX

*S*he waits in shadows and holds her breath. *The stars in the sky outnumber her a million to one, and yet she waits under their watchful eyes.*

*"It must be done," says a familiar voice.*

*"No," I say. "This is wrong."*

*He sighs. "It's the only way, or you will die."*

*A man lies at her feet. Lightning flashes, and her shadow holds up a dagger. The man raises his hands as if to plead for mercy.*

*"It must be done," says the voice.*

*My body tingles with cold. "This is wrong."*

*"Destroy him."* I wake with a start. "No, no..."

*"Destroy him."*

I jump at the sound, wondering for a second if it really is here. *It's in your head.* My lungs feel as if they're quivering in my chest.

Little beads of sweat have gathered all over my body, I feel hot and cold all over simultaneously. I stand and pace back and forth around my room. This apartment is too big for me. It's lonely and dark, the cold empty kind of dark that fills the hours just before sunrise.

My apartment is cozy in the morning, but at night, it freaks me out. My place on Virana was a single room. There's too much space here, and I can't help but feel like something lurks in the emptiness. Before I could open a window and be met with the gentle sound of waves crashing against the shore. Here, there's only the hum of transports that fly far overhead and the gentle rustling of leaves as the stale City air blows through the trees.

Maybe I've just been alone too long.

I try not to remember the dark images of my dream, the shadows and light, daggers and fear. The bits and pieces that flash before my eyes make me shiver.

My hands find my mattress in the darkness and I pull myself back onto my bed, sitting on the edge. I hold my head in my hands. It's not what I wanted. None of it. Take it all back.

The fantasy of what could be is constantly on my mind. Being with Dragon somewhere safe, anywhere but here.

It's dangerous and wrong. Most of all, it's cruel. I can't let myself believe, even if it's just for an instant, that things *might* be okay, that there's some chance he and I could be together. Why do I let myself hope when there is no hope at all?

My leggings lay crumpled on the floor. I fold them gently and place them in the closet. The closet door makes a gentle *click* sound as it shuts.

Sinking back into my bed, I take a nice deep breath and close my eyes. Just fall asleep.

*Click.*

My heart jumps a little at the sound, and I open one eye. The closet door is still closed. Maybe I imagined it. I close my eyes again.

*Click, click, click.*

A chill runs through me, and I sit up and look around the room. All that follows is silence.

My blood pounds in my ears as I count the seconds. Maybe someone is moving into a neighboring apartment. That's probably all it is.

It's okay.

It was nothing.

A thud and a clatter sounds a bit closer.

I hold my breath. The hairs on my body stand on end. There's something out there.

There's no crime in the Crystal City. The IAA makes sure of that. What if it's an IAA official? Would Liam have told his superiors some of the things I've said? He told me to be careful, but what if I stepped over the line?

I'm breathing so fast I feel dizzy.

*By the stars, Jaina, you need to calm down.*

I won the Trials.

If there really is something out there, I can handle it.

Right?

Standing up again, I open my room door and slink into the hallway. I quietly pull my scimitar off the wall, hoping more than anything I won't need to use it. I breathe deeply and glance into the living room. The outside city lights cast shadows of all colors upon the floor, but there's nothing unusual.

Something shiny catches my eye. A shard of glass lies sparkling on the floor. The wooden shelf that usually holds four wine glasses for decoration now only holds three. One must have broken, making the clatter I heard a minute ago.

My skin prickles all over. I may not be the most organized person in the galaxy, but I'm always sure to keep breakable things in places where even vibrations from upstairs can't cause damage.

The air feels different, more alive against my skin. It bends unnaturally to another presence.

There's definitely someone here.

Slowly, I work up the courage to walk into plain sight. I can hear the blood pumping through my veins, and it's like I've been thrown into the Trials again. I'm in one of the arenas, about to face some unknown enemy. Yet as I round the corner, I find nothing. I take a step back. *Shaav*, what's wrong with me?

My neck tingles. Maybe I'm going crazy but I'm too afraid to take that chance. I step backward, trying to keep myself against the wall. I brush against something warm.

Terror floods me.

A gloved hand grabs my wrist, reaching for my scimitar. The other covers my mouth with tremendous force. My attacker is armored. I can feel the reinforced plates against my back. I elbow my attacker in the stomach. The groan that follows is deep as my assailant stumbles back. A man.

I turn to face him in the darkness. All I can make out are vague lines. As he moves in the fragmented dim light, parts of his helmet shine back at me. I activate my scimitar and point it at him, but he pounces and pins me to the floor beneath him. He holds my wrists, pries my scimitar from my hand and shoves it away.

"Surrender, you stubborn *katiaj*," he mutters under his breath. His voice is electronic, like he's not fully human, but somehow, it's familiar.

I refuse to give in. My scimitar glitters in the soft light against the floor not too far from me. I lie there, panting for a moment, motionless aside from the rising and falling of my chest.

"What do you want?" I ask through gritted teeth.

He loosens his grip on my wrists just slightly, but it's enough to pry my wrist free of his grasp. My fingers just reach my scimitar, and I smash the hilt into his helmet. His neck cracks and he rolls to the side, moaning. I push him off me and lunge for him. Holding him to the floor beneath me, I press the tip of my scimitar to his throat.

"Hands up," I say, still panting.

He slowly raises his hands above his head. "Fine! I surrender!"

"Who are you, and why are you here?"

"Who knew you could be so energetic after bedtime?" he snaps back. "I know it's been a long week, but by the stars, you need to take a chill pill."

"Answer me! Remove your helmet now!" I press the scimitar closer to his throat.

His hands tremble. "Okay, okay. Easy." He slowly removes his helmet. His wry smile is instantly recognizable even in the darkness.

I lower my scimitar and stand, backing away from him. "What are you doing here? Why couldn't you have just knocked like last time!"

Liam sits up, grabs his helmet, and stands. "I'll explain later, but we've got to get moving." He looks me up and down in my revealing pajamas. "You might want to go get dressed."

I deactivate my scimitar and drop it onto the couch. "Yeah. Okay."

"Although, I don't mind if you–"

"Shut up," I shoot back.

I dash to my closet, trying not to think about how I was wrestling Liam in this little tank top. Why is Liam in my apartment in the middle of the night? And more importantly, why am I following his orders?

I change into my warmest black leggings and white long sleeve shirt with open shoulders. My black combat boots slip on easily, and I'm about to head out when my eyes flicker to the top drawer of my dresser in my closet. I bite my lip. It's better to be safe, right?

As quietly as possible, I open up the top drawer and sift through my clothes until my fingers brush the varnished wood at the bottom. I remove the tiny push dagger and its sheath from the drawer. Unlike my scimitar, it's here in my apartment illegally. The man I bought it from did not give his name, though I suspect he works for the IA Guard by day. By night, he sells weapons the Guard wouldn't miss. I'm not sure how else he would've gotten his hands on such a well-crafted little blade.

The knife is thin and no longer than my index finger. The back of the silver blade seems to have been carved perfectly to fit my hand. I shove the dagger in its small, black leather sheath into my boot, hidden from sight.

When I get back into the main room of my apartment, I pick up my scimitar from the couch and attach it to my belt. I look at Liam and find a second figure approaching.

"Jaina, I'm so sorry about this."

"Kavi? Why are you here?" I take a step back. "What are both of you doing here?"

Liam hesitates. "I wish I could tell you. Please just trust us."

"Why can't you just tell me? What the hell is going on?" My pulse throbs in my neck faster and faster. Don't they trust me?

Kavi looks worriedly at Liam.

Liam takes a careful step toward me and tries to take my hand, but I pull away. "Listen, Jaina, please. This is very important. We need you to cooperate."

"Why?" My hands are sweaty and cold.

Liam hesitates. "If I told you, I'm not sure you'd come."

"Cut it out, Liam. You're scaring her." Kavi rolls her eyes and turns to me. "Jaina, it'll be easier for everyone if you don't know anything."

"Tell me what's going on!" I cry.

Liam and Kavi exchange glances.

"Jaina." Liam's gentle voice pisses me off even more. "We're trying to help you."

"I'm sorry, Jaina," Kavi says. "We aren't permitted to tell you. Under any other circumstance I would, but please you have to trust us."

I scoff. "You aren't *permitted*? By whom?"

Silence.

Liam's brown eyes glimmer in the faint light.

"Am I in trouble?" I ask.

"Not yet." Liam laughs, but there's an edge of seriousness in his voice.

The whining of engines breaks the silence of the room.

Kavi reaches for something at her belt. I'm terrified she's going to pull out a gun. Instead, she presses something small to her ear. "Is that you, sir?" she asks through what must be a phonicom. "We're on our way." Kavi walks through the glass doors onto the balcony and out of sight.

"Jaina, this way." Liam grabs my hand.

I jerk back from him, but he doesn't let go. "No."

He pulls harder. "You're coming with me."

"No." I glare at him. "I'm not going anywhere until you tell me what's going on."

Liam grits his teeth. "Alright. Looks like we're doing this the hard way." He moves closer to me, but I back farther away.

"Liam, stop!" I order, unable to chase away the raw fear in my voice.

He shakes his head. "Jaina, this is for your own good. The next person who comes knocking on your door won't be here to help you."

My stomach drops at his words. I have every urge to fight him, but fear keeps me paralyzed. He storms up to me, grabs me by the waist, and awkwardly starts to carry me. His strength is so shocking and powerful I gasp in surprise.

"Let me go!" I struggle and push away while doing my best not to hurt him.

He drops me a bit, but he clamps his hand around my arm. "Come with me now," he orders in a very dark voice. "Or you will never see me or Dragon again."

My whole body trembles, but no words come to my lips.

Liam continues, "If you ever want to see *any* of us again, you must come with me. This is because we care about you. Because *I* care about you."

When he jerks me forward, this time I don't resist. He pulls me through the open doorway onto the balcony. A ship– not just an everyday transport, but a fully equipped IA Guard transport– hovers a few feet from us. A ramp opens up, leading into the belly of the ship. Liam pulls us toward it. There's a huge gap separating the edge of the balcony and the ramp. Between the two is a straight drop down, 300 stories.

"Wait! Wait!" I shout over the whining of the engines. Everything's moving too fast. What if I never come back?

"We've got to go!" Liam cries.

I'm not sure what I'm waiting for, so I make something up. "This ship is made for space travel!"

"No *shaav*, it better be!"

Liam pulls me up on to the railing of the balcony then puts his arm around my waist. He lunges for the ramp of the ship with me in his arms. I'm too afraid to scream. We close the gap between my balcony and the ship and fall into the dark interior of the shuttle. My feet hit the floor with so much force that I collapse under my own weight, propelled forward by the momentum of our jump. Liam crashes down with me in a tangle of limbs. Somehow he's on top of me, one hand on my waist and another just below my chest, while his knee is awkwardly between my thighs.

"They're in. We're a go," Kavi says from a little farther back in the transport.

The ramp closes, leaving us all in a dark airlock.

Panting, I look up into Liam's eyes. I almost shove him away, but as I tremble beneath him, I don't necessarily want him to move. My cheeks burn.

Kavi narrows her eyes in disgust as she looks at us on the floor. "Get a room."

Liam smirks. "Good idea."

I roll my eyes and clear my throat. "Is it just me, or did you *intentionally* land in this position?"

"Maybe the universe is trying to tell us something?" He grins.

"I don't give a *shaav* about the universe, get off me." I push him away.

He reluctantly rolls to the side, and I stand and dust myself off, desperately trying to forget the awkwardness. I couldn't have actually enjoyed be tangled up with Liam like that. There's too much going on, and I am so *shaavez* confused.

The rumbling of the engines echoes through my bones. The ship is moving forward and ascending higher into the atmosphere.

"Where are we going?" I ask.

Liam shrugs. "I'm kind of in the dark on this, too. Mister *I-know-everything-so-don't-question-orders* only said to get you out."

"Dragon's here?" I ask, a glimmer of hope sparks in my heart. "Liam, why couldn't you have just told me that instead of making a huge deal about it back in my apartment?"

He rolls his eyes. "You're pathetic."

"Liam, is he here?" I ask, sounding a bit frantic even to myself.

"I wish I could say no…" Liam sighs. "Don't make me regret this. *Please.*"

I glare at him.

Kavi walks over to us. "Liam, would you escort her to her room?"

"Kavi, please. I led us through the Trials. Why can't anyone explain a *shaavez* thing to me?" I ask.

She takes a deep uncomfortable breath and exchanges glances with Liam then looks back at me. "Jaina," she says slowly, "you may have been a leader in the Trials, but this is far more important. I don't take orders from you."

"This isn't about *orders*, Kavi. Why can't any of you just trust me?"

Kavi shakes her head. "I'm sorry, Jaina." There's only a cold, emptiness in her eyes, a mask to keep everything from me.

This is not the Kavi I know.

"We can't say anything," Liam says. There's a frustrated edge in his voice. "I'll take her to her room."

He takes my hand and approaches the wall of the cargo bay. A door opens, and he leads me through a long twisty hall. We lose Kavi somewhere behind us. My body moves on its own, and I'm unable to exercise my free will. I'm in utter disbelief. I was the leader. I was in charge of keeping us safe and alive.

Clearly, that isn't the case anymore.

With a jolt, my strength returns. I stop abruptly and pull back on Liam's grip. He doesn't let go, so I brace myself and yank hard. The jerk nearly pulls my arm out of its socket. I pretend not to feel the pain in my arm.

"*Shaav,* Jaina, that hurt!"

"Take me to Dragon," I demand.

"No." He attempts to pull me forward, but I hold fast.

"Why?"

Liam grits his teeth. "Kavi ordered me to take you to your room, so that's exactly what I'm going to do."

"I never thought you were one to follow orders," I snort.

"I'm not." He tightens his grip on my hand just a little. "If I were Dragon right now, you'd follow without question."

Red hot needles prickle at the back of my neck and I bite my cheek to try to hold back my anger. "Dragon would answer my questions," I snap back.

Liam raises his eyebrows and shoots me a half angry, half amused smirk. "Oh you think?" He yanks me forward, and this time, I don't do a good job of resisting. He's gotten so much stronger. It annoys the hell out of me.

"Why the *shaav* are we here, Liam?" I try to pry my hand out of his grip.

He keeps my hand in his, almost effortlessly. His expression is hard, yet there's a glimmer of terror in his eyes. "You're here because we care about you."

"That answers nothing," I spit. "I was your leader. I kept you all *alive*, I–"

"Listen to me!" He shouts. "I'm trying to save your life! From being stuck in a loveless marriage! Yes, you were our leader. You *were*. But things are different now, and it's time you trust us. It's time you trust *me*."

The racing drumbeat of my heart, the rhythmic pounding in my ears sounds like a death-march. "We're not staying in the IA..." I choke out the realization.

He doesn't answer.

My whole body trembles. "They're going to kill us..." The words roll off my tongue. "Liam, we can't just leave! The IA has eyes and ears all over the galaxy. They're going to find us!"

Liam takes a deep breath. "There are places the IA doesn't have a presence. Places that are safe."

"I thought the IA was in control of every habitable–"

"They're not." His voice is cold.

"Why are you going along with this if you're not trusted with details of this plan?" I spit at him. "How can I trust you when you don't even know what's going on?"

Liam's jaw tightens. "As much as I despise the man, Dragon has your best interests in mind. And whatever happens, I need you to know–"

The ship lurches to the right, and I'm flung against the wall with so much force it makes my vision go blurry, and I start seeing spots. Liam rams into me, and his body presses up against mine all over again. The armor on his chest slams into me so hard I can hardly breathe.

When the ship corrects itself, I have every urge to shove him away from me, but I wait to see what he does.

Liam smirks but doesn't move. "I swear this time it wasn't intentional."

"Pervert," I mutter.

His cheeks flush red, but his voice grows a little softer as his eyes linger on my lips. "Jaina, I swear."

I take a deep shaky breath, and my heart races in my chest. Looking up into his deep dark eyes, I'm speechless.

Yes, I know exactly what I need to do.

Instead of pushing him away, I let my left hand rest gently on his shoulder then softly move it to his neck. His lips are trembling and I know how badly he wants to kiss me. His breathing becomes heavier, and I lean in just a little closer.

"I'm sorry, Liam," I breathe.

"What are you doing?" he whispers as his eyes close a little.

Here's my chance.

Without hesitation, I lift my right leg, shoving my hand into my boot and clasping my fingers around the small push dagger I smuggled from my apartment. Before he can react, I wrap my fingers around his neck, push back on him, and slam him against the opposite wall. He grabs my wrist and struggles against me until he sees the dagger poking out from between the fingers of my right hand. The dagger I now tenderly press against his throat.

"You little *katiaj*." He sneers. "You really expect me to believe you'd slit my throat?"

"I don't know." I'm slightly breathless. "You look pretty terrified."

He clenches his jaw. "We're your friends, Jaina. I'm trying to do what's best for you. I swear by the stars I would never do anything to hurt you."

"I believe that, but if they haven't told you what's going on, we both might be in danger. I need to know."

His lips remain sealed.

"Liam, tell me where he is," I demand.

"Or what?" he chokes out. "You'll kill me?"

"There are a lot of debilitating places I could stab you without doing long term damage." I honestly could never do anything of the sort, but I try to keep my eyes dark, angry and determined.

He looks up at the ceiling then mutters, "The cockpit. He's in the cockpit."

"Where is that?" I press the dagger a little closer to his throat.

"Put the *shaavez* dagger down," he snaps. "We both know you're not going to use that."

After a moment of glaring, I lower the dagger and take a step back. My cheeks flush. I have no idea what he's going to think of me now. Not that it will matter. I don't care what he thinks of me. I just need to find Dragon. I need to find the truth. "Where is the cockpit?"

"Up ahead and to the right." He replies as he rubs his throat uncomfortably. "*Shaav*, Jaina, if you scarred up my gorgeous skin–"

I roll my eyes. "I wouldn't dream of it. Don't follow me." I shove the knife back into my boot, turn on my heel and run down the long hall in front of me. Finally, I reach the end and turn to the right. Behind the large metal door, I hear voices– frantic, urgent– but I cannot distinguish whom they belong to.

The green button on the panel to open the door calls to me, but for some reason I'm afraid. Of what, I'm not sure.

Curiosity wins out, and I press it.

The door hisses open, and I step in.

"In the name of the galaxy..." I choke out.

Out the cockpit windows, the Imperial Interplanetary Defender just above Crystal City airspace floats in the blackness of the outer atmosphere. The sheer size of the cylindrical ship is menacing, even from a distance. Hundreds of thousands of trained guards and soldiers live there, constantly prepared for battle. At a moment's notice, they could get in their fighters, fly toward us, and blow us into oblivion.

I want to scream, but I can't force a single sound from my throat.

Kavi turns around in her seat, and her face turns white. "Liam was supposed to take you to your room!"

"You didn't tell me we were approaching an IID!" I cry.

We're really leaving the Crystal City. I'm not sure whether to feel relieved or terrified.

Kavi's fingers fly across buttons on the control panel. "We've run into some trouble."

"Obviously!" I shout.

She grits her teeth, and her eyes narrow in frustration. "Take a seat and buckle up!"

I take the empty seat behind her. That's when I see him at the helm, and my heart stops.

"I repeat, we are an IAA Vessel. Requesting permission to depart the Crystal City," Dragon orders into the com.

I can't see him well, so it's no wonder I didn't notice him when I first walked in. He's sitting next to Kavi. Seth is sitting next to me, but I hardly recognize him. He looks thinner, less built than he did when we were in the Trials. He studies the navigation charts intently.

"Sir, have you sent the access codes yet?" Seth asks.

"Maybe they didn't go through." Dragon presses a button on the panel, and there's static. "IAA requesting permission to depart. Access code...seven, one, three, dash six, four two. This is shuttle A1-70 of the IAA, requesting permission to depart."

Kavi taps him, unable to take her gaze away from a screen to her left. "Sir, we've got three IA Furies on our tail. They're in attack formation but haven't made any aggressive—"

"They've been following us for the past few minutes. I don't think they'll make a move, at least not yet." Dragon leans back over the com and presses a button to send another transmission. "I repeat. This is shuttle A1-70 of the IAA, requesting permission to depart. Access code seven, one, three, dash six, four two."

There's a short silence.

"Incoming transmission from the Defender," Kavi says.

Dragon nods. "Authorize them."

Kavi presses a button, and the transmission plays.

"Shuttle A1-70, what is your assignment?" a male voice asks.

Dragon takes a deep breath and runs his fingers through his dark hair.

"Shuttle A1-70, please respond. Over," the man aboard the Defender says.

Dragon presses a button. "Sorry, sir. We've been experiencing communication malfunctions. We're heading to the outpost on Xiora to deliver reinforcements and prisoners. Over." He cuts the com.

There's some static at the other end of the line, and a cold silence fills the room. My skin prickles as our fate hangs in the balance.

"Permission granted. Over," says a gruff voice from the other end of the transmission.

Dragon, Kavi, and Seth simultaneously let out a deep sigh.

"About time," Dragon mutters.

Seth spins around in his chair. "I can't believe they bought that."

Dragon glances at Seth, smirking slightly. "Of course they bought it."

"So now what? They're just going to let us pass?"

Dragon takes a deep breath. "It won't be that easy, but I have a plan. Don't worry." His gaze flickers to me. His jaw tightens, and he looks away. He smiles a little. "Hi, Jaina."

My chest tightens. After so long, that's all he could manage to say to me? No *"I've missed you,"* no look of love, of longing, or even a glimmer of happiness upon seeing me? Not even a *shaavez* explanation? "Dragon," I manage to choke out. "What–"

He shakes his head. "Just hang in there. Everything will be explained."

My stomach sinks, and a cold sense of betrayal, anger, and fear spreads through my body, infused into my blood. How can he talk like this? He was my partner. By the stars, none of them trust me. Not even Dragon.

"The Furies are gone. Ascend from the upper atmosphere and switch to artificial gravity," Kavi says, her voice harsh, almost mechanical.

Dragon takes control of the ship and banks upward. His fingers glide across the control panel, and he presses a series of buttons. The sudden change of gravity is an odd sensation, uncomfortable at best. The pull toward the floor of the ship is different, less powerful. My heart beats oddly in my chest, like it's confused about the change as well. I'm not sure if it skips a beat or adds an extra one, but the feeling is slightly sickening. I close my eyes, take a deep breath through my nose, and exhale through my mouth a few times. *You're okay. You're not going to be sick. Just breathe.*

The sensation fades, but I keep my eyes closed. I clench my hands into fists to keep myself from trembling. Suddenly, I am so unbelievably afraid.

This is it. I'm never going back. I can't ever go back, or they'll kill me. They'll kill all of us. All we can do is run. Will I spend the rest of my life running from the IA? Running away from fear, from my duties and responsibilities to a nation I used to love?

I know what I wished for, and I know I wanted to leave. All I'm abandoning is a life full of lies.

But it was safe there. And the people I considered my friends don't trust me at all. I should feel safe with them, but I don't. I'm not sure I will until they can manage to tell me *something*.

I open my eyes. The Defender grows larger in the viewport as we leave the atmosphere of the planet.

"Another transmission," Kavi's voice trembles slightly.

Dragon clenches his right hand into a fist. "Here we go. Let's hear it."

Kavi presses a button, and the transmission plays.

"Shuttle A1-70," the same gruff male voice says coldly into the mic, "after further inspection, your mission to Xiora has not been confirmed with your base. Furthermore, there is a suspect IAA vessel on the loose, and we cannot allow anyone to leave Crystal

City airspace at this time. Your orders are to come aboard until the threat is neutralized. Over."

"I hope you made something up," Seth whispers.

"I'm working on it," Dragon mumbles. "Get ready to fire the drives, Kavi. We have to hit critical velocity. Get us into the hyperfield."

Kavi furrows her brow. "Are you *shaavez* crazy? Firing the drives this close to the IID and the City–"

"None of this is safe, Kavi," Dragon snaps back. "If you want *safe* I can drop you back in the Crystal City."

"Sorry, sir."

"Shuttle A1-70, please respond. Over," the man aboard the Defender says.

"I repeat," Dragon speaks angrily into the com. "We are experiencing communication malfunctions. It is urgent that we reach Xiora on schedule. There are lives at stake. Our mission has not been confirmed with our base because of the immediate need to depart but should be confirmed within the hour. With a suspect on the loose, confirmation will take longer. I urge you to let us continue. Over."

Seth rolls his eyes. "If they kill us, I'm blaming *you*."

"How are the drives?" Dragon asks.

Kavi's face is dark with worry. "Still charging."

Dragon turns his head ever so slightly to the right as if he wants to look at me but can't. He's hardly changed since I last saw him. His eyes still as intense, his hair maybe slightly darker. There's something wrong, something missing that I can't place.

The com goes static then comes to life. "Shuttle A1-70, permission to continue is denied."

Seth kicks the back of Dragon's seat. "*Shaav.*"

"Until your base has confirmed your mission, you are not permitted to proceed. Your orders are to come aboard."

"Of course." Seth curses. "We're dead."

"*Shaav,*" Dragon mutters.

"Sir," Kavi says, "there's no way we can get enough charge to hit the hyperfield threshold before they open fire on us."

A shadow of worry crosses Dragon's face. "I'll do everything I can to hold them off, but they've gotta charge faster if we want to make it out alive."

"We've got seven Furies on our tail," Seth reports, sweat streaming through his hair. "Guess those Furies *weren't* gone, Kavi. They can tell we're not planning on boarding."

"Can you identify their class?" Dragon asks.

"Interceptors, sir."

"Shuttle A1-70, if you do not correct your course, we will open fire," says the officer on the com.

"Kavi, how much longer?" Dragon's voice is harsh.

"Sir, we're only eighty-seven percent, and that's just for the threshold," she replies. "We aren't going to make it!"

"*Shaav!*" Dragon runs his fingers through his hair again. "We're not going to last much longer."

I unbuckle and jump out of my seat. "You have to cut the power."

They all turn to me, but no one moves.

Right.

They don't trust me.

"Kavi, give me your seat," I order. "We can't waste time."

Kavi stands but moves slowly, like she's not entirely sure if she should comply. She looks from me to Dragon a few times, then switches seats with me. I'm so close to him, now.

I start pressing buttons. The controls aren't much different from model ships I trained in on Virana. Dragon's eyes are on me, I can feel it. I'm not sure if he trusts me either, but I try to ignore it. Kavi and Seth are staring at me as well, and their gazes seem to cut into me like knives.

*Cut the power.*

I clench my teeth. "If I redirect the power from the rest of the ship to the drives, they will charge faster. Apart from coms, life support, and gravity, I'm shutting everything down. Now do you want me to get us out of here alive or as space debris?" I snap. "Open the com!"

Dragon presses a button on the control panel and opens a transmission to the IID.

"Defender, do you read me?" I ask. "Defender, do you read me? Over."

"Yes we read you. Now correct your course *immediately!*" the officer barks.

"Sir, our ship is out of control. I'm cutting all power within our vessel. We'll restore our course once we have control." My heart is pounding in my ears so loudly I can hardly hear anything else.

"Shall we tow you aboard?" the officer's voice crackles over the com.

"Negative. We have precious cargo, fragile medical units, and weaponry, destined for troops on Xiora. We cannot afford damaging it. Over," I say.

We wait a minute. When there's no reply, I start to wonder if I got the planet wrong. Dragon said Xiora, right?

The com opens once more. "Very well. Make it quick."

I cut the communication and return to switching off the power. The ship's engines stop completely. The lights power off. We're drifting in space.

"Help me transfer all power to the drives," I order.

"That could blow up the ship," Kavi warns.

"Not if it's done correctly," Dragon cuts in. "I'm on it."

This better work. If this doesn't charge them, I have no idea what will. My fingers are trembling. What am I doing? By the stars, what am I doing?

"Kavi, how are we?" I ask.

"We're ninety percent charged for a jump. Ninety-one, ninety-two and counting."

"Seth, get ready for the jump on my mark," I say. "Dragon, chart a course for..." I stop. I have no idea where we're going.

He doesn't look at me. "I got it."

"Ninety-seven percent charged," Kavi says. "Ninety-nine, one hundred!"

"Now!" I restore all power simultaneously.

The drives are activated. Time seems to slow. A whining sound slices through the sudden silence. Space around us bends and twists into a vortex. With a flash of blinding light, the shuttle charges forward into the hyperfield. The Crystal City and the Imperial Alliance, my dreams of the future and the painful reality they turned out to be are left behind, engulfed in the ocean of space.

I'm not sure if I'm ready for this.

# CHAPTER SEVEN

We're engulfed in a liquid blackness. It's an endless tunnel, like being underwater in the middle of the night, gazing up at a clear, starry sky. The hyperfield ripples with streaks of white, and it reminds me of home, of walking the beach at night and catching the glimmer of small, silvery fish in the waves.

It's not like I haven't been in the hyperfield before. Everyone has to pass through it to get to a system within a reasonable amount of time, but I've never been in the cockpit while passing through.

The whining of this ship is higher pitched than I'm used to. After a while, the sound disappears into the background.

Kavi sits awkwardly next to Seth, and the silence in the room is unbearable. They keep an eye on their sections of the dashboard, making slight adjustments here and there. In front of Dragon is a red screen and in the top right corner are the coordinates X 256, Y 879, and Z -044. I wrack my brain to pinpoint where in the galaxy that could possibly be. It can't be in IA space.

But there are no habitable planets outside of IA space. *Where the shaav are we going?*

When I muster the strength to glance at Dragon, his eyes are fixed on the windows. Is he pretending not to notice me, or does he really not care? The whole situation makes my heart sink deeper into my chest. We escaped the Alliance. Dragon came to rescue me, and yet for some reason, this doesn't feel like a rescue at all.

Seth clears his throat. "Kavi and I secured our trajectory through the hyperfield."

Dragon turns to Kavi and Seth.

"Thank you. Kavi, Seth, you're dismissed," he says politely. "We'll com you if we need you."

"Are you sure?" Kavi asks.

He nods. "Yes. Go help Luci with Avan."

Both Kavi and Seth stand up and leave the cockpit.

Now we're alone. I haven't seen him in four months, and yet he continues to ignore me.

By the tightness of Dragon's lips and eyebrows, I don't get the sense that he's happy I'm here. So why am I?

I'm not sure how to start up a conversation. It's all different now. With every second of silence, my blood boils hotter. What's wrong with him? He hasn't said a *shaavez* word to me, after four months this is all I get? When is he planning on telling me what's going on?

I can't take it anymore.

"Tell me." My tone is emotionless.

He stares out the cockpit. "Tell you what?"

The cold in his voice fills my body with a hot, sickening rage. I close my eyes and breathe in through my nose and out my mouth. *Stay calm.* My hands feel frozen. "Why?" I manage, refusing to look at him. "Why risk all of our lives, our futures... We're traitors now. For what? I want to know why."

The start of a smile plays at his lips, but he still doesn't face me. "Everything will be explained later." He casually flips a small switch. "We have betrayed a nation that was going to force you into marriage, a nation that was going to trap you there for the rest of your life and lie to you about everything. Does it bother you that we're traitors?" His voice remains steady, almost emotionless.

"I don't know." I keep my voice flat and try to conceal my anger. "I got us out of there alive, I deserve–"

"I had it under control." Dragon tilts his head slightly toward me. "I understand you want answers, and you'll get them. You're already taking this better than I thought you would."

"How did you think I'd take it?" I ask.

"Not quite sure." Dragon turns to me, but I look away the moment he does. I'm too angry, too afraid of what I might find in his eyes. "I was prepared for a lot."

"Where are we going?"

"Not Xiora," he replies, calmly as ever. "Jaina, trust me."

"How can I trust you when none of you trust me?" I snap at him. "What changed since the Trials? We worked together. You know I would've placed my faith in you."

He sighs deeply. "This isn't about trust."

"Of course it is." I grip the armrests of the co-pilot's seat. "You *abducted* me from my life. You could've just asked me and told me the truth. I would've come with you, and I would've been a lot more prepared."

Dragon hesitates. "Asking you was not an option, nor did it matter. I had to get you out of there regardless of what you wanted. You're important, Jaina." He speaks slowly, as if choosing his words with caution.

"What do you mean it didn't matter?" I aim to keep my voice steady, but it trembles slightly. "What if I had wanted to stay?"

"You would've come with us by force."

I grip the armrests of the co-pilot's chair even harder. It isn't just anger anymore. Cool prickly fear nips at the back of my neck, sending electric shivers down my spine.

"You are important," he says again, "so much more than you know. My *mission* was to get you out."

My body goes cold, and I want to throw up. Emptiness envelopes me, like someone took a shovel, cut me open and hollowed me out. Despite everything he's said, I hoped that maybe this was all because he cared. Maybe he saw the injustices of the Crystal City and was angry that I was being forced to marry. I swallow hard. "Mission?" I choke out.

"Yes."

I wait for him to explain, but he says nothing more.

"What are you?" *Dragon, by the stars, who are you?* My body trembles, and I think back to every moment I ever spent with him. Back on Virana, all the training, all the flirting in the Trials, the kiss...what was all that? An act? "Are you an assassin? A bounty hunter? A slaver?"

"You think that low of me?" he asks, his voice darkening. "That I could be a *slaver*? I just freed you from eternal slavery to the IA."

"Who do you work for?" My tone grows colder. "Are you a terrorist?"

Dragon runs his fingers through his dark, thick hair. "It depends on who you ask."

"I'm asking you."

"I'm a freedom fighter," he replies emotionless. "You know how on Virana, they'd tell us the era of Resistance ended?"

Chills run through me. All I can manage is a soft, timid, "Yes..."

The light from the hyperfield sparkles in his eyes as he stares forward. "They lied."

The door behind us slides open with a hiss. I turn around. Luci stands in the doorway. Her dark eyes meet mine for an instant. Her expression is menacing, and the corner of her lip twitches slightly. I can feel her annoyance from here.

Luci shifts her gaze to Dragon. "Sir, we're approaching the fleet."

Dragon nods. "Send the access codes."

"Yes, sir." She turns on her heel and starts to walk away.

"Luci," Dragon calls. "Once you've made contact, transfer all communications to the cockpit."

"Yes, sir."

The door slides shut, and there's silence.

Freedom fighter. My mind flashes back to news stories about the terrorists and the tales in the history books about the Resistance, about how they take people against their will and sell them into slavery in exchange for ammunition and supplies. They're ruthless killers, sacrificing their lives along with so many innocents just to get a point across.

And Dragon is a ruthless killer. In the Trials, killing didn't seem to bother him. *He said I'm important.* How the *shaav* am I important? By the stars, what are they going to do with me?

A crackle sounds over the ship's com, and a transmission comes through.

"Your access has been granted. State your name and rank," says a bored, uninterested voice.

"Altair Kasev, Commander of Operation *From the Ashes* assigned by the General of the GR," Dragon speaks confidently as if he'd recited the line a thousand times. The words leave his lips without hesitation, devoid of emotion.

GR.

That's what they called it.

The Galactic Resistance.

There's a short silence over the com. "Commander Kasev, it is an honor to have you back." The man's voice has become excited, alert.

"Thank you."

"Who would you like me to contact, Commander?" the man asks.

Dragon takes a deep breath. "The General."

"Of course. One moment please."

There's a *click* as the com dies, and words burst from my throat before I have time to reconsider them. "Tell me everything *now*." I can't help the panic in my voice.

Worry flickers across his face. "Jaina, I'd much rather wait and let the General explain everything," he says quietly.

"No," I counter. "I want you to tell me. The Resistance is gone. You couldn't possibly–"

"Jaina, the Resistance has survived. Citizens of the IA are kept unaware of our existence."

"Does the IA know?" I breathe.

"Of course they know," he snaps back. "They call us terrorists to make people fear us, to make us sound like a small band of organized crime. But we have an army that's growing every day. Soon, they'll have to face us for what we are."

"Dragon, stop!" I put my hand on his shoulder. "You can turn us around. We can find somewhere safe–"

Anger flashes in his eyes. "You have no idea how hard I worked to get us here, what I've had to sacrifice to get you out. This is who you are, Jaina. I am not going to disobey orders and abandon my life's work to find safety." His voice is sharp, even sassy.

"You have no idea who I am," I snap back. "I've spent my life worrying about you, missing you, and now we could go somewhere where we never have to worry about the Alliance, we can stop fighting. Life in the Crystal City was miserable with it's fake perfection, but that doesn't mean I wanted to escape and become an outlaw, a *traitor*. Now we have a chance–"

"A chance at what? To hide? To spend the rest of our lives running, in fear?" He replies. "And I know you better than you know yourself," Dragon pauses, "my orders are to deliver you to the General."

"What if I refuse?" I ask.

Dragon only looks away, back to the ships settled in the backdrop of the stars. "Don't fight me on this. You have to trust me."

"Why should I?"

"Because I care about you," he replies, his voice a little softer.

My stomach knots and I find myself speechless. Does he really care about me? I feel like I shouldn't trust him. Every bone in my body tells me not to.

But for some ridiculous reason, I do.

"Okay." My voice comes out in a whisper.

"Commander," a familiar voice crackles to life over the com. His voice is stern, commanding, and kind all at the same time. "Commander, do you copy?"

Dragon sits forward and presses a button to speak. "General?"

"Yes. By the stars, you're alright. Is Jaina with you?" he asks in an accented voice, like Shirez's voice. In fact, it sounds strangely similar to Shirez's.

Dragon looks from me to the com. "Yeah, she's here."

"May I speak with her?" He asks.

It sounds exactly like him, but it couldn't be. He's dead.

Dragon motions for me to come closer.

"Who is this?" I ask into the speaker.

"Jaina, this is Shirez. I want to apologize for all the deception. It was the only way. I'm glad you've returned safely."

My heart races in my chest. He's alive. The excitement coursing through my blood makes me dizzy. It's clearly Shirez's voice. I'd know it anywhere.

"Shirez, how are you..." I can't finish. "How–"

"I'll explain everything, Jaina. I promise," Shirez interrupts. "Altair, have Luci escort everyone to the living quarters. After that, I want you to meet me in the conference room. Bring Jaina."

Dragon nods. "Yes, sir. We'll be boarding momentarily."

*The Justice* seems much bigger on the inside than I thought it'd be, yet the ship looks like it was made more for a pleasure cruise through the galaxy than for battle.

I catch the faint scent of fuel and machinery. The impossibly low humming of the engines is faint beneath our echoing footsteps.

The crew members who pass us speak in cold emotionless tones. Every action they perform is precise and orderly.

Wine cabinets are awkwardly filled with sniper rifles and grenades. The white floors look like some sort of marble, but they're dirty and worn from troops filing down the corridors. Everything is fascinating, some weird twisted sort of contradiction.

It's the type of ship I'd expect a royal to own.

Maybe it belongs to Shirez.

Shirez is *alive.*

Dragon is a few paces ahead of me. He seems so far away. Distant. It hurts. I want to talk to him, the

Jessica K. McKendry

old him, the one I knew in the Trials. But the truth is I don't know who he is anymore. What will they do with me if they know I don't want to be a part of this?

It's been about twenty minutes since we got off the stolen IA transport. Luci led the others away when we disembarked, but Liam wasn't with them. As much as I hate to admit it to myself, I miss his presence. His comfort.

Dragon hasn't said a word to me. I need to break the silence. Dragon *had* to come for me, whether he actually wanted to or not. He said it was his mission, that I'm more important than I know.

*What about you, Dragon? Am I important to you?*

My stomach drops. I wish I could turn off my brain and prevent myself from thinking.

"Dragon."

He acknowledges me with a glance but continues walking.

I clear my throat. "What happens after we speak with Shirez?"

"Whatever my next mission requires me to do."

"Your next mission?" I choke out. Is that all I am to him? A mission? A lump rises in my throat, threatening to make me burst into tears or punch the *shaav* out of him.

Dragon stares forward into the distance. Past the walls. Past the ship. Past the stars. He doesn't even have the decency to turn around and look at me. "Yes."

I try hard to rein in the angry burning sensation at the back of my neck. "And where the *shaav* do I fit into this?"

He stops and finally his gaze meets mine. "Everything is changing. It has to change. Shirez will explain everything to you."

For a moment, I get the sense that he wants to say more, but he doesn't. The darkness returns to his crystalline eyes, and he turns away. He continues walking at a much quicker pace now, and I struggle to keep up with him.

My whole body trembles. His cold numbness ricochets off my bones and through my blood. It makes me shiver, and I have nothing left to say.

Dragon stops at a large, double door and inputs a code into the control panel on the wall. The door slides open and reveals a large conference table where a man studies a silverscreen.

Seeing him catches me off guard. I can't help smiling as Shirez stands from his seat at the right hand side of the head chair.

He strides up to me and gives me a hug. "Jaina, I'm so glad you're safe."

I pull away after a moment. "Shirez, what happened? We all thought you were...how did you..."

Shirez takes my hands in his. "All will be explained in due course, I promise, but first, you should have a seat."

I follow Shirez to the end of the table. He takes his seat, and I sit across from him. A glass of water rests to his right, and there's one in front of me. Who normally sits at the head of the table? Why isn't it Shirez?

Dragon hasn't advanced into the room, still standing at the entrance.

Just looking at Shirez floods me with relief. "It was so horrible hearing about you. I-I'm so glad you're alright. I just don't know what's going on, and no one is giving me any answers." I shoot Dragon a glare.

"Jaina, we have some serious matters to discuss." Shirez's eyes seem a little darker than I remember, a little more sunken in too. The hard lines of age that scar his face are deeper than before, like someone took a chisel and hammered away at it for the past four months.

Dragon nods. "I'll leave you now."

"Get ready for your assignment," Shirez says.

"Yes, sir." Dragon gives Shirez a weak salute then leaves. The doors slide closed behind him.

Shirez's brows are furrowed in all seriousness. There's a short breath of silence. "So..." he finally says. He leans back in his chair and places his hands on the armrests. "Welcome to the Resistance."

My fingers tingle, and my stomach drops.

Silence hangs over us like an ominous ghost in the room.

"I mean you no disrespect," I hesitate, trying to find a nice way to put it, "but I was under the impression that the Resistance had been destroyed and reduced to, um...terrorists." I avert my gaze to the table. If this truly is the Resistance, if this is the band of *terrorists* the IA broadcast warnings about so many times, saying something wrong could seal my fate.

"The Alliance lied about many things," he replies. "Clearly, we exist, and we are not the terrorists they make us out to be, I can assure you of that."

"How do I know that's true?" I choke out, my hands trembling. My brain hurts, I'm so confused. "How do I know you won't hold me hostage or sell me into–"

"Jaina." Shirez's smile is kind and comforting. "We extracted you from the Crystal City for a reason." He leans forward and sighs. "This is a fight for freedom. We don't sell people into slavery."

I swallow hard. He sounds convincing, but isn't that exactly what a terrorist would say? No, not Shirez. So far, he's the only one giving me answers. "How have you survived all this time?"

Shirez takes a deep breath. "Sixteen years ago, the IA could have defeated us. They would have destroyed us, actually." He interlocks his fingers and places his hands on the table. "Our forces were weak, our only defense was to run."

"What happened?" My lips move on their own.

Shirez keeps his gaze on me. His eyes are steady, yet they're filled with pain. "They captured our leader, the Phoenix, the one who united us, held us together. When they took her to be executed, we amassed our forces in preparation for a large attack on the capital. We would've lost the fight, but the Alliance panicked and made a deal with us. As long as we made no offensive move toward them, they would keep her imprisoned, but she would be safe. And we agreed."

"Did they keep their word?"

Shirez sighs. "Jaina, we need her. The Phoenix knows more about the Alliance and the Resistance than any of us will ever know. She plays a crucial role in the fate of the galaxy and is by no means safe in their hands, but they have kept her alive." By the soft tone of his voice, it's clear the memory is still fresh in his mind, as if it all happened yesterday.

I shift in my seat. "You're a prince."

"I was," he corrects. "Up until my 'death.' My father was the chosen Prince of Earth in 370 ASW. I was born as the sole heir to the throne. When I was twenty-five, I was appointed in place of my father. It was never a position I wanted, and my arranged engagement pushed me over the edge. I was trapped, and I needed an escape."

"How? Aren't they watching you at all times?"

"There's always a way out." He clears his throat. "I found an escape with the Resistance. Once my fate had been sealed with my marriage, I became obsessed with finding them. It was the only way out. At that time, they were an organized band of pirates of sorts. They kept themselves well hidden and would perform strikes, attack Alliance bases, steal ammunition, more of a nuisance than a threat. For years I searched in vain. Then they attacked *The Unforgiven*, one of the IA's most powerful battleships at the time. The ship and the entire crew disappeared near my planet. That's how I found them."

I look at him. "And they trusted you?"

"Oh goodness, no. Most certainly not. I was the Prince of the Earth. It took me quite some time, and a lot of expensive supplies to win their trust. I have been an insider for the past twenty-two years."

My eyes narrow. "You faked your death. Why?"

"It was time for me to go," he says carefully.

"Why *now*?"

"Because of you. This has always been the plan."

"What do you mean?" I grip the armrests of my chair a little tighter. "How does this have anything to do with me?"

A soft breath is purged from his lips, and he runs his fingers through his salt and pepper hair. "We had to get you out. On Virana, everything was so closely monitored that it just wasn't possible at the time. We needed to show you the Crystal City and the injustice there. It was hard to get your team together–"

I sit up straight. The pit of my stomach tingles. "You wanted me here? This whole time, the Trials, everything, was all to get me here?" My voice trembles.

"Yes. That's why we sent so many to extract you in case things went wrong. Kavi, Seth, and Luci were easy to get into Virana, but Altair..." He stares at the glass of water next to him but doesn't pick it up. "They found his presence disturbing. He made them suspicious."

My heart wrenches in my chest, and my stomach constricts. I can't help but feel betrayed.

He knew. All this time. This whole time, they've been planning to get me out of the IA. How far would they have gone to get me here? How far *did* they go to get me here?

My stomach twists, and I feel sick. I shake my head in disbelief. "Why me?"

Shirez looks down. "You have a lot more to do with the Resistance than you think."

Fear bubbles up inside me. It grows warm, like hatred. I want to know the truth. I've been lied to by everyone.

Dragon's the one who said there shouldn't be secrets between us but kept them all to himself. And I knew he was keeping things from me, but I couldn't have expected anything like this.

I grit my teeth. "You didn't answer my question."

There's a cold, suffocating silence.

"*Why. Me.*" I demand.

Shirez shifts uncomfortably. "The IA lies to their people. I don't want to become the enemy and withhold the truth from you, but before I tell you, ask yourself this. Do you really want to know? The truth can be painful, a great burden, even dangerous. The answer you seek is something you can never go back from."

Breathing suddenly takes such a huge effort. How bad could it be? What could possibly be so painful? So dangerous?

"Tell me. I want to know the truth."

He clenches his fist in a futile attempt to hide his trembling hands. "When the Phoenix was captured, the Alliance also took her child. The child was to be kept safe under Alliance eyes. The child was their... insurance, you could say. To make sure we wouldn't go back on our deal. To make sure we'd never try to break her out of prison. If we were ever to free her, her child would be executed. If that were to happen, she would have nothing left to fight for. She never asked to be freed, Jaina. She's remained in prison for her daughter. She remains there for you."

The hairs on the back of my neck stand on end.

"This is who you are, Jaina. The Phoenix is Amara Indera. She's your mother."

# CHAPTER EIGHT

My defenses are gone. They fall. Crumbling through the floor, melting into the ship and the vastness of space. But they don't stop there. They go on and on, to the bottom of the universe, and burn away until they are nothing. Sucked into a black hole or torn apart by a supernova.

No.

I misheard him. There's no way I could be...

I'm gripping the armrests of my chair for dear life, as if letting go would mean following my defenses through the universe and ultimately to destruction.

"No." My voice is no more than a whisper. "That's not possible."

My mother was a common citizen of the IA. That's what they said. She wasn't some *Resistance* leader.

Shirez's eyes are sullen with what looks like stress. "The truth isn't always what we want to hear. It's a burden we must carry, a burden we can live with or reject."

"Why should I trust you?" My voice is dark.

His expression hardens a bit, and I suspect he was expecting me to reject the words he had to say. "I'm not asking you to trust me, Jaina. You wanted to know the truth, and that is what I gave you. Ask yourself this…why do you think we'd go through the trouble of bringing you here, risking the lives of children in the process, if you weren't important to us?"

Dragon's words replay in my head, and I finally understand what he meant. It all makes sense. In the second Trial, when he told me he couldn't afford to lose me, he wasn't talking about *love*. This was his mission. He probably didn't give a damn what happened to me after we got out. And the rest of them? Did any of them care about me for *me* or only as an asset in their game?

Goosebumps rise up all over my skin as I remember my conversation with Sean in the park.

"Her eyes," I blurt out. "What color are they?"

Shirez's eyes narrow, he looks confused. "What do you mean?"

"Tell me what color her eyes are!" I demand frantically.

"Blue," he replies quickly. "Icy blue, but warmer and more kind than you can possibly imagine."

The pieces of the puzzle come together in my head to form a picture that makes me sick.

"How..." is all I manage to choke out. "...not possible..."

Shirez moves a hand forward but stops short and retreats. "Jaina, give it some time. It's a lot to take in."

His words barely process in my mind. All I feel is angry. By the stars, Dragon knew all along. Why the *shaav* didn't he tell me? He could have warned me or helped prepare me for what he knew was coming. Instead he left me here in this room to fend off my feelings alone. He's a coward.

"Where is she? My mother?"

Shirez's hard expression is on the verge of shattering. There's so much pain in his eyes. "They made a deal with us. If Amara was rescued from prison, you'd be killed. She loved you, Jaina. She was willing to sacrifice everything for you. Even her life."

There's a pause. I don't dare think because if I do, the only thing I'll feel is pain.

"Amara warned us that if we wanted to rescue her, we'd have to come for you first. Your mother is still in prison."

"She's alive?"

Shirez nods, but his expression doesn't brighten. "Not for long. Once the Alliance discovers you were one of the seven who escaped the Crystal City, she'll be executed."

My throat constricts, but it doesn't surprise me. Azad's words echo through my thoughts. *"It is not a painless death for a traitor..."*

My heart races in my chest, and the hairs on my arms stand on end. Part of me wants to ask what they're going to do to save her, if they're going to save her. Another part of me wants to scream, back away from the table in denial of it all, and curl up in a ball so tightly until I shrink into nothing.

"She isn't my mother," I finally choke out.

"Jaina." Shirez's face tightens a bit more.

"She gave birth to me, but she didn't raise me. She is not my mother."

Shirez's fingers squeeze together a little more. "She had no choice, Jaina. You were kidnapped. She did everything she could for you. Amara is risking her life and the fate of the galaxy to save you."

"She doesn't know who I am." My voice sounds desperate even to me. "If *this* is who she was, I am no daughter to her, either."

"You're just like her, Jaina," he says quietly. "You have her light. Her devotion. Her passion."

I clear my throat. "You knew her well."

"She had me promise to take care of you until you were ready. Unfortunately, there was no way I could get to you before the Trials."

"What do you want from me?" I ask, dark and demanding.

"For the time being," he says carefully, "we need you here. We need to keep you safe from the IA until we find her."

"And then what?"

Shirez shakes his head. "I don't know."

"What if you fail?"

"I don't know."

My breath trembles as I lean forward on the table, running my fingers through my hair. I stare down at the gray metallic surface of the table.

"I'm not going to sit here and wait." The words spill out of my mouth.

"Do you want to join us?" Shirez asks.

"No. I don't." My answer comes out quick and stern. "But I want to find my mother."

Shirez sighs. "You don't have to join us, but I cannot let you go looking for your mother."

"I'm not a part of this, so I ask that you let me go." I bite my lip to stop the tears from streaming down my face. I am so unbelievably afraid. There's no way I can go back to the Alliance, they would kill me. But I still can't bring myself to fully betray them. All I know now is that I have to find her.

His fingers tap an uneven rhythm on the table. "Until your mother is safe, I cannot let you leave this ship. After that, you may do whatever you wish."

I clench my fist. "So what are you going to do?"

"Your mother is kept in a secret prison. We don't know where yet, but we've got people working on a lead. We would've liked to rescue you after we had a set location, but the risks were too high. If the IA found us gathering information on her prison, they would have killed both of you."

I nod numbly. "So what do you want me to do?"

"You'll remain here with your friends who've decided to join us. When you begin to understand, you'll join as well." He looks over me.

"I'm not joining you," I snap.

He takes another deep breath and shifts uncomfortably in his seat. "Even so, you will be safe here." He looks at me sadly. "Do you think you'll be alright?"

"I'll be fine," I lie. "Where's Dragon?"

"He should be in his quarters, getting ready to leave."

"Where is he going?" I ask.

Shirez's eyes turn cloudy. "I cannot say."

I bite my lip. He cannot say or will not say? My hands clench into fists in my lap. "Where are Dragon's quarters?"

Shirez's gaze is on the table. "I'm afraid speaking to Dragon may not be the best course of action at this time–"

"I must speak with him," I insist. "Before he goes on his *mission*."

He closes his eyes. "Follow the corridor to the left then turn right. He should be there in room 0503." Before I can thank him, he adds, "You are dismissed."

I nod, stand without looking at Shirez, and follow the corridor. How could Dragon do this to me? I trusted him. I...I loved him.

A chill runs through me. *"He's lying to your face, Jaina. Why the shaav can't you see that?"* Azad had said, and he was right. Did Dragon ever feel anything for me at all?

Tears form, but I blink them away. I keep my eyes down as I move through the corridors, and when I finally look up, I can't breathe. Dragon's leaning against the closed door.

The moment he looks at me, I turn away and start down another hall. I thought I could face him, but the raging fire within me makes it impossible to even glance at him.

"Jaina," he calls, but I don't turn around, and I walk even faster. His footsteps quicken, and he appears at my side then steps in front of me.

I can't do this. I thought I could. "Stop following me."

"Jaina?" His hand touches my shoulder.

I grab his arm and I shove him violently backward. "Don't you dare touch me."

He raises his hands in surrender. In his eyes I find nothing but guilt. Not surprise. Not confusion or denial or fear. Just plain guilt. And that makes me even sicker.

"Jaina, calm down," he pleads. "Please."

"You lied to me!" I cry, holding back tears. "You... you..." I bite my cheek and can't finish.

He shakes his head and can't look me in the eyes. "Jaina, I'm–"

"All of it was a *lie!*" I shove him harder into the wall. "How could you? I trusted you..."

"I had to." He grabs my shoulders. His hands are gentle, his grip stern. "I'm sorry, Jaina, but you wouldn't have come with us if you had known the truth about me."

"You know that's a lie."

"It's not a lie!" he spits back. "You wouldn't have come if you knew what I was. I needed you to trust me. If that meant lying and doing what I did, it had to be done. For you, for your mother." His voice is softer now.

I back away from him, and press myself to the opposite wall. So that's it then.

"You used me. You *manipulated* me."

"Jaina, no..." he breathes.

"Admit it," I snap. "Everything you did, was so that I'd care about you. So I'd blindly follow you. So that you could bring me here."

"You think I wanted this, Jaina? You think I wanted to hurt you?"

I don't reply, and stare at the ground.

He moves so he's right in front of me again, and brushes his hand against mine. "Listen to me. I lied, yes. But not about everything."

I grit my teeth. "Like what?"

Dragon falls silent. He's so close to me I could easily reach out and pull his lips to mine.

For the first time, that's not something I want.

"Like what?" My voice is softer this time, and it trembles as I speak.

He gently touches my cheek.

Before I can fall into his arms or be soothed by his touch, I catch his hand and push it away. "Don't touch me."

His shoulders are curved inward, his body looks weaker than I've ever known it to be. "I'm sorry."

I jerk away from his hand still resting on my arm. "No, you're not."

Without another word, I turn around and start back down the hall. Doesn't matter where I go so long as it's away from Dragon.

"Jaina wait..."

I move faster. He catches up to me, grabs my hand and pulls me to him with such force I don't have time to resist. Adrenaline courses through my veins, ready for his next move.

None comes.

"Let go," I order, refusing to look at him.

"Please," his voice comes out soft.

"I thought you were better than that, Dragon." Honestly, that is what hurts the most. "I thought you cared about me. I know now you had a mission, and that's fine, but you didn't have to pretend. You're a horrible person."

"Is there anything I can do?"

"No. Nothing at all." My tears are gone, and my body is hot with my rage. "Shirez said you're going somewhere. Don't let me keep you."

"Jaina, wait," he says. "Please, don't make me leave like this."

I cross my arms over my chest and finally meet his gaze. "Get me a ship."

He blinks once, twice, and his lips twitch slightly. "What? What for? You can't leave–"

"I'm going to find my mother. Get me a ship, and maybe the sliver of respect I have left for you won't disappear."

He takes a step back, his eyes dark. "Shirez told you?"

The rage burns through my arms and up the back of my legs. I clench my fists. "Yes, he did. I can't believe you planned on keeping my *mother* from me as well."

"No, Jaina, it's–that's not it. I just..."

There's an uncomfortable silence. There have been so many in the past few hours I decide they're not worth counting.

He speaks first. "There's a team going out to find information on her location. It's taken years to even get a lead on where she might be. We have an entire armada working on this. Going out and looking for her by yourself will only get you killed."

"I'm going to find her, Altair, with or without your help. She risked her life for me, *is* giving her life up for me. The least I can do to repay her is risk my life to save her."

"Stop." He grabs onto my shoulders. "This is not worth your life. If you fail, or if you don't come back, the Resistance is over."

I push away his hands but take a step closer to him with more confidence than I've ever known. "I don't care about your Resistance. You can deal with the fate of the galaxy, of the Alliance. In the Trials, we were family. My mother is the only family I have now. I *will* find her."

He sighs and runs his fingers through his dark hair, his face twisted like he's in pain. "Jaina...I can't let you do this. I really shouldn't."

"You shouldn't have lied to me either, but your conscience was fine with that."

"*Shaav*, Jaina, I–" He cuts himself off then takes a deep breath. "By the stars, I can't believe I'm doing this. Come with me. I have the leads. My mission is to find her. But you cannot say anything to anyone about this, or Shirez is going to kill me."

"You'd deserve it." My confidence and anger fill me again. "Alright, I'll come with you."

He cringes and runs his fingers through his hair again. "This is an incredibly dangerous assignment."

"I'm not asking for permission."

Dragon bites his lip. "I can't afford—"

"*They*," I correct. "*They* can't afford to lose me. Not you. I'm coming whether you like it or not."

"Jaina, I am not authorized to take you. This is breaking a lot of rules, and if you get hurt, if something happens to you, the entire operation will be compromised. Your mother knows how to defeat the IA. We need her, and we need you alive."

I grit my teeth and stomp toward him. "You think I give a damn about what you're authorized to do?"

"You need to think about this—"

I don't relent. "No. You don't know how much I missed you. You don't know how much I felt." I narrow my eyes. "You owe me because you're a dick. And a *horrible* kisser." My words shock me a bit, but at least the first part isn't a lie.

Dragon grimaces and rolls his eyes at the ground. "I'll take you to the shuttle."

He strides mechanically down the hall and I follow. What the hell am I doing?

Finally, we reach the hangar. He activates the door, and it slides open. We step inside, and before me is one of the biggest rooms I've ever seen. There are hundreds of ships stationed in the bay. Several large ships capable of holding crews of fifty or so, yet the majority of them are smaller, made for one or two people, and short distance fighters.

"Come on," Dragon urges from a few feet ahead of me.

I shake off the amazement as he leads us to a decently sized black ship. It's sleek and streamlined, a stealth ship. The front half is disc-shaped, parallel to the ground. A long shark-like dorsal stabilizer rests on top of the disk, and points backward toward the adjustable thrusters. I've never had a thing for ships and machinery like Liam does, but this is something I can't help appreciating. It's big enough for a small crew, maybe five to seven people. On the front is carved a small silver dragon, and below it the words *The Odyssey.*

Dragon's eyes are on me, but I continue looking at the ship.

"Hey." Liam's voice tears my gaze from the ship. "You okay, Dragon? You look distracted."

Dragon's gaze flickers to me, then turns to Liam. "I'm fine. Thanks." He presses a button, and a ramp extends from *The Odyssey* to the ground.

Liam nods toward me. "What's she doing here?"

"What are *you* doing here?" I retort.

Dragon clears his throat. "Jaina's coming with us."

Liam raises an eyebrow. "Little Miss Snappy is coming along?"

"Yes." Dragon scowls at me.

Liam rolls his eyes. "Did I tell you she tried to kill me earlier?"

"You did."

Liam sighs. "As if it wasn't bad enough you're here."

Dragon's jaw tightens, and he takes a threatening step forward. "If you didn't mean so much to this mission, I'd have you detained."

"You should be grateful Liam wants to help at all," I cut in.

Liam's expression brightens, and he raises an eyebrow. The corner of his lips perk up into the slightest amused smile, and he nods to me appreciatively. "Thank you, Jaina."

"Why are you coming?" I'm honestly relieved it won't be just me and Dragon, although the combination of the three of us may not work out so well.

"I needed a mechanic," Dragon says curtly, "as a safety precaution in case anything goes wrong."

Liam snickers, looking rather proud of himself. "Oh ho ho that's not what Shirez said. He wanted me to go as a pilot because Dragon's piloting sucks and he's bad at fixing things."

I choke out a laugh. "I noticed."

Dragon scowls. "I pilot fine. I just fly faster than Shirez likes. Now climb on board and make yourself useful so we can get moving. We can't waste time." Without another word, he enters *The Odyssey*.

Liam smirks. "I think it's his time of the month."

I roll my eyes.

"What happened? Didn't your reunion go as planned?"

I'm too frustrated at Dragon for Liam's comment to bother me, and since his expression is one of concern, I decide to reply. "I just learned the truth about a lot of things."

"Oh..." His voice trails off. "I'm sorry?"

"Don't be."

My soul is on fire. In the strangest of ways, it's wonderful. It feels good not to have that longing pull toward anyone. This rage makes me so strong. I let the flames cool down for the time being, turn it into little embers until I need it to burn again.

I follow Dragon into the ship, and Liam slowly enters behind me. The ramp shrinks back into the ship, and the airlock doors close. The ship looks surprisingly bigger on the inside. We reach the cockpit where there are four seats: one for the pilot and copilot, and two more directly behind them.

Dragon sits in the pilot seat, pressing some buttons to prepare the ship.

Liam stands slightly behind me and clears his throat, but Dragon ignores him. He moves a bit closer to Dragon and clears his throat again.

Dragon continues to press buttons on the dashboard, not bothering to look at either of us. "You got a cold?" he snaps.

"If I'm not mistaken, I've been ordered to pilot," Liam says.

Dragon shrugs. "This is my ship. I've had her a long time, and I've always been the pilot."

"Get over it. Orders are orders," Liam replies.

Dragon shoots him a glare then stands. He switches to the copilot chair, coldness radiating from him. I take the seat behind Dragon so we can't see each other.

"Just be careful with her," Dragon mutters as he buckles up.

Liam quickly takes his seat as pilot and huffs. "It's just a ship."

"It was my mother's."

Liam scoffs. "If I break it, ask her for a new one."

"She's dead."

Did he know his mother *and* his father? I'm not sure if I should feel sorry for him or be even more enraged. He told me nothing, never said anything about his life, about his parents. How could I have been so blind to his lies?

"Oh." Liam's voice completely changes to a serious tone. "I'm sorry. I'll be careful."

Dragon nods. "Thank you."

Liam sits still. "How did you know your mother? Do you remember her?"

"It doesn't matter. What does matter is finding the Phoenix, so you should fly now."

Liam nods then glances at me. "Last thing. Why is she coming along?"

My gaze flickers to Dragon for a moment, and I'm not really sure what to say. "It has to do with my family."

"That's vague," he says suspiciously. "Are you gonna add anything to that?"

"Liam. Fly," Dragon orders.

Liam shrugs and presses a few buttons on the dashboard. The ship groans in reply. He twists around in his seat. "Okay, seriously though, I'm curious."

"It's about her mother," Dragon replies without emotion.

Liam raises his eyebrows. "*Jaina's* mother?"

Dragon nods. "She's our leader."

"Who is?"

"Jaina's mother," Dragon says, obviously annoyed.

Liam looks absolutely confused. "What?"

Dragon sighs. "Just *fly!*"

Liam takes his hands off the dashboard. "Just explain, and I'll stop asking questions!"

Dragon moans and runs his fingers through his hair. "The leader of the Resistance, the Phoenix, is in a secret prison, and our mission is to locate it. You were supposed to be paying attention in the briefing. Our leader's name is Amara Indera. She's Jaina's mother."

A glimmer of realization sparks in Liam's eyes. "Whoa. Wait. So Jaina's mom is the leader of the Resistance?" He looks at me with a mixture of shock, maybe even fear. "How long have you known?"

I take a deep breath. "Less than an hour, thanks to all the secrecy."

The muscles in his face tense. "Wow. Okay. Well that's definitely reason enough for you to come along." He stares out the viewport and adds, "Also, I'm not entirely sure what happened, but you guys have to stop. Your icy glares are making the ship like twenty degrees colder, and I don't do well in the cold, so can we break it up a little?"

"That's a good plan," Dragon says through his teeth, glancing back at me.

I clench my fist. "I can't promise anything."

Dragon shakes his head. "I think we can go now. Strap yourselves in."

Liam presses buttons on the touch-control panel faster than I can figure out what they mean. Dragon's eyes flicker to me. I don't want him to look at me. I don't want to feel his presence or his gaze. I probably shouldn't have decided to come along with him, but how else could I go about finding my mother? *I will find her.*

As I fasten my seat belt, my mind shoots back to my conversation with Sean on the roof. Maybe she has the silver ring I think I remember. Maybe she will have answers.

The ship lurches to the left, and I grab the side of my chair to keep from falling out.

"Careful," Dragon says nervously. "It took me a while to get used to her flight pattern–"

"Don't worry," Liam interrupts. "I've done this before."

By the stars, this isn't good. Maybe I should've stayed back and gone looking for her with Kavi instead. I'm not entirely sure she'd take me though. Who the *shaav* knows what Kavi is qualified for? She lied to me about *everything*, pretending to be my best friend and then going behind my back like this.

The ship heaves to the right a little harder than I expect and I'm nearly flung out of my seat. I grit my teeth. *The Odyssey* jerks to the left again as we exit the hangar and into the breathtaking vastness of space.

"*Shaav*, Liam! Be careful!" I bark.

Dragon holds on to his seat to keep steady. "It's okay. She's hard to control."

Liam smirks as he glances out the viewport then presses a few more buttons. "Just how I like 'em."

"Jaina, set a course for Keducia." Dragon's voice is dry.

Liam furrows his brow. "I thought we were going to Kashia."

"We are, but we'll need to stop to refuel along the way. Our tanks aren't large enough to make it the whole way. Set a course, Jaina."

The control panel next to me is a mess of colors and flashing lights. Somehow, though, when I focus, it seems that half of the chaos has been cleared. I remember the symbols we learned on Virana in flying classes, and it starts to make sense.

When I touch a button on the screen marked with an arrow, a map of the galaxy hovers over the screen. I type in *Keducia, Kashia system.* The hologram zooms in to a planet just outside of the Alliance. A cool tingling runs through me. We were always told there were no habitable planets outside of Alliance territories. How many worlds are there?

Lightly, I touch the planet. Two courses light up from our current destination. The shorter of the two goes through IA space, while the other is about two parsecs longer. I select the second path and the ship begins to steady itself.

"Are we set to make the jump?" Liam asks.

"Not yet," Dragon replies. "We need to wait for confirmation."

Liam nods. "I'm guessing Shirez doesn't know she's with us."

I hate that they're acting as if I'm not even in the room.

Dragon shakes his head. "He doesn't."

Liam sighs dramatically. "How did I *know* you were going to say that? What is it with you and breaking the rules?"

I raise an eyebrow and can't help feeling a bit amused. "As if you didn't break every rule you possibly could on Virana."

"Well, yeah, that's my job. He doesn't have to go stealing my spotlight," Liam mutters, pressing a few more buttons for course correction. "Dragon, did you brief her on the mission?"

"I'm getting to it," Dragon grumbles. "Jaina, can I talk to you without setting you off?"

His words sting beyond belief, and that in itself almost ignites me again. "I'm not going to let my anger get in the way of our mission," I reassure him flatly. "Be honest with me, don't *shaav* with me, and I'll hold back."

Dragon looks down at the floor. "Thank you. Only three people in the galaxy know the location of your mother's prison."

"What do you mean?" I ask, careful to keep my voice monotonous. "What about the builders? The prison guards?"

"The crew who built the prison as well as the architects mysteriously disappeared soon after it was completed. The guards are not in contact with anyone from the outside world during their commission there."

"What about the pilots who take new recruits out there?" Liam asks.

"I don't know. The whole thing is weird. They've probably got some unmanned stealth ship that transports them," Dragon replies.

"What about retired guards?" I ask. "Or the ones that have completed their commission?"

Dragon shakes his head. "Liam and I were assigned to the CCPD. I asked around, but none of the men seemed to know anything except that anyone who goes there doesn't remember a thing when they come back. I assume they drug them or make them forget somehow."

A tingling of uneasiness fills me. "But *someone* knows where it is."

"Yes. There are a few."

"Four, to be precise," Liam cuts in.

Dragon's expression relaxes, but his eyes shoot fire at Liam. The fire remains when he turns back to me. "Three– The Emperor, the Emperor's Advisor Major General Raval Tazrin, and Prince Tariin Sivva of Moris. Obviously, we can't go after the Emperor–"

"What about Tazrin?" I ask quickly.

His face hardens. "Why?"

"Why not? He'd be easier to get than the Emperor, and I'm sure he'd know a lot more than this Prince Sivva. Liam and I ran into Tazrin in the Crystal City. He was very polite too, he can't be that hard to find."

Dragon coughs out a laugh. "You ran into him? Raval Tazrin? Are you sure it was him?"

Liam nods. "It was definitely him."

Dragon pinches the bridge of his nose and then rubs his eyes. "Either way, Tazrin is out of the picture. The man is a killer and far too difficult to locate."

"But," I begin, "if we found a way–"

"Even if we did, we can't hurt him," he says sternly.

"Why?"

He shakes his head. "I don't know. Those are our orders. Hang on. I'm going to open the com. Jaina, be absolutely silent." Dragon presses a few buttons then clears his throat. "*Justice*, this is *The Odyssey*. Do you copy?"

There's static. "We read you, *Odyssey*."

"We're on our way."

Liam heads for a fairly clear area of space and prepares to enter the hyperfield.

"State your crew members," the girl on *The Justice* orders. "By the way, you're late. You should have left half an hour ago."

Realization hits me, and I have to ask. "Is that *Kavi*?" I keep my voice as quiet as possible.

Liam nods.

"Altair Kasev and Liam Rodan," Dragon answers. "And yes, we're late. There were a few…" he glances at me then turns back to the speaker. "Complications."

"Jaina's with you, isn't she."

I can tell it's not a question.

Dragon hesitates. "No, she isn't. If you see her, tell her I said hi."

"You know Shirez doesn't want her going," she says in a hushed tone.

Dragon leans over the dashboard. "Don't tell him."

Kavi moans. "I can't lie to him if he asks, but I'll hold out as long as I can."

"Thank you."

"Also if you need anything, information about people or coordinates, *anything* at all, feel free to contact me. I put like seven privcoms in the cargo hold. So if you and Liam and *you know who* need one, they're there."

"Thank you, Kavi," Dragon says.

"Not a problem. You're cleared for the jump once you're out of range. Good luck."

The transmission fades.

Liam clears his throat awkwardly. "So I continue forward a bit, right?"

Dragon nods. "Yes, until this light turns orange. Then you can make the jump." He faces me without making eye contact. "As I was saying. There are three people–"

"*Four,*" Liam interrupts again.

Dragon ignores him. "Three people who know the location. The Emperor and Tazrin are out of the question, so that leaves Prince Tariin Sivva of Moris."

"How do we find him?" I ask.

"We've located his friend, a trusted member of the Moris counsel named Draco Haidryn. He's on Kashia, doing business for Sivva. We'll locate him and interrogate him about Sivva's whereabouts. Then we track Sivva down, steal the information about the prison, and get the hell outta there. We go back to the Resistance, and from there we will inform Shirez, drag the fleet to wherever the Phoenix is being held, and rescue her before the IA kills her. That's the plan."

"Quite an intricate plan for someone who likes to wing it," I murmur.

"It's Shirez's plan," Dragon corrects, mimicking my tone. He turns forward to press more buttons on the control panel, prepping the ship for the jump.

A red light flashes to my right, the signal to prepare the drives. I check the fuel, the tank is full. "Liam said there's a fourth," I say quietly.

Dragon groans. "It's just a rumor."

Liam smirks. "The Shadow Hunter."

"Who's the Shadow Hunter?" A shiver runs through my body, like I've spoken a curse.

Dragon shakes his head. "The Shadow Hunter isn't real. It's just a fairytale to scare people into abiding by the law."

"You heard the stories back in the City," Liam says to Dragon. "The men talk about him like he's real."

"That doesn't mean anything."

"What is he?" I ask.

Liam clears his throat. "The Shadow Hunter is the Emperor's most skilled assassin. He never fails a mission, is friendly with the ladies, and is probably rich as hell."

"Shut up," Dragon mutters.

"For galaxies sake, Dragon, let me tell the damn story at least," Liam snaps. "Sheesh. Anyway, I was talking to the guys back in the City, and they say that when the IA first began, the first Emperor had a half-brother. The Emperor's half-brother was jealous of the Emperor's power, so the Emperor murdered him."

I raise an eyebrow. "Okay?"

Liam sighs. "The story goes that after the Emperor killed him, he somehow brought him back to life to live eternally in servitude of the crown."

"There are a lot of weird things in the galaxy, but you can't bring someone back to life," Dragon says. "Dead is dead. The story is at least partially invalid. But yes, legend says he's immortal and has served the IA since it's creation."

Liam tightens his grip on one of the throttles. "Thanks for ruining the story," he mutters. "We're far enough from the fleet to jump into the hyperfield. Buckle up."

I do as I'm told, and Liam waits for Dragon to get situated, although I get the sense he wants to make the jump before Dragon's ready. Dragon nods, and as he presses a button, the stars twist and stretch around us. A tunnel forms ahead. The darkness before us grows and reforms, and we're shot into the hyperfield. My stomach drops. No matter what happens now, there's no turning back.

# CHAPTER NINE

The silvery ripples of the hyperfield dance around us like lonely souls. Unlike the impossibly low humming of *The Justice* and the higher-pitched whining of the police shuttle Dragon stole, *The Odyssey* is silent. I'm not an expert with machinery or ships, but even I can tell that this one is a work of art. I've never seen anything like it, not even in Alliance databases on Virana.

Dragon gives out an occasional order that Liam follows with great reluctance and annoyance. After a while, Liam smirks, and I get nervous. He presses a few buttons, and some soft music begins to play.

"Dragon," Liam begins as he starts going through the different radio channels. "What's your favorite kind of music?"

He shifts uncomfortably. "Heavy metal."

"Oh, heavy metal. That's cool." Liam changes the station to some twisted dark Duranian polka song and bobs his head up and down to the music.

Dragon looks at Liam but I can't see his expression. Liam doesn't acknowledge him, and Dragon starts massaging his temples.

Liam laughs. "You don't like this music?"

"I can't say I do," he replies coldly. "I just told you I like heavy metal."

"Oh, right. Sucks. This is my jam." He keeps his head going to the music.

"What the hell? This is my ship, turn it off."

"But I'm the pilot, so I get to pick the music," Liam replies.

"I was supposed to pilot anyway!" Dragon cries.

Liam glances at me. "Jaina likes this song, though."

Honestly, I have no idea what this song is. It does sound kind of cool to me, but it's different from anything I've heard before. I'm about to protest, just because I don't want to admit I kinda like the same music Liam does, until I see Dragon's face all tight with frustration.

"Yeah, I love this song. Keep it on, Liam. This is great."

Dragon's jaw twitches slightly.

Liam keeps the dark polka music playing for a while then switches to some very *very* old rock music for a few hours. Surprisingly his choice in music isn't so bad. One of the songs I'd actually heard before, though I can't remember the title. Something to do with Cydonia, a beautiful mountainous region on Mars.

While the music plays, I start to drift off. The music consumes the silence and helps me forget the tension for now. I close my eyes and my body temporarily becomes numb to the uncomfortable chair. To be fair, the chairs aren't so bad, but after sitting here for so long, I kind of want to curl up and sleep. My muscles relax, and each breath becomes slower and longer. If I fall asleep at some point, I don't realize it.

After a time, I notice that something isn't right.

It's the silence.

I open my eyes. Dragon is leaning back in his chair, and though it's hard to see much of his face from where I'm sitting, I catch a glimpse of his eyelashes as he blinks slowly. Relaxed. Liam's arm appears from behind the back of his chair, and for a time, it's all I can see of him. He presses a button on the dashboard, and I'm glad to see he hasn't been sleeping on the job.

Liam turns in his chair slightly to face Dragon. "We'll reach Keducia in about an hour," he says softly. "Where's the best place to land?"

Dragon keeps his focus on the control panel. "Com Kavi and ask her. The privcoms are in the back. Storage unit to the left."

"Could you get them for me?" Liam asks.

Dragon's jaw tightens. "No. You're the pilot."

"Well, you're the person just sitting there," Liam snaps back.

"Because you insisted on being pilot."

Liam's hands grip his armrests a bit tighter. "I was *assigned* to be the pilot."

Dragon nods. "Exactly. So you have the biggest responsibility."

Liam wrinkles his nose and opens his mouth, but he stops himself and groans. He stands and walks past my seat to the back of the ship, muttering, "Hate this job."

Dragon's gaze falters to me as he watches Liam go. Dark rings of exhaustion encompass his aquamarine eyes, more gray than blue. I turn and stare forward out the window.

"You look like you need sleep," I say, my voice emotionless.

"I do," he murmurs, "but that isn't a luxury I can afford at the moment."

I gaze out at the hyperfield, at the spirals of light and dark. "You should trust him. Liam's stubborn, and a jerk sometimes, but he's a good guy."

Out of the corner of my eye, I watch Dragon look away and stare out the viewport. "You thought I was good, too."

"In all fairness, I've known Liam a lot longer than I've known you, and after all he's done for you, you should trust him."

"All he's done for me?" He laughs. "He almost majorly screwed up my plan to get you out of the City."

"He succeeded anyway."

"Could you trust him with your life?" He looks to me again.

I glare at him and raise my chin. "I could trust him with my heart."

Dragon's face darkens, and he shakes his head. "Fine. I'll go rest. I don't wanna be out here with you two anyway, but if he screws up my ship, you both pay for repairs."

He stands and walks past me to a thin door behind the cockpit on the port side. The door hisses softly shut behind him. As he leaves, Liam returns.

"Here you go, Jaina. This one's for you." He hands me a small privcom, and I gently place it in my ear. He glances over to the now empty copilot's chair. "Where was Dragon off to?"

"He needed some rest."

Liam nods. "I could tell. Who got his panties in a bunch?"

I shake my head and switch to the copilot's chair. "Can we not talk about this?"

He takes the pilot seat next to me. "Alright."

I can't help smiling as I replay his words in my head and laugh softly. "Panties in a bunch?"

He grins out the viewport. "Don't be hatin'."

I let my head rest on the back of the chair in defeat. "You're so weird, Liam."

"So I'm told." He adjusts some of the controls on the touchscreen. "I wonder what it's like to have parents."

"I don't know. I never thought about my parents until I got here. Never used to care."

"None of us did." Liam stares forward as if in a daze. "Everything they taught us was wrong."

He doesn't have to say more. I understand so completely that I hate it. Ignorance made us happy, and I wonder what life would be like had I not been influenced by Dragon.

The rage I feel toward the IA is everlasting. They had the impertinence to lie to the people who trusted them most. The people who had no choice but to believe in them. Sort of the way Dragon lied to me.

"It was lie upon lie upon lie. And we blindly accepted it," he continues.

The cruel awareness of the truth makes my stomach knot. "You know what the worst part is? Even though we know the truth, everyone else is still there. Like Maria and Garr, Roshiva and Ana...they're still blind. All of them. Everyone we knew."

He raises an eyebrow, and a sickly smile marks his face. "Well, I wouldn't mind if *they* stayed in the IA. Roshiva and Ana were both awful."

"Liam!" I nudge him in the shoulder.

He laughs. "Be careful, I'm the one driving the ship!"

"It's on autopilot."

"*Shaav.*"

I furrow my brow. "You're so mean."

He throws his hands up in the air, like he's been accused of stealing the last chocolate from the Masters' candy stash. "Oh, right. I'm the one pushing the driver around," he says sarcastically.

"Shut up," I tease.

He laughs again and returns attention to the hyperfield.

"What made you want to join the Resistance?"

His soft expression darkens. "I found out you were engaged two weeks ago."

"Two weeks?" I cry. "I found out one day before I was supposed to meet him! How did you know?"

He smiles slyly. "I was in the Guard. I had access to almost everything that happened in the Crystal City, but we weren't really kept up to date with marriages. That's when I got an order from General Tazrin."

"You spoke to him?" I ask.

"Not directly. I received a message on my silverscreen one night. He wrote to me and said there was a risk of a security breach, that Jaina Indera had to be protected until further notice. That until she was married in two weeks, it was likely that she was in great danger. I told Dragon about it the moment I found out, and he knocked me out. That's when I found myself tied up in what must have been a basement. Kavi, Seth, Luci, and Dragon were all there. They questioned me for a while and told me we had to get you out. They thought I was going to resist them, but honestly, the idea didn't sound bad to me. My job sucked since I was stuck with Dragon, not that it's any better now, but at least..." He sighs. "At least I thought there was a chance you might be happy. So I was in, and everything just kind of happened from there."

"By the stars," I murmur. "They didn't say anything about the Resistance to you, did they?"

"No. They thought there was a chance I might defect. I knew what I needed to know to get you out in time. Luci later explained everything to me on the stolen police shuttle."

"Why would they let you spend the night with me? How did the Alliance not find out?"

A cocky grin splashes his face. "So *that's* what we're calling it, now, darling? I spent the night?"

I scoff. "You know what I meant."

He laughs. "That's not what you implied."

*Shaav.* "I..."

His smile falters. "They were going to make you get married quickly, even if the tests failed. And I had to look around your apartment to see where the best place to break in would be. You-know-who was the first

to volunteer for the mission, but with his sketchy re-
cord from Virana we agreed it would be less suspicious
for me to do the job."

"You mean Dragon?"

He rolls his eyes dramatically.

My eyes grow dull. "You could have just said his
name."

"I didn't want to," he mutters.

I stare at him a moment. "You really hate him,
don't you?"

"*Shaav* yeah. Son of a *katiaj* thinks he's *shaavez*
perfect."

"Not even close," I admit. "I'm pretty sure I'm going to hate him for a long time."

"Is that so?"

I nod. "I don't want to go into it, I'm angry and
hurt."

"Whatever. I'm sure it'll pass, since he's just the
greatest."

"Liam, please." I touch his shoulder.

He laughs, but his hands are balled up together,
resting on his lap. "He doesn't deserve you."

I bite my lip.

"I joined the Resistance because of you, Jaina." He
forces each word out, as if every breath caused him
pain. "But you still treat me like the guy you knew on
Virana, like the guy who hurt you. That guy doesn't
exist anymore. I'm different now."

My chest hurts. It all comes crashing down on me and it's too much. "I'm sorry."

"I don't want an apology. I just want you to accept mine." His voice is so soft and steady I hardly recognize it. "I was mean and ignorant. I hurt you and I broke your heart." He looks me in the eyes. I don't see pain, or anger, or the sadness I expect. Instead, there is only confidence and strength. It's unnerving to see him like this. "Jaina, I'm so sorry. I always have been."

Is he apologizing because he still likes me? If he doesn't want something from me, why bother? It's not like him to ask for nothing in return for a sacrifice, yet all he wants is acceptance. Maybe he has changed.

"It's okay," I say softly. "I forgive you."

He lets out a long breath of relief and leans back into his chair. "Thank you."

For the first time, I feel like things might turn out alright between the two of us. The silence isn't awkward. It lasts a few moments until I break it.

"What do you think she's like?" I ask, trying to take my mind off Dragon. "Amara. My mom."

He smiles and blushes a little bit, staring into the hyperfield. "I assume she's a lot like you. Beautiful, like you. She's probably tougher than you..."

"Oh stop." I laugh.

He raises his hands in surrender. "Okay, she's probably intelligent, caring, and brave, like you."

"I'm not brave," I whisper. "I might be the most scared person in the galaxy at the moment. I'm not a fearless warrior."

Liam laughs. "I'm glad. You'd be an idiot if you were a fearless warrior."

"What do you mean?"

"Being fearless is idiotic and dangerous. There's a big difference between being fearless, and being brave. Being fearless is just having no fear. There is nothing noble about that. Bravery is being afraid and still facing your fears because that's what's right. Bravery is a rare quality. But you have it."

I feel warm with his words. "Thank you."

His brown eyes glitter a little as he gazes into mine. With the silence, our eye contact feels a bit awkward and I laugh softly. He laughs and looks away, back down onto the control panel.

"How long until we reach Keducia?" I ask, still smiling a little.

"About forty-five minutes. We've got some time."

I nod sleepily. A deepening pit begins to burrow itself into my stomach. When was the last time I ate? "You think there's anything to eat back there?"

Liam shrugs. "You wanna go check?"

"Sure. I'm starving."

"Me too."

I make my way out of the cockpit. The door to the right is closed, concealing Dragon in his sleep, while the one on the left remains open. Past the small cabins is a small open area. To the left are two circular tables with a cupboard over it. It opens with a *click*, and out falls a bunch of paper and scraps of random things. Hmm. Maybe Dragon needs to clean up a bit.

Among the things that fell onto the floor, I find a box of medical supplies, but other than painkillers, there's nothing to eat. My stomach grumbles. When *was* the last time I ate? When I had dinner, after Liam abandoned me to go home alone!

Thoughts of the Crystal City go shooting through my head. The aching in my stomach is momentarily replaced with thoughts of Sean. By the stars, it wasn't right to just leave him, was it? I hope he finds his love.

The empty sensation in my stomach increases to the point where I feel like I'm going to pass out, but I've gone this long without food. I should be fine.

"I couldn't find anything," I report when I return to Liam.

He groans in annoyance.

"We'll eat when we get to Keducia."

"Remind Dragon when he wakes up."

"Okay, I'm going to get some sleep." If I stay awake, I'll end up passing out.

Liam nods. "I'll be out here if you need anything."

I smile then leave him. I walk to the cabin on the left, and I'm asleep the moment my head hits the pillow.

*Pain.*

*Only pain.*

*I want to cry out in agony as it courses through my veins like wildfire. My blood slows, like lava in my body, refusing to flow.*

*This is a dream. I've had enough to know what they feel like. Despite the pain, I take comfort knowing this isn't real, that the moment I wake, it will all fade away. If only I could open my eyes, bring myself back to consciousness, it would all come to an end. But there's no waking, not yet.*

*It's here with me. The Shadow, the dark figure that haunts my dreams. It points forward, and I run through a tunnel and into a large room. I have to reach him. I have to reach him before it's too late.*

*By the stars, we were all wrong.*

*He can't do this.*

*He's at the other end, his back to me, yet the farther I run, the farther away he is from me. It's like I'm moving backward.*

*"Please!" I scream. "Stop, this isn't right. You can't do this, please stop!"*

*His shadow moves and transforms on the ground. Finally he looks at me, his pupils red, tears streaming down his face. "I had to," he says, his voice unfamiliar, harsh, raspy. "I'm sorry, Jaina. It was all I could do to save you." His shadow grows, and the spidery fingers reach toward me and close around my throat. Pain ricochets through my body, through every bone and every nerve. I can't breathe, but I don't want to. I see him standing there, with fire in his eyes and darkness in his heart. I can feel the tears streaming down my face, but I can't manage even a sob as the shadow crushes my throat. My will to fight disappears, and I let the darkness in.*

*I open my eyes.*

The room is exactly as I left it. The only thing that bothers me is the light, or actually the lack of it. I don't remember turning the lights off. Maybe Liam came in to check on me and shut them off.

I sit in the darkness and an uneasy feeling floods me. My skin prickles, and every hair on my body stands on end.

I'm not alone.

# CHAPTER TEN

"I was waiting for you," says a low masculine voice. My body freezes, I don't dare move. The dark prevents me from seeing the man behind the voice. "Who's there?"

A short, angry laugh bursts from him. "You haven't forgotten me already, have you?"

"Show yourself!" I shout.

A dark frame near the wall moves closer. His deep green eyes become barely visible through the sheet of darkness between us, but that's enough for me to recognize him. My breath catches, and the scar on my arm burns like a fresh wound.

"How does it feel to know the truth, my love?" Hot, endless rage is slightly audible in the steadiness of his voice. "I warned you."

My chest tightens. I want to protest, to tell him he was wrong. But he wasn't. A shiver runs through me.

"Let me go." The words stick in my throat like they're dried out and overused. Trapped in the past, I feel the grip of fear he has on me, feel his fingers in my hair, the knife on my skin, and his lips are on my throat. It's cold and electric, fiery and unforgiving.

I'm unable to wash my mind of his memory. I've tried to forget him, tried to stop him from haunting me every moment I live. I still hear Xana's cries as she begged for her life, hear how she asked me to apologize to Liam for her, the horrible ringing of Azad's dagger as he dragged the knife over her throat, and the soft gurgling behind her lips as the light drained from her eyes.

Azad touches my cheek. "Still as beautiful and naïve as before," he purrs. "You thought death could separate us, but I'm always with you. I will have revenge."

A voice comes from outside the door. "Jaina, wake up!"

What will Dragon and Liam do when they come in? Surely they'll stop him, right?

Azad kneels before me and grabs my arm. He studies me, his tan skin looks even darker with the lack of light. His black hair is barely visible, yet his eyes are almost glowing. I'm unable to move. He runs his fingers up my arm and to my shoulder. Azad smiles as his hand reaches my scar. "In the end, you can't win. Darkness will destroy you. And it will be beautiful."

"Why are you here?" *Shaav*, my voice shakes.

"By the stars, Jaina, don't be so afraid." He takes my hand and shifts his body closer, forcing me to back up farther onto the bed. Azad kisses my hand, but I'm still unable to move. An alluring smile tilts the corners of his lips. "I'm here to warn you. Someone's coming for you." His eyes flicker over me. "Not a friend, but not an enemy. Coming to take you back. Do not let her."

"Back where? Why are you telling me this?" My voice is nothing but a whisper.

The voice behind the door calls again, "Jaina, please."

"I want you to trust me, Jaina," Azad says. "I want to make Altair hurt so much he'd rather burn in hell. And your friend who's still in love with you...Liam? Is that his name?"

I don't answer; I can't answer. My heart is pounding restlessly, and my body trembles like I'm stuck in a cold rain.

"You have no idea what he's capable of," Azad says.

I pull away from him, finding strength in my anger. "You can't hurt them."

He furrows his brow. "Why not? Liam broke your heart ages ago, and Altair won't stop lying to you. Why would you forgive them?"

I can't speak.

"He's a liar, Jaina! You think this minor betrayal was all? You're wrong. He'll do it again, and again, and again," he says in a soft, seductive whisper.

"You're dead. You can't be here. It's impossible."

Azad sneers, pulling me closer. "*Nothing* is impossible. I'm more alive than ever. I'll find you. All of you. And when I do, you will suffer." He glares yet smiles. "And everything you will come to stand for will be destroyed."

My stomach shifts in place, and I try to pull myself away from him, but he doesn't let me go. "Stop," I beg. "Please."

"I will win, Jaina." He gently strokes my hair. "You know I will."

Rage overwhelms my senses, and I yank myself out of his arms. I elbow him in the stomach then kick him hard in the groin. He gasps in pain and crumbles to the floor. Azad moves toward me, but I reach the door and press my fingers to the button to open it. It's cold and hard against my hand as I smash it into the wall. Light floods the room, not the yellow-orange light from the insides of the ship but a white light. Like the light from the sun. It burns through my eyes, and the searing agony from my dream returns.

Fingers close around my throat, and he whispers, "This is just the beginning."

I scream.

My eyes shoot open.

"Jaina. Jaina, are you alright?"

Liam's brown eyes hover over me, and I jump back, only, I can't *jump back*, because I'm lying down.

I'm. Lying. Down.

Azad.

He was *here.*

Suppressing a scream rising in my throat, I sit up and press myself to the back wall as fast as I can. I bolt out of bed, I'm covered in sweat, and I can't stop shaking.

Liam rushes over to me and touches my hand. "Jaina, it's okay! It's alright, it's just me."

I shake my head, struggling to swallow the lump rising in my throat. It's not okay.

"He's-he's here!" I stammer through strained breaths.

Liam looks around the room. "You're okay, Jaina," he says, rubbing my arms. His hands warm my skin, but when they brush the scar on my shoulder, I recoil from his touch.

I'm freezing cold, but I'm still sweating like a fountain.

"Who's here?"

I swallow hard, turning my head to examine every part of the small cabin. "He was-he was in my room." I gasp. "He's on the ship."

"Jaina, I think you had a bad dream." Liam sits me back down on the bed.

A dream? No. That was real. I know what dreaming feels like, and that was anything but.

How did I get back in my bed? I opened my eyes after I thought they were already open. The pain was so real. Azad was so real.

The bedroom door opens, and I shrink away next to Liam, fearing Azad, but it's only Dragon. His presence irks me, but I am glad to know he's not bleeding out under Azad's knife.

"What's going on?" Dragon walks up to me and places a gentle hand on my forehead.

I turn away from him.

Liam shakes his head. "I heard her screaming so I woke her up. I think she was having a nightmare."

Dragon turns to me and I can see the worry in his eyes. "What happened?"

I breathe deeply. It *wasn't* a dream. "I'll be fine." My voice comes out mechanically like an automated voice message. I'm not ready to open up to either of them.

"You didn't seem fine," Liam says tentatively.

Azad had been here, hadn't he? He was on this ship, but he's nowhere in sight. I slow my breathing. "I'm okay. Really. I'm one hundred percent fine. It was just a bad dream." My voice quivers as I speak. "You can go back to whatever you were doing. I'm alright."

Liam and Dragon exchange concerned glances. A soft beeping starts, and Liam scowls. "Dragon, stay with her. I'll dock the ship."

Once the door hisses shut behind Liam, Dragon takes a seat on the bed across from me. His gaze is intense, demanding answers. His wide eyes show no hint of weakness, and neither does his expression. The interrogator must have the upper hand, and to do that, he's got to act confident.

I take a sudden interest in the floor.

"What happened, Jaina?" His tone is soft and stern all at once.

Despite how real it was, it *had* to have been a dream. Azad is dead. To admit he still haunts me would be cowardice.

"Nothing." I say it more to annoy him. I don't expect him to believe me.

He leans forward. "I know from experience that when someone wakes up screaming, something's wrong."

*Shaav*, that's true. Do dreams torment him, the way they do me?

The muscles in my face tighten. My gut knots and squirms beyond my control. "You wouldn't understand," I try.

His eyes grow dark. "Why are you trying to keep this from me?"

"You have your private life, I have mine. We're not friends. We don't have to tell each other about those sorts of things," I snap. "Forget it and let's move on."

For the first time, his indifferent façade crumbles. He's hurt, but of course he can't let that show, so it's no surprise when his lips twist into a sort of sorrowful sneer. "That's how it starts, you know. The visions."

He doesn't look like he's lying, but how the hell would I know. He's deceived me enough already.

"It wasn't a vision."

Dragon intertwines his fingers and rests his elbows on his knees. "It felt real, didn't it? You thought someone was here. What did he tell you? Did he warn you or threaten you?"

He'd think I'm crazy to still be haunted by Azad. After what Azad did to me, after Azad *murdered* her in front of me... I am scarred for life, and my mind will never heal from that, just as his initials in my arm will never completely fade.

"You could never understand." My voice shakes with rage and fear. "It's none of your concern."

Dragon grits his teeth, stands, and walks up to the door. "Keep telling yourself that."

"Get out," I order. By the stars, I just want him to go.

"Let me warn you," he says softly. "The dreams grow more real with time, and the pain gets worse. So much worse." He leaves, and the door closes behind him.

A sick twisting sensation in my stomach turns my body cold. My breath is squeezed from my lungs, and I choke out something between a sob and a moan.

The door is closed. I'm in here alone. Again.

Azad was here.

He *was*.

Whether he was physically here or not, it doesn't matter. It felt real enough for me.

But Azad is dead. I killed him.

And yet, the question still haunts me; how much more of what he said was true?

None of it.

Why am I letting Dragon get into my head? I don't have visions. I envy the people who dream of sunshine and flowers and happiness. Not that I'm that kind of girl, but it would be a whole lot better than dreaming about Azad.

I stand and head into the cockpit.

Liam pilots the ship; Dragon sits next to him. I take a seat behind him without a word, and they continue their conversation as if I'm not here.

"I'm telling you he's real," Liam argues, his voice taking on a persuasive tone. "At least *some* of the legends have to be true. I mean, the Shadow Hunter has killed so many people and it's been recorded. People have seen the mask he wears, the one from the legends. That has to be worth something."

Dragon presses a few buttons on the control panel and sighs. I'm not sure if he's annoyed with Liam, or if it's because of me. "The fact that no one has survived an encounter with him except for the Emperor is impossible. Maybe *some* parts of the legend are true, but he's not some immortal super assassin." His voice is dull and unemotional.

"Jaina, what do you think?" Liam raises his eyebrows. "People have seen him."

"It doesn't really make a difference whether he's real or not, if the legends are true," I respond.

Dragon glances at Liam. "Besides, he's gotta have a family. A wife, kids."

"I'm sure he's got a *ton* of kids," Liam laughs. "The Emperor grants him any woman he wants. Wouldn't that be wonderful?"

Dragon shakes his head, a numb, disgusted glint in his eyes. "Shut up, Liam."

"He's probably allowed to have more than one at a time..."

I let my head drop into my hands as embarrassment fills me. My cheeks feel hot, and my palms are unnaturally warm. "By the stars Liam, can we just focus?"

Liam waves his hand at me, as if to tell me to butt out of the conversation. "Yeah, sorry, I know." He turns back to Dragon. "Just admit you're jealous of the guy."

Dragon leans back in his chair defeated, letting out a long breath of irritation. He rubs his eyes uncomfortably and runs his fingers through his hair. "If he's actually real, then yeah of course."

My jaw drops. I can't help being baffled by Dragon's honesty in front of Liam, moreover, in front of me. I really have the urge to punch *both* of them. "By the stars," I mutter, "you are both disgusting."

Liam shoots a seductive glance toward me. "What? Aw I guess she can't handle that kinda talk."

"I can handle it fine. It's just weird!"

He shrugs and pats me on the shoulder affectionately. "It's okay, most girls are uncomfortable talking about—"

"Shut up, please!" To my dismay, I smile slightly, making my pleading much less convincing. "Just stop talking about it, okay?"

Liam raises his hands as if in surrender. "Fine, fine. Sorry. Didn't mean to make you feel so uncomfortable."

I roll my eyes and gaze out the viewport at the planet growing larger before us. "So anyway, this is Keducia?"

"It better be." Liam presses a button on the control panel and reads some information. "Is that the right pronunciation? Keh-doo-shee-ah?"

"Yes Liam." Dragon replies.

Liam waves his hand. "Whatever. Thank the stars we're stopping here. Tank is almost empty. Oh, and you might want to buckle up again." He grabs a joystick on his left, and shifts it slightly, tilting the nose of *The Odyssey* directly at the planet. "Landing on a planet with high gravity can be rough."

I do as instructed. The last thing I want right now is to be flung around like a helpless mammal in a cage. "How much bigger is this planet than Earth?" I ask.

Liam shoots me a quick glance. "You mean how much more *massive* is it?"

"You don't have to get all technical."

He smiles. "It's about ten percent more massive. What do you weigh?"

I sneer at him. "I'm sorry? That really isn't something you go around asking girls. You of all people should know that, since you flirt with them so often."

Oh, what I would do to wipe that terrible grin off Dragon's face right now. *Restrain yourself.*

"It's okay," Liam says. "You think Dragon and I will go around telling everyone your weight?"

"True, Dragon's good at keeping secrets." I shoot him an icy look. "I'm forty-six kilograms."

"Ow," Liam says in a high-pitched howling voice. He laughs. "Seriously?"

"Why?"

Liam shrugs. "Just makes it that much easier to sweep you off your feet." Before I can snap at him, he continues, "Anyway, you should feel about...five kilograms heavier."

"That's not too bad, right?"

Liam shrugs. "Depends. You'll probably get tired a lot quicker, but the two of you rested at least."

Dragon nods, but I remain motionless. I'm not sure I can consider what I went through *resting*. I wonder if Dragon was dreaming while he slept. Is he still tormented by them?

The descent into the atmosphere is as rough as Liam said. *The Odyssey* shakes and jolts left and right and I'm not sure what would happen if I wasn't buckled into my seat. Nausea knots its way into my stomach, and I close my eyes, holding onto my chair for dear life. The atmosphere is similar to Earth's. The sky is blue, and we pass through multiple gray clouds on the descent. We slow, and the flying becomes much smoother. I spot a small refueling port ahead, and Liam positions the ship to dock. Landing takes nearly an eternity, and I'm relieved the flight's over. I unbuckle my seat and stand but lose my balance and crash into the wall.

"Whoa, slow down," Liam says. "It takes a while to get used to the new gravity. Try not to move quickly, alright?"

My feet feel like they're being pulled into the ground, and my heart struggles to pump blood to other areas of my body.

Dragon takes my hand. "You okay?"

I nod and free my hand. "Yeah. Just stood up too fast."

"Liam's right. Move slowly, and take deep breaths." He heads to the back of the ship, opens the airlock door and the ramp, then leads us outside.

So it turns out the port isn't so small after all. The station is huge, probably around twice the size of the Crystal City Mall, and that's saying something.

Around us, an array of aliens and people from all different corners of the galaxy wait by their ships that range from one-manned transports to full-sized interplanetary cargo transports. Most of them are humanoid, many of them probably branched off from humans thousands of years ago when people started colonizing other worlds. For many colonies, the only hope for survival was genetic splicing, resulting in new forms of humanity. Others are completely alien with shimmery blue skin, or insect-like bodies. A few of them wear strange suits with helmets and tubes connecting to small box-like things on their backs. Maybe they can't survive in such an oxygen rich atmosphere.

"Let's get this over with as fast as we can," Dragon says. "We don't have time to lose."

"There's a café up ahead." Liam gestures to a large dirty-silver building on the edge of the refueling platform. "Refueling usually takes around twenty minutes give or take, so we'll have time to get something to eat."

Dragon's eyes widen a little. "I'm not trying to sound mean, but how do you know all this when you've hardly been anywhere?"

Liam places his thumbs under the strap of his holster belt and scrunches his shoulders. "I've always had a thing for machines. Everything the teachers wouldn't teach me, I taught myself. Learned a lot of other stuff in the process, like how to operate machinery that was unauthorized by the IA."

"Wait," I frown. "You got *terrible* grades."

"I did," he says, "but only because I was doing what *I* wanted to be doing. Not what the teachers wanted me to."

"I never would have known."

"Oh there's a lot you don't know about me," he says slyly. "Okay. I'm going to go pay for fuel. You two go head to that café over there and I'll meet you in a few minutes."

A shiver runs through me.

*"And your friend who's still in love with you...Liam? Is that his name? You have no idea what he's capable of."*

What Azad said in my dream meant nothing. Maybe I've had a few prophetic dreams in the past, but that doesn't mean anything.

Dragon and I continue on without a word.

A soft breeze breathes air into the station. It carries the pungent odor of fuel. The powerful stench clings to my throat and clogs up my lungs, making me want to cough. Just the smell makes me feel dirty and slimy.

I glance at Dragon. The silence between us is cold, dead, and stale.

Despite everything, I have to keep reminding myself that I don't really know him. I only saw bits and pieces of his true self during the Trials. He's like a puzzle that I won't ever be able to solve because most of the pieces are missing.

We walk up a large column of stairs made of dirty, silvery steel and approach the café. Dragon holds the door for me as we enter the café, but his every motion is mechanical.

The café is small and bright. Red leather booths and chairs line the white marble floors and walls. People and aliens of all colors chat together, the noise level is a nine on a scale of one to ten. It makes me a little uncomfortable with so many people around, but at the same time, it's nice knowing that whatever we say probably won't be overheard.

The two of us grab a seat at a small, silver table by a window where we can see *The Odyssey*, and Liam who is speaking with one of the workers. The two of them take turns nodding and talking, probably working out a price for the fuel.

We both avoid eye contact. The silence is cold. I want to say something, but the air feels stale in my lungs. I'm not sure if it's because breathing naturally takes more effort on this planet, or because of everything that's happened in the last twenty-four hours.

"Hello, there!" says a waiter with a strong accent. "Can I get you anything?" His voice is musical, and his words sound more like, "*ello, dah, san e get you anyding?*"

I don't fully look at the man. If he sees my face he might be able to recognize me.

Jessica K. McKendry

"What do you recommend?" Dragon asks, his voice flat and impassive.

The waiter explains a few dishes, but even after that, I'm not sure I really understand. They don't have many dishes native to Earth, and all of it sounds delicious. Of course, anything would after an entire day without food.

Dragon makes his choice.

The waiter turns to me. "What do you want, my dear?"

"I'll, um, I'll have the same thing, please." After all, Dragon must know something about what he ordered.

"Very good choice," the waiter says. "That is one of my most favorite dishes."

I smile, and the guy walks away. I hope it's good. Either way, food is food, and that's what I really need right now.

Dragon goes back to his quiet self.

I can't stand it any longer. "Okay. Talk to me. We're working together. Moping around because I wouldn't tell you about a stupid dream I had will not help us find my mother."

He sighs but doesn't say a word.

"Dragon, I'm not trying to be offensive, but the truth is you and I don't need to tell each other everything. You made that perfectly clear."

"I'm not offended," he says coldly.

I raise an eyebrow.

"I'm not," he insists. "I just…I just want to know what happened. Maybe I can help."

"Why? You don't have to. I didn't ask for help."

He furrows his brow and scoffs. "Why haven't you?"

"Dragon, I learned how to do things on my own in the Crystal City. I used to like having you around, but I don't need you. I can take care of myself. Besides, in the past twenty-four hours, I've found out you've been lying to me since the moment I met you. Why would I ever ask you for anything?" I stop myself. I don't need to be angry, annoyed is good enough for now.

"Oh, so this is your way of getting back at me because I didn't mention I was a traitor during the Trials? Cause that sure as hell would've gotten me killed. So I'm sorry that I felt like my life was a little more important than telling the truth. Or that I decided to complete my mission and save you from having to marry insane-revenge-crazed Azad's best friend?" His eyes are full with fury and annoyance, like he can't believe how ungrateful I am. "Everything I did, I did for you. My life has been a buildup to the Trials, to save you and get the *shaav* out of the IA. Yes, I lied to you. I had to gain your trust so you'd want to come with me when we tried to pull you out. I did it cause I had to. If you want me to apologize for that, I can't. Cause that was the right thing to do."

I glare at him. "How many wrongs did you have to commit to do something right?"

His jaw tightens, and he looks down at the table.

"How many people died just to get me through the Trials and out of the Alliance?" I ask harshly. "How many times did you lie or pretend to be someone you weren't? When you add it all up, does the good really outweigh the bad?"

He closes his eyes. "I hope so. By the stars, I hope so." He takes a deep, painful breath. "I honestly care about you. Putting all that aside—"

"'Putting all that aside?'" I mimic, my voice rising. "How can you put all that blood aside?"

"Because I am not you. If I didn't put it aside, I'd have to accept the darkness of my soul." His voice is as cold as his expression. A moment passes, and he lightens up a bit. "I want to help."

I shake my head. "You only want to help because I'm worth something to the Resistance. If it weren't for my mother, I'd be out of luck, and you'd have left me to my fate in the Crystal City."

"You're not worth something to the Resistance," he corrects. "You *are* the Resistance. Without you, the Phoenix would be dead. You were born for this. You were bound to join us eventually. I merely sped up the process. If you were someone else I wouldn't care as much, but you *aren't* someone else."

I have nothing to say.

Dragon inhales sharply then leans toward me. "I know you had a vision, Jaina. I know what it feels like, and I know that in our case, they can be dangerous. Now will you tell me?"

I don't answer.

"Who was it you saw?"

I keep my eyes away from his, for fear he'll read the answer in me.

"Was it Sean?"

"No," I mutter, looking down at his hands on the table.

He raises an eyebrow. "Was it me?"

I glare at him. "You wish."

"Was it Azad?" He says the name softly.

I should say no. It doesn't help that a small part of me wants to tell him. By the time I make up my mind about how to respond, it's too late. I've hesitated too long.

Dragon sits back in his seat and crosses his arms over his chest. "It's him, isn't it?"

I swallow hard. "Yes."

"In the vision—"

"It wasn't a vision," I bark. "Why do you keep saying that? How would you know?"

He moans, pressing his palms to his eyes, then pulls them away to look at me. "I *know*, okay? It has to do with something."

"That's real specific. Thanks. Just *shaavez* tell me." A thought occurs to me. "Do I have some fatal disease?"

His expression flickers with anger. "No, it's nothing like that."

I throw my hands up violently. "Why am I not surprised," I snap. "What is it with you and your precious secrets? Do you think it's fun? All these little games? You think it'll keep me around longer? Maybe the mystery around you will intrigue me so much that I'll fall in love with you? I know what you are. You're a liar. A damn good one too. This is the last thing I need right now. I need the truth. All of it. You owe that to me."

"The only reason I don't want to tell you is because it'd be too much. You just found out that your mother is the leader of a Resistance that you didn't even know existed, and now you're on a habitable planet outside of the Alliance, sitting across from me having a meal instead of getting married to Sean."

I clench my hand into a fist on my lap. "I know you think I can't handle this, but I'm a lot stronger than I look. Tell me something."

Dragon groans. "By the stars, Jaina, I…" He sighs then looks around, as if he's suspicious. "There is a prophecy," he mumbles.

"A what?"

He takes a deep, shaky breath. "A prophecy. Like, something that predicts the future–"

"I know what a prophecy is," I interrupt. "Are you *shaavez* out of your mind? A *prophecy*? You sound as insane as Azad."

"Jaina, this is real," he says quietly, "and it's dangerous. Please, you cannot go around talking about this."

"Why should I trust you?"

"Because I'm a major part of the Resistance. And this is extremely classified. This is supposed to be something your mother tells you."

I shake my head. "Tell me about this prophecy."

"I don't know much," he says, barely audible above the loud chatter of everyone else in the café. "This is sensitive material, so I can't give you much detail right now, but we think you are part of it."

"What could possibly make you think that I am a part of this? Why would you think this prophecy is real?"

"It's real. Do you remember the vicera flores? The glowing 'thought flowers' we encountered in the third trial?"

Yes, I remember. Xana pointed them out to us. I remember touching one, I remember it growing, and I remember Dragon pushing my hand away, saying I could've killed it.

I told him I was strong enough to handle this, so I need to act like I'm not freaking out, but my heart races, and my body grows warm. Memories of Azad flood my brain. By the stars, my blood feels cold. *You're the one, the Light. Anyone who's heard the prophecy knows it's you.*

No.

Please, Azad, don't be right again.

"It's a sign," Dragon says. "You're the Light, the one we've been waiting for."

Chills run through me. "What do you mean?"

"You're going to save us all."

"I'm sorry to be the bearer of bad news, but you've put your faith in the wrong girl. The only person I'm going to save is my mother. And this whole thing about the Light?" I glance out the window at *The Odyssey* so he can't see how much it bothers me. "Azad would call me that, and we both know how full of it he was. Dragon, I don't care about this prophecy. I really don't. If you wanna help, tell me about the dreams. What are they?"

He touches a deformation on the window sill next to us. "They're warnings, foreshadowing things to come."

The thick oxygen in the atmosphere makes it harder to breathe. Azad's voice rings clear in my mind, *"You are the Light."*

I keep my voice soft, and low. "What can I do to make them go away?"

"Nothing. There's nothing you can do."

My heart sinks. Will Azad always be present in my dreams? "I thought you said you could help."

Dragon shrugs. "Talking is helping."

"What do you dream about?" I ask.

His lips part, but before he can answer, Liam plops his skinny frame down in the seat next to me. Dragon shuts his mouth and returns to gazing at *The Odyssey* as workers begin the refueling process.

"What's with the intense mood?" Liam asks.

The waiter reappears with two dishes and gently sets them on the table before us. Despite the poor presentation compared to Crystal City meals, the smells get to me right away. It's celestial. The foreign spices mixed with some sort of red sauce and meat makes my mouth water.

The waiter asks for Liam's order, and only now do I realize the waiter isn't human. I've seen aliens all over the place, but this one is different. He's about the last thing I'd associate with the word *handsome,* but he's so otherworldly I can't take my eyes off him.

His light purple skin is pulled so tightly over his enormous head that his only facial expressions are through his thin lips. His eyes are way too far apart to be normal, even by alien standards. On top of his tall skull is a large ponytail of black...the strands are too thick to be hair. More like thin tentacles. I wonder if he has nerves running down them. If I touched it, would he feel it?

His sharp teeth click together as he waits for Liam to choose something.

Dragon clears his throat, and I turn to him with a start. His message is clear: *Stop staring.*

Oh no. My body goes into panic mode and I start sweating. I've been staring at the waiter, he can see my face now. Quickly, I glance down at my food and take a bite. Flavors burst in my mouth like fireworks on my tongue. The food in the Crystal City mainly focused on dishes from Earth. The Emperor's lineage is pure human, so naturally, it's the Royal Planet. I've never had anything like this in my life. What other things have I been missing out on?

Liam finally orders, and the waiter walks away.

Dragon leans closer to me. "He's a Keducian. They're the native species of this planet."

"Do you think he saw my face?" I ask nervously.

"You were staring at him for a full minute," Dragon replies. "Of course he saw your face, but I wouldn't worry about him recognizing you. They tend to have issues with short term memory."

"I hate to sound stupid," Liam cuts in, "but if his head is so big, why is he working at a café? Shouldn't he be like some interstellar genius?"

Dragon glances around the room and presses his fingers to his lips. "Shh! They're a violent species, so be careful what you say. They have thick skulls. Their brains are smaller than a human's."

"Like, how big?" Liam asks.

Dragon shrugs.

"Like, the size of a coconut? The size of a walnut?"

Dragon shakes his head. "I—"

"The size of a *pea?*"

"I don't know!" Dragon snaps back in a whispery voice. "I honestly have no idea. I just know it's smaller than ours."

"Guys, come on. Let's eat quickly so we can get back to *The Odyssey* on time," I interject. I scarf down the food as fast as I can. My ravenous hunger seems to grow with every bite.

Only then do I realize Dragon and Liam are staring at me.

I'm holding the fork in midair, halfway between my mouth and the plate. I set it back down. "Aren't you guys hungry?"

Dragon raises his eyebrows and continues eating.

Liam doesn't stop staring. "You can fit a lot in there, princess." He bites back a smile and stifles a laugh.

My cheeks burn. "I'm never eating in front of you again," I mutter before taking the last bite. Nothing remains except for a few pieces of something I'm a little too afraid to eat.

The Keducian waiter returns with Liam's food, and I can tell the only thing Liam's thinking is *pea brain*.

"Thanks," Liam mutters to the alien as he suppresses a grin.

The Keducian nods and walks away.

I slap him on the shoulder.

"Ow, what was that for?" Liam asks.

"I know what you were thinking," I shoot back.

"Stop listening to my thoughts. It's creepy."

"Just eat your food." I lean back against the booth and stare out at *The Odyssey*. The ramp is closed, and other Keducians stand nearby, refueling the tank. By the stars, it would be horrible if the ship got stolen. My anxiety rises in my chest, and I have to remind myself that to get past the airlock doors, you have to enter the access code. No one would be able to get inside without setting off an alarm.

I turn to watch the other customers in the small café. A woman with large purple eyes and skin the color of the sea sits on the other side of the room. Instead of hair, she has a large frill on the top of her head, decorated with jewels. Her cheekbones jut out fiercely, and somehow she is beautiful.

The door to the café slams shut. A figure clad in armor strides confidently into the café. The way he's built suggests his gender, but a black helmet conceals his face. He takes a seat two empty tables to my left. Now and then, he glances our way. It's impossible to tell if he's looking at one of us or keeping an eye on his ship somewhere out the window.

A waiter approaches him, but he waves the man off.

His black armor is peppered with blemishes of silver where the paint must have worn away. A few dents mark his chest plate. Either this man has seen a lot of battle or the previous owner did. A blood-red "S" stains his shoulder plate, though it looks more like a line that's slightly curved at the top and bottom. In the first lobe, there's a white dot, and just below it, within the second lobe is a red dot.

Liam finishes up his food and sighs heavily when he's done.

"You think they're done yet?" I ask, glancing toward *The Odyssey*.

"They should be," Dragon replies.

I feel a little bloated and heavy. The heaviness comes from the higher gravity, I hope, but the feeling that my stomach has stretched a few centimeters probably isn't.

"Come on. Let's head back," Liam says.

We pay for the food then walk outside. The silvery bronze flooring sparkles in some places, and in others, it's more worn.

Two people walk toward us. My gaze falls on the red IA symbol imprinted on the shoulder of their armor. I touch Dragon's arm.

"Keep your head down," he whispers to me.

Liam and Dragon walk ahead of me, and I stay behind. We continue forward, moving slowly into their range. My heart pounds in my ears. Their IA scout shuttle is two stations down from ours. Of all the places they had to land, it had to be near us.

"Hey!" calls a voice.

Instinctively, I look up. The moment I do, I curse myself for it because the two guards are locked on me.

They break into a jog and stop abruptly, now face to face with Dragon. His expression is calm. The only visible sign of fear is a slight quiver in his hand, but as he clenches it into a fist, even that disappears.

"Hello, officers," he says, not a tremble in his voice.

The guards nod.

"Um..." The younger guard sounds nervous. "Where are you headed?"

"That's not Alliance business," Dragon replies monotonously.

He looks to the older guard. They aren't used to being questioned.

"Listen," the older man says, sternly, "we just want to ask the girl a few questions. She matches the description of someone we're looking for."

"And who might that be?" Dragon asks.

The guards exchange glances.

"That information is classified," says the elder. "Now hand her over for questioning."

"Let me remind you gentlemen that this is not an IA territory. Your laws do not apply here," Dragon replies with a hint of darkness in his voice. "I suggest you move along."

"We aren't asking." The older man's hand subtly brushes the gun in his holster belt.

The younger guard reaches for me and I jerk back. A swooshing sound fills my ears. Dragon's scimitar touches the young man's throat, his eyes burning.

"I'm not asking either." Dragon's sword is steady. "Move along."

The older guard aims his gun at Dragon. Liam's gun is pointed directly at the older guard. A few people around us stop to gawk. No one screams or runs away; they act like this is a normal occurrence. The man in the black armor watches us with interest from afar. At least it seems that way. His hand rests on a gun in his belt, but he makes no move to retrieve it.

By the stars, if someone shoots, this could get very messy.

"Just let us ask her some questions, and we'll let you go in peace. Otherwise we'll have to call for reinforcements," the younger guard nearly pleads.

"You're not in any position to negotiate. You're outside of Alliance airspace, and by the looks of your vessel the two of you are traveling alone. The nearest Alliance planet is what...thirty-six lightyears away? Backup is going to take a few hours to get here," Dragon counters. "Now leave us alone, and I'll let you live."

A woman from the crowd raises her fist high in the air. "Kill that Alliance scum!"

A few others shout their approval, swearing and cursing at the guards.

Dragon raises an eyebrow at the younger man.

The guard takes a step back and clenches his teeth. They put their weapons away, and without a word, the two men continue on toward the café. I glance backward, to see the man in black, but he's gone. A cool, tingling sensation rushes through my blood like ice water.

Dragon deactivates his scimitar, and Liam returns his gun back to his holster belt.

Dragon touches my shoulder. "You okay?"

I subtly back away from him so his hand slides off my shoulder. "I'm fine."

Liam looks around suspiciously. "I had no idea the guard patrols out here."

Dragon shakes his head. "They shouldn't be here. We don't have much time to find the Phoenix before they execute her."

The three of us reach *The Odyssey*, and Dragon raises his hand to unlock the ramp.

"Wait!"

A figure jogs toward us. Dragon stops, and I rest my hand on the gun in my holster belt, just in case. The newcomer is a girl with tan skin and dark hair. Her features grow more familiar with every step.

"Luci?" Dragon cries in disbelief.

She reaches us and doubles over, catching her breath.

"What are you doing here?" I ask, unable to help the annoyance in my voice.

"The real question is, what are *you* doing here, Jaina?" she spits back, her eyes flaring.

"I told her she could come along," Dragon steps in.

"Why the *shaav* would you do that? Shirez specifically ordered you to stop her from coming!"

"Sorry," Dragon says sarcastically. "I guess I wasn't listening."

"He said, and I quote, 'Jaina will want you to bring her along, but do not let her go.' Does that ring a bell?"

Dragon shakes his head and shrugs. "Not really."

Luci's expression hardens.

"So..." Liam cuts in. "What *are* you doing here, Luci?"

"Shirez sent me to bring her back." She glares at me.

"You don't have to do that," Dragon replies.

"Yes, I do. General's orders."

My neck tingles. "I'm not going."

"What do you mean?" she asks. "You joined this Resistance, Jaina, and you have to follow its rules."

I step closer to her, taking on a more threatening stance. "I never said I joined the Resistance. I'm only here to find my mother, and I will not sit back and wait for something to happen."

"Regardless of your position, Dragon and Liam are part of the Resistance," she snaps.

Liam flinches a little.

"So," she continues, "you both have to follow orders. Hand her over."

Liam laughs. "Whoa, she's not some object we can *hand over*. And you're gonna have to get through me first. This is Jaina's mother, she has every right to be on this mission."

Dragon groans. "No one is fighting anyone. Shirez is wrong about this, and unless Jaina wants to go back with you, she's under my protection."

"*Our* protection," Liam corrects.

"I'm not going anywhere with you," I snap.

Luci grits her teeth. "He's going to kill you for this."

Dragon glances left then right as if he's suspicious Shirez is lingering around the corner. "I know."

Luci shrugs. "Fine. Then I have to come with you. You know I can't return empty handed."

*Shaav.* No. She is the last person I want tagging along. By the stars, they better not let her come with us.

Dragon shakes his head. "Luci, this mission isn't—"

"Oh one more thing." She grimaces. "My ship got destroyed. So either way, we're taking the ol' *Odyssey.* Just like old times."

Liam fidgets with something on his holster belt. "Did you get attacked, or did you just not land right? You seem like you'd be a sucky pilot."

Luci scoffs. "You're lucky you were assigned this mission."

Dragon nods. "That's what I told him."

Liam smirks. "It's not luck."

Dragon sighs. "Alright, Luci. Let's go."

# CHAPTER ELEVEN

As if it isn't bad enough having to be with Dragon, who alternates between sweet and angry, or Liam, who is constantly trying to get on Dragon's nerves, now I've got Luci to worry about, who is cold and harsh to me every chance she gets.

I shouldn't care what she thinks about me. She didn't think I was a worthy leader in the Trials, and maybe she was right. What's frustrating is that I still get the sense she's judging my every word.

Maybe it's because she has feelings for Dragon. It was more than just my leadership she was jealous of.

Luci and I have the back two seats behind Dragon and Liam. Liam, of course, is in the pilot seat, and Dragon is copilot again.

"Where are we headed?" Luci grabs onto the back of Dragon's seat.

Just seeing how comfortable she is around him kind of makes me sick. This whole time, she knew exactly who he was. She knew about the Resistance and the part he played in it.

"I'm surprised Shirez didn't tell you," Dragon bristles. He doesn't seem happy that she's here, so that makes me feel a little better.

"Shut up, Drag," Luci shoots back. "I followed you, Shirez didn't tell me where we're going."

"Stalker," Liam murmurs.

"I said shut up," Luci spits at him.

Liam raises his eyebrows and smiles. "You told *Dragon*, not me."

"We're headed to Kashia," I answer.

"Thank you." She sits back in her seat. "Was that really too much to ask?"

"Depends on who you're asking," Dragon replies.

Luci stares at Dragon so intensely I'm afraid lasers will shoot out of her eyes and disintegrate him. "Can I talk to you for a minute?"

He glances back at her, his voice emotionless while his eyes betray a slight hint of anger. "Go right ahead."

Luci crosses her arms. "Fine. I'll speak my mind. Why the *shaav* did you bring Jaina along? You completely defied the General's orders. If something happens to Jaina, everything is over."

"Shirez is wrong." He nearly growls as he talks. "I already told you that. She's Amara's daughter. This is what she would want."

"Oh really?" She laughs as she spits out the words. "How do you know *anything* about our leader?"

Dragon shifts uncomfortably. "Shirez tells me about her."

"Right." Luci slaps her hands down on her knees. "How typical of you to take the General's orders and toss them out the viewport. The only reason you feel like you can is because he's—"

"Shut up!" The pleading look on his face makes my stomach knot.

She raises an eyebrow. "So, you haven't told them about the General and *her* yet?"

I sit up with a start. "Told us what?"

"No," he admits. "I haven't."

Liam puts his hand in front of Dragon. "What haven't you told us?"

Luci doesn't shift her gaze from Dragon. "How typical of you. Of course you didn't think to bring that up before you made out with Jaina."

The following silence is as dark and frigid as a comet lost in space. Tingles travel up and down my spine as Liam's eyes wander in disbelief from Dragon to me.

My gaze finds the floor, and my throat constricts. The void of soundless cold suffocates me.

I look down, because it's easier than meeting Liam's gaze. I can't bear seeing the pain I know I'll find in his eyes. After everything Liam said and did in the Trials, about being there for me, maybe he thought a part of me would hold myself back from Dragon. Unfortunately, I didn't.

Luci scoffs. "Liam, why do you look so surprised? I thought you would've expected it. It was disgusting."

Liam ignores her, I only feel his stare burning into my face.

I quickly glance at him.

A mixture of disgust and pain registers on his face.

"What?" I retort harshly. "None of it matters. It was just a kiss. It honestly didn't mean anything."

Dragon's eyes flicker to mine then back to various deformations on the floor. He hides whatever he's feeling behind his natural mask so his expression is completely unreadable. He clears his throat and turns to Luci. "You know why I did it. The mission was at stake, and it was our last chance for her to trust us. You should be grateful it worked."

Sparks. Little flickering flames. Those embers I quieted down in my heart begin to light up again as he speaks the words. The urge to hurt him, cause him some sort of pain the way I feel pain right now is so unbelievably tempting. The muscles in my jaw twitch and my fingernails dig into my hands as I try to take a deep breath.

"That doesn't mean you can go feeling up the daughter of the Phoenix!" Luci snaps back. She grips Dragon's arm so hard her knuckles turn white. "You think just because you're *Altair Kasev* you can do whatever the *shaav* you want!"

I take that back. I want both of them to hurt right now. Want to say something that would make them crumble to their knees in tears, sobbing, hurting so much inside they want to tear their hearts out. That's how they're making me feel.

Instead I keep my teeth clenched, fingernails in my palms, trying so hard to brush it off.

Dragon meets my gaze with an angry fire then directs it to Luci. "I did what was necessary, and that's all!"

No longer able to contain it, my anger boils over. "It wasn't necessary!" I cry. It comes out a lot sadder and weaker than I intended. I feel as if I've been struck by an astroid. "I was your mission, not your conquest!"

Liam growls with rage. "That's it!"

He unbuckles his seat and lunges for Dragon. Dragon falls out of his seat to take cover, but Liam jumps to his feet and closes his hand around Dragon's shirt, pulling him up to face him. His fist hits Dragon squarely in the jaw. Liam punches him hard in the stomach, Dragon moans and doubles over, coughing as he tries to breathe. Liam shoves him back into the wall, pinning him there, yet Dragon doesn't strike back.

I'm too shocked to move.

Too shocked to breathe.

"Liam, stop!" I hear myself cry.

"You son of a *katiaj*!" Liam grabs Dragon's shirt and uses it to hold him to the wall. "Don't you ever touch her, do you understand me? You worthless *shaav*, you don't deserve anyone like her."

"Liam, stop it!" I shout.

Liam shoves Dragon harder into the wall. "If you hurt her, I'll kill you. Do you hear me?"

Dragon closes his eyes and nods. His whole body is quivering. His lip is bleeding down his chin, and a large dark purple bruise starts to form on his cheekbone.

"*Shaav* you." Liam punches the other side of his jaw.

Dragon groans, breathing slowly through his teeth. Blood drips from his mouth onto the floor. His teeth are crimson red.

"Liam, stop! Please!" I throw myself at him, pull on his shoulder, and force him away. I press my back to Dragon's chest, hoping Liam won't strike with me in his path. "What are you doing?"

Liam doesn't back down and shoots plasma bolts from his eyes at Dragon.

Luci wanted this to happen. Otherwise, she would have defended Dragon from the start.

"Are you crazy?" I snap at him. "What's done is done, there's nothing you can do to change it!"

"I don't *shaavez* care," Liam snarls.

"I care! We'll never reach my mother in time if we're too busy fighting each other! Liam, you have to pilot. Luci, you copilot," I order.

Panting, Liam holds his bloody fists tightly and he clenches his teeth. I'm afraid he's going to try to go through me to get at Dragon, but he coldly turns his back and returns to his seat. Luci's eyes are wide as she studies Dragon, but she does as I say and she takes the seat next to him.

Dragon keeps his steady gaze on the ground. Despite my frustrated rage, I can't leave him like this. Who knows what we'll be up against when we get to Kashia? He needs to be able to fight. I can't leave him alone with Liam, and I don't trust Luci. So I touch his arm and motion for him to come with me.

He follows me out of the cockpit and to the tables near the entrance of the ship. I make him sit, and he chokes out a laugh.

"What's this all of a sudden?" he asks. "One minute you're snapping at me, and the next you're trying to help...you confuse me."

I retrieve a medkit from a side panel in the wall and take a seat next to him. His face is really bruised. There's a cut above his left eyebrow, and his lip is still gushing.

He stares down at the medkit. "I don't need that."

"Yes, you do."

"I had it coming."

"You did. Believe me, I had the urge to do it myself. But if things get rough, you have to be able to fight when we land." I take a deep breath as I pull a small, silvery cooling sheet from the medkit. "Why didn't you defend yourself?"

Dragon sighs. "Evil will never go unpunished. The universe will bring all to justice in the end."

"Evil?" I ask, keeping my voice flat.

He smiles slightly. "It's an old saying. Evil could be anything that hurts anyone. Could be violence, could be a lie, a hurtful word. There's another quote like it, an even older one."

"What goes around comes around?" I smile slightly.

"Good enough."

I finally touch the cooling sheet to his cheek. He flinches and instinctively grabs my wrist.

"You don't need to use this," he says, his voice deep.

"Sure. I also don't need a cup of Tira coffee," I reply sarcastically. I move to touch the cooling sheet to his cheek again, but before I touch him, he stops me. Frustrated, I snap my wrist from his grasp. "How do you expect me to help you?"

"You don't need it because you are the Light." He studies my face very seriously. "The healer. The defender."

My throat tightens, and I break my gaze from his. "Stop saying that."

He looks down at the floor and furrows his brow. "But you are. I know it." Dragon purses his lips then meets my eyes. "You have visions, and you have a sense about people. You're able to read people easier than most. You will bring light and justice back to the people."

I shiver and shake my head. "It's a myth."

"Is it?" He takes my hand and touches it to his cheek. "Heal me, and tell me what you think."

"That's what I was trying to do before you grabbed me," I snap at him.

"No, I'll show you," he replies, reaching out for my hand.

Reluctantly, I let him take it. He lifts my fingertips to the cut on his left eyebrow. His skin is rough beneath my hand. I don't understand what he's asking me to do. My fingers touch the cut, and his warm blood makes my stomach knot. I have the urge to pull away, but I decide to humor him.

"Close your eyes," he says.

"This is stupid," I reply.

"Close your eyes and imagine your consciousness," he orders.

"What do you mean? Imagine my consciousness?"

"Keep your eyes closed," he scolds. "If you concentrate, you'll see it."

I close my eyes and attempt to "imagine my consciousness." The darkness behind my eyelids fades as memories flash before me, slow-motion pictures of Virana, the jungle trees, the warm air, and the feeling of freedom as I floated across the beaches at night.

"What do you see?" he asks.

Clearing the memories from my mind, I shrug. I have no idea what he's trying to prove. "I don't see anything."

"Take slow, deep breaths. Don't let anything distract you. Now what do you feel?"

I do as he says, and a soft breeze of thoughts swirls into my mind. I can't exactly decipher them, but I feel them there. "Refreshed, I guess."

I get the feeling that he's nodding. "Hold on to that feeling."

"This is ridiculous," I reply.

Dragon squeezes my hand a little tighter, reminding me that my fingers are still on his cut. "Move it," he says.

I raise an eyebrow. "Move *what?*"

"That feeling," he continues, as if that were obvious. "Concentrate."

"What are you talking about?" I ask.

"I don't know. Just put it where it's supposed to go. And get that annoyed tone out of your voice. You need to stay calm. Deep breaths. Focus."

*Deep breaths. Inhale, exhale. Calm. Stay calm.* Not exactly sure what he means, I try to "pull" the refreshing sensation with the force of my mind. I don't know where exactly, only "down." It moves slow, like it's floating through selak taffy.

Dragon moves his thumb over my hand, pulling me slightly out of my concentration. It isn't hard to guess that he's staring at me. Shutting my eyes even tighter, I do my best to focus.

"Do you see anything?" he asks.

"No, not..." I stop mid-sentence. A glow grows between my eyelids, and warmth fills my body.

Dragon squeezes my other hand tightly. "You see it, don't you?"

With a gasp, I pull my hands away from him and open my eyes. He's much closer than I expect, so I jolt backward and avert my eyes to the ground.

"You saw," he breathes.

I purse my lips, shoot him a glare, and then look away again. "I didn't see anything. You told me to imagine things, so that's exactly what I did. I *imagined.* That doesn't make anything real."

"You can hide it from yourself, but not from me." Intensity grows in his voice.

I grab the cooling pad again. "See? It's just as bad as it was before."

The healing properties built into the pad helps restore proteins to the skin. The swelling goes down pretty quickly, and I'm able to stop the bleeding so that his cuts become merely scabs. Whatever he thought I was capable of, I'm not.

He flinches when I bring the cooling pad to his lip.

"Hold it there for ten minutes," I instruct him coldly. "The bleeding should stop, and it should heal almost completely within the next few hours. Though don't be surprised if you're sore for the next few days. You're lucky you have a good medkit onboard."

"You could've done it yourself," he says quietly.

"I just did," I snap back.

He shakes his head.

"What about you, Dragon?" My voice flares. "You seem to be so sure that I'm the Light. When *you* touched the vicera flores, they shrank. What do you see within yourself?"

Dragon glares. "What I see within myself is of no concern to you."

What a surprise. "Of course."

A red light flashes overhead.

Dragon looks up and removes the cooling pad from his lip. "Has the bleeding stopped?"

"Mostly."

He closes up the medkit and walks away. I follow him into the cockpit and sit next to Dragon behind Luci and Liam.

Through the viewport, I stare at the planet before us. The atmosphere of Kashia is thick. We pass through its purply-blue clouds for a long time, and I start to wonder if this planet has a surface at all. Maybe it's a gas giant, like Jupiter, Saturn, or Neptune.

"Are you sure this is the right place?" I ask, cautiously testing the water.

Liam nods once without turning to me. "Yep."

"How far down do we have to go?" By the stars, I can still feel the anger radiating from him.

"The surface is inhospitable. To most species, the atmosphere isn't breathable." Liam's voice is controlled and monotone. "They created cities built on supports, and encased each one in a large, plexiglass bubble. It elevates the city enough so the air pressure doesn't kill everything."

"Are there natives?" I ask.

Liam shrugs. "Not that I know of."

"That's what inhospitable means." Luci sneers.

Liam clears his throat and then begins with a little more optimism, "I found a public landing platform equipped with free safekeeping for *The Odyssey*."

"Thanks." Dragon says emotionlessly.

In the distance, a silver speck appears. As we come closer, I realize it's a city. Nearby are many other specks of various sizes. Some are far away and disappear into the clouds. How many settlements do they have on this planet? Why would anyone want to live here?

"This is it," Liam says, circling above the largest city.

A plexiglass bubble made up of tiny, see-through hexagons encloses the entire city. Soon, it becomes clearer that the "tiny hexagons" are big enough to fit a ship ten times this size. Has anyone ever crashed into one of these "bubbles"? Because of the high air pressure, I'd assume everyone would have to evacuate the city or suffocate. That would be an awful way to go.

Liam positions the ship outside a hexagonal sheet of plexiglass. It opens without command or authorization. For people looking for a safe place to live, this isn't a good sign. Unless Liam received some sort of landing confirmation, anyone could enter the city.

He carefully guides the ship through the plexiglass and onto a small landing platform. I'm more than relieved when we touch the ground, I'm tired of flying.

Liam sighs as the whining of the ship's engines dies down. "Okay, Draco Haidryn," Liam says, turning his chair around.

"How are we going to find him?" I ask.

"We know he's been in this district," Dragon says. "He's notorious on this planet. If he's here, it won't be hard to find him."

I furrow my brow and can't help feeling slightly defeated. Hopefully the city is a lot smaller than it looks. "We can't just stroll around searching for him. Do we have somewhere to start?"

"We'll have to split up," Dragon replies.

Liam brings his hand to his forehead. "Do we have another way to go about this?"

"Yeah," Luci agrees. "I mean, your last plan to get Jaina to like you kinda backfired."

Anger consumes Dragon's eyes, clouding them and turning them a shade darker. "Listen," he hisses, "I know you're angry, but I need you to focus and suck it up. If not for me, or Jaina, do it for General Indera. Unless any of you have a better idea, don't *shaavez* complain." He rubs his eyes. "We just don't have another option. We'll wander the city, collect information without arousing suspicion, and then meet back here. We'll stay overnight and devise a plan."

"And if we don't find enough information?" Luci asks.

Dragon bites his lip and his eyes falter to the floor. "We don't have a choice. Time is not a luxury we can afford." His expression is pained. "We'll work with what we have until we succeed." He holds my gaze a moment before shaking his head and pressing a button on the control panel to unlock the airlock doors.

Chills run through me. Tonight, we decide the fate of my mother. We can't be late.

I remove my scimitar from the compartment near my seemingly assigned seat and attach it to my holster belt. Dragon, Liam, and Luci attach other various weapons to theirs. When we're ready, we follow behind Dragon and leave *The Odyssey*.

The purple-blue clouds press up against the plexi-glass protection, swirling and creating dark shapes in the air. If it weren't for a few rays of Kashia's star shin-ing through the thick clouds, I'd think we were at the bottom of an ocean.

A long metallic stairwell leads into the city, and I feel like we're facing some huge monster. By the angle of the light, I think it's sunset, but I'm not sure how long days last on this planet. Some places, like Venus, have days longer than their years. Could this sunset last that long?

"Here we are," Liam says mechanically.

Dragon stares down into the city. His face is still pretty discolored here and there from the beating he took. At least all of the bleeding has stopped. "Luci, you go with Liam?" he asks.

"I'm not going anywhere with him." Luci glares at me.

As much as I hate her disrespectful responses, I can't help but take her side on this one. I don't want to go anywhere with Dragon. Or Liam. Or Luci. But mostly Dragon. I'm not ready to forgive him, I'm not sure if I'll ever be.

Dragon nods slowly. "Alright then. Jaina and Liam, you take the west side. Luci and I will take the east."

The metal stairway from the landing platform takes us to the "ground level" of the city. Dragon leads, and I'm last in line.

When we reach the bottom, Dragon says, "Remember, the last thing we want to do is arouse suspicion. Blend in and get as much information as you can. If you need to contact me, you have your privcoms. Luci and I will contact you when we're headed back to *The Odyssey*."

I nod sort of blankly and turn toward the west where a long avenue filled with people and aliens of all sorts awaits. Maybe we should start there.

"Come on, Liam," I say. My feet carry me forward into the avenue, and I see Liam out of the corner of my eye following close behind me. I glance backward. Luci and Dragon have started heading east.

There's only one thing that matters right now, and that's saving my mother. The only family I have. The thought of her makes me want to run through the streets, to search every corner of the city for Draco Haidryn, but I take a deep breath.

Dragon's right. We can't arouse suspicion.

The air is cool but not cold. It's not fresh, either. It smells stale, like a thousand generations exhaled at once. I only wish there was more light, yet Kashia's star is so immensely large and it emits more radiation than any sun I'm used to, so maybe it's better we're shielded by the clouds.

The streets of the city are crowded, and I hope no one notices us as we pass. I lead us through an alley and into the large gathering on the next street over. Small buildings made of some sort of sandstone line the streets. It looks like a very sad market. Elderly men and women stand behind makeshift countertops. In front of them are displays of food and jewelry from places I can't name. The people in the street ignore them for the most part. Only the small swarms of children in rags with yellow or blackened teeth pay them any attention. Their lips are an unhealthy purple color, and their eyes are sunken in. They hold up small trinkets to the people in the shops. Sometimes, they're greeted with a nod, and other times, they're waved off. The richer-looking people don't seem to notice them at all.

My heart sinks.

These children need help. Why isn't anyone helping them?

"Liam," I choke out.

He moves to my side, follows my gaze, and shakes his head. "There's nothing we can do," he whispers.

"We have extra money," I breathe.

"We can't. If the Resistance succeeds in their mission, it will help everyone."

I take a deep breath. "It won't. There are always going to be people in need, no matter who is in charge or where we are."

"Which is why we can't help them, Jaina. That is not our mission, and no matter how many people we help, there will always be others. Not to mention, we will be noticed."

He's right. I hate it so much, but he's right. We can't be noticed, so I keep my eyes on the ground. I can't bear looking at the sickly children without feeling more guilt.

"Hold my hand," Liam orders. "Couples don't tend to stalk people."

I scoff. "Last I checked, we're not a couple."

"Jaina, please don't be so difficult," he says in a harsh sort of breath. "We can't risk being noticed."

I bite the inside of my cheek. "For the sake of my mother." Reluctantly, I grip his hand and squeeze it hard.

"Ouch! What the *shaav?*"

I don't let go of his hand as we continue down the street. "After what you did to Dragon, it's the least you deserve."

"Are you kidding me?" he snaps. "Dragon used your trust. He took advantage of you." He intertwines his fingers with my own, and then glares at me. If he's trying to make me feel uncomfortable, it's working.

I pretend to shrug it off. "You're making it sound worse than it is."

Liam keeps his eyes forward as we wander the streets. "He made you believe he loved you then betrayed you."

"That's not—"

Liam stops me and gently presses me into the stone wall of a building. "It's exactly what happened."

"You're making a scene," I whisper.

"We can fight. Just make it look romantic."

A few passersby glance our way, so I place my hands on his shoulders to make it look more "romantic."

Liam touches my cheek and gets real close, like he's going to kiss me, but anger blazes in his eyes. "I hate to say I told you so, wrong, is *wrong*." He shakes his head, knitting his brow. His lips curl into a painful smile, like he's sorry for me. "Why aren't you upset?"

I push myself out of his grasp away from the wall, grab his hand tightly, and continue forward down the street with him at my side. "Who said I wasn't?" I mutter.

He raises an eyebrow. "Then why are you defending him?"

"Because he didn't defend himself when you went at him," I snap back. "I found out about all this on *The Justice*. Yes, he betrayed me, but he felt guilty, and so I made him bring me along on this mission. As much as I hate to admit it, he is the only hope we have of finding my mother. We have to trust him, at least to a certain degree."

Liam runs his fingers through his dark brown hair.

We wander down a few more streets. I hope he remembers the way back, because I have no idea where we're going.

Up ahead, a group of about five or six tough looking men in armor gather outside a tavern. A blond guy in the center looks like he's in charge since he's talking to everyone else. My stomach knots, and I get this feeling, this sort of rush. My lungs constrict.

"Let's sit down." I yank Liam toward a nearby bench.

"What for?" He glances at the men. "That moon-shaped crest on their armor, that's Draco's symbol."

"How do you know?"

"I looked him up in *The Odyssey*'s records and saw his family crest. How did you know that?"

I shake my head. "I didn't."

"Lucky guess then. Draco hires mercenaries wherever he goes for protection, and they all wear his symbol." Liam nods toward the men. "Watch them."

I turn to face them.

He grabs my chin and forces me to look at him. "Don't *stare*! I meant out of the corner of your eye. They'll kill us if they realize we're following them."

I take a shaky breath. "Good to know."

From my peripheral vision I notice two of them are staring at us with such intensity I feel like their eyes are throwing daggers into me.

"They know we're watching," I say.

"I know." Liam smiles, staring straight forward at a shop across from us. "Just pretend you're relaxed."

He wraps his arm around my shoulder. Smiling along with him, I scoot closer to him and lean my head against his shoulder. What would I do if I were relaxed at the moment?

"So, how are things since leaving the Crystal City?" he asks.

I shrug. "Can't say things happened the way I would've expected, although anything is better than being stuck there."

"I hated it there." He shoots another glance at the men. "They're leaving."

They disperse into two groups of three and continue down the road on opposite sides of the street.

"Come on." He stands.

I grab his arm and hold him back. "Just wait a sec."

"If we don't hurry, we'll lose them."

"They split up. Why would they do that?" I ponder.

Liam scowls. "It hardly matters, we have to follow them or lose them." He pulls me forward through the mass of people.

"Slow down!" Maybe they're a lead to find Draco, but they're mercenaries and murderers. The farther we are, the better. "You've got to let them get ahead."

"There's information right here. We can just snatch one of them and question them in an alley," he says.

I make him stop and lower my voice. "Do you not see all these people around us? We're out in the open. If you tried to attack them, the police would be here in moments. Besides, it wouldn't take them long to notice one of their buddies is missing. That's a terrible plan. We should follow them and when we're in an area with less people around, we'll make a move."

Liam glares at me. "That doesn't sound like a great idea, either."

I hesitate. "There are three of them and two of us, and we won the Trials. I don't want to do this either, but it's the only way."

Liam glances at the guys slowly walking away from us. "He knows we're following them."

"How do you know?"

He nods toward them. "The guy just looked at us then turned away."

I glance toward the man then back at Liam. "*Shaav.* Okay. What should we do?"

"Let's keep following them. They'll probably try to create an ambush. Only, it won't be an ambush because we'll know it's coming."

"Where did the other three go?" I whisper.

Liam moves a little closer to me. "What?"

"The other three guys who moved to the left side of the street, where did they go?"

Liam shrugs. "See? Ambush."

I clench my hand into a fist. "On second thought, I don't think we should walk into this."

He raises an eyebrow. "Are you scared, Ms. Jaina Indera? Daughter of the Phoenix?"

I sneer at him. "Of course not."

The sky grows darker by the minute, and fewer people walk the streets. I'm not sure if they're thinning out because of the darkness or simply because we've moved to a less crowded area.

The night seems to have crept up on us without warning. The blue haze created by the blue and purple clouds becomes darker and even more menacing as the rays of the unseen sun set over the horizon. I wish it were only the darkness I had to be afraid of tonight.

# CHAPTER TWELVE

The three men turn into a dark alleyway and I shudder as I watch them turn the corner. Of all the places in the galaxy, a dark alley is the *last* place I want to be right now.

Silently, I approach the wall of the building next to the alley. They could be waiting just around the corner, ready to kill us any moment. The streets are nearly empty here. I've still got my privcom, but that's not much to rely on.

I press against the wall so hard that the rough stone scrapes against my back, but I don't dare step away from it.

"Jaina," Liam whispers.

His voice makes me jump, I wasn't expecting him to be so close. When I turn to him, he hands me an R&Y DE-420. It's small and fitted with a silencer. Perfect.

"Set for stun?" I ask.

"Of course. We're not murderers."

*Just breathe. It'll be okay.* I furrow my brow then turn to look back at Liam. "Wait, why did you hand me the gun?" I whisper quietly. "I don't wanna go in there first. You look around the corner. You're the one hopelessly in love with me."

Liam glares into my soul. "First, because you're the daughter of the Phoenix, and second because you just said that. I'm not doing it."

"Are you *scared*?" I ask, trying to pull the same trick he pulled on me earlier.

"I'm scared of you more than them. They're not as pretty. If you get shot in the face, you won't be as pretty, so I won't be as scared."

"You *kanta*," I hiss.

He laughs. "I didn't know you'd ever use that word."

"You *shaavez* deserved it. Now let me focus."

I close my eyes a moment as I lean against the wall. *It's going to be okay. Do what you feel.* My blood is pulsing in my neck, down my arms and into my hands clasped around the cold steel of the gun.

*Go.*

I quickly peer around the corner, then pull back.

"I'm not dead," I whisper to Liam.

"I noticed. Are they there?"

"No idea. I didn't see anyone, I don't think. I moved so fast, and it was dark, and no one shot me, so I think it's okay."

"By the stars, Jaina." He rolls his eyes, then jumps into the alley, holding his gun ready to fire. He doesn't shoot.

I do the same.

There's no one in sight. Old boxes and debris piled up high provide too many places to hide. I shift my aim and take an unsteady step deeper into the alley.

No one.

I'm ahead of Liam now. "You coming, or what?" I ask. I can hear the fear in my voice with each quick, nervous breath.

He takes another step, but remains behind me. Does he want me shot in the face?

I advance further into the alley and glance back. The street is empty. Dead empty. I wonder if anyone would hear me if I screamed.

"I don't think they're here," Liam says.

"Of course, they're here. We both saw them."

"And they magically turned themselves into heaps of garbage? There's no one here."

I continue searching, moving down the alley and keeping my gun trained on anything that might be a threat. As I walk, my hand trembles with uneasiness. I don't like this.

What's left of the dying sunlight is dim. I'd feel so much better with a flashlight about now. This dark alley gives me the creeps. What's worse, I'm about halfway to the back, so making a quick escape nearly impossible.

Liam's right.

No one is here.

Was there another alley they went into? Did it only look like this is where they went?

A cold, tingling runs down my spine. "Liam, look for a trap door somewhere."

"I'm on it," he whispers.

Why would someone put a junk pile here? Do they just throw their garbage out their windows? A broken table split down the middle rests on a few taped up boxes that look like they've been sitting here for centuries. On top is a pale white figure. It's a doll. A doll with white skin, a pink dress, and perfect blond hair.

A shuffling sound behind me makes me freeze.

I whip my gun around and aim. I don't have time to gasp. Before I can squeeze the trigger, the man rams himself into me and slams me into the wall knocking the gun from my hand.

He shoves the barrel of a gun under my chin. *Shaav.* This isn't good.

"*Leshka veqez tromana sthik,*" he says in a low, growly voice. His dark yellow eyes peer into my skull. The metal is cold on my throat and presses so hard into my neck I'm afraid it will start to ooze blood.

Adrenaline shoots through me. It pulses through my veins with every heartbeat.

That's when it hits me. What am I doing? I won the *shaavez* Trials, and I'm just letting this guy hold me against a wall? How pathetic.

I snap my head to the right, keeping my face away from the gun then let myself drop to the ground like a stone. Twisting to the side, I tangle my leg between his feet, and jerk it backward. He stumbles, and I snatch my gun off the ground and aim it at my attacker.

"Hands up!" I order.

He does as I ask, yet he doesn't look too surprised.

Someone else rams into my shoulder and pins me to the ground. He's on top of me in a flash, pinning my wrists to the dirty floor of the alley. He's the blond guy with the close cropped hair, the man who looked like he was in charge.

"Look what we've got here," he says through gritted teeth.

Another man appears and holds a knife to my throat. I try to struggle against the two men and get the blond man off of me, but he doesn't budge. The second man only presses the knife closer.

The blond one says something to the man with the knife, but I can't catch his words. The man with the knife grabs my arms and the blond man gets off of me. I let out a breath of relief, but it doesn't last long.

He stands me up and holds my back to his chest. The pressure of the cold, merciless knife returns to my throat. The sharp blade grazes my skin, and when I blink, I see her.

*"Any last words?"*

*Xana closed her eyes. "Jaina... I should've been kinder. Tell Liam I'm sorry."*

*He slits her throat.*

My eyes burn with fury at the memory, and despite my current situation, my stomach knots. Her words wrench my heart every time I think of those last moments. They make my eyes sting with tears of fury, hatred, and every kind of pain.

The blond rises to his full height, and suddenly I'm plagued with thoughts of doubt. Maybe following them wasn't such a great idea. He looked a lot shorter from farther away.

Down the alley, Liam's in just about the same situation I am.

The blond studies me for a moment. His closeness reminds me too much of Azad. It makes me nervous.

"Why were you following us?" he demands.

Instead of replying, I jerk to the left. I know I can't get away, but I can't give in.

The guy behind me pushes the knife deeper into my throat.

"Let me go," I moan through my quick breaths.

The blond laughs. "Why? So you can shoot us down? Tell me why you were following us."

I grit my teeth.

He nods to the man at my back, and the man behind me slowly twists my arm in a direction I'm sure it shouldn't be going. I hold my breath as the pain grows, trying to ignore it, but the farther he moves it, the more I'm afraid he won't stop until it's dislocated or broken. He quickly twists it upward, and I moan as the bones in my arm begin to buckle. Tears of anger and pain well up in my eyes, but I don't let them fall.

The blond nods again, and the pain lets up.

I suck in a deep breath of air. The one good thing about being tortured by Azad is that most everything else pales in comparison.

The blond is probably in his late twenties. His eyes are a deep purple, and I wonder if he colored them or if he was born that way. The word *Ranos* is engraved on the top of his shoulder plate. Maybe that's his name.

He grabs my chin and a look of recognition flickers across his face. "I know you."

"Don't tell him anything!" Liam cries, struggling against the others.

"Shut him up!" Ranos hisses to his men down the alley then turns back to me. "So, you wanna tell me?"

I hear a painful crack from Liam's direction and he moans. My heart wrenches at the sound.

The man behind me loosens his grip. This is my chance. Might be my only chance.

Before he can slit my throat, I grab his hand, pushing against his strength, while kicking backward. My boot makes contact, maybe his knee, and a sickening snap follows. His cry of agony echoes through the alley. Ranos lunges toward me, but I step out of reach. A man who has been helping out with Liam makes his way toward us. He tries to grab at me and I evade his attack by ducking and snatching the dagger out of his belt. With one swift motion, I lodge it into his side where his armor doesn't protect him. I turn away from him before I have a chance to feel sick.

*Stupid.* Luckily I have another knife tucked into my belt. My hand automatically rushes to my holster belt, but my gun isn't there. Right. I dropped it.

Another man stops in his tracks, retrieves a gun, and fires. The plasma projectile rushes past me. My shirt grows warm from such close exposure to the bullet, but I ignore it. He shoots again, but I duck and pick up my gun. I aim and pull the trigger. The bolt of energy hits him, and he falls to the ground, temporarily paralyzed.

I'm almost relieved until I realize Ranos is nowhere in sight.

A clatter above my head makes my eyes shoot upward. Sure enough, Ranos is making his cowardly escape up a ladder on the side of the building. Son of a *katiaj.*

I lunge toward the ladder. As I climb, I strain against Kashia's gravity.

Another plasma bolt explodes in the alley. With a sick wrench of my stomach, I remember that Liam is still down there. I just left him in the middle of his own fight!

Taking an uneasy glance down, I find, to my relief, that Liam's doing quite well. One man lies in a heap on the ground, and two others struggle to keep control of Liam. He'll be okay. Three men is a little too much to ask of anyone, but he can handle two on his own.

Good. I have to get to Ranos before he escapes. He could be our only chance if Dragon and Luci don't find anything.

Hauling myself higher up the ladder reminds me of the rock wall I had to climb on Virana. At least there are no spiders here. I tilt my head upward just as Ranos disappears over the roof of the building. *Shaav.* I've got to get there before he finds an escape route.

Sweat streams into my eyes, but I don't have time to wipe it away. When I finally reach the top, I feel like I've climbed the great Mt. Olympus Mons. I'm so tired I almost forget what I was climbing for in the first place. After stepping onto the roof of the building, I pull out my gun. Ranos is nowhere in sight.

I creep across the roof, aiming here and there. According to those unsatisfying dramas I used to watch in the Crystal City, the bad guy always sneaks up behind the heroine and catches her by surprise.

*Behind me.*

I spin around, but he's not there. Silly superstition. He's got to be around here somewhere. People don't just dissolve into thin air. Not normally, anyway.

Only a few meters away is an overused shed. Maybe it's where they store the nuclear reactors to help power the building, but I can't be sure. I really hope he's not in there. It looks creepy, and I'm not that eager to find out what's behind that big, metal door.

Maybe he got away.

It's dark now, completely dark. The only light is from one of Kashia's moons. It casts pale blue light through the clouds.

I hold up my gun and frantically search the place; I can't turn back until I'm sure he's not here.

The sound of plasma-fire fills the air, ringing loud and clear. The bolt of red light rockets toward me. A sudden pain sears in my thigh. A gasp bursts from my throat, and my hands fall to my leg, gripping my thigh tightly as I try to stand. I've dropped my gun again. I clench my teeth, trying to hold back the cry bubbling up in my throat. Tears burn my eyes.

A figure steps out of the darkness and into the dim light of the Kashia moon. "You still haven't answered my question."

My eyes have gone blurry with the pain, but I recognize Ranos's voice.

"*Shaav* you!" I spit back through bared teeth. My stomach churns, and I'm hot all over. I'm going to vomit.

He smiles then moves in with frightening speed, punching me in the abdomen.

My vision blurs even more and my head spins. *No, you are not going to pass out.* He *shaavez* shot me in the leg. He's going to pay like hell for this.

He grabs me by my shirt, pulls me up to face him, and buries the nose of his gun into my skull. "You don't answer this time, and I shoot," he hisses.

*Think fast.* I can't, though. All I feel is pain. The tears welling in my eyes trickle down my face. I moan in agony, hoping, praying that he'll have mercy. Through my blurry vision, I manage to catch a glimpse of the gun against my forehead.

Somehow, my eyes focus on the small blue zero on the side of his cartridge, and adrenaline kicks back in. My pain fades just enough for coherent thought. He's out of ammo.

With the new realization, I don't have time to feel the pain in my leg or my stomach. I smack the gun out of his hand and elbow him hard in the stomach. He starts to fall to the ground and grabs my wrist, pulling me under him to soften his fall.

My back hits the concrete with a sickening thud, and the breath is knocked from my lungs. He retrieves a knife from my holster belt. My fingernails dig into his wrist until they pierce his skin. A warm liquid trickles at my fingertips. He growls as the knife drops to the ground. I push him to the right, but he rolls back on top of me. When I try to throw a punch, he grabs my hand.

"They're looking for you, you know." His voice is deep and raspy, deranged, almost.

"Get off me," I snarl, attempting to wiggle free.

He smiles crazily, the strong, bitter smell of alcohol lingering on his breath. "You're worth a lot of money, you know. What'd you do to make 'em so angry, Indera-girl?"

My fingers go cold. By the stars this is bad.

"I don't know what you're talking about," I snap.

"I saw your picture in the bar. It's not very often that an individual upsets them so much. I heard they're sending their best hit men after you."

He loosens his grip and I use all my strength to press against him and flip him over. I pick up the knife then press it tightly to his throat.

"I'm following you for information," I bark. "That answer your question?"

Rage flickers in his eyes, but he doesn't try to fight me off. If he so much as moves... I spot my gun a meter away, but I can't risk grabbing it.

"Now," I demand, "tell me where Draco is and you'll leave this rooftop alive."

"What does it matter to you?" he chokes out against the dagger.

A *clink* sounds behind me but I can't look, afraid he'll try to make a move if I do.

"You got him." Liam's voice echoes softly. His footsteps softly thump on the concrete roof as he approaches.

Liam points his gun at Ranos. No reason for me to be on top of him anymore. I pick up my gun and tuck it into my holster belt along with the knife.

"You okay?" Liam asks me, his eyes locked on Ranos.

"Yeah, I'm good," I reply breathlessly.

Liam removes my scimitar from his holster belt and hands it to me. "Here. Must've fallen."

"Thanks." I take the scimitar, activate it and point it at Ranos. "Get up."

He does.

"Drop all your weapons and put your hands behind your head," Liam continues.

"I disarmed him," I reply quickly.

"Not completely. Don't be too impressed with yourself." Ranos tosses a small knife to the ground then puts his hands above his head again. "Happy now?"

"Not yet," Liam growls. "Tell us where he is."

Ranos raises an eyebrow. "*Who?*"

"You *shaavez* know who," I spit back.

He takes a cautious step forward, hands still raised above his head. "We can work out a deal."

Liam brings his elbow across Ranos's face, knocking him backward. "Nice try, but you're not in any position to ask for money."

"Here's the deal," I begin. "You tell us, and we let you live."

He swallows hard. Maybe he's not used to be being beaten. If this is really what the galaxy has to throw at us, if this is what it's like having to fight someone who hasn't been trained in a gifted school, the rest shouldn't be difficult.

Ranos shakes his head nervously. "Okay, I'll tell you." He laughs painfully. "What do you want with Draco anyway?"

"We probably won't kill him, if that's what you're worried about," Liam shoots back.

"That's not what I asked."

"For being our captive, you've got a lot of questions." I wave my scimitar around. "It doesn't matter what we want with him. Just give us the information, and we'll let you go."

He shakes his head. "He's in Rei'oud. The rich side of town. He's staying at a friend's house."

"What's his friend's name?" Liam asks.

Ranos shrugs. "I don't know. He doesn't tell us more than we need to know."

Liam bares his teeth. "Is there *anything else* you can tell us?"

"He's not here with the prince," he replies. "There's a bit of an emergency in the IA at the moment." Ranos shoots me a smile.

"We know," Liam snaps.

Ranos raises his hands in surrender. "Just thought it might help."

I nod and lower my scimitar. "Go."

Liam looks at me like I'm crazy. Maybe he didn't actually expect me to let him go, but I want to be someone who keeps her word.

Ranos glances from me to Liam nervously.

"It's okay. Get out of here," I say.

He takes a step forward, and I retreat to let him pass. Ranos walks across the rooftop, breaks into a run then disappears over the side of the building.

"What if he reports us?" Liam asks.

"Then we better make this quick. He knows who I am."

# CHAPTER THIRTEEN

My thigh is searing with pain. Even though the plasma bolt cauterized the wound, my fight with Ranos dislodged pieces of burned flesh. Blood drips slowly down my leg, enough to make me uneasy.

I'm afraid I won't be able to make it back to the ship. Thankfully, Liam wraps his arm around my waist and gently walks the two of us back.

Liam considered stopping a few times to see if any of the local shops had some medical supplies, but it would take too much time, and we can't risk being recognized again. I can't hold back the mission. We're already running late, and time isn't something we have right now. Besides, despite the pain, it's only a plasma wound. I can hold out. For my mother.

"Come on, Jaina," Liam says. "We're almost there."

The journey seems to last forever. I must slip in and out of consciousness while walking because when I look down, I see the silvery platform where *The Odyssey* is docked.

Liam inputs the password into a touchscreen on the side of *The Odyssey*. The ramp extends from the ship, and the doors hiss open. He helps me up the ramp, and agony rings through me with every strain of my muscles.

The moment we're inside, the ramp slides back and the doors behind us shut.

"Dragon!" Liam cries. "Are you here?"

Footsteps round the corner. "What's wrong?" Dragon asks. His face pales and his expression hardens. "I've got meds."

"I'm alright," I say. "All I need is some rest. It's not all that bad." My vision starts to go a bit blurry. Am I really okay?

"Liam, get her to lie down."

Liam leads me into the cabin on the right. He yanks the blankets off the bed on the end. "You heard him, Jaina. Lie down."

"This really isn't necessary," I reply through gritted teeth. "We don't need to waste the meds, we don't have time for–"

"Aren't you in excruciating pain?" he asks angrily.

I take a deep breath, pretending to ignore the heat in my leg. "I just got a little scorched. Can't it heal by itself?"

"It could get infected. Don't be stubborn. We need to sterilize the wound."

Dragon enters the cabin and shakes his head. "Lie down."

I do as I'm told and take a quick breath as the burned skin stretches ever so slightly across my leg. It stings, like a thousand tiny pins in my leg.

Dragon stands over me, puts on some plastic gloves, then places his hand on my knee.

"Absolutely not!" I shout. "Where did Liam go? I want him to do it."

He shakes his head. "I don't know, and we don't have time to find out."

I can already feel my pulse speeding. By the stars, this is going to hurt. This is really going to hurt.

His fingers gently brush the burn, and I wince. "Sorry," he says.

Luci enters the room.

"Luce, I need scissors."

I sit up with a start. "*Scissors?* What for?"

What is he thinking? I'm pretty sure he's not a doctor. If he was, why didn't he help anyone who was injured in the Trials? This is not good.

"Don't worry, Jaina," he replies calmly.

"I'm *shaavez* worrying," I snap back. "Since when are you a doctor?"

"You're going to be okay. It's a flesh wound, but Liam is right. It needs to be sterilized. I know what I'm doing."

Luci hands him the scissors. I don't care if my leg falls off or if it gets infected. If I die, at least Dragon won't have to use those scissors!

"Um," I interject, just before the scissors touch my skin. I jerk back a little, causing a searing pain to travel up my leg, into my spine and into the back of my skull. "Don't you have a sedative or something?"

Dragon smiles weakly. "I'm not going to amputate your leg with scissors, okay? Lie back down. Now...this might hurt a little. Just breathe."

I close my eyes and breathe.

In.

Out.

In.

Out.

"Oww!" Tears well in my eyes as I bite down hard on my lip. "Careful!"

"I'm sorry."

I turn my head to the side, and Dragon shoots me an uneasy look. He probably doesn't think it's the best idea to watch. Even I don't think it's a good idea, but I can't pull my eyes away as Dragon punctures a small hole in my pant-leg above my wound. He cuts an area big enough for him to get a good look at the burn. The fabric of my pants has melted into my skin to the point that it's hard to tell the difference between the two.

I bite down on my tongue and dig my fingernails into my palms, trying to cause enough pain on some other part of my body to make up for what I feel on my leg.

Luci hands him another tool that looks something like pliers.

I moan and pull away as the cold metal makes contact with my skin.

"Sorry," he mutters again. "Just don't move."

I close my eyes and attempt to focus on something else, anything else to keep the pain from taking over me. My heart races in a nervous panic.

"Where's Liam?" I bite my lip.

Dragon pulls another piece of melted fabric from my skin and doesn't meet my eyes. "You already asked, and I don't know."

"He went outside," Luci answers.

"You let him go out alone?" I ask.

"He said he wanted some time alone, so I left him alone," she replies.

I shake my head. "What if something happens to him?"

"He'll be okay," Dragon insists. "Please stop moving."

I swallow hard. I don't know if I'd ever be able to forgive myself for being so harsh toward Liam. *Shaav, stop it, Jaina. Don't think like that. He'll be fine.*

"Luce, I need the sterilizer," he says.

Luci hands him a syringe, and I start to feel queasy.

Dragon meets my gaze. "Don't watch."

I look up at the ceiling, but I feel the syringe poke into my fresh skin, and the entire wound flares up. My hands squeeze tighter, my fingernails dig farther into my flesh, and I shut my eyes tight, holding back tears.

Something cold presses against my skin and a moan escapes my throat. My eyes feel like they're going to water and I grit my teeth together so hard I'm afraid they'll fall out. My leg automatically jerks away, but he holds me still.

When he finally removes the cold, I open my eyes and see the wet cloth. I lie back down and relax my muscles. It stings, but it's not as terrible as it was before. There's a residue of charred fabric, skin and blood on the cloth and I shudder.

Dragon takes a step back. "You okay?" he asks.

"You tell me," I say through my teeth.

He nods and hands me a cup of blue liquid. His hands tremble. "This should ease the pain."

I gulp it down. It's bitter and tastes like copper, but immediately the pain begins to dull.

Dragon smiles a little and leaves the room. The door slides shut behind him.

"He seemed in a hurry," I remark.

Luci laughs. "Liam and Dragon aren't good with blood."

"I know. Why'd he do it then? Aren't *you* the doctor-nurse-person?"

She shrugs. "Beats me." She begins wrapping my leg with a bandage.

"Did you guys find anything?"

"Not much," she replies mechanically. "Dragon and Liam will look for more."

"What about you?"

She shakes her head. "Not while you're hurt."

"You can stop pretending you don't hate me. I know you do. You don't have to stay." My voice becomes a lot calmer as the pain fades to a dull throbbing.

Luci laughs and takes a seat on the bed across from me once she's done with my leg. "I don't hate you, Jaina. I just...I don't respect you."

"Not sure if that's any better," I breathe. "Why?"

"I don't know. Maybe it's because you're not with us. You know the evil of the Alliance, and yet you refuse to join our cause." Her voice is gentle and sincere.

I shake my head. "I can't join your cause. I'm only doing this for Amara."

"You know she'll want you with us," Luci replies. "The Phoenix is the Resistance."

I look at the ground and take a deep breath. "When we find her, I may change my mind. But until then, I don't know."

She nods. "Get some rest, Jaina. I'll be in the cockpit if you need me."

I smile weakly. "Thank you."

When I wake up, all I see are coffee brown eyes. I jolt upright.

"Hey, hey, it's alright." Liam gently grabs my arm. "Lie down. It's okay."

Blood pounds in my ears, but I settle down. I rub my eyes and wipe little droplets of sweat from my forehead. "I'm sorry," I whisper. "I thought it was a nightmare."

Liam smiles just a little. "Do I look like a nightmare to you?"

I raise an eyebrow. "Maybe."

He takes my hand in his. His is cool compared to mine, and he squeezes gently. "How are you doing?"

"Alright, I think. It's just a flesh wound."

His eyes are locked on our hands. "Jaina, I'm sorry about what happened. I'm sorry I wasn't–"

"Liam." I squeeze tighter. "Are you blaming yourself for this?"

He takes a deep, uncomfortable breath. "I just…"

"Liam, by the stars, this is not your fault. I'm okay. Are you okay? I was worried about you. Luci said the two of you went to look for more information, and I thought you'd be quick, but when you didn't return for a few hours, I was really worried. When did you get back?"

"Maybe ten minutes ago. Dragon and Luci went to sleep. We have a big day tomorrow. Luci told me not to bother you, but I just had to see how you were. I'm sorry."

I run my thumb over his palm. "Don't be. I was lonely."

A troubled smile dances across his lips. He brushes a strand of hair back out of my eyes.

I attempt a smile, but darkness washes over me. Not because of my leg, it's my scar. It burns, heating my entire shoulder to what feels just short of a thousand degrees. It's been on fire all night, and if I try to sleep, Azad is the only face that haunts my dreams.

"What's wrong?" he asks.

I study his eyes and the soft lines of his face. He's so close to me, but for some reason, it's not uncomfortable. It feels natural. Welcome.

"Nothing," I reply.

His soft brown eyes fill with concern. He cares about me. By the stars, he really does. All this time, I thought it was merely that he was selfish, wanting something he couldn't have. All the way back in the Trials, did he really mean it when he said he loved me?

Liam closes his eyes ever so slightly and presses his forehead to mine. Our noses touch. I don't pull away.

"I'm glad you're okay," he whispers.

I feel the warmth of his breath pass over my lips. In fact, I feel warm all over.

My hand slowly finds its way up his arm and to the back of his head. His hair is soft and warm and comforting. My eyes shut gently, and I pull him even closer. His lips brush against mine, the feeling sends warm shivers through my whole body. *By the stars, Liam, kiss me.*

He pulls away, removes my hand from behind his neck, and stares down at the ground. His eyes are sad and darker than usual. "No," he says quietly.

My face burns, and I clench my jaw, unable to help being incredibly embarrassed.

"Not like this, Jaina."

"What do you mean?" I manage to choke out. "I thought–"

"I want it to mean something." His voice softens.

"How do you know it wouldn't have meant something?" I whisper.

Finally he looks deeply into my eyes. "You're not okay. What happened?"

I start to feel choked, like he wrapped his fingers around my throat and squeezed as tightly as he could.

"You can tell me anything, Jaina."

I close my eyes a moment. By the stars, why? I open my eyes and stare down at my bed. "I've been dreaming about Azad," I manage.

He nods slowly. "And?"

"He says he's coming."

His light brown eyes turn darker with worry. "But you killed him."

"I know. I know. But while he was dying, he said he'd return. That he'd find me. That he'd...take revenge. He was so confident, too. He told me things,

Liam, things I didn't believe at the time, but have turned out to be true."

"Like?"

"He said Dragon would betray me. And in a dream, he said someone would try to take me back to the Resistance. That was right before we landed on Keducia."

"Jaina..." Liam sighs. "The man was insane. He was a murderer, a psychopath. He was trying to turn you against your team for his own sick purposes, so of course he'd tell you Dragon would betray you. Honestly, it was probably just a lucky guess that Dragon actually did. Azad still haunts you, so it's no surprise he came to you in a dream."

I shake my head. "It's not like that, Liam. It's always so real. I feel like it's real."

"Do you think he's coming?" Liam asks.

"It's not possible. He's dead. But...I don't know. There's something about him that lives on."

Liam touches my shoulder gently but does not lean in close this time. "It was just a nightmare, Jaina."

"But what if it's not? Dragon said they were visions."

"Visions are like magic, like some sort of other-worldly power. There's no such thing," he soothes. "Random prophetic dreams, maybe, but it was a nightmare, that's all. And if it's not, you might as well believe they are. At least that way, it won't haunt you."

I nod but don't look into his eyes. "Thank you."

He doesn't reply. I hear him stand and watch him leave. Liam doesn't turn around to look at me. "Get some more rest, Jaina." He closes the door behind him.

# CHAPTER FOURTEEN

"Jaina, wake up," Luci calls.

I open my eyes with a start to find Luci staring down at me. She touches my arm. Her hand is freezing cold, and I flinch from her touch.

"What's going on?" I ask, pulling away from her.

"Liam has information he wants to share with us."

With that, my mind immediately shoots back to last night. I remember how Liam came to me and spoke so gently. How tenderly he touched me and pressed his forehead to mine. How he lovingly held me to him and how I held him in return. How I wanted him to...

My stomach knots, but I'm not sure what I feel other than confusion.

By the stars, I hope he doesn't bring that up.

Ever.

"Okay." I get up slowly.

My leg stings when I start to move it, but I push through. Luci thinks I'm weak enough already. It feels a lot better than it did yesterday. The advanced meds Dragon has here work faster than anything I've known.

"What time is it?" I ask.

"Almost noon, but the days are only sixteen hours here. Noon is eight o'clock." She grabs me by the arm and yanks me into the cockpit.

Dragon and Liam are both talking about who-knows-what. I have no idea what they have in common.

Dragon half-smiles at me. "Jaina, how are you feeling?"

"I'm fine. Thanks." I shoot a slightly insincere smile back at him.

Liam only acknowledges me by nodding in my direction.

Dragon looks at Liam. "Tell them what we found."

"We've located Draco. He's staying at a friend's house in Rei'oud, a richer district. This house is heavily guarded."

"How do we get in?" I ask.

Dragon smirks. "Draco is holding a party. Tonight."

Liam nods. "Everyone is invited, so we'll go as guests. Of course we have to pay a fee, but a ton of people are going."

Luci raises her eyebrow, and her lips curve into an unsure smile. "How much is this fee, exactly? We can't use up Resistance money to get into a party."

Dragon and Liam exchange glances. Dragon clears his throat. "We can afford it. It's five hundred Ariks. For all of us."

My jaw drops. "Five hundred Ariks! You've got to be *shaavez* kidding me! How can anyone afford to go?"

"This is the *rich* district," Liam reminds me. "Most people can afford it. Anyway, we'll stop by the party, get Draco alone and find out where Sivva is. Jaina, you and Dragon will interrogate him while Luci and I distract his guards."

"I have more experience," Luci cuts in. "Besides, Jaina needs to stay safe."

I glare at her and grit my teeth. "This is my mother, Luci."

"If you get yourself killed, this whole operation is a failure," Luci snaps back.

"No." I look from Dragon to Liam. "I'm going. I owe my mother my life, and I will do everything I can to free her."

Liam's face becomes a little darker, but he nods. "You may have been in the Resistance longer, Luci, but Jaina was the best student on Virana. Dragon and Jaina work well together. They got us through the Trials, and I'm convinced they can get us through this."

I furrow my brow. Liam completely ignores the fact that I'm looking at him. Why the sudden change? I want to ask him so badly, but now is definitely not the time or place.

Liam continues, "After you interrogate him, there should be an underground safety zone in his basement with a passage to the public park outside his house. Luci and I will take *The Odyssey*, land in the park, and you'll escape that way."

"Whatever," Luci sighs. "It's a good plan."

Dragon shrugs. "It was Liam's idea."

Luci raises an eyebrow at Liam. "Then you're to blame if this fails."

"Thank you?" he replies.

"How do we convince Draco to speak with us?" I ask. "We can't just kidnap him in front of everyone."

"We can't casually interrogate him either," Luci adds.

Liam bites his lip. "So um, that's the one thing we kind of have to talk about."

My stomach sinks like I swallowed a boulder. "By the stars, what now."

"So, you or Luci might have to, um..." He looks at Dragon then back to me. "Seduce him."

"What the *shaav*?" I scoff. "You realize that *seduction* and I don't go hand in hand very well."

Luci rolls her eyes. "You're damn right about that."

Dragon shakes his head. "Jay, it's not that hard. Just say some things he'll want to hear, and you can easily get him alone and trick him into anything you want."

Gritting my teeth, I shoot back, "Oh right. I forgot. *You* would know."

"Look," Liam says, "we'll worry about all of this when we get to it. Luci and I will go get some stuff for all of us to wear. Dragon, you hang back while Jaina's healing."

"I don't need anymore healing. I feel fine!"

"Sounds good," Dragon answers over me.

Liam nods. "We'll be back shortly."

But Liam and Luci take forever. Time slows and leaves me tapping my foot as I rest in the copilot's seat. Dragon remains silent, reading through the database in *The Odyssey*. He glances up at me and asks how I'm feeling every now and then, but other than that, we don't speak. I don't want to talk. Maybe he picks up on that.

And after what happened with Liam last night, what the *shaav* do I do? It seems like an eternity has passed when they finally return. The pressure between Dragon and I seems to vent and dissipate. At least a little.

"We're back," Liam chokes out breathlessly as Luci follows closely behind him.

I stand and move to greet them, but when I catch sight of their faces marked with lines of exhaustion, my smile fades. "What happened? Was someone after you?"

Liam's face is pale, and his eyes are dull. "I don't know how we made it out of there alive," he whimpers. "It was horrible." Luci drops two bags onto the ground.

Dragon lingers close behind me. "Did someone try to rob you?"

"That lady who owned the shop tried to rob us!" Luci cries. "She was like 'buy this' and 'buy that,' and it was the most stressful thing I've ever done."

"There were so many," Liam mutters as if in a daze. "So many clothes." He takes a sloppy step forward. "Why so many clothes?"

"Well," I say, "people need clothes."

"But all those different sorts? No one needs that many..."

Luci nods and pats Liam on the shoulder. "It's okay. It was hard for both of us."

I bite back a grin and escort the two of them farther into the ship after closing the ramp. "So, did you guys get anything?"

"Yeah. Everything is in those two bags," Liam says, his eyes still dazed, but his face has a little more color now. He picks one up and tosses it to me. "Those are the girls' clothes." He picks up the other one and tosses it to Dragon after fishing out a dark blue shirt and a some black pants. "That's for you."

Dragon nods. "We should hurry. The party is starting soon and our window of opportunity won't be
open very long."

"Do we really have to go?" Liam asks. "I am so tired.
I don't think I'm alert enough for this."

Luci shakes her head at Liam. "Dragon is right. We
won't have long to complete the mission." She nods to
me. "You can change first. Yours are white."

I take the bag and walk into the cabin on the right
while Dragon takes the left. After closing the door, I
lock it and remove the white shirt and the tight white
pants. Sighing, I put it on. One sleeve extends to my
wrist, and on the other side, there's no sleeve at all. It
stops short, covering only my right arm and my chest,
leaving my stomach bare. Tiny crystals hang on threads
a few centimeters long from the bottom of the fabric,
tickling my stomach and making me feel like something
is crawling on me. The pants squeeze my legs. At least it's
something I can move around and fight in, if necessary.

In the bag, I find a pair of white shoes. Clear jewels
that hurt my eyes to look at are arranged in a criss-
cross pattern to hold my foot in the thin frame. But
what grabs my attention the most are the incredibly
tall heels on the back. I put them on, expecting the
worst. Standing still, I look ridiculous. What kind of a
person would put herself through this?

Keeping all of my weight on my toes, I reach the
door after nearly losing my balance. Carefully, I open
it and walk out to Liam, Luci, and Dragon.

_The Inferiors_

"How the *shaav* do you expect me to walk?" I ask, unamused.

The three burst out laughing.

"Liam picked out our clothes," Luci moans.

"Why'd you let him do that?" I ask.

Luci glares at Liam. "He didn't give me much of a *choice*."

Liam shrugs. "You look amazing."

"I look fragile and scandalous." I sneer. "That's what."

"I kinda like it," he replies, keeping his eyes on my chest.

I cross my arms. "You're disgusting."

He smirks slightly. "Not the vibe I got last night..."

Dragon quickly clears his throat and scans me up and down. "You look nice."

My face turns warm. "Thanks. You too."

His white shirt brings out his marine blue eyes, while a black overcoat and dark pants complete his attire. As angry as I've been, I can't deny that he looks good. Liam's outfit is almost the same, and if I'm completely honest with myself, he looks just as amazing. He doesn't seem to fill the suit as well as Dragon does, but he is no less stunning.

"Alright, Luce," Liam says. "Your turn."

Luci scoffs at him then walks into the cabin on the right. When she comes out, she's wearing a dark blue shirt that's similar to mine, except it covers her entire stomach. She's got silver leggings and high heels identical to mine, except they're black.

"And why did *Luci* get appropriate clothing?" I ask.

"Yours are fine, Jaina!" Liam cries. "Luci's clothes are more boring."

"That makes me feel great," Luci mutters then turns to me. "This is stupid, we have to get going, or we're going to be late."

Dragon laughs. "The sooner I can change outta this, the better."

"You think *you're* uncomfortable?" I scoff.

We make our way into the cockpit. Liam starts the engines and lifts the ship gently into the air, but he doesn't make an attempt to fly outside of the city's plexiglass bubble that shields it from the harsh atmosphere. Instead, he flies toward the inside of the city, closer to the center. There are buildings everywhere, and the sky grows darker and darker by the minute. He sets the ship down gently at the middle of a park. It's one of the few places within the city that's not crammed with buildings and people.

"That was short," Liam remarks. "Luckily, since this is public parking, we shouldn't have to worry about a fee."

Dragon stands as the whining of the engines comes to a stop. He leads the four of us outside and onto the gravely path escorting us to a white building ahead. The house is planted on a huge field of green grass, while bright red flowers pepper the lawn. A few other mansions dot the landscape, and I can't help gawking at the fact that some people are actually rich enough to live in places like that.

"Who in their right mind would need a home that big?" Luci murmurs. "It would be so lonely."

"I guess that's why he's holding such a big party," Liam replies.

I take a step forward, but lose balance on my heels and stumble forward.

Dragon catches my fall. "You alright?" he asks as he helps me up.

I can feel myself blushing as I regain my balance. "Stupid heels."

"Here." He takes my arm, like he wants to keep me close.

I can almost hear Liam rolling his eyes behind me. Luci's probably doing the same.

Finally, we approach a giant metal gate guarded by two men in light armor. I doubt they've seen much combat. Defeating these two men on my own would be a piece of shala cake.

"Are you sure they'll let us in?" I whisper to Dragon.

"They better. I paid the fee."

"Stop right there," says the guard once we're in speaking distance. "State your name."

My nerves spike, but I try to keep a confident look on my face. *Dragon knows what he's doing.* Everything will be fine. Everything will go according to plan.

"Alek Jesyn." He seems to choke on the word, clears his throat, then continues. "Alek Jesyn, honorable prince of Havera. These are my two servants." Dragon gestures to Liam and Luci.

Liam grits his teeth and fakes a smile.

"And," Dragon turns to me, "this is my fiancée."

The guards exchange glances. The taller one takes out a small silverscreen. When he looks up, he nods. "We're sorry for the inconvenience, your highness. You may proceed."

He opens the gate and steps aside. The gate closes behind us as we walk inside.

Dragon pulls me closer to him, and the meaning of his words slowly sink in. How can he think it's okay for us to pretend we're engaged? He could've said he was engaged to Luci or even Liam.

The skies are dark again. The days are much shorter than they should be. I know they're only sixteen hours here but it's confusing and doesn't feel right at all.

"Where did you get the name Jesyn?" Luci asks.

Dragon shrugs. "It popped into my head when I made the payment. They don't do background checks. They just accept a name and the money."

"What about your fiancée?" she asks darkly.

"Excuse me for not being creative under pressure. I didn't see you making any suggestions," he mutters. "Jaina, inside the house you'll have to call me Alek."

*The Inferiors*

"Whatever you say, master," I snap.

He cocks his head and furrows his brow. "What?"

"I thought that's what I was supposed to call you. You're the prince, this is a sad arranged marriage, and I'm the poor bride-to-be. Perfect plot line. Draco will think it's sexy."

Dragon's jaw twitches. "If you say so."

"Question," Liam interjects. "Why does Jaina get to be your fiancée while we have to be servants?"

Dragon raises an eyebrow. "Would *you* rather be my fiancé?"

"Um, yes?"

I can't help smiling a bit. "Cut it out, Liam."

"Everyone, just do exactly as I say," Dragon adds.

"Oh, right, because you're just the best at everything, aren't you?" Luci's face is tight. "I already know what we're doing. Liam and I will make a distraction while you get Draco. Simple as that."

"I don't think it will be that easy," I say.

We've reached the front doors. They're wide open, revealing a large entrance hall with polished floors made from expensive stone brought in from all over the galaxy. People of all different sorts fill the hall. Two staircases round the edges of the room, decorated with a velvety red carpet and shimmery gold handrails. Chatter and light Zallian music fills the air.

"Now, that's really a sight to see," Luci says, her voice softer than before.

Dragon tugs lightly on my arm. "Let's go find him."

"Should we split up?" Liam asks. "We'll privcom you if we encounter the target."

"Sounds good," I reply. "Let's get moving."

Liam and Luci break to the left of the room as Dragon and I head into the heart of the crowd. Most people are talking while others dance around like drunken lunatics across the floor. A red-skinned Fallen man holds a girl in a bright, starlight-yellow top and a black skirt against a wall. She grasps him tight, pulling him closer to her, kissing him violently.

Dragon gently brushes his hand against mine. "Draco's known for his parties. People can do whatever they want here."

We pass through the entrance hall and enter another room with tables crammed to the edges with food and drinks. The lights grow dimmer as we move deeper into the house. Dragon and I reach a room where the music booms so loudly that the ground shudders. The lights are dark purple and blue, flashing on and off.

Dragon jerks me to the side, spins me around, and pulls me to his chest. My heart jumps into a nervous flurry. I try to pull myself out of his arms, but he doesn't let me.

"Dragon," I breathe. "What are you–"

Dragon leans in his mouth close to my ear. "Act like nothing is wrong. Go with it. Pretend you're enjoying this."

"I'm not enjoying this, and you're freaking me out. What the *shaav* are you doing?" I ask harshly.

"Those guys behind me. See them?"

I glance over his shoulder at the ever-changing crowd. "Who?"

"The Seravas. Pale, chalky skin, tough looking..."

I nod. "Yes."

"I know them. Resistance sent me on a mission three years ago to retrieve stolen money." He winces. "They weren't so happy when I stole it back."

The toughest looking one catches my gaze. Dragon sways back and forth to the music, keeping me close to him.

"They saw me," I whisper. "They might be coming this way."

"Are they close?"

The three men eye the two of us, drifting nearer and nearer.

"Not as uncomfortably close as you are right now, but yes. They're getting close. They're getting really close. What do you want me to–"

"Kiss me."

"*Absolutely not*," I hiss.

"Hurry, Jaina," he says. "We'll be less conspicuous. Just until they pass. We're getting married, remember? I'm sure you can handle it."

"I'm not as good at acting as you," I snap back, "but I'll do my best."

I glance from the guys behind Dragon to his lips. Slowly, I move my hand up his shoulder and onto the back of his neck. I glare at him. Dragon smiles and doesn't hesitate. His lips close around mine. His warm hands rest on my waist, and he pulls my body against him. I feel warm all over. Angry all over too. *By the stars, why is he such a good kisser?* How many girls has he kissed? How many girls has he been with and gone even farther with? I open one eye and glance to the three men. They're still watching. Of course.

Dragon's lips momentarily part from mine but just barely. "Are they gone?"

"Unfortunately no," I breathe, and he kisses me again.

Deeper this time.

Closer to me.

My fingers wander through his soft brown hair as his hands climb my waist. Again, I open my eyes. This time, they're gone. I grab Dragon's hand, which has steadily risen up my ribs and near my chest.

"Dragon," I say, trying to pull away.

He kisses me again.

"Dragon, they're gone," I continue as our lips part. I'm breathing heavily.

Dragon pulls me back to him, pressing his lips to mine once more.

I'm warm all over, but I force myself to pull out of his arms. "Damn it, it's over!"

He blushes. "They might've still been watching. You were convincing."

"I learned from you," I shoot back. "By the way, I feel incredibly violated. So thanks."

He focuses on something behind me. "There he is."

I follow Dragon's gaze.

A man dressed all in black enters the room. His blond hair is slicked back, and a cocky grin rests on his pinkish lips. He's probably in his late twenties. A few age lines mark his face, and his deep brown eyes hold a glimmer of suspicion, like he knows someone's here for him.

"What do we do?" I ask.

"Get him to like you, and get him to lead you to his safe in the basement. We'll interrogate him there. I'll contact Luci and Liam and keep an eye on you."

"*Seduce* him?"

He places his hand on my shoulder. "You have to."

"Do I have to? Why can't you do it?" I retort.

Dragon raises an eyebrow. "The guy isn't into men, I'm sorry."

"And you know that how?"

He sighs uncomfortably. "Jaina, you can do this."

"Whatever," I moan. "What if you guys can't get to me in time?"

"I'll be there, Jaina," he whispers. "I swear on my life I won't let anything happen."

By the look in his eyes, that crystal sincerity, that flicker of light, I know he's telling the truth. As much as I've been trying to deny it, I do know he cares about me. Maybe he didn't ever love me, but he cares. He'll keep his word.

"How are we going to get him to notice me?" I ask.

Dragon thinks for a moment. "Everyone loves a damsel in distress. Come with me. He's going to a different room, so we'll follow him. I'll pretend to hurt you and Draco will rescue you. He'll be your hero. Talk to him a bit, try to get him alone, then interrogate him. We'll come to you."

My stomach churns with anxiety. "What if he doesn't fall for it?"

He takes my arm and begins to lead me toward Draco. "Make him fall for it. Is your phonicom working?"

"I'll check." I press on the tiny earpiece. "Test one, two, three."

Dragon nods. "You're good."

We make our way behind Draco. Luckily, the next room is lighter, and most of the people here are drunk or too busy doing their own thing to notice us. Draco is easy to spot. He speaks quietly to a Hazbash man, and the two of them share a laugh.

"You ready?" Dragon asks.

"Ready as I'll ever be." My ankle buckles, and I stumble into Dragon slightly.

"Let's just hope you make it across the room," he breathes.

"You can wear these if you want," I snap.

"Fair enough. Acting starts now. Just play along."

We make it a few meters away from Draco. Dragon puts on a half-crazed grin, grabs my arm, and pulls me to him. I can only stare back in slight shock at the sudden change.

He rolls his eyes. "Come on, Jay. Struggle or something. Make a scene."

I half-cry in annoyance. With that, I try to yank myself away from him. "Let me go! Alek, please!"

"Stop it," he hisses.

"Please, stop. You're scaring me. Get away from me!" I push myself out of his arms.

A hand touches Dragon's shoulder and pries him from me.

"Sir," Draco says. "I believe the lady wants to be left alone." His voice is heavily accented, similar to Shirez's, in the way that he pronounces his R's like 'ah'.

"Excuse me, *sir*," Dragon snaps, "but I'd like to be left alone with my lady."

Draco reaches into his pocket and pulls out a few Arik chips then hands them to Dragon. "Buy yourself a drink and give it a rest, alright?"

Dragon bites his lip and fakes a sneer, but he takes the money and walks away. He shoots me a reassuring glance when Draco shifts his gaze to me, but after that, he disappears into another crowded room.

"You alright?" Draco touches my chin.

I nod. "I'm-I'm fine. He gets like that from time to time."

Up close, he looks older. Probably early to mid-thirties.

Draco touches my arm, and I do my best not to flinch. "Did he hurt you?"

I shake my head. "I'm alright. Thank you, sir."

"Who was he?"

I fake a painful laugh. "My fiancé."

He gently takes my elbow. "Does he always treat you like that?"

"Yes," I breathe. "I hate the man."

A bit of static in my ear from the privcom. "I can still hear you," Dragon says.

I smile. Oh yes, I know he can hear everything I'm saying.

"Is there anything I can do for you?" Draco asks.

I hesitate. *Tell me the location of Prince Sivva. That's what you can do.* "No," I reply casually. "I think I just need to get out of here."

"Wait. Before you go, let me get you a drink."

I have to make this his decision. He can't think I'm giving in too easy. "Oh, you don't have to–"

"Really, I insist. This is my party, and I can't have you going home like this. Come with me." He takes my arm and directs me into a crowded room. "What's your name, love?"

I almost flinch. No one seems to know the meaning of that word, *love*. They say it to strangers they lust over. Instead, I force a smile. "I'm Jaina. And you're Draco, I presume?"

He takes a seat at the bar, grinning. He orders something for both of us then turns to me. "Who's your fiancé?"

I hesitate. "Prince Alek Jesyn of...Havera." That better be what Dragon said. Far as I know, Havera isn't even a real place so we better keep our facts straight.

"Prince? For a prince he seems quite..."

"Immature?" I cut in. I've never loved technology more. "He's always like that."

"So, what's an unmarried royal couple doing at my party?"

I lean forward placing my elbows on the counter and face him, sort of squeezing my chest between my arms. "What do you think? This is a party, isn't it?"

His eyes glance down at my breasts that are slightly popping out of my shirt. "I think a prince wouldn't bother coming to a party of such small magnitude. Which is why I don't think you're here to party."

"Really?" A slight nervous sensation begins to tingle in my stomach.

Draco nods. "Yes, really. I think you're here to get away."

I can't help but sigh in relief. Our drinks come, and Draco nods for me to take a sip. Gingerly, I pick it up and gulp down half of the blue shiny liquid in the small cup. My throat burns, but I try not to let it show. At least it's not as bad as the Myrym.

"Well, you're right," I breathe, smiling gently at him. Before he can say anything else, I add, "Thank you for saving me, by the way."

He laughs quietly like he's trying to be shy and humble but it comes out more turned on than anything. "It was my duty as a gentleman."

Oh he thinks he's so smooth.

The privcom in my ear comes to life again, and I jolt upright with a start as screeching fills my ear.

"You okay?" Draco asks.

I bite my lip. "The music from next door is really loud. Maybe we could go somewhere quieter?"

His eyes darken with passion. "As you wish my dear." He picks up his drink then leads me through a few corridors.

"Jaina," I hear Dragon's voice through the privcom. "We're tracking you from my silverscreen, we should be able to find you wherever you go."

Draco watches me intensely, continuing to scan me up and down. "Have you been to Kashia before?"

"No. It's a beautiful place, from what I've seen." Every few steps I make sure to brush against his arm. His skin is clammy and hot. Ew.

"It is," he replies, slowing down then coming to a stop in a fairly empty room.

The music is faint, and at the far end of the chamber is a large metal door that's completely sealed shut. His secret escape route maybe?

"Is this quiet enough?" Draco asks.

"It'll do. Though I was thinking even quieter…" my voice trails off.

His hand is shaking a little as he touches my arm just above my elbow. "It's a shame your freedom is limited to the end of the week. If there's anything I can do…"

I have to force a sensual laugh from my throat. Gentle, and breathy. "You've done so much already, I can only hope there's something I can do for you." My eyes meet his, and I try to imagine it's someone else. But it isn't Dragon's face that flickers into my head. My cheeks feel warm, and I find myself looking at him longingly. "It's my last night here." I step closer to him and feel his alcoholic breath on my face.

Draco's hand moves up to my neck as I watch the desire grow in his eyes.

*I've got you in my trap. Hah.*

"*Shaav*," Dragon curses in my ear. "We lost your signal."

Why can't anything ever just work out? For once? I'm doing my part, rather well I'd say. And I have to admit it's kinda awesome knowing I could control a guy with just a few suggestive words and motions.

"Come with me," Draco says, his voice low and raspy. He doesn't take his eyes off me as we move toward the large silvery door. When we get there, he looks down and enters a passcode into a small panel. 4189. I have to remember that. The door slides open with a hissing sound. It's protected in a thick metal coating. He takes my hand and gently tugs me through the door. It shuts behind us.

*Four one eight nine.*

The room is small, decorated with red carpet and dim lights. A huge red couch and a coffee table fill the room. I can hear my heart beating in my ears. Okay, the fun seducing part is over, now I just feel trapped. *Stay calm, Jaina. Stay calm.*

"What is this place?" I ask, trying my best to mask my fear.

"The safe room," Draco replies.

"Oh, the safe room," I repeat, hopefully loud enough for Dragon to hear. "It's nice."

"Found it in the blueprints," Dragon says. "We're on our way. Are you alone?"

"You going to finish that?" Draco gestures to the drink still in my hand. I forgot I still had it.

*Four one eight nine.*

"Yes," I reply, answering both Dragon and Draco.

"Good," Dragon replies. "Keep him there."

"So," Draco says. "How do you like it?"

"It's impressive." The blue drink helps a bit, but it's going straight to my head. I'm warm all over, and as I take another sip, my anxiety becomes a bit duller.

Dragon better get here soon. Draco's going to realize this is a ruse once I don't follow up with my words, and it's not going to be pretty.

"Not as impressive as you, love. Have a seat?" He gestures to the red couch that looks a little too comfortable.

I quickly down the rest of my drink, hoping its effects kick in quickly, then let myself fall into the too-comfortable-couch. He sits next to me, taking the empty glass from my hand, and places both of our glasses on the table in front of us.

"You don't deserve to be treated the way he treats you. You deserve so much better." He puts his hand on my thigh.

Resisting every urge to push his hand away, I scoot a little closer into him instead. "It wasn't my choice. Royalty is never given a choice."

He nods, moving his hand a little farther up my leg. Mid thigh. "You have a choice tonight."

*Damn it, hurry Dragon.*

"Do I?"

"You have a choice to make a memorable night with someone who helped you," Draco says.

There's the sense of entitlement I was expecting. Should I kiss him? If I kiss him for a while that could hold him off, but it could also lead to a lot more than kissing a hell of a lot faster. Quickly, I decide against it.

"If my fiancé found out, he would hurt me," I pout.

His face inches closer to mine. "I'll make sure that doesn't happen, Jenny."

Jenny? *What the shaav.* He doesn't even remember my name! By the stars if any other man treated me this way, he'd have three broken bones already.

He looks into my eyes, and for a moment, I fear he can see right through me. I run my fingers through his blond hair. It isn't very soft. In fact, it's kind of gelled back and stuck to his head.

*Four one eight nine.*

Draco takes a deep breath and leans in closer to me. He presses his lips against my shoulder, and I have to fight the urge to kick him in the balls. His desperation for quick and easy pleasure is more than a bit disturbing. He starts to kiss my neck, and I put my hand on his shoulder, pushing him away a little bit.

He stops and looks at me. "What's wrong?"

"Um…" I look around the room, starting to panic. "I should find my fiancé."

Draco caresses my arm. "You don't need him."

"No, I just don't feel good," I say, trying to stand up.

He yanks me back down onto the couch next to him. "I know something that will make you feel better," he breathes darkly.

That's enough. With all my strength, I close my fist and punch him in the jaw. I untangle myself from him and jump off the couch. He can't reach me from here, but he's still too close for comfort.

Draco's eyes narrow as he holds his jaw in his hand. "You little *katiaj.*"

"Jaina," I hear Dragon's voice in my ear. "I'm right outside. I need the code."

"Four, one, eight, nine!" I shout.

Draco's eyes change. I see shock and the fear. Then anger tortures his face again. Before he can make a move, the door hisses open behind me.

"Hands up," Dragon orders, aiming a gun at Draco. "I'll make this plain and simple. Give us what we want, and you'll live."

I expect Draco's face to go pale, or become even redder. I expect him to beg. To lash out or *something.*

Instead, he shrugs. "We'll see."

Now, I'm terrified.

He presses a button on the wall. Sections of the wall retract into the ceiling and reveal silvery, metal pathways in two directions, and at the end of one, there's another metal door. Four guards appear seemingly out of nowhere and hone in on Dragon and I, guns aimed at us.

"Where's Luci and Liam?" I whisper to Dragon.

"Getting the ship," he replies.

"Drop your weapon, or we shoot the girl," says one of the guards.

Dragon takes a deep breath and drops his weapon onto the ground.

The guards form a tighter circle around us. I hear the blood pounding in my ears. Dragon has to have a plan. He always has a plan. But he's glancing around at the guards, his eyes a little panicky. I start to freak out. *By the stars, Dragon doesn't have a plan.*

I knew this outfit was a horrible idea. I couldn't hide weapons anywhere with this skimpy thing!

The guards grab me, their meaty hands gripping tightly to my arms. Struggling will do me no good, so I don't. The other two guards take ahold of Dragon.

"Well, that didn't go according to plan," Dragon mutters.

"Does it ever?" I snap back, not appreciating his humor.

"Silence!" shouts one of the guards holding Dragon.

Draco nods. "Kill them."

The guards ready their weapons, and even though I heard the order, I can't quite comprehend what's happening until I see the gun pointed at the back of Dragon's head. My stomach drops four meters into the floor. They're going to kill us.

No. I have to save my mother. I have to help the Resistance. I have to tell Liam I'm sorry. This can't be how it ends. I will not let it end like this.

My heartbeat slows. My breathing grows deeper and slower as well. I hear a voice in my head, my own voice. My gaze flickers around the room, and I feel like I'm in a dream, but I notice everything. The couch, the yellow lights in the ceiling, the metallic walls where the guards were summoned from. Draco pressed a button on the wall. It made the doors open. There's another button, barely noticeable all the way to the left. A secret escape route? With our luck, probably not, but it's worth a shot.

A voice interrupts my frantic thoughts, and things speed up to normal time again.

"Wait," Draco says. "Kill the boy. The lady might be valuable. I recognize her."

I clench my teeth together so tightly that it hurts. So they're just going to kill Dragon in front of me and sell me back to the IA? My entire body burns like I've already been shot a hundred times, although I probably won't be shot at now. Unless I do something crazy.

The two guards holding my arms pull me back. The guard at Dragon's back puts his finger on the trigger. The guard is trembling. In one horrible moment, Dragon will be gone. It's horrifying, but there's the trembling. He must not be well trained.

*Come on, Dragon. Do something, please. By the stars, please.*

"Get it over with," Draco orders.

"Altair," I call.

Dragon glances at me calmly. "It's okay."

What the *shaav* is he waiting for?

I try to pull away from the guards holding me, but they've got me secured in their grip.

A gunshot sounds.

My knees go weak, and my stomach drops. The guards keep me standing, but I'd be on the ground if it weren't for them. The guards holding Dragon ram into each other, and Dragon breaks free from their grasp. The terror from hearing the gunshot fades, and the adrenaline kicks in. A guard tries to move toward Dragon after he untangles himself from his friend, but Dragon shoves his boot in his stomach, and the guard tumbles to the ground. Dragon picks up his gun lying on the floor and fires a shot at the first guard.

The guard's body goes limp as the plasma catches him in the dead center of his forehead. The two men holding me fire shots at Dragon with their free hands and try to drag me out of the battle, but they hold on to me with a bit less force. Enough for me to yank my arm free from one and elbow the other in the stomach. He stumbles backward but doesn't let go of me, so I ram myself into him and force him to the ground.

My hand finds the extra pistol in his holster belt and I press it to his throat and fire without hesitation. I roll away from the dead man and bring myself to my feet.

"Jaina!" Dragon steps in front of me.

A plasma bolt moves toward us, and he pushes me to the ground. After the shot disappears, Dragon pulls me up and fires at the guard.

"You okay?" I ask breathlessly.

He nods. "Draco." Dragon pulls out his scimitar, charging at the guard.

I bring myself to stand. There's a large opening in the wall that hadn't been there before. So I was right about the escape route. Breaking into a run through the new hallway, I find Draco charging toward the door at the other end. He's halfway across the corridor. My body moves on its own, lifting the gun, aiming at his leg, and firing in fractions of a second. The first shot misses, but it's close enough to make him jump. He doesn't stop running. *Stupid idea.* I fire again, and this time, I'm dead on. His left leg gives out, and Draco cries out in pain and tumbles to the ground.

I catch up to him, but he continues trying to get away, scooting himself across the floor like a baby.

Anger and adrenaline shoot through my veins like bullets. He was going to kill Dragon right in front of me. The urge to aim my gun at his skull and pull the trigger is nearly overwhelming, but I hold back. He has information we need.

I grab him by the ankle and pull him backward about half a meter. He lashes out at me, kicking and fighting me off with his uninjured leg. By the stars, he's heavy, but in the end fighting is no use.

The shooting in the other room ceases, and my lungs burn. Footsteps rush toward me, and I turn toward the sound, aiming my gun. Relief floods me. Thank the stars he's okay.

My feet are swept out from under me, and my body hits the ground with a thud. Spots appear in front of my eyes while I struggle to breathe. My ears are ringing, and I start to panic. I turn on my back to find that Draco has managed to get back on his feet.

Dragon aims his pistol at Draco. "Don't move." He shifts his gaze to me. "Are you alright?"

"Yeah." I cough. "I'm fine." The ringing in my ears has died down, but I can still hear my heart pounding in my head from the lack of oxygen. I'm slowly able to stand.

Dragon grabs Draco by the collar of his shirt and plants him firmly against the wall.

"Let me go," Draco says, his voice shaking.

"I'll let you go if you tell us what we need to know," Dragon says. "Otherwise, I'll have to ask her to shoot your other leg. You don't want that, do you?"

Draco shakes his head. "No, please," he pants. "Don't, just-just tell me what you want. Please, I'll do anything. Do you want money? I can give you money, whatever you want, just let me go."

Dragon turns to me. He's got that look, the one that says, *you insisted on coming, so you ask the questions.*

"Where is Prince Sivva?" I demand.

Draco looks from me to Dragon twice over, his face growing paler. "I...I don't know."

"Jaina." Dragon nods toward the pistol in my hand.

I swallow hard but bring the nose of the gun to Draco's uninjured leg. I know what it's like to be tortured. How could I put someone else through that? I grit my teeth. This isn't meaningless torture. This is war.

"No, please!" Draco begs. "I don't know where he is! Don't shoot me!"

"We're looking for information," I say, my voice burning with fury. "Now where is he?"

"Where is Sivva?" Dragon orders.

"By the stars, I can't tell you!" Draco cries. "It's treason, they'll kill me!" He's drenched in sweat.

"Well," Dragon says darkly. "That's an easy choice, isn't it. Die now, or later. Believe me, later would be much less painful. I've got all night and about a thousand ways I can get this information out of you, so you better choose wisely."

"You–you wouldn't..." Draco manages. "You're both young, you couldn't."

Dragon raises an eyebrow. "Wanna bet?"

Draco continues panting, and I shove the nose of the gun harder into his good leg. His jaw twitches. "Go ahead!" His teeth are clenched as perspiration drips down his hair. "Kill me, torture me, they'll do so much worse."

Dragon nods to me.

I pull the trigger.

The gunshot echoes through the corridor, as does Draco's cry of pain that follows. Dragon lets Draco fall to the floor, then kneels beside him.

"It doesn't matter if you're more afraid of them," Dragon says calmly. "There's only a certain amount of pain the human body can endure before you break. So let's try this again. *Where is Sivva?*"

I shiver at the sound of Dragon's voice, and almost drop my gun. What have I done? What has this man ever done to deserve this?

"I'll give you money, I'll give you anything," Draco cries, cradling his thigh in his hands.

Dragon retrieves his scimitar and points it at Draco's shoulder. "Talk, or you lose your arm."

Draco trembles as tears stream down his face. I'm frozen with fear, hoping with all my heart Dragon won't take his arm. The thought makes me sick.

"Need a little more of a push?" Dragon asks, his voice rising with anger.

Without hesitation, I touch Dragon's shoulder. "Stop. Let me."

Dragon's eyes meet mine for an instant, glittering with shards of doubt. But showing any sign of weakness or uncertainty at this point in the interrogation would be detrimental for everyone involved. He doesn't say anything, but nods, then stands and backs away, giving me room.

I kneel beside Draco and gently touch his hand. There's a strange warmth inside me and I'm not sure where it comes from but it's like a river, flowing from my core to my fingertips.

"Draco," I say softly. "Someone I love very much is going to die if you don't tell us where Sivva is. No one needs to get hurt, and your involvement will remain unknown." More than anything, I wish I could give him a bit of calm and a bit of courage. My fingertips feel warm and Draco's face seems to relax ever so slightly. "Please," I continue, "you don't need to suffer anymore. But if you can't tell me anything, I'll have to turn you back over to him and he will not show you mercy."

Draco closes his eyes, and his body shakes. "Vera," he says quietly. "He's in the Vera system."

My hand that's touching his arm starts to sweat. The rest of my body is fine, but my hand is so warm. I consider pulling back, but he's talking and I can't risk changing anything about the current situation that might make him stop.

"What planet?" I ask carefully.

Draco swallows hard. "Vera Kaas. I don't know what he's doing there. The Alliance called him there for an emergency meeting." His voice becomes frantic. "I don't know what it's about, something about a security breach."

"Why would Sivva be allowed in an Alliance meeting?" I ask.

"His father is in the Senate," Dragon answers, taking a step closer to me. "The Alliance does a lot of trading with him, so even though he's not officially IA, they treat him that way. But if what you say is true," Dragon's voice grows a bit more harsh, "he'll have the information with him. Where can we find him?"

Draco shrinks back, seemingly trying to push himself into the wall. "That's all I know."

"You sure?"

"I don't know anything else!" He cries. "By the stars, I'm only an employee. I don't have access to that kind of information."

"Thank you for your cooperation. Jaina, contact Liam. Tell him to be ready." He turns to Draco. "Hopefully we won't meet again."

With that, he takes the hilt of his gun and hits Draco in the back of the skull. Draco collapses to the ground.

Dragon takes a deep breath. "Let's get out of here."

I turn away from Dragon, trying not to think about how he was about to brutally torture Draco, and press the button on my privcom. "Liam Rodan," I say into it.

Dragon grabs my wrist and pulls me toward the door at the end of the corridor.

There's a short ring tone. "Hello?"

"Liam?" I ask.

Dragon yanks me through the doorway and into a dark hall made of stone. The door locks behind us with a click. There are no windows. The air smells dry, like ashes.

"Yep," Liam replies.

"Get the ship ready." I have to run to keep up with Dragon. "We need a quick escape."

"We'll be ready. Are you alright?"

"Oh, you know," I reply breathlessly as I run. "Same as usual."

"That bad? *Shaav*, I'm sorry. See you in a few, and be safe." He cuts the com.

A deep rumbling makes the ground tremble.

"Dragon, what is that?" I have to shout to be heard over the noise.

He comes to a stop, and I finally catch up to him. His face glows slightly orange, there's an angry fire in his eyes. I wish I were being metaphorical or just imagining it, but the reflection of the fire in his eyes grows brighter and brighter until I have to turn around.

Flames race toward us with so much speed I'm frozen solid with fear.

Dragon grabs my wrist. "Hurry!"

I can see the end of the tunnel from here, but no matter how fast we run, the flames will reach us before we make it. Instead of running, Dragon jerks me to the side and shoves me into a hollowed out portion of the wall. The flames are moving too fast to round the corner, but the space is only big enough for one person. Dragon backs away from me and stands exposed to the oncoming flames.

"Don't move, Jaina," he orders. "If you stay still, you'll be okay."

"What are you doing?"

He only looks back at me, a painful glimmer in his eyes. Horror floods me, and my stomach drops. The light in the tunnel grows brighter, and Dragon becomes more orange by the minute.

"The Resistance needs you."

"Dragon, stop!" I try to reach out to him, but he backs away.

The fire has almost reached us. Closing my eyes, I rush into the tunnel of light. The heat is racing in. My fingers find the soft fabric of his shirt, and I don't let go of him. I force him back into the only safe place in the entire tunnel, and press him to the wall, keeping him as far away from the fire as I can.

Yellow and orange flames streak passed us.

The heat is unbearable.

Dragon pulls me closer to him, wrapping his arms around me and squeezing me tightly to his chest. In that moment, I feel safer than I ever have in my life.

The fire keeps coming, and my back is throbbing with pain. It's much worse than it was in the volcano in the second Trial. Tears stream down my cheeks as the heat dries out my eyes. Cool droplets trail down my face through the menacing heat before they evaporate. The air is so hot that it almost seems cold, like a blanket of icy rain against my body.

Dragon's fingers grip my hair tightly as he keeps me close.

He's shielding me.

Protecting me as he's always done, no matter the costs.

The roaring stops abruptly, and the heat slowly dies down, but Dragon doesn't move.

Finally, it's over.

"I think it's done," he says, coughing. "Are you okay?"

I open my eyes but my vision is clouded, and I can barely see. All I can make out are various shades of blurry gray. "I'm okay," I try, but the words stick in my throat as I cough violently instead. A steady stream of tears pours from my eyes, by the stars it burns. "I can't see," I choke out.

Though I can't see Dragon, I can hear him wheezing. His hand somehow finds mine and he pulls me forward.

My body is drenched in sweat, and my back is throbbing with pain. Fear trickles into my stomach as

I wonder how bad the damage is. Without my vision, I'm too afraid to ask. I'm not entirely sure if I could ask even if I tried, my throat is clogged with smoke.

Without my sight, running is hard enough. But add to that the lack of fresh air, my lungs tremble as if they'll collapse. I'm gasping, hoping against all hope we can get the *shaav* out of here. Luckily, the gray fog that seems to hover over my vision starts to lift as my eyes continue to water. I can see shapes again, the outline of Dragon heaving us forward despite the smoke that's suffocating us.

Every breath inflicts deeper pain inside my chest.

Ahead, there's a staircase. Or maybe there isn't, and I'm just hallucinating with my lack of oxygen. When my foot lands on the first step I almost expect it to fall through, to shatter the illusion, but I'm propelled upward until we reach the top. The air is only slightly better here.

The wall before us is black, but there's something strange about it and I don't understand why until Dragon places his hand on a small lever on the side.

A door.

This is our way out!

He jerks his hand back and inhales deeply. "Hot," he coughs out.

"Hold on," I manage through a painful breath. I grab onto his shoulder to stay balanced as I remove my shoe.

Dragon holds onto me, and I press the bottom of my shoe to the door handle. It makes a clicking sound, and I ease the door open. I hop forward and into the grass outside and make sure to keep the door open for Dragon.

He walks through, and we finally let go of each other. I attempt to put my shoe on but I start to lose balance and tumble forward into the grass.

Drinking in the cool, fresh air makes my mouth water. My face is wet with tears, my body drenched in sweat. The air is sweet and gentle like the green grass. Every breath that fills my lungs takes a bit of the pain away, and I've never been so thankful to breathe.

Dragon laughs.

"Don't ever do that again," I say darkly. My eyes burn with a bit of anger.

Dragon takes my hand gently in his and squeezes it.

I don't react.

"It's okay." His voice is raspy. "Here they come."

"No." I slowly pull my hand out of his grasp. "No."

The sound of an engine rumbles a few meters ahead, and never in my life have I been so glad to see a ship knowing Liam is inside.

*The Odyssey* is prepped and ready for takeoff. The ramp is still open. Dragon and I make our way toward it, and I trip as I get inside, but I don't stand up. I'm aching all over, and I'm exhausted. The cool metal against my hands feels so good. I just want to lie here and fall asleep.

I cough a few more times before I catch my breath. Dragon is on the floor next to me, staring up at the ceiling, panting for air. He looks at me and smiles. "We made it."

# CHAPTER FIFTEEN

"Luci, take control of the ship for me." Liam's voice is close.

I hear his footsteps coming toward us, so I force myself to stand. Dragon looks at me a bit dazed then stands up, too.

Liam rounds the corner and almost runs into me. He wraps his arms around me in a tight embrace. He pulls away slightly and looks me in the eyes. "By the stars, I was worried. You were taking a while. You guys okay?"

"We're fine," I reply.

His eyes widen a little. "Jaina, you're bleeding."

I follow his gaze. There's a blob of dark red blood on my chest just above my heart, and droplets of red trickle down my shirt. Was I shot? How didn't I feel the impact? My body shifts into panic mode, and I touch the wound. Except, there's no pain, no gash or even a small cut where blood could escape me. I'm still out of breath from the smoke, and my back still feels like it's on fire but my chest feels alright considering everything. I place my hand against the wall for support. "It must be from Draco," I breathe.

Liam looks at me, as if asking permission to check, and I nod. He places his hand where the wound should be, but there's no bullet hole, not even a scratch. "Oh, *shaav*," he says nervously. "What happened?"

My whole body tingles and I start to feel sick. "What's wrong?"

I spin around, following Liam's line of sight. I feel dizzy.

Dragon pulls his hand away from his arm. It's coated in blood. I want to gag.

It all comes back to me. Dragon shouting my name. The crackle of gunfire. He jumped in front of me. By the stars.

"Why didn't you say anything?" I cry.

He shakes his head. "It wouldn't have done any good. I'm okay."

"You aren't okay," Liam says. "I'm going to get Luci."

Dragon nods. "That might be a good idea."

Liam disappears around the corner.

"Dragon." I take his hand, "How bad is it?"

"Not bad," he says quickly.

"The *truth*."

His jaw twitches. "Honestly I don't know. I'm too scared to look."

Remembering how tightly he held me to him in the tunnel when the fire was passing by, I look down at my hands. My fingertips are coated in blood. His blood.

"Dragon, I'm sorry, I'm so sorry," I say, fighting every urge to be angry with him. I don't know what else to say, but the horrible truth is that he's hurt, and it's my fault. I'm always in the way, and he always has to be a hero and save me. Someday it will get him killed. I want to yell at him for his stupidity, but I decide to save it for later.

"Jaina, stop. You didn't have anything to do with it."

My head is spinning, I feel like I'll collapse. "If I hadn't been such an idiot...I should have gotten out of the way!"

Luci runs over to us, followed by Liam.

"Dragon, what happened?" She turns to me. "What did you do! *Shaav*, Jaina, if you hurt him–"

"Luci, look at me," Dragon interrupts.

But Luci just keeps glaring at me, as if I'm the cause of every problem in the galaxy. If I don't end up saving my mother, that's probably what I'll become.

"Luce, calm down. It was a bullet, not plasma, and it just grazed me," he insists.

"That definitely explains why you're bleeding all over the place!" She hisses. "Why is Jaina covered in your blood?"

"Luci, I need you to hurry and sew me up or something, it stings like hell," he orders. "Liam, we were nearly trapped in a fire, make sure she's okay."

Liam takes my arm as I choke out another few coughs. "Hurry, we need to check you for smoke inhalation."

He pulls me aside into the small cargo hold and has to hold me up as the ship goes all wobbly. My vision gets spotty as he sets me carefully on the ground and walks away. What's wrong with me? Thinking hurts.

Liam is at my side again and slaps my cheek lightly. "Stay with me."

"Ow." I hear myself make the sound but I don't feel fully present.

He places a plastic mask over my nose and mouth. "Breathe."

I close my eyes and do as instructed. My hands are shaking, my lungs seem to burn with every breath. As the cold oxygen floats into my chest, my head stops spinning, and eventually I stop hearing my heart thumping away in my chest. I'm not sure how long I sit there sucking in air, but eventually Liam removes the mask and sits back on the floor.

His face seems to relax. "You good?"

Everything becomes more clear, and I realize the ship has stopped shaking. Maybe I just imagined it?

I nod. "I'm good."

"The oxygen is mixed with some medicine, it should help your lungs heal faster. You'll need another dose of it in twelve hours, but until then you should be okay," he says. "Let's get to the cockpit."

We move silently into the cockpit, and as we pass Dragon's room, I hear Luci talking but I can't make out what she's saying.

Liam and I take our seats, pilot and co-pilot, but I can't bring myself to say anything. I just stare forward out the viewport and watch the city move beneath us. The sky is still dark as the void between the stars.

This is all my fault.

Dragon is hurt, because of *me*. Because of my stupidity.

First, I fell for him when I shouldn't have.

Then, I was completely numb toward him. Enough to let him fight off the guards by himself. I was too eager to catch Draco and find my mother. I should've just stayed with him. Who the *shaav* would care if Draco got away?

And even then, he was going to sacrifice himself to save me in the tunnel. He would have died to protect me. How could I have let it come so close to that?

"Well," Liam says. He keeps his gaze on the viewport, but he smiles. "At least you look nice."

My white outfit has been colored slightly gray from the heat of the flames, and I'm still covered in blood. A few burns are visible on the cloth where plasma bolts just missed me. I try to pull the cloth of my shirt low enough to at least cover my belly button, but it doesn't do any good. It only results in pulling the neckline down, and, well, there's only so far it can go without becoming dangerous.

Liam laughs. "I don't mind."

"Of course you'd say that. You thought it would be okay to join the Resistance in my pajamas." My voice is harsher than I mean it to be, maybe because my lungs are still recovering. I'm not even mad at him, just at myself.

His lips curl into a smile. "How could I forget? That's the night you tried to kill me."

"If I remember correctly, it was *you* who tried to *attack* me. And then I ended up cornering you."

He shakes his head skeptically. "You're remembering wrong."

I don't reply, and I don't smile.

"So," he says gently after clearing his throat, "you wanna tell me where we're going?"

"The capitol," I say monotonously.

He hesitates. "Of Kashia?"

"No. Vera Kaas."

Liam laughs nervously. "Wait, *where?*"

"Vera Kaas. Capitol of the Imperial Alliance. Sivva is staying at the Senatorial Hotel."

He stares back at me, his eyes a bit wider. "You're joking, right?"

"I wish I was," I mutter. "Apparently they called him to a meeting–"

"I know," he interrupts. "I found that out from one of the girls at Draco's house. Jaina, that place will be packed with security. All of the leaders are there, so maximum security is an understatement." His face is almost colorless.

"Yeah, well, that's where we have to go," I retort.

Liam's entire aura is tense. I feel it in the air, like a physical expression.

"What?" I ask.

"You're the daughter of the Resistance. That's what."

"Don't say that." I turn away from him. "It would be my luck that she doesn't even believe I'm her daughter. What if I'm *not* her daughter?"

"As much as I hate to say it, if the Resistance wasn't sure you're her daughter, they wouldn't have bothered rescuing you."

"I know."

"Jaina." He leans closer to me. "The Alliance wants you, and when they find you, they'll do a lot of awful things before they decide to put you out of your misery."

"They're looking for all of us. I'm not the only one you need to be worrying about."

"But you especially, Jaina."

"Either way, we have to do this. You have to trust me. Everything will be okay," I insist. I can't say I actually believe it. But we've come this far. Who says we can't make it the rest of the way? Maybe we *can* make it across the galaxy in time to save my mother.

Liam nods slowly. "Alright. I'll set a course for Vera Kaas."

The silence that follows is long and deep, like there's a gulf of water between us.

I can't stop replaying the events in Draco's house and I keep returning to how Dragon took a bullet for me. For some reason, I'm more angry than thankful. Angry that he would risk his life for me, angry that I owe him my life.

"What's wrong?" Liam asks eventually.

I shake my head. "Dragon is what's wrong."

"What do you mean?"

The scene flashes back into my head, Draco begging, Dragon's threats.

*Dragon's scimitar is pointed at Draco's shoulder. "Talk, or you lose your arm. Need a little more of a push?"*

"Sometimes I wonder if Dragon feels anything at all," I say. "He threatened to take Draco's arm, and I think he meant it."

Liam tilts his head, his eyebrows bent with worry. "Can't say I'm surprised. He's a dangerous man."

"It's worse than that," I reply. "It's...contagious."

"What is?"

"The violence." My voice is quiet as I stare forward. From the corner of my eye, I see Liam glance at me. "Did he make you do something?"

I shrug. "I shot Draco in the leg for information."

"Well it worked."

"That's not the point," I sigh.

I gaze out into space as we leave Kashia's thick, poisonous atmosphere. The stars poke out of the final layer of clouds one by one, like eyes.

"You should get some rest," Liam says. "You look exhausted."

"Yeah, I probably should." I stand.

"Jaina," he says gently before I can leave. He stares out at the stars. "Do you ever get the feeling like the universe is trying to tell you something, but you can't quite grasp it?"

"Like what?"

"I don't know. It's like there's a sound that echoes across the stars that we can't hear, but we can feel. It's speaking, and you feel it, but you don't actually have a way of interpreting it. Do you ever feel that?"

I think for a moment. "I don't know."

"One more thing... I don't think it's a good idea to trust him," he says in almost a whisper, his gaze fully locked on me now.

I feel like I've been physically struck, but I stand still. "What makes you say that?"

He shrugs. "Just a feeling. There's still too much we don't know."

"Vera Kaas," I remind him. "Goodnight, Liam."

I leave before he can reply.

Sleep is fleeting, seemingly lasting only a matter of minutes. I've changed into an incredibly comfortable gray armored tank top and black kevlar pants. The blankets are bunched up at my feet on the bed; I've had enough heat to last me a while. I lie flat on the bed, staring at the ceiling, wondering how much time we have before we reach Vera Kaas. Capitol of the IA. Long ago, before the Century of Darkness and the Great Stellar Wars, Vera Kaas belonged to the Galactic Alliance. It was a free society governed by the people, from what I've heard. The wars were what forced us into a dictatorship.

It feels like we've been flying a long time.

*Knock knock.*

"Jaina," Dragon says. "Are you awake?"

"Yeah. Come in." I sit up and hang my legs over the side of my bed.

The door hisses open, and I notice how Dragon carefully presses the button to shut it behind him. He takes a seat on the bed across from me.

"How's your arm?" I ask.

He glances at the white bandage around his arm and smiles. "I'll live."

He'll be fine. He's not even pale from the loss of blood.

"Don't you dare do that again," I blurt out.

The muscles in his face tighten and one corner of his mouth twitches slightly. "Do what?"

"You don't have to keep saving me. I can handle myself."

Dragon takes a deep breath. "Why'd you save me?"

My chest tightens, and my stomach tingles with anxiety. I have to focus all the strength I have left to answer him. "Because, I had to."

"You didn't have to, after all I've said and done to you, you could've just let me—"

"No. I couldn't." That fire burns in me and grows hotter, angrier. "You know I couldn't."

"I would have deserved it."

Despite myself, my eyes begin to fill with tears. I feel searing heat and so completely cold at the same time. How can he talk like that? What has he done to make him think he deserves to die? Yes, he tricked me and lied to me, he hurt me and destroyed my trust but he doesn't deserve to *die*.

"Hey." He kneels before me and takes both of my hands in his, but I can't make eye contact. "Jaina, what's wrong? I'm alright, and the mission was a success."

"You were going to *die* for me." My voice quivers. I have to get out of here before I start falling apart right in front of him. I stand, but he grabs my hand and steps in front of me.

"Jaina, wait. Please."

I look up at him. "Dragon, promise you'll never do that again."

I see complete guilt on his face. He shakes his head. "That is something I cannot do."

Frustration and annoyance course through me. Their cold tendrils growing on the back of my neck. "Yes, you *can*. Don't risk your life for me."

Dragon only looks back at me calmly. "I'd do it a thousand times over to save you."

"Don't talk like that. You lied to me before about everything. The least you can do is make a simple promise!" My heart crawls up into my throat, and pain seeps into my voice. "Promise you won't do it again, that you won't-"

"Jaina." He strokes my hair.

I catch his hand, stopping him. "Why would you risk so much for me? Is it because of my mother? For the Resistance?"

"No." He shifts his weight. "I just..."

"Don't die for me. I'm not worth it."

He pushes me back slightly so he can look me in the eyes. "You are. If something happened to you, I couldn't live with myself."

"You kissed me because it was necessary. Because I wouldn't have come along, and now you're talking like you have feelings for me."

"I don't know why I kissed you. I care about you. I know I said a lot of things during the Trials that weren't true, but when the Masters took me, I constantly thought of you. And...when Shirez rescued me and told me I'd return to you, I looked forward to that day."

I turn around and glance into his eyes. "So you lied when you said it meant nothing to you."

He swallows hard, eyes pleading, begging me to understand him. "Yes. I lied. I'm a liar, Jaina. I don't know why the *shaav* you still trust me."

"I don't really have a choice," I reply.

"Please, just try to understand."

"Do you love me?" I whisper bravely. "Did you ever?"

Dragon keeps his gaze on the floor and sits down on the bed. "I..." He looks like he's struggling, almost choking on his words.

I can hardly see him through my watery eyes. *What did I expect?*

There's a knock, but the door slides open without invitation. Liam steps through the doorway and his gaze shifts from Dragon to me, a mix of worry and confusion on his face. "What's going on?"

"Nothing." Dragon's voice falters.

Liam's gentle eyes study me. "Are you okay?"

"I'm fine." I sigh.

Liam glares at me, and I know he'll ask me about this later. No. Not ask. *Demand.*

"I'd tell you to get more sleep," he begins, "but we're almost there."

"How long do we have?" Dragon asks.

"About forty minutes."

Dragon nods. "I'll be out in a minute."

Liam acknowledges it with a slight nod then leaves, closing the door behind him.

Dragon looks at me carefully. "Last time I fell in love, bad things happened. I can't let it happen again. Not with you."

"What happened?"

His eyes close a moment. "It's not something I expect you to understand."

"Of course." I cross my arms and shake my head with disgust. "I'm not surprised."

# CHAPTER SIXTEEN

"So what's the plan?" Liam asks as he presses a few buttons on the cockpit control panel.

I automatically turn to Dragon. Our gazes meet for an awkward moment until I break it. My body feels tense and anxious, and I take a deep breath and try to hide my anger.

Dragon hesitates. "I'm open to suggestions."

"How the *shaav* did I know you were going to say that?" Liam asks, his voice a bit snappy. I wonder if he can tell how angry I am.

"I didn't exactly have much time to come up with one since I was shot in the arm," Dragon retorts. "I'm sorry for the inconvenience."

"*Grazed*," Liam corrects as he rolls his eyes. "Does anyone else find it a bit odd that he acts like a leader until he's upset and then just sits there?" He glances from the viewport to Dragon. "You should be prepared for this sort of thing."

"Shut up. You're just about the *last* person I'd go to for a lecture on leadership. And if you wanna talk to me about getting shot at, you can take on the next dangerous mission."

"I'm just stating the obvious," Liam shoots back. "I'm actually tired of listening to you. You've got stupid ideas anyway."

"Sounds good to me. I'm tired of having to plan everything," Dragon replies. "I already said I was open to suggestions."

Luci shrugs. "Once we reach the planet, we have to be careful. Chances are we'll be recognized by the police if we go anywhere public."

"We'll have to find a way to extract the information at night," I add. "It'll be easier that way."

Dragon doesn't look at me. In a way I wish he would, just so I could show him that I honestly don't give a *shaav* about him.

Liam presses a few more buttons to his left. A silvery light glows on his face, emanating from a screen on the control panel. He takes a deep breath then turns back to Luci and me. "So I broke into the records, Sivva is staying at the Senatorial Hotel, room 71203. So that's the seventy-first floor."

"You what?" Dragon cries. "You realize–"

"Yes," Liam replies quickly, typing into the control panel. "We only have a matter of time before security traces the security breach back to our location. But, hey, I work well under pressure."

*Breathe in. Breathe out.* This is where it starts, where the adrenaline kicks in. By the stars, here we go again. "Thank you, Liam." I look to Luci. "You and Dragon can scout the area. I don't know how effective it'll be, but–"

"I got this." Luci nods. "Maximum security isn't a problem for us, is it, Dragon?"

Dragon's jaw twitches. "We've never had to deal with anything like this before. You realize how serious this is, right?"

Luci glares at him. "What the *shaav* is up with you?"

"Nothing." He glances at me then back to Luci. "Nothing," he repeats. "Okay, we'll do it."

"I'll break in, since Dragon doesn't wanna put himself on the frontline anymore," Liam says.

Dragon sighs. "There are tons of cameras in that building. Detectors can match a single face with a name in an instant. It will be dangerous for anyone to go in there."

"Which is why it'll be perfect for me," Liam replies. "I'm not known in the Resistance, and I'm unrecognizable to the Alliance."

"Fine," Dragon says anxiously, "but when you go in, you have to keep your head down."

"I know how to break in." Liam rolls his eyes. He presses something else on the control panel and brings the ship out of the hyperfield. Before us is a beautiful planet, filled with colors, mostly green, gray, and blue. "Wow," he breathes. "Is this really the right place?"

Dragon nods. "Yeah. Vera Kaas. The green is artificial grassland, and the gray areas are cities. Some stretch across continents. Liam, how good are you with repairs?"

"Oh, so now you wanna join in?" Liam spits back.

"Do you want my help or not?" Dragon bristles.

Liam rolls his eyes. "What kind of things?"

"Remote controlled probes?"

Liam's eyes brighten. "Do we have one? They're easy, but I need all the parts."

"There's a broken one in that storage unit over there that I haven't been able to fix."

"What do we need a probe for?" Luci asks.

"It'd be really helpful for finding the information we need." Liam stands and heads to the small storage unit. He opens it, and removes a small remote probe. It's black and spherical with a few holes around the surface. "This will work. What's wrong with it?" Liam asks as he takes a seat on the floor.

"No idea," Dragon replies, "but now I'm piloting."

Liam shoots him a glare. "I swear if you *shaav* this up–"

"It's my ship. I've got it."

I clear my throat. "Okay, so we have a probe. Once Liam has it fixed, we could send the probe in to find the information we're looking for, right?"

"How will it know what we're looking for?" Luci asks.

Liam doesn't look up from the probe. "I can program it to scan all electronic files it comes in contact with. Once we confirm that what we need is in there, we'll make a move."

"Which is?" Luci asks.

"Someone goes inside to retrieve it."

"If someone is going inside, it'll be me," Dragon says.

"Stop trying to be a hero," I snap. "I'll go."

"Jaina I love you, but that is actually the worst idea I've ever heard," Liam counters.

"Liam is right," Dragon says, not bothering to look at me.

Liam shakes his head. "If you actually listened to me, Dragon, you'd find that I'm right most of the time."

Dragon scowls and glares back at Liam.

I glare at Dragon, fighting every urge to protest. They do have a point, as much as I hate it.

"Jaina," Liam says calmly, "you really can't go out there. This is the capital. The security is crazy, and you've got a bounty on your head. I'll go in and retrieve the information. I know how to work the system."

"Wait a minute," I say. "If we have a probe, why does someone have to go inside at all?"

Dragon sighs. "The drive on the probe isn't big enough. It can't download the whole file."

"At least let me go with you," I say, ready to get on my knees and start pleading. "You might need backup."

"Just me, Jay," Liam replies. "I'll be fine."

Luci touches my arm. "It's best for you to stay."

I swallow my anger. No matter what I say, it's clear that none of them are letting me go.

"So..." I pause. "You want me to stay here? In the ship?"

Dragon nods. "That's the best idea. Liam goes in to retrieve what we need, and Luci and I will keep an eye out for Sivva. He's a partying type of guy, so he'll probably be out late," Dragon replies. "We shouldn't have to worry about him, but just in case, we should be ready."

"What time is it?" Liam asks.

"It's 2100 hours at the Senatorial Hotel. Nine o'clock."

"I know how to translate military time," Liam mutters.

Dragon shrugs. "Jaina, you take care of the ship."

I nod before I realize what I'm doing. And I hate it. Is he making me do the stupid job because he's annoyed with me? Because I'm angry with him and because I told him not to risk his life for me? Because he wants to keep me safe?

No.

*Liam* wants to keep me safe.

Dragon just wants me alive so that we can find my mother.

"Landing sequence commencing," says a computerized voice.

"Here we go," Luci breathes. "Worst part of the flight."

"What are you doing?" Dragon barks. "They'll shoot us down before they let us land."

"So we free fall," Liam replies.

"We *what*?" I panic.

Dragon's mouth slightly opens and his eyes are squinted.

"Do you have a better idea?" Liam raises an eyebrow at Dragon.

Dragon raises his hands off the control panel. "You do it then."

"*Shaav* no!" Liam replies. "This is your ship, remember?"

"I'm not gonna be responsible for the death of Amara Indera's daughter," Dragon snaps.

Liam quickly puts the probe back in the storage unit, takes his place in the copilot chair, and presses a few buttons. "You're right," Liam says, his voice focused. He looks at Dragon seriously. "You're going to get us down there safely with my help."

"I'm usually more prepared for this sort of thing." Dragon presses buttons on the control panel at his side.

"Dragon." Luci leans forward in her chair and squeezes Dragon's arm. I can hear her very controlled breaths, but her hand trembles. "You're not actually considering this, are you?"

"*The Odyssey* is one of the best stealth ships ever created," Dragon replies, "but IA scanners will pick us up. The only way we can make it down there relatively safely is by conducting a free fall."

Luci and I exchange worried glances.

"Is it possible?" I ask carefully. "Has anyone ever done it before?"

Liam nods but doesn't look at me. "It's a very old trick. It was practiced in ancient times, when people had just discovered space travel. It wasn't used for stealth though. They used it to land in the ocean in a pod."

"But we're not landing in the ocean, right?"

Dragon takes a deep breath. "No. We're cutting the power, since all systems have to be shut down as we enter the atmosphere. Otherwise they'll be able to track us. Once we're low enough, we can restore power, but we have to do that before we crash into the plateau."

"Wait a minute, once we're safely in the atmosphere, won't they be able to track us anyway?" I cut in. Liam shakes his head. "Once we start the free fall, we'll just look like debris or a small astroid burning up in the atmosphere. When we're close enough to the planet's surface, we turn the power back on and go into stealth mode. They'll never know."

"Dragon, no." Luci squeezes his arm tightly. "Absolutely not, there has to be another-"

"There's not," Liam cuts in quickly. "Besides, I've always wanted to do this."

By the stars, I'm slightly horrified to see a grin on Liam's face. He starts pressing buttons frantically. Every light in the ship goes out at once.

"Everyone, buckle up. This is going to get rough," Dragon says.

"The cloaking device!" Luci cries in desperation. "Can't you use that?"

Vera Kaas grows larger in the viewport. I take a deep breath. My stars, I don't want to die. I really really don't want to die. I double check my safety belt and tighten the straps.

"That was destroyed," Dragon replies. "We don't really have a choice." He presses buttons at high speed, and the ship lurches downward with such force I'm afraid it'll tumble out of control.

My whole body is trembling, but I decide not to protest. This is the only way.

The lights on the control panel go out, and Dragon lifts his hands. "Here we go." He glances to Liam. "Are you ready?"

Liam's grin freaks me out. "Oh yes." He laughs. "Let's *shaavez* do this."

"If you mess this up," Luci starts, "I'm going to kill both of you."

Dragon smiles a little. "Sounds fair. If we mess up, we'll all be dead anyway."

"By the stars," I breathe. "Just don't, please." I start to feel sick. This is not good, this is really not good.

"Here we go," Dragon says. "This won't be pleasant. Just hang on. It'll be over in about ten minutes."

As if timed for Dragon's words, the seats start vibrating, and the ship lurches left then right, slowly at first, but harsher as time goes on. I lean back against my seat. A horrible buzzing sound makes everything worse. My vision goes blurry from the vibrations, and I close my eyes. My teeth chatter against each other, and it gives me a headache. I peer out of my eyelids at the rapidly approaching surface of the planet.

That's when I realize Luci is screaming, but I have no idea what she's saying. I don't even bother trying to understand.

The circular frame of *The Odyssey* glows red against the backdrop of the plateau. We're overheating. I take a deep breath, but in all honesty, I feel like crying. I'm not ready to die. *I'm not going to let us die.*

"Is this supposed to happen?" I shout.

Liam turns to me uncomfortably but nods. He looks about as worried as I feel.

"None of this is supposed to happen!" Luci cries. "I'm not supposed to be here, I wouldn't be here if it weren't for you three idiots!" She continues shouting, but her words fade from my consciousness.

I grip my seat as the painful descent makes my body tremble down to my bones. I'm not sure how long it lasts, but it feels like forever. When I glance out the viewport, all I see is green.

Green grass. A meadow grows before us with such speed that I don't have time to realize what's happening. Gravity seems to increase in fractions of a second as Liam turns the power on and pulls back on the controls. I feel like I'm being melted into my seat.

And then, it all stops.

A grassy field moves quickly below us, only a kilometer down.

"We're alive." Liam gasps.

"Yeah," Dragon says breathlessly. "Holy *shaav*."

Tears stream down Luci's face, and I realize they're streaming down mine too. I try to get enough air into my lungs, but I can't. Deeper and slower breaths don't seem to help. I hear them talking, but I don't understand them. I'm dizzy, I feel sick, and I start to cough.

"Jaina," Dragon says for the second time I realize. "Jaina, go lie down."

"I'm-I'm okay," I hear myself say. "I'll be fine."

"You need to rest now," he orders. "Luci, please take her back."

"I don't take orders from you, Kasev," she snarls, "but I'm not gonna let her puke all over me. Come on, Jaina." She stands.

I start to follow, while Liam gets out of his seat, muttering something to himself. He opens the storage unit again and removes the probe. I take another deep breath, feeling uneasy and shaky. By the stars, why does my body have to rebel against every stressful situation we're in?

"Go lie down for a few minutes. If you're going to puke, feel free to use the bathroom," she says angrily. She points back through the ship past the cabins.

"Thanks." I stand up and walk into the cabin on the left, lie down on the bed, and close my eyes. My mind dozes in and out of sleep, but the sickness rises again. Maybe I should go to the bathroom before I throw up in here.

The bathroom is small and uncomfortable, overall claustrophobic. But it's nothing I can't handle. My reflection in the mirror stares back at me. My skin is pale, even for me. I turn on the faucet and splash water on my face.

*Take deep breaths. You're okay. Just breathe.*

"You can run," he says.

I look in the mirror and see him.

Before I can scream, I turn around and touch the hilt of my scimitar on my holster belt, but he's already gone. My body is crumbling into panic mode, and even the flutter of my eyelashes when I blink makes me jump. *By the stars...*The sickness makes my stomach churn.

*Shaav,* I'm going crazy. I'm actually going crazy.

I turn back around, shut off the faucet, and wipe my face with a cloth. *Everything is fine.* My body shudders as I hold back tears. I'm frozen, I refuse to stand up straight to look in the mirror, and yet I can't turn around and leave.

The hairs on the back of my neck stand on end. The air grows cold. I feel him behind me. I know he's there.

"Leave me alone," I say quietly. Slowly, I reach for the hilt of my scimitar.

A hand wraps around my wrist.

I try to scream, but he covers my mouth with his hand.

"Just a little too slow," he breathes as he shoves me into the wall. His green eyes shine brightly into mine. My chest tightens. Tears stream down my face. I want to fight him, but the absolute terror has made me weak.

"Haven't you learned by now that struggling is pointless?" He removes his hand from my lips and strokes my neck.

My voice is gone. My whole body trembles. There's a warm trickle in my hand and the burning in my shoulder returns. I'm going to vomit.

He looks exactly as he did last time I saw him. His black hair is messy, and his shirt is torn beneath the sparse patches of his armor. Blood oozes from the stab wound in his side and even though I'm not touching him, blood pools in my hand and drips to the floor. Not my blood. His.

I close my eyes. "It's a dream. What do you want from me?"

"Nothing. Only to help," he replies. "While the imbalance remains, fate will try to destroy him. The shadows are coming tonight. If you do not interfere, he will die."

"Who?" I ask.

"It would ruin the fun if I told you."

My voice grows angrier and darker. "You're not real, get out of my head!"

"Not *real?*" He throws me against the opposite wall and pulls a knife from a sheath on his belt.

My back hits the wall, and I crumble to the floor. I need to escape. I need to get out. By the stars, I need to wake up. My legs force me to stand, and I press the button to open the door. *Go away!* After a few seconds, I realize the door won't open. I'm trapped inside my head.

Azad grabs my wrist and traps me against the wall with his body. I moan in pain with his force. "Not real."

Laughing, he takes my left hand and touches the knife to it. "Tell me, Jaina, does this feel real enough for you?" He drags the dagger over my open palm.

Pinpricks of pain shoot through my hand as he separates my skin. I try to kick him, to lash out, *something*, but my body doesn't move.

He takes a fistful of my hair and pushes my head into the wall. He cranes his neck so his lips nearly brush mine. His forehead touches my own, and his hand slowly rises up my waist. "You can't hide from me."

I blink, gasping for air. Something's wrong. I'm staring up at the ceiling–the bedroom ceiling. I'm in bed. I sit up, but Azad is nowhere in sight. All I hear is the humming of the engines, and all I feel is our motion through the atmosphere.

It was another dream.

Despite my shaking body, I stand and walk out of the cabin. I can't be alone anymore. How long had I been asleep? My heart still pounds restlessly in my chest.

"Jaina?"

I jump backward, half-screaming. My bones don't feel supportive, and I'm suddenly afraid I might topple over.

Dragon stares at me strangely from across the hall. "You okay?"

The air is crisp and cool, almost electric in my throat. "Sorry. I'm fine." I start to walk toward him, to move past him into the cockpit, but he stops me.

"Jaina, I'm sorry about earlier," he says. "I'm sorry about making you stay here in the ship. I'm just worried about you."

Does he really mean that? There's no trace of a lie etched into his expression, but he does too good of a job hiding it, so I can't be completely sure.

"It's okay." It's really not, but what else am I supposed to say? Nothing is going the way I thought it would. I don't even get to go on this last mission with them.

"Are you ready?" He shoots me a confused look when I lift my eyebrows. "For the mission."

"It's not like I have to be ready," I reply.

His eyes scan my face. "I'm only doing this for your safety."

"You're doing it for the Resistance. Not for me."

Dragon looks into my eyes a moment longer than necessary before dropping his gaze to the floor. "If any of us are in trouble, we'll call you, and you'll pick us up, okay?"

I nod, not agreeing with a single word. "Okay."

"Can you do this?"

I nod again. "I could do a lot more."

"Did you rest well?" He ignores me.

I look away, nervously. My dreams are my burden to bear, he doesn't need to know how tormented I am, how afraid I am. "How long was I out?" I ask instead.

If he knows I'm avoiding the question, he doesn't mention it. "About half an hour."

"When do you leave?"

"Liam just fixed the probe. After we send it into Sivva's room to find what we need, we'll have to go inside. I was just coming to get you." He looks down at me but not at my face. He tilts his head a little and furrows his brow. My cheeks grow warm, and I cross my arms over my chest. "I'm sorry," he says. "I wasn't-I wasn't looking there. I was just–" He takes my left hand. "What the hell did you do to your hand?"

I look down, a bit pissed off. "I didn't–" All the warmth drains from my body, and the dizzy sick feeling returns. My left palm has a small cut across the surface, and only now do I realize the stinging pain. But I *dreamed* I was in the bathroom and Azad–

"Are you okay?"

By the stars, what's happening? Maybe because of my stressful dream I dug my nails into my skin, but fingernails couldn't make such a clean cut...

"I just...I just cut it while I was sleeping." I push past him and enter the cockpit. I can't be alone right now, but I don't want to talk about this.

The moment I'm there, my body relaxes a bit. Outside the viewport is the largest city I've ever seen. The buildings are more than skyscrapers. More like sky-breakers. They poke through the clouds and are large enough for thousands of people to live or work in.

I gasp. "In the name of the galaxy."

"Breathtaking, isn't it?" Luci asks.

Glowing signs flash across the tops of buildings and on floating billboards between airways. Women with big puffy lips and other enlarged body parts stand proudly on balconies, showing themselves off to the rest of the city. I wonder if they actually *like* living here. Life in the Crystal City isn't anywhere near as perfect as they said it would be. Is it the same here?

"It looks like that's it." Liam points to a giant, cylindrical building up ahead.

"The Senatorial Hotel," Dragon adds.

The building grows in the viewport, and for a few seconds, I can't process anything other than complete and utter amazement.

"That's a hotel?" I ask, astonished. I rub my palms together, wince, and try to conceal the small cut on my hand, wanting to think of anything and everything besides that.

Twilight is upon the city, and darkness closes in. Buildings surround the Senatorial Hotel. How are we going to get in?

Liam turns to me. "When we get to the balcony, you and Dragon will cut a hole in the glass for the probe."

"Are we going to get inside?" I ask Dragon.

Dragon looks at me intensely. "*Liam* is going to get in by using this special formula he came up with. Apparently it's capable of unlocking any door in the galaxy."

"It is," Liam mutters. "Trust me. It'll work."

"You and I will get in as security guards?" Luci asks Dragon.

Dragon nods in affirmation. "There's an underground road where the servants work and sleep beneath the hotel. We'll locate two servant guards and take their clothes and ID."

"You're going to take their clothes?" I ask. "Isn't that a bit...I don't know...rude?"

Luci scoffs. "By the stars, Jaina, we're stealing vital information. We're not trying to be polite."

"You're just going to leave them naked?" I can't help feeling a bit uncomfortable. If someone knocked me out and stole my clothes, I'd be pretty upset.

Luci's long, shiny brown hair shimmers as she shakes her head. "That doesn't matter. We dress up as guards and claim that our master called for us. We go to Sivva's floor, stand outside his door, and pray we don't find him there."

The Senatorial Hotel grows larger in the viewport until the tiny little squares all over it become large one-way windows. Liam pulls a lever and adjusts a few things on the console. The windows become larger and I'm just a bit worried about possibly crashing into the building. *The Odyssey* rises slowly until Liam presses a button, and we stop, floating in the air.

Dragon takes a deep breath. "Liam, perform a bioscan of the room."

"Just a sec." Liam watches the control panel and presses a lever down. "Done. No life forms detected. We're all clear."

Dragon nods. "Let's go, Jaina."

I stand and press a button in the back of the cockpit. It opens to reveal a small compartment filled with small pistols. I take one with a silencer attached and strap it into my holster belt.

"Liam, position the ship so we face the balcony. We'll be in touch with you over privcom."

The two of us leave the cockpit. The ramp of the ship opens up to Sivva's balcony. The cool night air rushes into the bowels of the ship, tossing my hair behind my shoulders. The airways behind us, beyond *The Odyssey*, are crowded and full. It smells foreign, a bit like the Crystal City, but more alive.

Dragon steps off the ramp down onto the balcony, and I follow. The engines of *The Odyssey* are almost silent, apart from the soft *shh* of the air around it. We walk up to the glass window that actually serves as a door.

"Why would a guy *ever* need this much space?" I ask, a bit in awe of the size of the apartment.

"People are attracted to wealth. And what good is money if you can't show off your riches?" He hands me a small laser cutter. He removes a small handlebar like thing from his pocket and presses it to the glass. "Cut a large circle in the glass around this. This handle will keep it from shattering. Just do one half, and I'll do the same with the other. Move in an even distance around the handle."

I nod. Carefully, I turn on the laser and start cutting away at the glass. The cut glass glows a bright blue, the same as the beam from the laser. I'm about halfway done when I feel Dragon's gaze on me.

"What happens when we find my mother?" I don't look at him as I ask the question.

Dragon looks at me then back at the glass. "That's when the real fight begins."

"What happens to me?" I ask.

"That's up to you. You could join us…"

I shake my head as I continue to work. "I don't want to fight anymore."

He laughs gently. "Of course you don't."

The slight cockiness in his voice irks me. "What's that supposed to mean?"

"Nothing." He clears his throat, turns off the laser, and takes the handle in the center of the glass circle we've cut. "Keep cutting. When you complete the circle, slowly back up."

Once I finish my work, I turn off the laser and back away. He inhales sharply, and pulls the handle to lift our glass circle out of the window, and places it on the floor of the balcony.

"Now what?" I ask.

He takes a seat on the balcony, next to the glass circle. "Now you tell me what happened to your hand."

The question makes me shiver. The cut has become a thin line of irritated pink skin. There's no cut, not even a scab. I look up at Dragon, not sure what to say. "Nothing," I end up choking out."Just a little scratch, that's all."

His eyes are trained on mine, and his gaze doesn't budge. "What did you see?"

"Stop. We have a mission to accomplish. We can't spend our time talking about stupid dreams."

"Tell me now and we don't have to waste any more time on it," he orders.

I cross my arms and look away from him. At the buildings around us, the airways filled with ships, the lights and advertisements. "It was Azad again," I breathe. "He said he's coming back to haunt us or whatever. I don't know. And then he cut my hand, because I told him he wasn't real." I shake my head then glare at Dragon. "I was stressed out, so I cut myself in my sleep, and I incorporated it into the dream."

"Why are you almost healed, then?"

I scoff but feel my breathing quicken. By the stars, is he *trying* to make me feel crazy? "I don't know! It wasn't a very deep cut. What matters is that I'm fine!"

Dragon takes my left hand in his and he studies the red mark where my strange cut was present only a few minutes earlier. Even the faint line of pink is fading. "This is dangerous, Jaina."

I clench my jaw and suddenly I'm freezing cold. "How is it dangerous?" I ask, trying to remain strong, but my voice comes out trembling.

"Jaina, you need to listen to what he tells you," Dragon says. "He may be dead, but that doesn't mean that what he's saying isn't true."

"So what? He'll come find us as a ghost?"

Dragon shakes his head and backs off, finally releasing my hand. "No. But someone else might. Azad is giving you a warning."

"What do you mean?" I ask frantically.

Dragon shrugs, turns away from me, and starts to walk back toward *The Odyssey.*

"Dragon."

He faces me again. "We'll talk about it later. The moment this mission is over." Dragon presses the button on his privcom. "Hey, we're done here. Have Luci bring it out, and we'll put it through."

I take a deep breath and look up at *The Odyssey* hovering at the edge of the balcony. The ship adjusts, lowering itself slightly. I worry that the open ramp will smash into the balcony, but so far things are alright. The airlock doors open, and Luci comes through, sliding herself halfway down the ramp with the probe in one arm.

"Be careful. We've only got one shot," Luci calls. "Don't drop it." She tosses the probe down to Dragon.

He catches it easily. "Have Liam lower the ship below the balcony so we can get back in."

She smiles. "Got it." Luci climbs the ramp and enters the code to open the airlock.

Dragon looks at me as *The Odyssey* starts to descend. "Come with me. I might need your help."

I want to roll my eyes, but I follow him back to the glass door.

He holds the probe up to the hole we made. "Take this for me."

The probe is heavier than I expect, and I have to rest it on my leg to support the weight. It's covered in buttons too, so I have to be careful I don't accidentally press one. "Please make this quick. I don't like being up here out in the open."

"Which one…" Dragon mutters.

"What are you looking for?" I glare at him.

He sighs. "The 'on' button."

"How about that one?" I point with my eyes.

Dragon takes the probe out of my hands and turns it around a few times until he finds the universal "on" symbol I gestured to. I smile knowingly as I cross my arms. He presses the button, and a soft humming fills my ears. Dragon lifts the probe up to the glass and drops it through the hole we made.

I gasp as it plummets to the floor, but the probe catches itself and begins wandering the room. A blue scanner appears when it approaches something in the darkness.

Dragon smirks, a cocky, stupid look on his face. "I know what I'm doing."

"Sure..."

He looks toward *The Odyssey*. "Let's go."

I run across the balcony with Dragon at my side. The ship seems a bit farther away than I'm comfortable with. In fact, I don't think I'll ever be comfortable jumping anywhere from a balcony. I close my eyes for a moment, and remember jumping from my own balcony onto the stolen ship with Liam. *I can do this.*

Do it before Dragon.

The smooth stone railing is cold under my hands and I push myself up to stand on top of it. With a leap of faith, I land in *The Odyssey* on both feet. I glance back at Dragon as he takes a gentle step onto the ramp from the balcony. My cheeks feel a bit warm. The distance between the balcony and the ship is actually small enough to step over.

The airlock hisses open, and Liam walks through the door. "You got it in? It's safe?"

Dragon nods. "We're all set."

"Good. I'll drop you and Luci off at the servant entry," Liam says. "The IA will realize we've hacked the floor plans for the hotel within a few minutes. I uploaded a virus to the system so it should be about an hour or two before they can figure out where the hack came from."

"We'll tell you if anyone's approaching the door or going inside while you're still in there," Dragon says. "We'll do our best to distract them. Do not risk your life to get it. Understood?"

"Aw, isn't that sweet?" Liam grins mockingly at Dragon. "Jaina, he actually cares about my safety!" His smile disappears, and he scowls. "Don't pretend you give a *shaav*."

Dragon jerks past Liam into the cockpit. I give Liam a gentle smile before continuing into the cockpit with him and taking a seat next to Luci. Liam takes the controls. I buckle up quickly as Liam banks to the right. The ship moves down through the atmosphere closer and closer to the ground. My insides shift in odd positions, but it's nowhere near as bad as the freefalling. Everything inside me slides downward when we level out and come to a stop.

"We're here." Liam presses a few buttons and opens the ramp and the airlock.

Luci unbuckles her seat and stands. "Stay safe, you two," she says to us.

"You too," I reply. "Good luck."

"Jaina," Dragon says, "the information from the probe is being fed directly to the ship. A red light will start flashing when it finds what we're looking for. That's when you send Liam in."

I nod. "I'll watch for it."

Dragon smiles a little. "Don't forget to pick us up."

With that, Luci and Dragon exit the cockpit and move through the airlock. The door closes behind them, and when the hissing stops, I shut the airlock. They've left the ship, and we have a job to do.

# CHAPTER SEVENTEEN

"So that's it then?" Liam asks.

For the past half hour, we've been waiting for this stupid light. And now that it's flashing red, I wish it had taken longer. "Yeah, that's it." More than anything, I want to stop Liam from going in. It should be *me* instead of him.

I glance back at the building outside the viewport. We're hovering in an empty airway, doing our best not to arouse suspicion. It's dangerous out here. Who knows when Sivva will be home? Maybe he's the partying type of guy, but he *could* get home early. What if Liam gets hurt while he's inside? If there were guards in there, they would have destroyed the probe already, so that's not something we need to worry about at least.

"Jaina, did you hear *anything* I just said?" Liam's voice fades into my mind.

I snap out of my daze. "What?"

He's putting on his silvery-black armor. His hair falls gently around his forehead, and he taps his foot a few too many times for it to be habit. He's nervous.

Liam sighs. "Never mind."

"I'm sorry," I breathe. "I'm just really worried."

Liam takes a deep breath. "You've got nothing to be worried about."

I shake my head and stand, making my way over to him. "I'm worried about *you*, Liam. It would kill me if something happened to you."

He raises an eyebrow. "Really?"

I scoff. "You think I *want* you walking into an Alliance-infested building?"

"I dunno. Maybe?" His humor only makes me feel sick to my stomach.

"Stop it, Liam. It's not funny," I snap back.

He smiles. "Yeah, it is."

I grab a pistol out of the storage unit next to me and hand it to him. He shoves it into his holster belt.

Liam shrugs. "Just trying to make you smile."

"It's not working," I breathe.

We make our way past the airlock doors and into the small cargo bay.

"Jaina." He places his hands gently on my shoulders. "I'll be fine, okay? I promise."

I look down at the floor. My whole body feels cold. "Let me come with you. That way I won't have to be so *shaavez* worried about you."

"No, Jaina. You've got your orders, and you're too valuable."

"As if *you aren't?*" A terrible aching shoots through my heart. "You're the best mechanic they have. The Resistance needs you, too."

"Jaina, what did I tell you? I promise you I'll be alright. Besides, I like having someone worried about me for once."

I look away from him. "You always have someone worried about you."

"I can't let you come with me. You know how much I care about you."

"I care about you, too," I insist. "I just don't want anything to happen to you."

"I promise. And unlike Dragon, I'll follow through with my promises. Everything will work out."

"It better, or I'm going to be really mad at you."

"Oh, I'm *so scared*," he says sarcastically, smiling.

I pull him close and wrap my arms around him. "Just don't do anything stupid."

He hugs me tightly. "When have I *ever* done something like that?"

"Oh, shut up." I pull back and put my hands on his shoulders. "You better get going now."

"I'll be right back." He begins to walk toward the ramp of *They Odyssey*. "You know how to fly a ship, right?"

I shrug. "I know enough."

"Good. There's a landing pad over there, so once I'm off, that's where you'll wait for us. You've got a pretty clear view of the building, so you shouldn't have much trouble getting to us if we need you."

My heart sinks a little as he steps off the ramp and onto the balcony.

I rush back into the cockpit and press a button to close the ramp. I know all the basics of flying; it's just the quick maneuvers I have trouble with. This will be easy.

The airway remains crowded with passing ships, and I'm a little nervous about making it across. *The Odyssey* is bigger than most of the small planetary transports, so it won't blend in very well on the freeway, but I hope it won't matter since there are so many rich people here. With a sigh and a boost of courage, I lift the ship into the air.

It's easy to control. The slightest motion in the manual steering joysticks make it turn. I feel every motion of the ship through my hands, feel the engines rumbling beneath me. Once I've joined the other vessels on the airway, I realize I have no idea what the traffic rules are. On Virana, we never needed to know them, and in the Crystal City, we used public transportation.

Ships zoom past me, and it makes me jittery. Ships behind me start honking their horns. I have to speed up, so I engage the power a bit more. The landing area Liam gestured to is close. Thank the stars I don't have to stay in the airway long. When I finally manage to make it out of the airway, I enter the automated landing sequence into the main computer. I can only hope that this little station isn't privately owned, but a few smaller ships rest here, and there's no private property signs. *The Odyssey* does a good job of landing itself, and I take a deep breath.

What now? I just wait here until someone is in trouble or dies? The thought makes me sick. I have my orders. I can't compromise the plan. If I *shaav* up, they could all be killed.

Anxiety rushes through me in waves. I can't stop jiggling my legs. My body feels hot and cold at the same time.

*Everything will be okay.*

I glance around the cockpit, and my gaze rests on the main computer of *The Odyssey*. If I looked up my name, would it say anything about me? The GalaNet is censored by the IA in Alliance territories, especially here. I wouldn't want them to trace any searches back to my location. Though Liam said we're practically untraceable until the IA destroys the virus blocking their system. Hmm.

Without a second thought, I switch to the co-pilot seat so I can access the main computer. I turn it on with a wave of my hand.

"Indera," I say.

A blue holographic dot jumps up from the computer system, swims around in a circle for a moment, and then disappears. A picture pops up in full color, and my heart stops. It's me. No, not quite. It's me in twenty years. The woman's hair is curlier than mine, but the same color. Her eyes are blue.

Under the picture, a small caption reads: *Amara Indera.*

"Mom," I breathe softly.

She's beautiful. She has an intense look in her eyes that is so familiar.

"Mirror," I say to the computer.

Next to the picture of my mother, a computerized mirror pops up. That's where I've seen that face. I make that face all the time. Her skin is pale like mine, too.

I close out of the mirror, and I scroll down from the picture. There is a short article underneath:

*Amara Indera, resistor of Alliance authority, was imprisoned for treason at age thirty-four. She admitted to her crimes and was sentenced to death. For reasons unknown, her sentence was changed to spend the remainder of her life in prison. After her suffering is complete, she will be executed.*

Chills run through me. Maybe I *have* been the only thing keeping her alive but I'm also the cause of her suffering.

What if she's gone crazy? Being in prison for seventeen years doesn't help a person's mental state. What if she's tortured relentlessly? What if she's already dead?

No, they would've made that public.

Out the viewport, a hovercar slows down as it passes Sivva's suite. My blood begins to race and somehow I feel every vein in my body. What if they call the police? What if they already have?

I tap my privcom. "Liam Rodan."

There's a short ring tone.

"Liam, Liam, come in. Are you there?" I ask breathlessly.

"Jaina, what the *shaav*? I'm here. What's wrong?"

I sigh and lean back in my chair. False alarm. "Is everything alright?"

"So far. Should I be worried?"

"Maybe. Hovercar just passed by slowly, seemed to be checking things out," I breathe. "Did you find it yet?"

"Mmhm. I'm downloading everything to the ship. Is someone coming for me?"

A police hovercar flies by. I want to start the engines, fly to Liam, and make him climb aboard, but I know he wouldn't. The car passes by without stopping. *Shaav* I need to stop worrying.

"No, you're fine," I manage. "How much more time do you need?"

"Just a bit longer." He goes silent.

"Liam?" I say intensely. "What's going on?"

There's a bit of static on his side. "I'm not alone here," he whispers. "Don't come for me. Hang on."

By the stars, why did I let him go in there by himself? I panic and before I realize what I'm doing, I start the engines and fly to Sivva's balcony. I set *The Odyssey* to hover. All the risks can fall to me.

I tap the privcom again. "Liam Rodan."

Ring tone.

"Liam, are you there?"

Static.

Burning acid rises up from my stomach and into my throat. No turning back now.

I force myself to stand and strap a holster belt around my waist. My hand automatically snatches a gun from the closet and I hook my scimitar onto the side. In another moment I'm in the back of the ship, but burning anger takes over me when I realize I haven't opened the ramp yet.

I rush back into the cockpit and press a button to open the ramp.

Everything will be okay.

Somehow, I'm in the air falling toward the balcony. My feet hit the ground, and I bend my knees to absorb the shock. *Everything will be–*

The glass door we sent the probe through is broken. Completely shattered. That must be why the other car stopped. Our cut was clean and smooth. Barely noticeable. And with Liam's code, the door should have opened without force. This is reckless.

I take the pistol from my belt and step through the doorway.

The room is huge. Actually, it's more like five rooms interconnected with a kitchen and a fully equipped bar, couches face the windows and large holoprojectors, and doors leading into more rooms. There are far too many places for an enemy to hide.

I press the privcom again. "Altair Kasev."

"What?" Dragon asks.

"Something's wrong," I whisper, turning a corner and aiming my pistol at multiple targets. I find nothing except for the lamps and couches. "The glass is broken the way we came in, and Liam won't answer," I breathe into the privcom. I feel like the slightest sound will make someone jump out at me.

"Where are you?"

"I'm *inside*," I snap quietly. "He said he wasn't alone. Tried to call him several times. No answer."

I turn another corner.

No one.

Unlike the main room, some of the furniture here is tipped over. "Looks like someone got into a fight in here."

"So, you're *inside* the room?" Dragon asks harshly.

"I'm not going to let Liam get killed! He's—"

A thud to my left.

"Are you okay?" Dragon asks.

"Hold on."

"I'm coming up."

"No. Stay in position. Over and out." I hang up on him and listen for the sound again.

*Thump.*

*Boom.*

*Crash.*

A soft moan filters through the walls. Yes, I hear it clearly now. I fling the door open and look for something to shoot at, but there's only a computer on a desk. A holoscreen reads *download complete.* Liam must have gotten the information already.

Another door at the end of the room catches my gaze, and I run for it. I yank it open, and sure enough, Liam is on the floor. He's alone. I run to his side and fling myself to the ground next to him.

I hold his face in my hands. Blood gushes down his temple from a cut on his forehead. To inspect the wound, I take a small flashlight from my holster belt a shine it on his face. The cut isn't deep, not enough to worry much. I shake him a little. "Liam. Wake up!"

His eyes roll around a little. I check his pulse and it's stronger than I expect. Good. I might need him to fight again if his attacker is still present.

My hand touches my gun, and I yank it free from my holster belt and stand. I direct my aim toward the bed, then the nightstand, then the door. This must be Sivva's room.

A creaking noise sounds from behind me, and I turn in time to see an armored fist jolt outward toward my face. Pain explodes in my jaw. I stumble and grab the corner of the bed as I fight the dizziness. Pinpricks of color appear in my peripheral, and I will myself to stay conscious. My legs feel weak.

The room is silent, and it occurs to me that I've been expecting to be hit again. It hasn't come. I look up at the man in black armor. A red S is printed on his shoulder plate, and my mind shoots back to Keducia and the man in the café. The man who stood and watched as the two IA guards stopped us.

"Surrender." His modifier makes it impossible to identify his voice.

"Who are you?" I try to buy myself some time as I overcome my pain.

He moves closer. "I think you know." His voice is emotionless.

"What do you want?"

"The whole Alliance is looking for you, Indera-girl. You're worth a fortune."

My fingers go cold. "So you're an executioner? A hit man?"

He cocks his head a little, so I take my chance. I snatch my scimitar from my belt, activate it, and then lunge for him.

Reacting on cue, he sidesteps my thrust, grabs my wrist, and tosses my scimitar to the ground. He shoves me into the wall and closes a powerful armored hand around my throat, slowly suffocating me. I grab his hand and claw at his body, but there's not a single weak point in his armor.

"Assassin is a more accurate term," he replies mechanically. He loosens his grip enough for me to squeeze a few breaths of precious air into my lungs before tightening it once more. "Where are your accomplices?" He releases me but grabs a gun and aims it at me.

"How'd you find us?"

"I ask the questions," he snaps. "Turn yourself in, and I won't kill you."

My strength slowly returns as I catch my breath along with my confidence. I can defeat him. He's not planning on killing me yet, so what do I have to lose? The fire returns to my body. Everything happens on it's own.

I grab his hand and twist the gun from his grasp. My legs propel me forward and I kick him in the chest, knocking him backward into the wall.

He groans, takes a stun pistol from his belt and aims it directly at me. I duck even before he takes the shot.

"Hands up!" Dragon orders from behind me.

The assassin shifts his aim and fires with no hesitation. Luci takes the shot to the stomach and as a wave of blue light flashes over her body, she collapses to the ground. He's using a stun pistol.

Dragon pulls the trigger, and a bolt of plasma rockets toward the assassin. He avoids it just in time and shoots at the window. As the glass shatters into millions of tiny shards, he makes a run for the window and jumps.

I run to the window and watch him plummet down the side of the Senatorial Hotel. Only moments before smashing into the ground, a pair of jet burners ignite on the back of his calves and the palms of his hands. He rockets forward and disappears into the crowded streets of the capitol.

Dragon touches my arm. "We have to get outta here before he returns."

Liam moans and I go to sit next to him.

"Did I get him?" he mumbles.

"No, you sorta saved that for me," I reply.

He rubs his eyes. "I was trying to warn you."

"Did you get all the information?"

He nods. "Wouldn't have left without it."

"Good," Dragon replies. "We have to hurry, the police are probably on their way."

Luci's eyes are open as her body twitches a bit.

"Is she going to be okay?" Liam asks.

Dragon nods. "She'll be fine in about half an hour."

Dragon picks Luci's lifeless frame carries her onto *The Odyssey* while I help Liam to his feet.

"Are you going to be okay?" I ask him.

He nods.

"Where does it hurt?"

"I took a bit of a beating, but it's really just my head," he replies quietly. "Is it bad?"

I shake my head. "It looks worse than it is."

We make our way back toward *The Odyssey* and the glass from the broken window crunches under my feet as I walk to the balcony and climb into the ship with Liam's arm around my shoulders. Inside, Dragon carefully sets Luci down on the bed next to the one I've been sleeping in.

I try to lead Liam to the room across from Luci's but he refuses and sits in the co-pilot seat. So I grab some ice and a cloth for his head and hope for the best.

"I may have a slight concussion," Liam says.

"You should rest your brain," I reply. "Keep the cloth on it and apply pressure to stop the bleeding."

"I'm not stupid." Liam rolls his eyes and takes the ice and the cloth. "Dragon, the ship is yours. Get us out of here before we're traced."

Dragon sits in the pilot's seat. Of course I'm left sitting in the back again. Dragon quickly turns on the thrusters and lifts *The Odyssey* high into the atmosphere, above the clouds.

"Who was he?" I ask. "The assassin? He called me *Indera-girl.*"

Dragon shrugs. "You've got a memorable face, Jay. I'm not surprised he knew you. He's probably one of the Emperor's men."

"Dragon," I start. "Do you think…" I let my voice trail off. Saying it would make me sound like an idiot.

"The Shadow Hunter?" Liam asks my question for me. "Was it?"

Dragon shakes his head as he accelerates higher into the atmosphere. The darkness of the cosmos starts to envelope us. "The Emperor has hundreds of assassins. Makes sense, since he has so many enemies."

"Don't tell me you didn't see his armor," Liam says. "Jaina, I know you're observant like that. It had that red S on it with the two dots. That's his symbol."

Dragon shakes his head. "Everyone knows that's his symbol. Some crazy person could have it printed on his armor to strike fear into others. Besides, this guy jumped out the window when I shot at him and didn't kill *any* of us. Good for us, but really bad for your theory."

Liam helps guide the ship into the last layers of atmosphere.

"Okay," I say slowly, "but what if he's following us? What if that wasn't the end of it?"

"He couldn't possibly be following us," Dragon insists. "Sure, my cloaking device is broken, but *The Odyssey* is still hard to trace."

"Don't be so sure," I murmur.

Dragon raises an eyebrow. "Why?"

Liam glances back at me, his hand still holding the cloth tight to his forehead. "I thought I imagined that. You saw him too?"

I nod. "He was on Keducia with us and must have traced us here. He was next to us in the café, and watched us when we were stopped by the guards."

Dragon hesitates. "Why didn't anyone tell me about this? Maybe it was a coincidence."

"Coincidence?" Liam jeers. "Okay, so the guy who was sitting next to us in the café just happened to come all the way to Vera Kaas and break into the same hotel room on the same night?"

Dragon sighs. "I don't know. Just do your job and prepare us for the hyperfield. We've gotta get back to the Resistance. Coordinates X50, Y108, Z-99."

"Got it. Buckle up, we're jumping," Liam says.

And with that, the fabric of space shrinks before us and we shoot into the stars.

# CHAPTER EIGHTEEN

No matter how much rest I get, I can't shake the feeling of exhaustion. I'd go to the cabin, but I don't think it would do much good. Most likely I would wake up tired all over again.

Luci woke from her stun wound a few minutes ago, and she's back to her normal snappy, arrogant self. We should reach the Resistance in about an hour, but Dragon informed us it might take a bit longer since they don't like to keep the fleet in one place for too long.

Liam sits comfortably in the pilot seat; he insisted earlier that flying with a concussion would be easy, though I feel like he was just annoyed with Dragon's flying. Luckily the bleeding has stopped and all that's left is a large scab.

Luci has taken copilot duties.

Dragon is behind me, sitting on the floor, leaning against the wall. It doesn't look comfortable, but he doesn't seem to care as he studies the silverscreen in his hand, making sense of the information Liam stole. Unfortunately, the silverscreen batteries are running low, and the only outlet capable of recharging a silverscreen without exploding is in the wall.

"Jaina," Liam says. "I forgot to thank you. You disobeyed orders to save me. You're my hero."

"Not really that heroic." I laugh.

"Disobeying orders is insubordination." Luci's voice is hard. "And insubordination is not in the least bit *heroic*."

Dragon stands and pulls a few wires and memory chips out of the closet behind us. "Don't listen to, her," he says casually. "I disobey orders all the time, and I'm fine."

"You rebellious idiot," Luci scorns. "You're really going to encourage this?"

"Just stating the facts," he says.

"So, are you saying it's okay for us to disobey you?" I ask slyly.

He smiles. "I'm not saying that at all. I have to make decisions that will carry out quick and effective strikes with minimal casualties. So, most of the time, my orders will keep the majority of people safe, but, there are times when I've got no idea what I'm talking about."

Liam shakes his head. "Okay, that's not exactly the most inspiring thing I've ever heard you say, but at least you admit."

"Just don't tell anyone else I said that when we get back," Dragon mutters. He sits back down in the corner, plugs something into the silverscreen, and then continues reading.

"How is it coming along?" I ask.

Dragon raises his eyebrows and smiles a little. "There's a lot more information than we thought. I'll show you."

I take a seat next to him on the floor, my back resting against the wall. I consider scooting away a little, but I can't see the silverscreen as well, so I let myself rest against him, our shoulders lightly touching.

He pinches the screen, and it zooms out to view all the files. He presses a few buttons and selects a file. A map of the galaxy appears. He presses another button on the side, and the map pops out of the screen, in holographic mode. "We're headed here." He points to a smaller star system on the 3D map. "Multiply resolution by ten."

"Multiplying resolution by ten," the silverscreen repeats in a soft mechanical voice. "Would you like to expand map size?"

"Yes."

The map of the galaxy grows about five times the area of the silverscreen, spreading itself a few inches above the floor of the cockpit.

"Zoom to Sol Veya System," he says.

The map shifts, spinning toward us slowly. It then zooms in on a small system.

"Sol Veya System," the silverscreen says. "Relaying information...G-type main sequence star. Absolute magnitude is equivalent to 9.21. Consists of one habitable planet–Sol Veya. Distance from star is ten light minutes. System is located 8.54 light years outside of Imperial Alliance space. Sol Veya was previously occupied by the Galactic Alliance before the Great Stellar Wars for mining. Due to its importance to the Imperial Alliance, the Sol Veya system is not programmed into any other map. Would you like me to search for more information on planet Sol Veya of the Sol Veya System?"

"No thanks," Dragon replies.

"Sol Veya," I mutter. "So the IA just erased it from every map and database?"

Dragon shakes his head. "It was never in an Alliance database. It must have been forgotten in the Great Stellar Wars. It's strange...I expected your mother to be kept on one of the core worlds."

"Ten light minutes from the sun," I remark. "Is it cold there?"

"Cooler than Virana, I'm sure, but I wouldn't expect it to be covered in snow."

"How far is Sol Veya from the fleet?"

"If they are where they're supposed to be, just a few parsecs away," Dragon replies.

Liam's eyes widen. "Sol Veya, I know that name. A few years ago I hacked into the main computer on Virana just to see if I could do it. I read through some classified files, a lot of it was in code and over my head, but there was this tiny file that caught my attention and I'm never gonna forget what it said."

"And?" I ask.

He clears his throat. "It said, '*Sol Veya. Reduce security. Annual reinforcements are no longer required. Send new recruits to IAA or the Guard instead.*' And then it mentioned how the message would erase itself within twenty-four hours."

"How the *shaav* did you remember that?" Luci asks in disbelief.

Liam shudders. "It felt important, and it made me uneasy."

"Why would they cut security?" I narrow my eyes as if it will help me find an answer.

"The rest of the Alliance has been told that the Phoenix is dead," Dragon replies. "They probably didn't want people to get suspicious about continuously securing a planet that only a select few know about. A planet that's location is only known to three people in the galaxy."

"So," Luci cuts in, "if they've kept security low, we can mobilize the fleet and make a surprise attack."

Dragon rubs his right eye. "Since the Crystal City breakout two days ago, they might have changed things."

"Do we have the layout of the prison?" I ask.

"I'm still looking for it."

He retracts the map back into the device and begins searching for more information. I let myself lean into him a little more. His eyes flicker across the screen, reading every small detail and rereading things he missed the first time through. When he doesn't understand something, his eyes will slow and backtrack a little. His lips move sometimes, like he's going to say something.

Dragon sits up a little. "Luce, that guy we talked to in the Hotel, he said the emergency meeting was called because of the Crystal City thing, right?"

She nods.

"Okay," he says thoughtfully. "So we escape the City with Jaina. The Alliance calls an emergency meeting, which means they're getting worried."

"Why do you say that?" I ask.

He turns to me. "You, the daughter of the Phoenix, won the Trials. Then we got you out past all of their high tech security that *no one* has been able to get past before. Of course, if it weren't for the help of insiders, it never could have been done."

I shrug. "Okay, I'd be nervous if my enemies were running around wreaking havoc in my galaxy, but the Alliance is powerful. They've got *millions* of troops against, I don't know, a few thousand?"

"Three *hundred* thousand," Luci corrects. "That's including generals like Shirez and commanders."

"Still," I cut in, "that's three hundred thousand against millions. What do they have to worry about? Why do they need to worry at all even if we are able to free her?"

"First, you better not talk like that in front of the troops," Dragon says sternly. "It's bad for morale. Second, not many know about the prophecy. But those who do see the first signs of its coming. And that's what scares them the most."

"Whoa, whoa," Liam interrupts. "*Prophecy?*"

"Hold it there," I snap at Dragon. "I'm not part of this crazy prophecy you speak of."

Dragon ignores us. "Jaina, the prophecy states that if you are the Light, you will be born of two worlds. You will save lives instead of waste them. You will bring people hope instead of pain."

"Two worlds?" I ask. "What's that supposed to mean?"

Dragon shrugs. "I'm not entirely sure, but Shirez knows something about it."

"What are you talking about?" Liam shouts. "Can someone *please* explain to me what's going on?"

Dragon sighs, his eyes resting on the ground. "A long time ago, there were a people called the Dalivan. They still exist today, but only in small numbers. Have you heard of them?"

"I didn't know they still existed," Liam replies. "Can't they see the future?"

Dragon nods. "The majority of the species can see a few minutes to a few days into the future, but every once in a while, a truly great Dalivan is born with the ability to see a future a thousand years away." He stops nervously and takes a breath. "Before the Imperial Alliance, before The Great Stellar Wars, during The Century of Darkness, there was such a Dalivan. And he had a vision. Over the years, it occurred and reoccurred to him. Dalivan after saw the same thing. That vision became the prophecy."

"Can the Dalivan be wrong?" I ask slowly.

"Yes," Luci replies, "but if the same vision reoccurs for others down the line, the more likely that future will come to pass. Three of the most powerful have seen it. They've all seen different versions, but overall, it's the same."

I swallow hard and turn to Dragon. His blue eyes are dark with worry, and he refuses to meet my gaze. "Does Shirez believe in the prophecy?" I ask.

"No."

"What exactly is the prophecy?"

"Dragon," Luci says sternly, "telling her isn't a good idea. We don't even know if she's the one they speak of."

"Yes, she is," he shoots back.

"And how would you know?" She asks.

"Because I can see it. She and her mother are symbols of hope. Jaina brought hope to me when they took me from Virana. And...I know because I think I'm part of it too." He looks at me sadly then turns back to Luci. "Luci, you know there's a chance I could be the other. As much as you want to deny it, to believe I'm not like that, my power is dark."

I touch his arm carefully. "What are you talking about? What power?"

"Yes," Liam urges. "Please explain."

Dragon glances down at the floor. "In the prophecy, three forces are supposedly born as people. The Light, the Dark, and the Shadow. The Light is a healer and defender, one who chooses love over hate, even when things are hard. The Dark is a fighter and a killer, one who chooses hate over love, who does what has to be done despite feelings. And the Shadow is justice. You are the Light."

"Just because a flower grew when I touched it?" I ask scornfully.

"So if Jaina is the Light as you say she is," Liam begins, "does that mean she can heal people? Like... with her mind?"

Dragon nods.

"I tried that, remember?" I say, touching Dragon's shoulder. "You went through all these random steps with me and absolutely nothing happened."

"Clearly you didn't do it right," Dragon replies.

"Can we test this?" Liam asks. "Like, if I cut my finger a little bit—"

"Don't you dare cut your finger or you're healing it yourself," I snap. "I'm not going to perform little experiments for you. And you're absolutely crazy if you think I actually possess some freakish mind power."

Dragon's expression remains solemn. "Too many things have happened for this to be a coincidence. When we save your mother, she'll tell you."

"Oh, my mother is crazy too? I don't believe any of it."

"You believe in a long dead ghost that can hunt people down without being seen. You think you saw the Shadow Hunter. What makes this any different?" Dragon asks.

Liam looks at me. "He has a point, Jaina."

"Do you believes this, Liam?" I ask.

He shrugs. "I'm not sure."

"You will." Dragon glances back to the silverscreen. "Enough of this, we need to focus. If any of you want to be there when we rescue General Indera, you have to be prepared, and you'll have to attend the briefing."

"I'll be there." I stand and take a seat behind Liam, leaving Dragon alone on the floor.

I pull my legs up onto the chair and hold myself curled up in a little ball. Taking some deep, controlled breaths, I try to let everything sink in. The prophecy, the Dark, the Light, and the Shadow. None of it makes any sense. Maybe if he explained more I would understand. But all his riddles, the way he avoids answering me by changing the subject, how can I ever understand?

If he ever wants me to trust him, the lies must end.

"Incoming objects," Liam says. "They're not in the hyperfield."

Dragon moves into the seat next to me, behind Liam. "That might be them. Drop out of the field."

"And if it isn't?" Liam asks.

"They could be pirates but not the Alliance. Not this far out," Luci replies.

"I'll prepare the forward cannons just in case," Liam mutters. "Coming out of the hyperfield now." He presses a button then slowly decreases the speed. Space around us seems to warp and thicken. Silvery dots approach from far away.

When we're close enough, *The Justice* comes into view. There's a large ship to its left and another to its right, and hundreds more that range in all different types and sizes behind them.

Dragon points to the one on the right. "Shirez says that's your mother's ship. *The Unforgiven*. Best warship in the fleet."

The ship is larger than *The Justice* and darker. Like a stealth ship, like it was built for battle. "Is that an Alliance ship?" I ask.

He nods. "It was a long time ago."

I laugh gently in disbelief. "How the hell did she get her hands on an Alliance warship?"

"She used to be a soldier in the Alliance," Dragon says. "Someone high up in the IAA. The ship was hers. When she joined the Resistance, it was her gift to us."

"Incoming transmission," Liam says. "Should I open communication?"

"Yes," Dragon replies.

Liam presses a button. For a moment, there's only static.

"*Odyssey*, come in," Kavi's voice echoes through the transmitter. "*Odyssey*, is that you?"

Luci gives up her seat to Dragon so he can sit in the front. Dragon takes the chair and holds down the button to keep coms open. "We read you, *Justice*. This is *The Odyssey*. I repeat, this is *The Odyssey*."

"Thank the *stars* you're still alive!" she cries. "Is Jaina with you?"

"Of course," Dragon replies.

"Good. Commence landing sequence immediately. Shirez will want to see you right away. He's not in a good mood."

"Thanks for the warning, Kavi," Luci says into a secondary mic near her seat. "How are things going with the troops?"

"Everything's alright. They were getting anxious since you hadn't returned, and Jaina was missing."

"We'll see you soon," Luci replies.

"Over and out."

The com fades, and Dragon leans back in his seat. "Well, Shirez isn't happy."

"What a surprise," Luci mutters sarcastically.

"Shirez might not want any of us to be on General Indera's rescue mission." Dragon pinches the bridge of his nose and closes his eyes. "We have to be extremely careful if we want a part of the assignment."

"He can't exclude me from that mission," I interject. "I'm not a part of the Resistance. I will be there."

"I like your determination." Dragon stares out the viewport as we approach *The Justice*. "But I'm not sure if that'll work on him."

A light on the control panel flashes.

"Landing sequence commencing," the computer says.

Dragon sighs. "Here we go."

# CHAPTER NINETEEN

I never thought of Shirez as a scary person, but in the end, I don't know anyone anymore besides Liam. Dragon is still a mystery to me; it's like he's not even fully real in my head. Luci seems to be showing her true colors. I guess she always has. The only difference is that now I know she's part of the Resistance. I may not know what kind of person Shirez is at all. He's been Prince of Earth ever since my mother was put in prison, maybe even before that. How long has he been pretending to be part of the Alliance? How long has he been someone he's not?

Aboard *The Justice*, we approach a large door. By the tension radiating from Dragon and Luci, I decide I should probably be scared.

Dragon turns to Liam and I. "Both of you keep quiet, okay? Let Luci and I do the talking."

We nod together. Dragon hesitates before pressing a button on the control panel. The door seems to slide open in slow motion. It gives me a few more seconds of calm before the storm. Whatever the storm may be.

Shirez stands as we enter the small conference room. He looks anything but pleased. A shiver runs through my body. Shirez's gaze rests intensely on Dragon, his eyes are unemotional and as hard and frigid as stone.

"Close the door, Altair." Shirez looks to us. "Have a seat."

I want to say something. Apologize and get it over with. It's not like I have to mean it. Just saying it usually does the job. But by the angry, tense look on Shirez's face, it's clear he wants to have a long, painful chat.

The four of us sit in a straight line across from him, with Dragon directly across from him. Luci's beside Dragon, then Liam, and I'm last in line. I'm glad I'm farther away.

Shirez sighs. "Information about Amara Indera's prison was in the hands of Prince Tarin Sivva of Moris. Your mission was to retrieve that information quickly and decisively, without causing commotion, and yet your mission failed. Would you like to explain?"

Dragon's jaw twitches, and he knits his brow. "We didn't fail. We retrieved the information and a bit more with minimal casualties."

"Oh, really?" Shirez asks harshly. "I asked for a clean, quiet mission. Instead, the Alliance called an emergency meeting regarding your escape from the Crystal City, *and* in a recent government publication, it was exposed that a Resistance ship was traced from Keducia to Vera Kaas. Altair, *The Odyssey* is untraceable. Can you tell me what the *shaav* happened?"

Dragon looks from Shirez, down to the table. He flushes red but doesn't meet Shirez's cold gaze. "Sir, the plan was that we'd break into Sivva's house when he wasn't there. The bioscans didn't come up with anything, so we thought it was safe to enter. But when we went in, we were met by an assassin who got away before we could–"

"You were careless! How were you followed?" Shirez shoots back.

There's silence. Cold, aching silence. Honestly, none of us have a clue.

"Sir," I interject in the strongest voice I can muster, "the assassin in Sivva's apartment, we saw him on Keducia. He didn't follow us to Kashia. Somehow he knew. He attacked Liam in Sivva's place. He must have known exactly what we were after."

Shirez rubs his eyes. "Where were Altair and Luci when you retrieved the information?"

355

"They were keeping watch," Liam replies. "We hadn't expected anyone to be home, so Dragon and Luci were stationed outside to warn me if Sivva returned. The assassin arrived shortly after I finished the download. He wasn't there when I first entered."

Shirez turns back to Dragon. "I don't know what the hell happened on your mission, but it has caused chaos. The IA has a fleet commissioned to arrive at the prison within the next forty-eight hours."

"Sol Veya," Dragon says. "That's where they're being sent to. I transferred the information to *The Justice*'s main computer. Our pilots have already started adjusting courses."

"You're not off the hook," Shirez says. "I gave you strict orders *not* to bring Jaina along."

"It's her *mother*," Dragon shoots back. "She had a right to come."

"You disobeyed my orders *again*. You could have gotten her killed."

Dragon's fingers curl into a fist on the table. "But I didn't. She's fine!"

"You risked all of our lives and the fate of the galaxy for this," Shirez snaps.

Dragon stands with anger burning in his eyes. "If there was someone in a higher position and they told you to leave General Indera behind, would you?"

"That's different." Shirez glares at him. "Her life is in danger, and my mission is to protect her. You put Jaina in danger."

I'm on my feet before Dragon can say another word. "With all due respect, sir, I threatened to search for her on my own if he didn't take me with him. If he hadn't taken me, I could be back in the hands of the Alliance by now."

Shirez grits his teeth. "Take your seats."

Dragon and I exchange glances. As if in mutual agreement, we both lower ourselves back into our chairs.

Shirez turns to Luci. "Adelina, you were ordered to bring Jaina back. Why didn't you?"

"I told her I wasn't coming with her," I cut in. "Sir, I'm going to do anything and everything I can to save my mother. She sacrificed so much for me. I couldn't handle the guilt I'd feel if something happened without me even *trying* to save her."

Shirez runs his fingers through his salt and pepper hair. "There's nothing we can do about this now. What's done is done. But, Dragon, you can't think that just because of your position you can get away with things. There will not be a next time. Do I make myself clear?"

Dragon glares at him, his entire expression dark and clouded. "Understood, sir."

Shirez nods. "You're dismissed. Be down in the main hangar when the alarm sounds."

I stand when Luci and Dragon do, and we leave the room without looking back.

"That was intense," Liam whispers.

Dragon shakes his head, his expression strained. "It went better than I thought it would. Luci?"

"Yes?"

"Take Liam to the hangar," he orders. "Jet wanted to meet him."

Luci nods. She takes Liam by the arm. "Come on, let's go."

"Um, okay," he replies. "Jaina, I'll see you soon."

Luci pulls Liam away, and they break off into another corridor, leaving Dragon and I alone. I stand facing the way they left, missing Liam more than anything and wishing he had kissed me back on *The Odyssey*. I push the thought away the moment I think it. This isn't a time for romance or comfort. This is about finding my mother, the leader of the Resistance.

"Are you alright?" Dragon asks.

I shift my gaze to the ground. "Yes. Are you?"

"Everything is fine." He doesn't try to hide the annoyance and anger in his voice.

"Do you think he'll let us go?" I ask.

Dragon shakes his head. "We're going either way." He opens a door on the side of the hallway to reveal a small room filled with computers and three chairs. The screens of the computers provide the only illumination in the room. He falls into one of the chairs and moans as a computer lights up, demanding a password. I take the chair next to him. He types something in a few times. On the third try, he gets it right and the computer unlocks. It reveals files on officials, and the layouts of various Alliance buildings, the ones with strategic value I assume. He taps the screen and pulls up all the information on Sol Veya.

Finally, he looks down at the desk and exhales a long, unsteady breath. "He's my dad."

Everything stops. "What?" I ask.

"Shirez," he continues, his eyes slightly glazed over. "He's my father."

My jaw drops open. It feels like it's falling to the floor. No way. No. *Shaavez.* Way. "Stop screwing with me."

He looks me in the eyes. "Does it really surprise you?"

I feel like I'm choking on my breath, like someone slammed into me full force and knocked the air out of my lungs. "He's your *father?*"

Dragon nods carefully. "I thought you would've guessed by now…"

It's coming back to me. All of it. I don't know why I hadn't thought of it before, but it's all coming back to me now. Shirez always treated Dragon differently than anyone else, and he placed him as the team leader because Dragon is his *son.* He talks to him like a strict parent, and Dragon defies him like angry teenagers do in all the stories. And they make the same faces, too.

"I mean, you're both good at lying," I manage.

"I learned from the best." Dragon shakes his head. He leans back in his chair and stares at me. It doesn't feel weird or awkward, which surprises me a little.

I stare back at him. "What about your mother? Who was she?"

He shrugs. "I never knew her. She killed herself after I was born."

"I'm sorry."

He cuts me off. "It's okay. I don't know what I was missing. Having a mother."

"What was her name?" I ask.

"Nalia. Nalia Kasev Melohem. She cheated on Shirez often."

I struggle to breathe normally. My heart is racing in my chest as it all falls into place. "That's how you know your father. When I was arranged to marry Sean, he said your father would come pick you up during the summers. You went to the Uncharted Lands in the summer with Shirez. That's how you were in Virana. You're-You're *royalty*."

Dragon laughs. "Absolutely not. To be royalty in the Alliance, you have to be approved by the Emperor. Besides, I was meant to be on Virana."

I nod slowly. "Did you know my mother?"

"I know what Shirez told me about her, but he doesn't like to go into detail. I've seen pictures of her. She looks a lot like you."

I manage to smile a little bit. "I saw a picture of her on *The Odyssey*."

"She was beautiful," he says. "Like you."

I roll my eyes but warmth floods my cheeks. "Compliments will get you nowhere."

Dragon shrugs and shakes his head, but he refuses to meet my eyes. "Alright, I see how it is. I won't then."

I smile slyly. "Good, I don't want them."

"What if I mean it?"

He still doesn't look at me, but I wish he would. It would be a bit easier to read him if I could see into his eyes. "You'll need more than words to prove it," I reply.

Dragon laughs a little this time. "Very true."

I clear my throat and glance at the blue computer screen. "Tell me more about my mother."

He smiles sadly. "Shirez says she never forgot a face."

"Do you think she'll know who I am when she sees me?" I ask.

"She'll know the second we find her."

My pulse throbs in my throat. Anxiety starts to course through me. "What if she doesn't like who I've become?" My voice is softer and shakier than I intend it to be.

Dragon sighs. "I think she'll just be happy that you're alive." His eyes cloud with what looks to me like worry. "How are you feeling?"

"Afraid," I whisper. "Determined but definitely afraid."

"That's a good thing."

"Have you ever had to do this before? I mean any-thing like this at all?"

"Not like this," he replies carefully. "Never like this. In the summers after Shirez was done training teams for The Trials, we would disappear and join the Resistance. I would carry out smaller missions now and then, things to prepare for the role of commander. All of it was a test. Even The Trials."

A soft silence fills the room, pleasant and natural. Fulfilling, too, as more pieces of the puzzle fall into place.

"Does Shirez love her?" I ask.

Dragon takes a deep, uncomfortable breath. "I don't know. Maybe, but maybe it's just that they're friends. I really don't know. I haven't seen her in six-teen years. Back then, I didn't know what was going on between them. I was too young to understand. It'll be weird when she gets back. Shirez will want to spend time with her, and she'll want to spend time with you, so that leaves me alone, I guess."

"You won't be alone. Things are complicated. You've lied and tricked me and hurt me beyond any-thing words can describe, but that doesn't mean we can't be friends."

"You think *friends* is possible for us?" The look in his eyes softens a little. He's got a slight smile, like he's not sure if I'm crazy.

I smile gently in return. "I think it's worth a shot."

A siren-like noise screams above my head and I jump.

"There's the alarm." His face hardens once again, and a shadow passes over him. "We're approaching Sol Veya. Let's go save your mother."

"Listen up!" Dragon's voice echoes across the hangar. "I know you're all excited, but unless you want to end up dead or as an Alliance prisoner, pay attention!"

Laughter ripples through the soldiers around me. Dragon stands in the center, and I'm part of the circle. Kavi and Seth are here. I'm pretty sure I saw them holding hands when they walked in. I don't go up to them, since I'm not sure what to think of our friendship anymore.

"We've got thirty-seven people here, not including myself," Dragon says. "Team Cala, you've got six people with you, right?"

A Martian boy at the head of the group of six people nods. He looks familiar, not just in the sense that I think I've seen him, I *know* I've seen him. He's a little ways away from me. Maybe if I got a closer look…

"Good," Dragon says. "You're in charge of taking out communications inside the prison. You go in, set charges, and destroy it. Jet, you're in charge." Dragon turns to a larger group. "Team Nova, Lieutenant Luci

Adelina is your leader. You'll be clearing the perimeter.
When the air strike starts, that's when you make your
move. Do not take action any time before then." He
shifts his gaze to the largest group, containing about
twenty, maybe thirty people. "Team Comet will keep
in contact with the Resistance. You must not let any
IA reinforcements past you. Without you, we lose our
advantage. Now, because all communications will be
dead, you have been provided with an old fashioned
satellite to send messages to *The Unforgiven*. Apart
from your satellite, no other communication will take
place."

Luci steps forward. "Commander, how will we
know when to retreat?"

"I'll send up a blue flare in the northern part of
the valley. When you see it, you'll know we're safe. Any
more questions?"

Liam steps forward. "After we take out the communication tower, where do I meet you?"

Dragon nods. "I'll get to that in a moment. The
rest of team Cala, once you take out communications,
you join the Comets. There are too many guards for us
to hold off forever. If everything goes to plan, I should
be the last person out of there with General Indera.
Anything else?"

No one makes a sound.

"Good. I've sent maps of the prison to a silverscreen aboard each of your shuttles. It has an outline

of your mission and where you should be and when you should be there. The atmosphere down there is much thinner than anything you're used to, so make sure to take enough breath beads with you. Get to your ships. We'll leave in twenty minutes."

The group disperses and I move closer to Dragon. Liam hangs around the two of us and takes a seat on a crate of ammunition.

"Breath beads?" I ask Dragon quietly.

"You chew it and take a deep breath before you swallow. It coats your lungs with Aluuna oil that allows you to breathe on planets where you would normally suffocate. Each bead wears off after about an hour, so we have to take a few."

I nod nervously. "Alright. Who was the Martian?"

"Jeton. You met him in The Trials, I think. People call him Jet."

I wince as the memory resurfaces, my nervousness spiking a little. *He tried to kill me.*

Dragon turns to Liam and gestures for him to come closer.

Liam saunters in so that the three of us are standing in a triangle. "So what's the rest of it?"

Dragon looks from me to Liam. "We'll need your skill. So does team Cala. We're all landing a few kilometers away from the prison to avoid their scanners. Jaina and I will stick with Cala and Nova for a while until you're both dispatched on your missions. Once communications are out, you get the hell out of there. Jaina and I will be at the bridge. It's the only door they leave open, because no one knows about it besides the guards. You'll have to scale the bridge. When you make it to the top, we need you to open impossible doors. Without that, we'll never get to General Indera."

Liam nods. "I'll be there."

Dragon takes a deep breath. "You can still back out of this if you want."

"I'm sticking this out to the end," Liam replies sternly.

Dragon bows his head slightly, and Liam shows him the sloppiest salute I've ever seen, but the gesture is a good one. With that, Liam heads to his own ship with his designated team.

"So," I breathe. "I assume we're not taking *The Odyssey* since Shirez was so upset about us being tracked."

He smiles gently. "Liam had the cloaking device repaired. We'll be invisible."

I frown with suspicion. "Really?"

"He said if we're all escaping Sol Veya in *The Odyssey* he'd rather not be shot down." Dragon laughs, but his eyes darken. "Though I have a feeling it's more to protect you."

I tilt my face down so my hair hides the warmth in my cheeks.

Dragon leads me to the other side of the hangar where *The Odyssey* waits for us. He presses a few buttons on the outside, opening the ramp and airlock doors. We climb aboard the majestic ship and I realize how much it feels like home.

"You wanna be my co-pilot?" Dragon asks as he sits in the pilot's chair.

"I'd be honored." Smiling, I take the seat next to him and look out the viewport into the hangar. There are so many people. No one matches; there's no official uniform or attire. In the Alliance, everyone wears uniforms, and everyone has to dress to a certain code. Here, it's so colorful. I could almost call it *beautiful* if we weren't all marching into battle. Some wear expensive suits of armor. Others wear simple clothes that hardly have protection at all.

Dragon hands me the silverscreen. "Here you go." A small, holographic map of the prison floats above the silverscreen. He makes it a little bigger so I can see the entire layout of the place.

"It's huge." I gasp. "How many prisoners?"

"We can only guess. Maybe hundreds. The place is built like a barracks, so it's assumed the guards vastly outnumber the inmates.

"How are we going to get her out?" I ask.

Studying the hologram, it becomes clear that the prison is in the center of a valley. Its cubic shape gives it a large roof, allowing guards see anything or anyone approaching. Little red markings here and there all over the map reveal strategic lookout points and small stations near the prison where guards patrol more frequently.

"As I said, we'll stick with Nova and Cala until both are dispatched on their missions."

"Why are we taking different transports?" I ask.

"The truth is, they'll probably leave before we get out," he replies. "More likely than not, they'll presume we're dead and will have to leave. Going inside is basically a suicide mission. That's why it's me, you and Liam."

"If anyone can survive, it's us."

He laughs. "You ready?"

I nod. "Absolutely."

"We're going to win this, Jaina," he says reassuringly. He presses a few buttons on the control panel.

I smile at him nervously. "Don't get too confident."

"If you're truly the Light, we'll win," he says, smiling wryly back at me.

The good feeling starts to fade. "That's comforting."

Dragon points to an area on the holographic map a few kilometers away from the prison, deep in the heart of the valley. "Our ships will land about here," he says. "We'll be safe from detection. According to the files we extracted, there has only been one major breakout attempt since the prison was built, and it failed. As long as we can get there before the Alliance

Fleet does, we should be fine. So, we'll land *here* then begin the journey to the prison. It's cooler down there, so you'll want a coat. We'll spend the night in the valley then attack before dawn. Once Nova and Cala are dispatched, we'll head in. We'll move around to this side of the prison. There's a single bridge running from the prison and into the wall of the valley. It's a supply line."

"This is where we meet Liam?"

"Yes. It's the one place that the gates are always open. Of course, the doors beyond that are locked, so that's where Liam's skill comes in."

"And after that?" I ask.

"We get your mother."

"Departure in T-minus three minutes," says a computerized voice over the loudspeaker.

Dragon presses a button to close the ramp and another to activate the engines. They rumble as they come to life, sending tiny vibrations throughout the ship.

"Have you co-piloted before?" he asks.

I shake my head.

"All you need to know is that if anything happens to me, there's a second set of identical controls on your side. They only become active if you press this button." He points to a dark orange button in the center of the dashboard. "When you press this, you're captain. Other than that, you're in control of the weapons system, which is there." He points to the upper half of my side of the panel. "These are plasma cannons, these are forward automatic turrets, and these are the back ones. Got it?"

"I'm ready to go."

My half of the control panel lights up.

"Departure in T-minus one minute," the computer echoes.

"We're going to be okay," he says.

"I know." My voice comes out prickly. I just want to get this over with. My head is swimming, almost drowning in thoughts and worries while my stomach performs backflips.

"All ships depart," the computer finally orders.

Dragon lifts the ship into the air and out of the hangar. Space engulfs us, and pinpoints of light break up the vast darkness. The planet Sol Veya is already huge in the viewport.

My heel is thumping on the floor. I notice my movement, but don't do anything to stop myself. Maybe it'll help my nerves.

Dragon leads the Nova, Cala, and Comet teams down to the surface with us. The ride into the atmosphere is rough, which is saying a lot because *The Odyssey* has generally been smooth except during our free fall into Vera Kaas.

"What if she's crazy?" I ask suddenly. "My mom. What if she's gone crazy? Prison can do that to people."

He sighs. "If your mother has gone crazy, then there isn't hope for any of us. She had such a strong will. She was a legend. Her imprisonment made her even more so. It showed the people that she was willing to do whatever she could to save the ones she loved, and that she wouldn't give up. If the Alliance has broken the Phoenix, they might as well break the rest of us."

"You talk about her like she was a god."

"Not a god, Jaina. Gods are like dictators, demanding blind trust, belief, and sacrifice with little proof they deserve it. The Phoenix was nothing of the sort. She didn't ask people to trust her, believe in her, or to make sacrifices. Her actions made you trust and believe. And she sacrificed everything to keep you and the rest of us alive." Dragon gazes back at the planet's surface, slowly approaching us. He pulls up so we're not angled to crash into the yellow grassy plain beneath us.

The sun is already setting outside. Dragon said it's supposed to be cold here, but it looks more like it'll be dreadfully hot. So far, Sol Veya is mostly flat ground with an occasional hill here and there. The lack of physical features makes passing over the valley so much more incredible. It's much longer than it is wide, and it resembles a horrific scar in the face of the earth. Even from our altitude, it looks huge.

"Is that it?" I ask.

"Yep. The prison is three klicks north of our landing position." He brings the ship down deep into the heart of the valley and sets it in the tall, golden-brown grass. "Well, it's been uneventful so far," he says smiling a little. He stands once he shuts down *The Odyssey,* pulls a crème-colored jacket out of a compartment to his left, and hands it to me. "For the cold, and for blending in. Unfortunately we're short on funding, so we can't afford one for everyone. The Resistance can only supply weapons and fuel hatred for the IA."

"Isn't that kind of what the Alliance does to their citizens?" I take the jacket and slip it on. It's warm and fuzzy on the inside, and the hood in the back is lined with expensive maliz fur. "They just make people hate and fear everyone else who thinks differently."

Dragon cocks his head a little. "Good point, but the Alliance gains power through lies."

I zip up the jacket. "It seems like both the Resistance and the Alliance tell one-sided truths to their people about each other. You both lie."

"Are you on their side now?" He spits back.

I shake my head quickly as my pulse speeds up. "No, I didn't mean that at all. I was just saying what I thought." I take a deep breath. "Where'd you get the jacket from?" I ask, trying to change the subject.

"It belonged to my mother." Dragon's voice is a bit softer this time, thank the stars. "Just try not to get plasma burns all over it."

"I'll do my best," I say, hoping he doesn't make any more comments about our previous conversation. "Can we go outside now?"

"Wait." Dragon grabs my arm. "Breath beads."

"Right."

He lets go of my arm, reaches into another compartment, pulls out two small boxes, and opens them both. The boxes contain these beautiful little pearly white spheres that look like they should be jewels. "Take one, chew, and breathe in through your mouth before you swallow."

I take one and I slowly place one of the beads on my tongue and I let my teeth sink in. There's no flavor, just a sudden coolness, like air is filling my mouth without having to breathe. I inhale until my lungs feel like they're about to burst. The coolness fills my lungs, and I start to choke and cough. Tears well in my eyes, and I swallow the remains of the bead. Once it's down, the choking stops, and I hold my hand to my throat, slightly shocked.

"Was that supposed to happen?" My voice is strained and weak.

"You're supposed to swallow it faster, but it tends to do that. You okay?" Dragon takes both small boxes of breath beads and puts them in his coat pocket.

"I am now." My breath feels weird in my lungs, like something isn't quite right.

"Now we're ready to go."

Dragon opens the airlock doors, and we walk down the ramp. A cool breeze floats inside the shuttle. Never mind what I thought about it looking warm outside. I step into the open, and a shiver courses through my body. The golden grass measures up to my chest. A few of the taller grasses are about Dragon's height. At least this gives us good cover.

A few clouds dot the horizon. Three black and silvery objects descend from space and land softly in the grass around us. The ship nearest us opens, and Liam steps out with Jeton and his crew behind him.

Liam and Jeton approach us. "We're here for the night, correct?" Jeton asks, his shimmery gold eyes on Dragon.

"Yes. The nights are cold, and we can't risk our lives or our strength before we see battle. Keep the heat on in your ships, and rest. We'll begin tomorrow at 0300 hours, so get to sleep as soon as you can," Dragon replies.

Liam stands straighter and stronger than I've ever seen him before. His expression is gentle, but his eyes are solemn and determined. Liam bows his head slightly then joins a small group of men a few meters away, leaving Dragon, Jeton and I alone. I'm not really sure what I should do. Pretend I don't recognize him?

Jeton grins "Nice to see you again." He reaches out to shake my hand.

I glance at Dragon, trying to find an answer. "It's, um…nice to see you again, too."

Jeton nods appreciatively, I think. After a bit of an awkward pause, he looks at Dragon. "Commander, how long is a day?"

"Thirty," Dragon replies. "It's hour twenty-five right now."

"Thank you, sir," Jeton says, smiling again. He turns to me. "Commander Indera, I would like to apologize for my behavior during The Trials. I'm glad you made it out safely."

His politeness is stunning compared to what I knew of him before. "It's fine, really." I laugh nervously. "And I'm not a commander. Just call me Jaina."

"Well, Jaina, good luck tomorrow." He turns to leave us.

I wait until he's far enough away and ushering others back into their ships before turning to Dragon. "Why did he call me *commander*?" I ask.

Dragon smiles a bit sadly. "They all look up to you. You're a leader to them. They think you're on our side."

I cock my head, feeling a pinch of annoyance. "What's that supposed to mean?"

He crosses his arms. "You made it clear that you don't want to be a part of the Resistance."

"I didn't say that. I don't want to fight anymore and I said I'm not sure. I'm not eager to join the fight."

Dragon gently bobs his head, nodding slowly. "That's alright." He's standing in the tall grass, and I hear him breathing. "We should check out the area."

"I thought we were supposed to be going to bed."

"Yes, but we should also scout out the area. It's to protect the troops," he adds.

"If you insist." I sigh. Something tells me that it really isn't about the troops or scouting the area. More like, maybe he wants to spend some time with me outside. In this beautiful valley that could turn into a bloodbath tomorrow.

"You look suspicious," Dragon says. "Don't you trust me?"

I cough out a laugh as we begin walking together through the tall grass. "You want the long answer or the short one?"

Dragon rolls his eyes. "Touché. I guess I walked into that one." His expression becomes more serious, even a bit sorrowful. He takes a breath, like he's going to say something, but he doesn't. Maybe he thinks I should've forgiven him by now.

I should pull back and stop him. We really will need our rest, even though the days are longer here. But for whatever reason, I don't.

The valley seems to close in as darkness tightens its grip on the land. The cool frosty air on my face makes my cheeks and nose freeze, but I hardly notice.

"You okay?" Dragon asks after a moment.

"Are you?"

"I'll be fine," he says a little too quickly for it to be sincere.

"Do you wanna talk about it?"

He shakes his head. "It's a lot."

"I can handle a lot," I reply carefully. "Is it about the whole prophecy thing?"

He remains silent. The valley grows darker with each passing minute, and one by one, the stars appear in the sky. A chilly eastern breeze floats over us, as if urging us west to the prison, like it's pushing us to my mother.

"I don't know what happens when this is over," Dragon says finally. "A lot will be revealed, a lot of things I'm not looking forward to."

"Things about yourself?" I ask.

Dragon nods. "Yes."

"In The Trials," I begin, "you told me you had done terrible things."

"I have." There is no emotion in his voice. "I've hurt more people than I've ever helped."

There's a long pause. His words about the prophecy surface again in my head like waves. It all hits me at once.

"You think you represent the Dark," I say very softly. As the words come out, I shiver. The cold night air is getting to me.

Dragon inhales sharply.

"Why?" I ask.

He hesitates. "I told you that the Dark is a fighter. The Dark chooses hate over love, logic over emotion. I do what I have to do despite how I feel. No matter how many people it hurts. I've always been like this."

"No you haven't. You haven't always been like that. You were always sweet to me, and you protected me when we were young."

Dragon takes a deep breath. It's dark now, but I can see his hand tremble slightly. Maybe he's just shivering. "You're the only one I haven't completely screwed over."

I can't help smirking. "I might have to disagree."

He looks at me with the most depressing sad smile I've ever seen. "At least you have the intelligence to keep yourself emotionally distanced from me."

"It hasn't been very hard after what you did, but like I said, it would be nice if we could be friends."

"That's what I'm trying to say though." He stops walking and faces me. "Jaina, if you're the Light, then just being friends with me could destroy you."

My face tightens. "Let's just say this prophecy *is* true. The Light is supposed to heal, and love, and be kind." I take a deep breath. "And if you are the Dark, that means that your only salvation is finding the Light."

"I wish it were that simple."

"Why isn't it that simple?" I ask, my voice growing a bit harsher. I can see my breath in the light of the stars.

He runs his fingers through his hair. "Every time I try to do good, it turns out all wrong."

I touch his arm. "That isn't darkness. That's being human."

"Azad's sister is dead because of me," he says darkly.

"I'll be the judge of that." I cross my arms over my chest and cock my head. "Tell me what happened."

Dragon shakes his head. "I've put it out of my mind."

"Clearly you haven't. Azad said you killed her..."

He takes a deep, painful breath. "I did. It was an accident, but I killed her." He's looking down, yet he's not focused on the ground. It's more like he's looking through the ground, through the core of Sol Veya and into the stars on the other side. "Rasha Viraak will never breathe again. She will never have another heartbeat. She will never smile or laugh. She'll never fall in love again, or watch another sunrise or sunset. Because I was careless."

"How did it happen?" I keep my voice soft.

His body seems to stiffen, and his eyes go cold as they meet mine. "I'm not talking about this anymore. The point is, I am The Dark."

My fingers are numb, and I rub my hands together to bring some warmth back into them. Dragon turns forward and continues walking. I follow him through the tall, golden grass until we reach the small clearing where we landed our ships.

He keeps his eyes on the ground. "You know I get the dreams, too."

I don't look at him either. "Do they scare you?"

He nods. "Every time." Dragon takes a step forward then gazes up at the stars. "If you try and tell yourself that the visions—or dreams—aren't some sort of warning, if you try to deny their reality, they'll do something to prove you wrong."

"The cut on my hand..." I take a shaky breath.

"The dreams are warnings," he says. "I've awakened with cuts and scratches, even a stab wound once."

"The dream *stabbed* you?"

He finally looks at me. "It healed within about twenty minutes. There's not even a scar."

I meet his intense gaze. "Can you stop them from hurting you?"

He nods. "Just accept that it is its own reality. That it's a warning."

I look down at my left hand where Azad cut me in my dream, where I had a gash when I woke up. The pink line is gone now. No scar. "I dread sleeping now."

Dragon takes a deep breath. "Speaking of, we should rest."

I choke out a laugh. "Comforting."

He leads me back into *The Odyssey,* closing the ramp and airlock doors behind us. The warmth inside floods my senses.

"Dragon?"

He turns to me. "Yes?"

"I'm afraid of dreaming again." I keep my eyes on the ground.

Dragon nods slowly as I glance up at him. "I know," he pauses. "Do you think…"

"What?"

He sighs anxiously. "There's an extra bed in your room. If it makes you more comfortable, I could sleep by you. Not *by* you, but you know, in the other bed."

Warmth floods my cheeks.

His cheeks redden. "If that's weird–"

"No, it might help." I smile gently at him.

I open my cabin door and walk into my room. He presses a button to close the door behind us. I quickly lie down in my bed on the left side of the room, and he lies down on his after turning out the lights. I don't bother taking off my jacket. My shivering hasn't stopped yet, and I'd feel weird taking anything off while I'm alone in a room in a bed next to Dragon.

"Dragon," I start, my voice echoing in the darkness. "Are you sure they won't detect us out here?"

"I'm sure. Get some rest Jaina."

"Goodnight, Dragon."

"Goodnight."

I close my eyes and fall into the deepest sleep.

# CHAPTER TWENTY

"Jaina, wake up." Dragon's gentle voice brings me out of the murky depths of sleep. "Wake up."

I open my eyes sleepily. Dragon looms over me, his hand on my arm still shaking the last bit of sleep from my tired body.

"What time is it?" I ask slowly as I force myself to sit up.

"It's 0300 hours. I already gave the order for team Nova to move in with Cala. Once Nova is in position, they'll give the signal, and then it's time for us to go."

I nod slowly, still a bit out of it, and rub my eyes.

"Did you rest well?" He asks.

I don't remember any dreams or waking up in the middle of the night terrified, and I smile. "Nothing. No bad dreams. I slept really well I think. You?"

He smiles too. "Me too. No dreams."

Something beeps in the other room. Dragon stands and heads for the door.

"What's that?" I ask, my heart beating a bit faster now. Every tired part of me comes to life.

"It might be the signal. Could be a transmission, too."

"You think they could have cleared the perimeter already?"

"It's possible." With that, he's out the door.

I get out of bed. A slow wave of fear courses through my veins as reality washes over me. We're about to break into a prison from which we may never escape.

Taking a deep breath, I walk out of the room to find Dragon sitting in the pilot's chair, issuing orders into a com. Or rather, taking orders.

"Yes. Yes, sir. I understand. Over and out," he says.

"What is it?"

He turns to me. "Shirez. He said we should get moving immediately."

"How are the other teams?"

"Liam's about to cut communication. An Alliance fleet is coming out of the hyperfield, but they're still far off so we have time. Our fleet is headed to the other side of Sol Veya so that the Alliance can't track us. We have to move quickly and get inside before the Alliance sends reinforcements." He stands, straps a holster belt around his waist, and attaches two 75 caliber stealth pistols, his scimitar, a dagger, a stun pistol, and a poison dart gun. Then he slings a silenced DE-90 assault rifle over his shoulder. He hands me another holster belt with the same array of weapons. "Here, take these."

I attach my scimitar to the holster belt. "Can I have one of those?" I gesture to the DE-90.

Dragon raises an eyebrow. "You know how to use it?"

I choke out a laugh. "Turn off the safety, point and shoot."

His face relaxes but his eyes seem annoyed as he hands an extra DE-90 to me. "Strap it to your back."

I nod appreciatively. When he pushes the gun into my hands, my body tightens as I try to compensate for the weight of it. With a jolt of strength I lift the weapon over my head and strap it onto my back.

"Come on. We have to move along the wall of the valley until we reach the supply line. We'll scale the bridge, and hopefully Liam will be there on time. Make sure your weapons are silenced. We can't let anyone know we're inside."

"With the battle outside, won't they be expecting us?" I ask.

He shakes his head. "They're arrogant and overconfident. If we had an entire army here, they might be on higher alert, but for three people to make it past their defenses and break out with our leader? They assume it's impossible, that it wouldn't even be attempted."

Dragon and I take another breath bead. The sensation is just as strange as before. Dragon presses a button on *The Odyssey*'s control panel to open the airlock doors and the ramp. He sets a timer so both will close behind us, and we rush out into the frigid morning air.

The sun hasn't risen yet. It'll be a few hours until sunrise. Stars glimmer in the sky, and looking up at them, I feel so terribly small.

We walk quickly side by side through the thick grass toward the prison. Even in the darkness, I can see it. The building is black, so black that it makes the night look bright. Spires rise into the sky as lookout posts.

My breath fogs in front of me, and my fingers are starting to go numb. We continue through the field for about an hour. After some time, Dragon suggests we take another breath bead so that we don't start choking on the thinner atmosphere. Something howls in the distance, and a moon appears above the valley. Silvery light fills the space like the ghost of a river that once cut this scar into the land. It's haunting. The ground makes tiny crunching noises under my feet, like I'm stepping on fine crystals of glass. A thin layer of frost covers the earth like a cage, like a prison, trapping new growth under the earth, keeping everything cold.

"Get down," Dragon orders suddenly.

I do as he says, and he crouches with me.

"Don't make any sudden movements," he whispers. "We're close enough for their snipers to be able to find us."

"How much farther?" I ask quietly.

"Just over two hundred meters. This is the hard part."

I close my eyes a moment, adrenaline coursing through my veins. What if we go in and never come out?

"Hey." He kneels beside me on the frosty ground and takes my cold hands in his. His are only a little warmer than my own. My teeth start to chatter. He brings me closer to him. "We're going to make it."

"For all you know, we could be dead by the time we reach the prison."

"Don't talk like that," he says sternly. "Have faith."

The freezing air scrapes at my lungs as I follow him farther through the grass. The guards on the spiral towers scan the area with spotlights, searching for intruders or escapees, I'm not sure.

"Stay out of the lights," Dragon whispers. "If one comes near us, don't move and keep your head down."

I can't muster the strength to say anything, but I nod.

We move stealthily, trying to make as little disruptions in the grass as we can. Luckily, the wind is on our side, flowing in from the east, moving the grass with us. I'm grateful for that cover.

One of the spotlights trails toward us. This isn't good. The frozen morning air breathes over my face, and I shiver. I struggle to keep myself from bolting toward the wall of the prison, the only place where the lights can't reach.

The spotlight gets closer to shining on us. My lungs draw air in and out faster than I'm supposed to. Blood pounds in my ears like battle drums.

"We should move," I whisper to Dragon. I look to my left, but he isn't there. Panic floods me, washing over me like cold water.

The spotlight stops, a mere two meters to my right. A red light flashes on top of the prison, and the screaming wail of an alarm sounds, shattering the air like glass. Guards begin shouting as the other two spotlights shine on the area near me.

They found him.

They found us.

The alarm is deafening in my ears. Do I run to Dragon? Or do I continue this mission without him?

"This way," Dragon's voice says to me. Somehow, his voice comes from the left. "Slowly."

I'm shaking uncontrollably. The sound of the alarm seems to draw my sanity away from me, and I struggle to hold onto it. I want to scream.

"*Jaina*," Dragon says again.

I slowly move to my left while trying not to cause too much of a disturbance in the tall grasses. Finally, I see him. He takes my hand.

"What's going on?" I ask over the loud siren.

"I don't know," he says, "but I'd rather not find out."

A buzzing sound whirrs in the air. A bolt of plasma rains down from the prison and strikes the ground next to me. I jolt farther to the left, nearly knocking Dragon over.

"We have to run." Panic floods me as I speak. "We have to go now, they know we're here, they–"

"Stop." Dragon looks past me.

I follow his gaze. There is motion to my right. Not the soft motion of the wind caressing the tall grasses. This is the motion of someone- or something- in terror, trying to get away. Another bolt of plasma rains down, but this time the bolt lands within the spotlight.

There's a piercing scream, a wail of pain that cuts through the alarm. The noises that follow sound like a dying animal. Shrieks fill the air. After a moment, I realize the animal-like screams are forming words.

"No!" it cries. "No, my gods no, don't let them take me!"

The voice is crazed. Horrified. It raises the hairs on my neck and arms.

Shouting echoes from the top of the guard tower.

"Jaina," Dragon whispers. "We have to get out of here."

He gives me that look. The look that says, *Jaina, ignore this or we will die.* But I can't bring myself to move.

Whoever is over there, he or she is in pain. We should do something, we *have* to do something. Drawn to the cries of pain, I inch closer to the spotlight. I need the screaming to stop.

The sound of the alarm rings distantly in my ears, and I hear the clanking of armored guards. They're getting close. Before Dragon can pull me away, I dash toward the light and peer through a few stalks of grass.

A man lies motionless on the ground, his clothes torn and dirty. His face is covered in grime and sweat. He moans, and my gaze rests on the plasma burn on his chest. His hands quiver, from old age or shock, I don't know. Maybe both. His stunning gray eyes lock with mine.

I should save him. We have the ability to save him, we have to help him.

His eyes widen, and fear courses through my blood. He's going to call out and warn everyone that the prison is being attacked.

"Go," he moans softly.

His voice shocks me. I can't move. I can hardly breathe. I try to speak, yet no sound escapes my throat.

"*Go!*" he shouts.

Dragon grabs my arm. "Jaina, we have to go *now!*"

I snap out of my daze. The guards are coming for the man, not for us.

"We can't just leave him," I say.

Dragon looks at me painfully. "We have to."

I try to pull back, but Dragon yanks me into motion. His hand is clamped around my wrist, and he doesn't let go. We don't stop running until we reach the rocky wall of the valley. He pushes me against the wall and holds me there.

"*Shaav*, Jaina, what were you thinking? You could've gotten us killed!"

I stare back at the spotlight in the golden grass. Guards stand around the man. I'd like to think they're helping him, that he'll be alright, and they will nurse him back to health. But I know the Alliance. He was confined here for a reason, and that reason was to die.

"Dragon, we left him," I reply angrily. "We could have carried him. We could've—"

"He would have slowed us down," he snaps. "We would have been caught. This is war. He gave us an opportunity. Because they caught him, we were able to get away."

The guards still stand in the spotlight. Another scream rings across the valley. A gun fires.

I flinch.

Dragon's gaze falls to the ground. He takes a deep breath then slowly looks back to me. "It's the best fate he could have asked for. Death doesn't normally come quick with the IA."

"We let him die," I murmur.

Dragon's eyes remain strong, and his expression stern. "If we hadn't, we'd be over there lying dead next

to him. We couldn't have stopped it. It's not our fault."
Dragon pulls back and releases me. "I'm going to see if the coms are down. When they go out, that's our signal." He turns away and pulls out a silverscreen.

"Do you think Liam is inside yet?" My voice is soft.

"He should be on his way here. The alarm was probably triggered by his team."

My insides twist. "Why isn't he here yet?"

Dragon sighs peacefully. "He's a smart man. He'll be fine."

The sound of the alarm echoes throughout the valley. It sends chills through my body. Every blood vessel pulses with adrenaline and anxiety. Why isn't Liam here yet? I start biting my fingernails. This isn't good, this really can't be good.

Something rustles in the grass. A figure moves in the darkness toward us, making a dangerously obvious disruption to the wind pattern across the field.

*Let it be Liam. By the stars, let it be Liam, safe and unharmed.*

All my muscles tense. What if it isn't Liam?

Dragon raises his hand slightly and motions for me to get down. My body follows his order without even thinking about it. He gets down, too, and points his DE-90 toward the oncoming target.

The dark figure moves cautiously closer then stops. "I am an idiot. You guys hear that? I said it. Now please don't shoot," whispers the figure.

I look at Dragon, unable to stop the confusion ricocheting through my brain.

Dragon smiles and stands. "You made it."

Relief floods my body. I run over to Liam, and finally, he isn't a dark figure anymore. The small strands of his hair twist in the wind as he approaches.

"Thank the stars you're alright," I say quietly. "What was the whole *I'm an idiot* thing?"

Liam shakes his head. "Dragon made that be my codeword to rendezvous with you. Figured no one in the Alliance would dare to admit it." He glances at Dragon. "Or maybe he just wanted to hear me say that."

"What took you so long?" Dragon asks.

"We set off the alarm. They had their communication unit rigged so that if someone hacked in, the alarm would sound. Guards showed up, but we got out in time."

Dragon nods. "*Shaav.* We'll be okay but our troops outside the prison will have a harder time. We have to hurry before the Alliance sends down reinforcements."

"We cut off communication," I reply. "Why would they send–"

"They'll try to contact the base," Liam says. "When the fleet doesn't get a response, they'll know something is wrong. This could turn into a full scale attack."

My breath trembles as I nod. "Let's go." The sooner we get this mission over with, the better. I can't stand the churning in my stomach.

Dragon looks up at the incredibly tall bridge hovering over us. "You guys ready for some climbing?"

I reach upward to grab the next bar and close my fingers around the icy metal. If I look down, I know I'll freeze up and fall. The more I think about looking down, the more I have the urge to. But I refuse.

"Liam, Dragon, are you alright?" I ask quietly. I feel the soft vibrations of their ascent on the metal bars beneath me. They're close.

"We're fine. Just keep going," Dragon replies.

"How much farther?" Liam asks.

I glance up to the top of the bridge. "Only a meter or two."

By the stars, we must move quickly, only it sounds like a horrible idea as I climb the frost-covered supports of a bridge towering high above the ground.

The cold metal burns my skin. My hands beg me to let go, but I hold on tight.

"*Shaav*," Liam curses.

My heart jumps. Instinct makes me look down at him, hoping more than anything he's not going to fall. My head spins. The ground is so far away. "What's wrong?"

Liam glances up at me worriedly. "Nothing. Keep moving."

I'm not sure whether to believe him or not, since he sounded in pain. For the time being, I let it go so I can focus. My muscles burn from climbing. Despite the cold numbness in my hands, the rest of my body is drenched in sweat. The DE-90 strapped to my back pulls me down, whispering to me to let go. I force myself to push on, keeping a steady rhythm in my head.

Reach. Grab. Breathe. *It's okay.*

Reach. Grab. Breathe. *Almost there.*

Reach. Grab. Breathe. *One more bar.*

My hand reaches up, and I press my palm onto the comforting, flat surface of the top of the bridge. With a final burst of strength, I pull myself over the ledge and let myself lie there for a moment on my stomach in the darkness under the stars.

As an afterthought, I twist myself around so I'm facing the ledge and reach down to help Liam up. He takes my hand and sighs with relief when I help him onto the bridge. Dragon manages just fine on his own.

"Hey," someone calls.

I automatically grab my stun pistol.

"Hey, you!" the guard calls again. "Freeze!"

The guard rushes toward me. I take aim and fire. He falls to the ground and doesn't move. The muffled sound of the silenced shot fades under the wail of the siren.

Another guard raises his weapon, but a bolt of light rockets toward him and hits him squarely in the forehead. He falls backward to the ground with a soft thud and then a quiet *crack.*

I look back at Dragon. His gun is remains pointed at the man, as if he expects the guard to sit up and try to shoot. He has a dark look in his eyes as he approaches the guard I stunned. Without a second thought, he points his silenced weapon down at him, and before I have a chance to interfere, he fires into his skull.

My stomach knots. "No! Dragon, why?"

"Jaina, shh…" Liam breathes.

Dragon looks back at me, slightly perplexed. "You stunned him. He would have been awake within half an hour. He would have alerted other guards to our position of entry, and we cannot have that. This is war."

"That was not an act of war." My voice waivers with anger. "That was murder. He was defenseless. That was unfair and wrong."

"Now is not the time to debate right and wrong," he snaps. "We have a mission, and we must take every precaution."

I push down the horror and moral pain coursing through my veins. There is *always* time to debate right and wrong. Doesn't that weigh on his soul?

"Jaina, take off your coat," Dragon says. "We don't need to blend in with the grasses, and the fabric restricts some movement. We can't risk that." He takes off his jacket and tosses it over the bridge. It lands softly in the grass below.

Despite my anger, I follow orders and unzip my jacket. None of my weapons come loose from my belt, but I have to adjust my DE-90 strapped to my back to remove the coat. Once I've escaped from its warm embrace, I throw mine over the edge as well.

"Liam," Dragon says in a commanding voice, "get to work on the door."

Liam approaches the large metal door in front of us. There's a small silverscreen built into the side of the hexagon shaped doorway. He takes a small device out of his pocket and holds it up to the silverscreen.

He hasn't said a word since we reached the top of the bridge. I turn away from the door and step toward the lifeless form of the guard Dragon murdered. I crouch down next to him, studying him. His face is pale as death wraps its cold arms around him. Clues of his former life remain. His grey eyes are locked forever in a moment of fear and determination. His thick lips are slightly parted, and a soft trickle of blood stains his forehead.

My head spins, and I'm afraid I might topple over. I wonder if he had a girlfriend. Or maybe a wife. What if he had children? Alliance families aren't given much money if they don't live in the Crystal City. What if he was the only support for his family? What if they starve now that he's not here to provide for them?

"Forgive me." My fingers touch his eyelids, and I gently press them closed. "Peace be with you, my friend." The words that leave my lips surprise me. I'm not sure where they come from, but the words feel right.

Footsteps behind me.

"Jaina, what's wrong?" Dragon asks.

"You wouldn't understand." I have to grit my teeth to stop myself from saying anything more. Without another word, I walk away from the dead man.

Dragon moves to stand next to me as we wait for Liam to do his job. He takes a deep breath. "Your mother won't be strong enough to escape this way, down the bridge. She's been here so long that she might not have much strength left."

My soul seems to grow heavier in my body. What if we get to her cell and she's too weak to leave?

I turn to Dragon and decide to change the subject. "Why did he tell me to go?" I ask myself more than Dragon. "Why would he say that?"

He shrugs. "We'll never know."

A chill runs through me. "It was like he recognized me," I whisper.

His gaze falters from the hexagon door. "What do you mean?"

"He looked at me like," I hesitate. "Like he knew who I was."

Dragon's face turns a shade paler. "If the guards followed him, he could've told them we were near. It could've been a setup."

My blood boils under my skin, and my face grows warm despite the cold. "He told me to *go*, Dragon. If it was a setup, I think he would've begged us to stay and save him."

"What if it was all planned out?" Dragon ponders. "What if the Alliance knew we were here, and they sent that man out to locate us?"

I scoff in disgust. "Dragon, they shot him!"

"I got it," Liam says.

A light turns green, and the doors hiss open, revealing a hall shaped like a pentagon. The artificial lights inside are a sickly yellow-green.

"Thank you, Liam," I breathe nervously.

Dragon and Liam step in front of me, their weapons at the ready. I remove my gun from my holster belt and move down the hall after them. We approach a corner, and my heartbeat doubles in speed. Dragon peers around the wall and then jumps into the new hallway, searching for a target.

"Coast is clear." He motions for us to follow, then reaches into his holster belt and produces a small silverscreen. "Take it," he says, handing it to me. "You tell us where to go. Stay behind us. Whatever happens, you need to survive."

"It feels good to be needed," I mutter. I turn on the silverscreen, and a map of the prison appears. Locating the large bridge is easy, and I follow the path to the hall we're currently in. There's a red dot near the center of the map marking our destination.

"We have a long way," Liam breathes.

We approach the end of another hall.

"Which way?" Dragon asks.

I study the map with careful precision. I can't risk making a simple mistake. "Right. We go right. At the next one, we go left."

"Are you sure?"

I take a deep, angry breath. "Are you doubting me?"

Dragon shrugs. "Should I?"

"I trust you," Liam says. "Light the way."

His confidence in me makes my cheeks turn warm.

"Right," I repeat.

The metal floors and walls are all a deep, dark gray. Even though the electric lights above my head are bright, it's not nearly enough to light up the room. The entire atmosphere of the place creeps me out. The hairs on my skin stand on end. I feel distant, like this is all a dream, like I'm not really here.

I glance back at the map. We're in the living quarters for the guards.

"We need to get down to the prison level," I whisper. "She's ten levels below us."

"Do you see a staircase or an elevator?" Liam asks.

I zoom in to our position. "There's an elevator in the next hallway to the left."

Dragon nods. "Got it."

We reach the end of the hallway and turn to the left. Why are the halls are so empty? Maybe they're too busy defending the fortress from the Resistance outside. Shirez's reinforcements must be wreaking havoc on the place.

"Is this it?" Liam stands in front of a large door.

"Yep," I reply. "This is it."

Dragon cautiously moves to press the button on the side of the door, but stops at the last moment and looks to me.

"Why are you hesitating?" I ask. Only now do I realize the severe nervousness pressing down into my chest.

He takes a deep breath. "Get in position. Who knows what's beyond this door."

"I'll open the door, and you get your weapons ready," I respond. "You might have better aim than I do."

Liam raises an eyebrow. "We *do* have better aim than you."

I shake my head. "Depends on the situation."

Liam takes aim at the door along with Dragon. Without any further hesitation, I press the button. The doors slowly open, and the sound of two gunshots echo through the room.

I peer into the elevator. A guard leans against the wall, staring back at us. His throat is seared, burning black from the plasma. There's another burn mark over his heart. He staggers to the right then falls down, collapsing on the floor. One of his hands moves to his neck, just below the injury. His body starts convulsing, and then he finally goes still.

Liam extends his hand to Dragon, his palm facing the ceiling. Dragon glances at Liam, smirks, and slaps his hand onto Liam's.

I stare at the two of them, utterly disgusted.

Dragon takes a step forward and gets into the elevator.

"Shouldn't we do something with the body?" I walk into the elevator behind him and he presses the button, closing the doors.

"Like what?" Dragon asks.

I scoff. "Like bury it?"

"When do we have time for that?" Dragon cries, clearly frustrated.

My face becomes hot, but I press on. "It's just disrespectful."

"The Alliance will send the body back to his family," Liam responds. "It'll be alright."

"What level are we headed to?" Dragon asks.

"One," I reply.

"Level one?" Liam asks. "Let me see the map."

I hand him the silverscreen, and he studies the hologram.

"Level one. That's deep. Level five is already underground," Dragon says.

Liam shrugs. "The only way we can get to her is to get through a higher level of the prison."

Dragon presses the button that indicates level one on the side panel, and we begin the descent down through the prison.

"There's only one door on that level," I say, continuing to study the map, which is still in Liam's hand. "We'll need your skills again, Liam."

Liam nods. "I'd be honored."

Dragon takes a deep, pained breath. "Your device could set off a lot of alarms. If that happens, every available guard would retreat to General Indera's cell."

The elevator stops, and the doors open to reveal a dark room. The dim lights on the side of the walls do little to illuminate the place. Down here, the walls are no longer made of metal. Everything is stone. The thick, musty air sticks to my skin.

There's a downward staircase at the opposite end of the room, and whispered voices seem to echo through the halls. Like ghosts. The breath leaves my lungs, and I get the sudden urge to run, as if there's an invisible barrier between me and the staircase.

A chill runs down my spine. Are the echoes from another room? Or are they the words of people who once passed through this dark place? People who have met their fate too soon at the hand of the Emperor?

Some of the voices sound closer than others. Some even pass by my ear, and I'm able to catch a few words.

I turn to Dragon, and he looks just as afraid as I do. I glance back to the staircase, and the whispers fall silent.

Then one, clearer than the rest, speaks. I feel the breath gently touch my cheek.

"The shadow follows."

Shivers run through my arms and legs. But no one's there except for Dragon and Liam. I swallow hard.

"Did you hear that?" Liam asks.

"Please tell me that wasn't real," I manage.

"This is absolutely terrifying," Liam breathes. "Do we have to go down there?"

Dragon nods slowly. "Yes."

*Shaav,* that's not what I wanted to hear. Going down a dark, stone hallway in a dark prison controlled by the enemy who outnumbers us isn't sounding like such a great idea. But to think my mother is just through this passage…I cannot turn around.

I lift my gun and begin down the stairs. Dragon walks next to me, with Liam directly behind me. The sound of my boots on the floor is hardly noticeable, but I can hear their faint echo from the ground. We pass a torch fixed to the wall.

"Since when does the Alliance use *fire* for the sole purpose of light?" I ask. "They're all about the future and diving into scientific discoveries, not the *old* way of doing things."

Liam only takes a shaky breath.

"It's for effect," Dragon replies in a whisper. "This is a fortress of darkness and terror. The Alliance is known for experimenting on men and women under the death sentence before execution. The fire is a symbol of power, of the pain to come."

His words strike me harder than if he had punched me in the face. What if they've done experiments on my mother? What if they made her forget me?

Dragon, Liam, and I round a corner.

Light pierces my eyes and temporarily blinds me. I shield them until they adjust. The stone floor spreads out to form a huge room, lined with mostly empty prison cells. The bars are thick, probably seven centimeters in diameter.

The stench is unbearable. The smell of waste and decay fills my lungs, and I almost gag. I cover my nose with my hand and try to breathe, struggling to mask the smell of death.

The entire room has a greenish-blue glow. The light. It comes from a large, four meter-high doorway at the opposite end of the room. There's no door. I find myself walking toward the room unintentionally, like it's drawing me in. Somewhere deep inside myself, I know this is where I have to go.

"Jaina, wait," Liam says. "What if she's in one of these cells?"

"She's not." My voice comes out dazed.

"How do you know?"

"I just know," I whisper. "Somehow I know."

Dragon looks into my eyes, holding my gaze for a few moments, and nods. Slowly, I walk with them on either side of me through the open doorway. The smell isn't as bad here. In fact, the air almost smells fresh.

In the center, where the light emanates from, is a huge glass cylinder. It's filled with some blue, shiny liquid.

"What the hell is that?" Liam gasps.

The glowing blue liquid makes my stomach churn. The longer I stare at the cylinder, the more afraid I am. *What are you?* my mind wills it to answer.

I turn toward Dragon, and the look on his face nearly makes me gag. He doesn't move, just stares horrified at the cylinder.

"*Dragon?*" I beg him to respond.

His gaze falters, but he doesn't look at me. "It's an oxygen-rich liquid. Like amniotic fluid." His face is pale. "Used improperly, it can be implemented as a torture mechanism. I've seen blueprints for this device before, but it's all experimental. I didn't know the Alliance could build this yet."

I feel like I'm going to choke, but I force myself to speak. "She's in there."

He turns to me, an unbelieving expression on his face. "Okay, maybe I didn't say it right. This is only an *experiment*. No one actually *knows* if a person could actually survi–"

The liquid swirls unnaturally to one side. I run up to the glass and press my face to it. The oxygen rich liquid isn't clear, and it's hard to see through it, but sure enough, there's someone inside. I see hair. Dark brown hair.

"She is in there!" I cry.

"What if it's not her?"

It is. I know it. Is she conscious? Is she suffering?

I search the room. There's a control panel next to the tall, thin tube, and I run over to it. None of the buttons have labels on them, and I start to panic.

"Liam!" I call to him from across the room. "Do you know how to figure this out?"

He rushes over and studies the control panel. He nods quickly. "Yes, but this looks terrible."

"What do you mean?" I ask frantically.

He hesitates. "These different controls are hooked up to really bad things. This is for electrocution. This one here is for severe heat, this one releases acids into the tank...Dragon's right. This is being used for torture. But there are a whole bunch of chemicals for healing, too. The subject probably is forced to endure trauma then forced to heal only to be tortured again."

"Deactivate it," I order. "Drain the liquid."

"Liam," Dragon calls, "make it transparent first, just so we can make sure if it's her."

"It doesn't matter if it's her or not," I snap. "Someone is suffering, and they need to be saved."

Liam does as he's told, though, and a red light turns on inside the tank. The liquid becomes semi-transparent and reveals a woman floating in the middle of the tank.

I can't move. I'm frozen in my place.

It's me.

No.

It's her.

By the stars, it's her.

Her eyes are closed, and her skin is pale. She looks young. Too young to be here. There are dark circles under her eyes, like she hasn't slept in years. Have they kept her in this exact tank for the full sixteen years of her imprisonment?

"Drain the tank," Dragon orders. "Make sure it goes slowly. Once it gets close to the end, stop the draining. If she's been in there for a long period of time, she won't be used to breathing air."

Liam presses another button and the tank slowly begins to drain. I watch her carefully in the cylinder. Her hand twitches.

Dragon rushes over to Liam and takes over at the control panel. He glances at me. "You get over there. When the fluid has drained, she'll need an oxygen tank for a minute until she's used to breathing natural air again."

There's an oxygen pump on the side of the wall, probably used for helping her breathe whenever they had to take her out...if they ever took her out at all. Her feet touch the bottom of the tank, and her eyes shoot open. She presses herself against the glass and opens her mouth as if to scream but no sound comes out. Her fist slams against the glass then brings both of her hands to her throat like she's suffocating.

"What's happening?" I cry.

"Break the *shaavez* glass!" Liam shouts. "Draining the tank set off some failsafe, the oxygen is being sucked out."

The room is relatively clean. There's nothing lying around, so I reach for my holster belt, and pull out my scimitar. After activating it, I step tentatively toward the glass.

The woman with my face thrashes around in the tank.

If I break the glass, she'll fall out and hit the ground. She might not be strong enough to catch her fall.

*How long has she been in there?*

I slam my scimitar against the glass with as much force as I can muster. The glass crackles under my blow. Grooves appear in the cylinder but not enough to break it. I hit it over and over again until my hands burn from the force of every impact. Each blow reverberates into my fingertips, and I have to grit my teeth to keep them from chattering.

The glass shatters.

Everything moves in slow motion.

Shards of the broken cylinder crash down on me. I cover my face as the liquid spills over me, soaking my body. It's cold. *Freezing cold.*

And then I remember my mother.

Her body falls toward me, spilling out with the rest of the liquid. I drop my scimitar and let it float away as I position myself to catch her.

She hits me hard, knocking me down, and I land in the freezing fluid on my back. A shooting pain turns the back of my shoulder warm. I wait for the rest of the watery substance to pass over us before I sit up, shivering. My arms wrap around Amara's body, her back to me. She's gasping for air, and her eyes are closed.

"The oxygen tank!" I cry.

Liam rushes toward me after grabbing the tank. He kneels in the puddle of cold fluid. Dragon follows suit, and he drags me away from the breaking point with my mother in my arms.

"*Shaav*, it's freezing!" Liam complains.

I shudder. "You're not the one who just got it dumped on your head!"

He grits his teeth as he shivers.

"Give her the tank," Dragon says quickly.

Liam puts the mask over her mouth, but she pulls away.

"General." Dragon leans closer to her face. "You have to breathe," he coaxes.

"Enough," she chokes weakly. "Please, *enough!*"

Dragon looks up at me. I can sense his gaze on me, but I can't tear my eyes from her. She looks just like me. Long, dark hair with only a few gray strands. Her chin is a mix between pointed and round, just like mine.

"General," Dragon continues. "We're here to rescue you."

She keeps her eyes closed as she struggles to breathe, but when Dragon tries to put the mask on her this time, she doesn't resist.

"Kill me," she says. Though her voice is weak, her tone is strong. This woman once led soldiers into battle. "Please, kill me."

"General..." Dragon gets down on his knees. He holds her face in his hands. "Open your eyes. Don't you remember me?"

Her eyes flicker open slightly. They're a deep, crystal blue. She studies Dragon for a moment, and she sits up as far as she can. Her weak muscles only allow her to make gentle movements, but her will seems so strong.

Dragon shakes his head, sadly. "Do you remember?"

"My stars..." she breathes. "You have Shirez's eyes. And his hair." She has an accent, one I can't quite place, but it makes her voice so beautiful. "Why are you here? Where is my daughter?" The kindness in her voice has disappeared. "Is she alive? Is she safe?"

Dragon glances at me. His mouth moves as if he's trying to say something, but he can't.

Her face turns to me, stricken with fear. *Even her expression of fear is the same as mine.* She stares into my eyes and lets her gaze flicker over my face. "No..." Her voice is barely a whisper, so small and weak. "It can't be...Tell me your name, my love."

My eyes fill with tears, and I don't know what to say. This is my mother. Even shivering, cold, and wet on a prison floor, she is beautiful. What am I supposed to say?

I can't bring myself to move or speak. Just seeing her shock makes the weight of the situation sink in. This woman, who's been kept in this prison for sixteen years for *me*, is my mother.

Words fall from my lips. "Jaina. I'm Jaina Indera."

"My baby..." Her voice cracks as a tear streams down her face. "Oh gods, my baby!" She wraps her arms around me as tight as her frail form can manage. "You are so beautiful. You're all grown up..." She turns to Dragon. "Altair, thank you. I wasn't sure if you'd ever make it."

He blushes. I can tell, even in the dim lights of the room.

Liam remains silent, slightly stunned maybe.

Another siren starts to blare. But this one is much, *much* louder than the first.

"ATTENTION: INTRUDER ALERT. INTRUDER ALERT. CELL 00001 HAS BEEN BREACHED." The mechanical voice repeats this message on a loop.

Liam looks up at the speakers in the corner. "*Shaav,* we need to go."

Amara's eyes widen slightly. "I know a way out."

"Can you stand?" Dragon asks.

She nods. "I will try."

"How-How long have you been in there?" I ask, helping her to her feet.

"I don't know," she says quietly. "How old are you my daughter?" Her eyes fill with a mix of joy and sadness.

"Seventeen," I breathe.

Tears well in her eyes, but she blinks them away.

"How are you feeling?" Liam asks.

"Dizzy and weak, but I think we can make it out of here before I collapse," she replies. "The guards kept me well fed until recently. Who's your leader?"

"You are, General," Dragon replies.

She shakes her head. "Who is currently in command?"

"General Melohem."

Her body is frail, and clearly she hasn't been fed enough in the past week. But her movements suggest she's been prepared for this for years.

"Good," she manages. "I need a gun."

Dragon, Liam, and I exchange glances.

"Your honor," Liam says awkwardly, probably not sure how to address her. "Are you really in any shape to be handling a weapon?"

She smirks, her tired eyes showing sparks of life. "I can handle anything."

Despite not knowing her, I trust her completely. I hand her my stealth pistol, and she takes it with a firm grasp. It's a good thing I brought an extra one. My scimitar is lying on the ground and I pick it up. It's still cold and wet from the liquid, but I'm already starting to dry.

"What side of the prison did you come from?" Amara asks.

"We came from the east," I reply.

"Do either of you have a charge? Or a grenade?"

Dragon and Liam exchange glances once again, but Dragon reaches into his holster belt and prepares to hand a magnetic charge to her. Before he does, his eyes meet hers. "What do you have in mind?"

"You think I'm crazy," she states gently.

"General, I meant no offense-"

"I don't blame you, Altair. No one leaves Alliance prison completely sane. Do you trust me?"

"Always, General." He hands her the charge.

She nods graciously, then steps toward the door. Her legs buckle, and I grab her arm to keep her upright. "Help me to the door," she says.

She wraps her arm around my neck and I walk her toward the doorless doorway we came through to get to her. She plants the charge on the wall next to the door. "Trigger?"

Liam tosses her the silverscreen and she catches it. Her reflexes are surprisingly quick.

She pulls up a hologram. "They really updated this tech," she mutters under her breath. Her gentle, long fingers dance across the screen. "Do any of you know how to reprogram this?"

Liam steps forward. "General, whatever you need, I can make it happen."

Amara smiles sweetly at him. "Your name?"

"Liam Rodan," he says without hesitation.

"Reprogram the camera to detect changes in distance. I need this within two minutes. Can it be done?"

"I'll get it done in one." Liam smirks and immediately gets to work, expanding holograms, then shrinking them back into the two-dimensional screen. He finishes within a minute and proudly hands it back to her. "The camera will detect change in distance. Any change, once it's in position, will set off the charge."

"How is that going to help us?" I ask.

"The door," Liam cuts in, glancing to Amara.

Amara gives him a tired smile. "Well done, Rodan." She places the silverscreen into a small, unnoticeable groove in the stone floor.

I look up to the top of the doorway, and, sure enough there's a thick sheet of metal, waiting to close off the room. She presses a button on the control panel on the side of the wall, and the door begins to close.

"Care to explain?" Dragon asks. "Just curious."

"When the door opens," Amara begins, "the charge will go off. Sections of the wall will collapse, making it difficult to enter for the time being."

Dragon's face is still skeptical. "And how are we getting out?"

"Follow me." Amara leads us toward another wall at the back end of the room and touches a stone. She presses it into the wall, and a secret door opens.

"How did you find out about that?" Liam asks.

"I made friends with a guard. Come. We must hurry."

# CHAPTER TWENTY-ONE

The sound of an explosion rings through my ears. The ground vibrates beneath our feet, and small chips of stone shake free from the ceiling. The guards have made it through the door, at least, the ones that weren't blown away by the charge.

The corridor is long and too narrow to move in more than a single file line. Amara is in front, and Dragon insisted on being last, just in case the guards found the secret passage. Luckily, Amara was able to close the door.

*How can she be my mother?* A moment later, my heart answers, *Look at her. Feel the unconditional love pouring from her soul? Do you not see the resemblance?*

The hairs on my arm stand on end. It's not every day that someone gets to meet their long lost mother, who turns out to be the leader of a resistance movement.

Another explosion ricochets through the walls of the building. The vibration in my boots makes my bones quiver. Our troops must be doing a good job holding them off.

Amara seems to be growing stronger by the moment. She drags her hand along the small corridor to keep her balance, but it seems she can mostly stand on her own.

"Only a bit farther," Amara whispers, but then she stops and holds out her hand in front of me, motioning for us to stop.

Liam nearly runs into me, and I consider making some curt remark but the sound of muffled voices ahead cuts me off. Light shines in from the ceiling and the hall opens up to a large room with a ladder attached to the wall.

"Here we are," she says in the softest voice I've ever heard. "If I'm not mistaken, this should lead to the prison commanders' dining hall."

"Why would we want to go there?" I ask.

"It's the quickest way out of here, other than the bridge," Liam cuts in.

Amara nods. "Very good, Rodan. There are guards ahead. If we can, we'll sneak around them. If not, we'll have to fight our way through. I'll go first."

"No," Dragon, Liam and I say in synchrony.

"I'll go." Before anyone can stop me, I grab the first rung of the ladder and start climbing. This is my job. This is my duty to the people, to my mother.

The ceiling is only a few meters up, not anywhere near as bad as the height of the bridge. I reach the top quickly, push the stone plate that closes us in to the side and peer out into the world above. There's no one in sight, but from the looks of things, we're under a table. At least it gives us good cover.

"Coast is clear," I whisper down to the others.

I climb out of the hole, sling the DE-90 forward, and peek my head out from under the table. Still, there's no one there. I swear I heard voices before.

Could the Resistance really be putting up *that* much of a fight so every guard in the entire prison is focused on them? Something's wrong. We might be good at this, but we shouldn't be this good. Rescuing her is terrifying but it hasn't been extraordinarily difficult so far. There has to be something more to this, something we've missed.

Stepping out from under the table, I search the room for something to shoot at. Nothing, not a sound or smell follow or even a visual lead as to where someone could attack us from.

"All clear," I say again.

Dragon, Liam, and Amara come out to join me. Liam helps her out of the small hole.

"Now where?" Dragon asks.

"This way," Amara replies.

The sound of a cocked weapon stops me, and my body automatically goes still.

"Freeze," a deep, masculine voice says.

Amara turns around, and so do the rest of us. Seven. Seven guards, all with guns aimed at us from the doorway beyond. I swallow hard but try to retain a look of calm. We can do this. We've been through worse.

"Let us go," Dragon says. "And we will let you live."

The man in front laughs. "Amara Indera." He sighs with a mocking smile. "Sixteen years of imprisonment and you've sent children to rescue you?"

"Cermain, do not underestimate me," Amara responds without emotion.

"You must realize you're gravely outnumbered."

"Only physically. Not in spirit." Amara stares coldly back at the man. "I'll give you ten seconds before I shoot."

Two guards start to break away from the group.

Cermain stops them. "Don't fall for her treacherous ways."

"General," a soldier next to him says. He's trembling. "The legends are true. She has the phoenix heart. It doesn't matter what we do now. We are damned!"

"Silence!" Cermain shouts. "She is an Inferior, and a woman at that!" He snaps his dark gaze back to

Amara. "You and your daughter will pay for your sins. I'm sure the Emperor has her right now, torturing her, disfiguring and abusing her until she begs for death!"

Amara's jaw twitches, and she nearly growls. "My daughter is standing next to me." She raises the pistol and fires. She strikes him right above the heart. Cermain stumbles backward, and the other guards pause, looking between Amara and me.

"Fire, you idiots, *fire!*" Cermain orders from the ground.

Before they have the chance to fire, Amara knocks the table on its side and ducks behind it. Dragon pulls me to a wall behind a thick bookcase, and Liam takes shelter behind a doorway. Gunfire bolts across the room toward our positions.

"Jaina," Dragon says quickly. "Use your scimitar. They won't be expecting it."

"A sword is nothing against gunfire!" I reply over the deafening sound of gunshots.

"Not if you're the Light."

The firing ceases, and footsteps approach. Dragon grabs his gun and jumps into plain sight. He fires a few times then finds cover behind a chair. Two more bodies drop to the floor with a thud. Three down, four to go.

I put my hand on the hilt of my scimitar. What the *shaav* does Dragon mean? A sword is a sword, no matter who's using it. Frustrated, I grit my teeth. Of all moments, he brings up the damn prophecy *now*. I hold my breath. They must have seen where we took cover.

A guard steps around the corner. I activate my scimitar. The blade shoots out of the hilt so quickly the man has no time to react as it pierces the soft skin of his belly and emerges from the other side. Before he can fire his gun, I kick him to the ground.

Two more shots are fired, one from Liam and one from another guard.

How many left?

I slowly work up the courage to look around the corner, out from behind the bookshelf. A plasma bolt rockets toward my head, and I pull myself back around the corner before it can hit me. Three left.

I catch Liam's eye. He nods.

This time, when I move around the corner, I don't stop. I jump out from behind my cover and fire my DE-90 at Cermain then at the guard standing next to him. He dodges my shot and returns fire. The plasma bolt comes toward my face, and I jerk away.

The bolt flies passed me, but I don't have time for relief. Another bolt comes toward me, and I duck, letting it fly over my head. I glare at the guard, aim, then fire. This time, I don't miss. He hits the ground with a repulsive *crack* and lands in such an odd position, I know that he's broken bones. It makes me nauseous to look at him, so I turn away.

Everyone else is dead, except for my mother, Liam and Dragon. The rest of the men lay in a pile on the floor.

One of the dead coughs. Not so dead after all. He reaches for his gun. Amara aims and pulls the trigger. The plasma shot echoes through the room, and his body goes still.

"We have to move," Amara says. "This way."

"How do you know your way?" Liam asks her. "Haven't you been locked up this whole time?"

"I've been busy. I stole a map once."

We follow her to the balcony, and the blinding morning sun strikes me like daggers in my eyes. I look over the edge, and my breath catches.

"That's...a little far," Dragon says.

A *little* far? It must be a fifty meter drop.

Amara shakes her head. "No. Knowing Shirez, I can guess his strategy. We'll be safe, assuming the Alliance Guard will be busy fighting reinforcements over there." She points across the valley.

The Resistance reinforcements have come in, trading fire with the Alliance. People lie scattered on the ground, dead or wounded.

"Hurry," Amara says. "They'll send up more guards when they realize where we've gone." She grabs a grappling hook from Liam's belt without asking, wraps it around the stone balcony, then drops the rest of it down to the ground. "I'm going first this time. I'm not letting you go down on a cable that hasn't been checked. Understood?"

When none of us reply, she nods, obviously satisfied, then climbs over the edge of the balcony. It's a long drop. Enough to kill someone if they jumped.

"Once I'm down, one of you can start after me," she says calmly.

She tests the strength of the cable and slowly but surely lets herself down. I hold my breath throughout her entire descent. It's so easy to picture her slipping and crashing into the ground. At least it's not concrete or stone, just the golden grass that surrounds the entire prison.

Amara finally makes it to the ground, and I'm able to breathe again. She gestures for one of us to follow. I beg Liam to go after her, so that she can be more easily protected. He agrees, and follows suit.

A bullet zips our way. I hear it crack, the *sffft* of it making contact. The cable shudders.

On the ground, Amara's gun fires, a man cries out then he falls silent as he hits the ground a few meters from them.

"*Shaav*," Dragon curses. "The bullet hit the cable. It's still stable, but only one of us can safely make it down. Go."

"No, you go," I reply quickly. "More guards are coming. You can't fight them off alone."

"Neither can you, now go."

"*Shaav*, Dragon, I'm not letting you risk your life for me again!"

"I'm ordering you to go!" He shouts. "I am your commander, and you'll do what I say!"

No matter what it takes, I can't let him do this. I walk over to the balcony and grab the cable in my hands. When Dragon faces the room with a gun in each hand, I take my scimitar, slice through the cord, and let it fall to the ground.

"Jaina!" Amara cries.

"You have to get *The Odyssey*!" I shout. "Liam, take her there now! One klick east!"

Dragon turns back to me. His mouth drops open, and fury rises into his eyes. I've disobeyed a direct order, but I don't care.

Liam and Amara take off into the golden grass and disappear beyond my line of sight.

Dragon forcefully grabs my wrist and pulls me up to face him. The power in his hands crushes me slightly. I don't flinch. "Why would you do that?" he cries. "You've put the entire mission in jeopardy! If Amara doesn't make it to the ship–"

"She will," I say sternly. "She will. We just need to hold them off long enough for her to fly back for us."

"By the stars, Jaina, why!" There's so much pain in his voice.

If only I knew.

Just like that, my body moves on it's own.

I pull him to me, melding his lips with mine, pleading desperately for him to understand. At first, he doesn't move, and I almost hope he pulls away. Slowly, he returns my kiss, leaning into me and keeping me close to him. I pull away, and by the way he moves back in, I know he doesn't want me to. He opens his eyes as our lips part, a confused look on his face. What did I just do? What did that mean?

Movement out of the corner of my vision catches my attention. I turn to see four guards round the corner, weapons raised, and ready to fire.

"Hands up," says the one in front of us.

I swallow hard. Now what? I start to second guess my brilliant idea of staying behind, but I wouldn't have left Dragon. I wouldn't have left anyone here alone.

"Hands up, or I shoot!" the guard cries.

Dragon meets my eyes then glances down. I follow his gaze and see his thumb pointing to a pocket on his holster belt.

Understanding, I slowly put my gun on the ground but make sure my scimitar is still on my belt. I raise my hands above my head.

"You, too. Hands up." The guard glowers at Dragon.

I sense Dragon moving, but I don't dare look at him again.

"You want me to drop my weapons?" Dragon asks. "Or would you rather come over here and take them off me yourself?"

The man's jaw tightens. "Remove your weapons. Make no sudden movements. Girl, get over here."

I don't move. I'm not leaving Dragon.

My plan? I look from Dragon to the guard, feigning confusion. "*Nal anna shari?*" I ask, speaking a rarely used dialect of Cora.

"She doesn't speak the national language?" the guard asks.

Dragon shakes his head.

"She's of no use to us then," the guard says. "Kill her."

At that moment, Dragon reaches into the pocket on his holster belt, tosses a silver object onto the floor in front of them. It beeps once then bursts into a million pieces. Something smashes into me, and I feel like I'm falling. The *boom* of the explosion is all I process before a high-pitched tone rings in my ears, fading in from the silence. I realize I'm on the ground. Dragon's hand pulls me up as the sounds of the world slowly return. Gunshots fire in the distance, and finally everything rushes back to me.

"Jaina, get up!" Dragon pulls a knife from his holster belt and throws it at the only guard that's managed to survive the explosion.

For a moment, all is silent.

"Don't move," a voice calls from behind the pile of dust and rocks that used to be a hallway leading out to a balcony.

I take my scimitar in my right hand and my pistol in my left. "Show yourself!"

A dark figure approaches us. He's head to toe in black armor, and a helmet covers his face. A dark red "S" is painted onto his armor.

"Nice to see you again," he hisses. "Do you really think I'd let you leave without dropping by?"

"Remove your helmet and tell us who you are!" I shoot back.

The man cocks his head. "You naive little girl. I'm stronger than the two of you combined. Now surrender, or I'll open fire."

"Never," I spit.

"I'm not joking, Jaina," he says softly.

His use of my name only angers me and I grit my teeth.

The man laughs. "I know everything about you."

Dragon takes a stance, raises his gun, and fires. The man in black armor moves out of the way as the bolt flies passed him, simultaneously pulling a small, metal object from his holster belt and throwing it.

I don't have time to move.

Dragon falls to the ground, a throwing star lodged deep in his shoulder. He clutches the wound, moaning and taking quick, painful breaths.

"He's going to die now if you don't save him," the armored man says. "The poison on that doesn't let its victims die painlessly."

Every cell in my body urges me to kneel on the ground next to Dragon, but I don't. I activate my scimitar and stalk toward the man.

"I'll make you a deal," he says. "Surrender, and I'll give you the antidote."

Rage builds up inside of me, and I raise my scimitar. "I will not."

"If that's how it's going to be…"

I bring my weapon down upon him, but he backs away just in time and pulls out a sword of his own. He stops my blade from coming any closer, and pushes me backward into a pile of rubble. It only takes me a moment to regain my balance but in my few seconds of distraction, I've given him the advantage. Without hesitation, he charges me and knocks me to the ground. I try to kick him but when my foot makes contact with his armor, it hurts my toe more than anything.

He pins me to the ground and wraps his gloved hand around my throat. With all of my strength I attempt to push him away but he doesn't budge. My arms move on their own, fighting him with all my strength, but he grabs my wrist then runs his hand down my arm and onto my left shoulder. My vision starts to go blurry as my fingertips lose sensation. My head feels like it's going to explode, and dizziness takes over. He digs his fingers deep into my arm.

Into the AV carved on my skin.

Horror floods me. My body screams but the air is trapped in my lungs so I can't make a sound. Electric pain shoots through my whole body. I try to kick, to lash out in any possible way, but the lack of air makes it hard to move.

The whining of an engine fills my ears.

A gunshot sounds, and the bolt skims his shoulder. The force makes him recoil, pushing him off me and onto the ground. He stands but I grab his ankle. The armored man trips, and I climb on top of him, a dagger to his throat.

I could kill him.

By the stars, I could so easily kill him and I would enjoy it.

"Where's the antidote?" I demand, pressing the dagger close to him.

A mechanical sickening laugh escapes his vocal modifier. "I don't have it, darling."

Rage. I plunge the long dagger into his arm and press it deeper until I feel it hit his shoulder blade. Blood gushes relentlessly from his armor, I must have hit an artery. He cries out and kicks me away.

Scrambling to my feet, I see *The Odyssey* hovering just half a meter above the balcony. There's plenty of space to land but the half-blasted stone won't hold. My arm burns with pain where he pressed his fingers into my skin. I glance back at the armored man and he's fumbling with something on his holster belt.

Need to hurry.

Dragon's face has gone pale and sweat covers his forehead. I kneel beside him. "Dragon, get up. We have to move."

"It's not–" he breathes. "Not deadly. Poison."

"Jaina, we have to go!" Amara calls from the ramp of *The Odyssey.*

"Help me!" I cry, taking Dragon's arm.

Amara jumps out of the ship and runs to my aid. For being weak, she's a lot stronger than I am, and together, we pull him to the ship and lift him onto the ramp. After that, she rushes into the cockpit.

The armored man slowly gets up, and fires three shots at *The Odyssey.* One bolt misses, the other two hit the hull leaving dark burn marks.

"Better run, little girl!" He shouts over the engines, holding his bloody shoulder. "This is far from over!"

The ramp closes as we rise into the atmosphere.

I stay with Dragon on the ramp. I can't bear leaving him alone like this. Holding him in my arms, I stroke his hair.

"Jaina," he manages. "The...the poison. It's not deadly."

Is he delusional? Why would the man in armor lie?

"What is it, then?" I ask. My voice shakes.

"Torture mechanism." He coughs, and his body tenses. His eyes shut tight and he moans in agony.

"Dragon," I whisper, "you're going to be okay."

His tenseness lasts another moment then fades. He swallows hard and looks up at me. "Jaina," he says softly, "you have the power." The pain rises up in him again, and I hold him close to me, keeping my cheek to his forehead.

Suddenly, his body goes still. I freeze, close my eyes, and block the tears that want to roll down my face.

"Amara!" I half-scream, examining him again.

She rushes around the corner and falls on her knees next to me.

His eyes are closed, and his hands are cold. Deathly cold.

"Is he–" I can't finish.

"No," she quickly says. She touches the throwing star, still buried in his shoulder, then pulls out a silverscreen from a compartment in the wall. "I need a chemical identification of this poison," she says, pressing her fingers to the silverscreen.

It takes a minute for it to process, but it feels like a lifetime. "Chemical analysis complete. Klorazyne. Causes death-like symptoms and nearly halts breathing and heartbeat. Inflicts great pain on the victim, including burning or stabbing sensations on all nerve endings. Has been known to be deadly to a few species, but humans will live after suffering side effects. Symptoms fade after ten hours. Would you like me to continue?"

Amara shakes her head. "No."

"There's nothing we can do?"

"Remove the blade and see if you can bandage it or stop the bleeding. When we get to *The Justice*, the doctors there can help. Until then, take care of him."

I nod, and she gets up, heading back to the cockpit.

His breathing becomes more noticeable, and his body starts to warm. I almost don't want him to wake because at least if he's unconscious, maybe he won't feel as much.

He barely opens his eyes. "Are you...are you gonna do it?"

I touch his shoulder, and he winces. "I don't want to hurt you."

"It'll hurt more if you leave it," he insists. "You can do it. I know you can."

"How?"

With his right arm, he unbuttons his shirt and slides off the armor beneath it, revealing his broad chest and toned stomach. The blade is lodged just below his shoulder but too far up to be near his heart. Blood gushes down his trembling arm, and it makes my stomach churn.

I touch the throwing star, and he shuts his eyes.

"Do it fast," he manages. "Please."

I suck in a deep breath and gulp down the burning fluid rising in my throat. With a quick jerk, I free the blade from his body. Dragon slams his head backward into my legs and moans painfully through his gritted teeth. He clutches his shoulder as blood runs through his fingers. Gently sliding him off my lap, I stand up and charge toward the storage door a few meters away. I yank the door open. My fingers quiver while I frantically pull things out, searching for a bandage or cloth or *something* to stop the bleeding. My hands are covered in blood and my stomach convulses.

I grab a small medical cloth kept in a box as well as an anesthetic and rush back over to him. "I'm sorry," I manage, holding the cloth to his skin.

He jerks away from it and shakes his head. I take his arm and inject the anesthetic into him. Immediately, he begins to go still, but he doesn't stop shivering. I pull him into my arms and hold him tightly to me. My hand wanders to his shoulder, and I hold the cloth to his skin.

His body is warm against me as I keep pressure on his wound. I close my eyes and concentrate. A cool rush floods me, and somehow I know what to do. Removing the cloth from his shoulder, I lightly press my fingers to the gash and focus. There's a brightness. An entire star within me. There is warmth, there is peace.

And then I feel everything alive, the energy. I feel Dragon's heart beating, not against my skin within his chest, I feel it pumping blood through his veins. Our veins. I am part of it. No, I *am*. I am the blood, the lungs, the heart. Somehow a part of him, within him and without, I urge the wound to close.

When I open my eyes, I don't know how much time has passed. A cold, nauseous feeling spreads through my body when I see it. The large, bloody gash, the terrible wound…it's healing. The blood has clotted, faster than I could have ever imagined. I keep my fingers pressed to him, and focus once more, but this time, the cool rush doesn't come.

I look down at him and sigh with relief. My body is drained, and I'm lightheaded like I've been holding my breathe. My vision is off, like the whole world is a little bit more gray. The nausea seems to grow worse, and I'm not sure if it's because of the stress or because of this odd, supernatural thing I've just done. What have I just done?

I run my fingers through his hair. Trembling, I press my forehead to his and hold his face in my hands.

"Please be alright, Dragon," I whisper. "You have to be okay for me."

He breathes slower now and his trembling softens. I wonder if he'd be proud.

# CHAPTER TWENTY-TWO

They take Dragon and the rest of the wounded to the to the hospital once we're aboard *The Justice*. He's still unconscious, but it's clear he's also still in pain. It hurts me just thinking about it.

It doesn't feel right being back so soon. We should be moving somewhere, going somewhere new. Instead, I find myself sitting around in various places, waiting for something to happen, waiting for someone to confirm that Dragon's alright.

I bite my fingernails as I wait in the hangar bay. After standing outside the hospital for an hour, the nurses told me to get some rest and forced me to leave. Then they admitted Amara to the hospital. Now I'm alone.

Three ships are in a docking process, and two more are right behind them. I can hardly stand the tension. There's no way I'm going to leave this hangar without seeing Liam, without confirming with my own eyes he's still alive. After he landed *The Odyssey* safely in the hangar, he took another ship back down to the battlefield to aid the evacuation.

*Please, Liam. Please be alive.*

The first ship lands safely in the hangar, and the engines slowly die.

Jet steps onto the ramp before the ship is settled and slightly loses his balance as it touches down. He rushes down onto the metal floor of *The Justice*. "Come on, guys!" he calls, turning toward the ship. "What are you waiting for?"

The other troops start to exit the ship, and I become more and more frantic as I search for him.

I rush up to Jet. "Jet, where's Liam?"

He keeps a straight face. "He's coming. He refused to leave until every last soldier, even the wounded were safe. His will be the last ship."

I nod and lie on crates of ammo, trying to stay comfortable. The minutes drag on into hours, and fear fills my blood. What if his transport was shot down? No. There would have been an alarm, a signal to evacuate the airspace.

Every few minutes another transport lands in the hangar. The sight isn't pretty. Some of the men and women need to be carried out on stretchers. One man has something shiny and white lodged into his bloody leg. It takes me a moment to realize his bone has snapped and that's what's protruding from his body.

Another has blood all over his face. A red cloth hangs over the side of the stretcher. The cloth is dripping with blood. No, not a cloth. It's his hand, or whatever is left of it. Blown to pieces, mangled and destroyed.

I can barely muster the strength to keep myself from vomiting.

Finally, the last ship lands. Still I don't allow myself to feel relieved. I need to see him. Exhausted troops file out of the ship, while the most severely wounded are quickly rushed into the hospital wing on more stretchers. The hangar smells like blood and death.

Then finally, I see his face.

"Liam!" I shout.

His eyes lock on mine and I sprint to him. He traps me in his embrace, so tight I have to push him away to breathe.

"Liam, I was so worried about you!" Tears fill my eyes.

"Is Dragon alright?" he asks immediately.

I nod, pulling out of his embrace slightly. "He'll be fine, but I haven't heard back from the doctors yet."

Liam hugs me again. "Are you okay?"

"I'll be fine," I say softly. "Liam, I–" I stop myself, unable to keep from shaking.

He glances down at me and gently places his hands on my shoulder. "What's wrong?"

My lips curl into a smile, but I can still feel the tension in my face. "I saw him again," I breathe, looking around skeptically. "The Shadow Hunter."

Liam's inhales sharply. "You're sure?"

I nod. "I'm sure. When I sent you and my mother away to *The Odyssey*, he's the one who hurt Dragon. I think he knew about my scars."

He cocks his head to the side slightly. "What scars?" When I don't answer, his eyes widen. "*The* scars?"

I nod.

"How would he know?" He continues. "There's no way he could know unless he saw you naked."

"Liam!" I change my voice into a whisper. "He did *not* see me naked! No one has!"

"Not true," Liam shoots back quickly. "I used to watch you in your dorm on Virana. You *never* closed your curtains!"

My face is hot, and I resist the urge to slap him. "You're telling me this *now?*"

His cheeks redden, and he grins. "You've got a nice–"

"Enough!" My whole body grows warm, and I start to sweat nervously, but, by the stars, his words make me smile.

"There we go," he says, grinning.

I raise my eyebrows. "What?"

"You should smile more."

"I would if you were around more." I look down after I say it, but it's the truth.

"Jaina." Liam brushes his hand against my cheek. "I'll be around whenever you need me. I'm always here for you."

"I'm serious," I breathe. "Liam, I think he knew. How?"

Liam shrugs, a pained expression across his face. "Jaina, when we went into the Crystal City, we were all profiled in the Alliance database. Maybe...maybe they added something about your scars. It's a distinguishing feature. Remember, if it really is the Shadow Hunter, he knows how to do his job. He probably read your profile when you went missing."

I'm not sure if I feel better or worse. "Thank you, Liam."

"Anything for you."

He takes me into his arms. His body is strong and warm against mine. I feel more comfort than I have since the old days on Virana, like I can stay here in his arms forever.

Looking into his beautiful brown eyes, I run my fingers through his soft hair. "Did you really stand on the beach outside of my dorm?"

He turns a bit more pink. "Yes, and I don't regret it."

I playfully slap his cheek. "No more peeking."

Liam smiles. "You should get some sleep."

"Thank you." I stand on my toes and kiss him on the cheek. Without another word, I lazily make my way to my new room.

⇒⇥ ⇤⇐

Sleep doesn't come, not even after six hours tossing and turning. I lie on my back, on my side, on my stomach, and then the other side, but I can't get comfortable.

I listen to the ship as we move through space like a bullet tearing through flesh. The whirring of machinery is muffled but recognizable through every wall. When I put my head on the pillow, I hear the vibrations coursing through the floor, and into my mattress.

Deep down, I know it's not the lack of comfort or the omnipresent sounds of the ship that keep me awake.

Every time I close my eyes, I see Azad. His dark green, vengeful eyes. Those eyes that promise death and pain. I see the dark, mysterious warrior. The dark "S" painted on his shoulder drips with blood. Shadow Hunter or not, he's a killer. A murderer. I feel him pressing his fingers into my scar.

*Who are you?*

As I slip into sleep, dreams of pain and cold haunt me. My mind is speeding through every fear, every crime I've committed or witnessed. I hear knives being sharpened and guns being fired. The sound of my dagger entering Azad's flesh. The squelch of tissue against the blade. I taste blood on my tongue and the smell of death from inside the prison overwhelms my senses. The sound of the bolt Dragon sent through that prison guard's head echoes through my mind.

I can't sleep.

My head is spinning.

And all I reach for before I awaken from my nightmares...

Is Liam.

He's the only one who makes it all go away. Dragon might take away the dreams, but Liam takes away all the pain. He makes me forget the horrors of the world. His gentle smile, full of life and kindness engulfs me and fills me with peace. He shades me from the terrifying rain of darkness that surrounds us all.

I stare up at the ceiling. It's metallic, like the walls. Boring and clearly not built for looks.

Finally, I give up. There's no way I can sleep. I leave my room and wander through the halls, which have become quiet since the troops are sleeping.

When I reach the hospital, I'm relieved to see doctors aren't swarming the area as they were earlier. The past ten hours since the battle started, the medics have been busy. Now, only the nurses are on patrol, while the doctors treat the last shipment of wounded Liam brought in.

I glance through a few of the patients in the infirmary but can't find him. Worry starts to course through me. Dragon and the computer on *The Odyssey* could have been wrong. What if the poison *is* deadly?

Frantically, I charge into the recovery room. My body instantly relaxes as I rest my eyes on him. He's sleeping soundly, cloaked in hospital attire. An IV bag rests nearby, trailing down to a large vein in his arm.

I take a seat in an empty chair next to him. My gaze traces the lines of his strong jaw, his chiseled features, and I place my hand in his. I squeeze his hand as I glance into the corridor and a thought crosses my mind; I really didn't check if I was allowed to be here. And I also didn't check if anyone was around to catch me.

Slight pressure in my hand makes me look back to him. His eyes flutter open, and he moves his thumb gently over my fingers.

"I didn't mean to wake you," I whisper. "I shouldn't have-"

"I'm glad," he replies, slurring his words a bit. "Is everyone okay?"

"Yes." I smile.

"Amara," he breathes. "She's alright?"

I nod. "She's safe. So is Liam. Everyone's okay."

He rolls his eyes. "I hate this hospital gown. It's sticking to me, but that lady wouldn't let me take it off. Can you fire her?"

I can't help letting out a slight laugh. "You're on a lot of medication."

"That's right, but I feel good." He grins. "You know, you fought really hard, and you were really sexy, sexy. Can I have another kiss please?"

"Dragon." I sigh, smiling. "That was only to make sure you wouldn't be mad at me. I shouldn't give you another one."

"Please?" he asks drowsily.

I shake my head. "I ran out of kisses."

He nods, closing his eyes. "Did you have bad dreams when you went to sleep?"

"Sort of."

He sits up a little, but he hesitates and grabs his injured shoulder. "What happened to me? My shoulder has a headache."

"You were hurt. You're going to be fine."

"Oh good," he exhales. "Well, goodnight."

He lies down in the cot and falls asleep. Have to admit, I'm a bit jealous he can sleep so well. I stay in the uncomfortable chair for quite some time. I'm not sure how much time passes before my eyes close. I wake to the sound of someone calling my name. I feel like I'm swimming up from the depths of the bottom of the sea. With every moment, the voice grows clearer.

"Jaina?"

It's Dragon's voice.

My eyes open, and I take in a nice gulp of air. Dragon is sitting up more, and his eyes are clear. His face isn't as relaxed as it was before. More relieved, but not playful and joyous anymore.

"Hey, you feeling okay?" I ask.

He blushes. "Physically, yes...but my honor depends on what the hell I said to you when I was drugged."

"You didn't say anything too bad." I try to hold back a laugh. "Did the doctors come in while I was resting? How long have I been here?"

Dragon shrugs. "I woke with a clear mind about half an hour ago. The doctors did come in to speak with me..." His hesitation makes me nervous.

"And...?"

"They found the strangest thing." He looks down at his hands, sort of absentmindedly playing with his fingers.

"You're making me nervous."

"They said a wound like that should've taken me weeks to recover. But they found that I had significantly healed before I even arrived on *The Justice*. They even asked me if I was sure I got it during the battle." His eyes pry. "I'm going to be released in three days."

I take a shaky breath and manage to smile. "That's wonderful, Dragon. I've been so worried about you."

His gaze doesn't falter. "You did it, didn't you."

It isn't a question.

I rest my elbows on my knees, my head in my heads. "I don't know. I honestly don't know."

Dragon raises an eyebrow. "How?"

I study the tiny imperfections in the metal of the floor. "I don't know what happened. I just touched you, and when I looked, you were healing. I didn't *do* anything. It was a miracle."

He shakes his head in visible disapproval. "How many miracles will it take for you to see the truth?"

"A lot more than this," I reply curtly.

"You are the Light, Jaina," he says. "You always have been."

"What if I don't want to be?"

"You were chosen."

"You don't know that," I shoot back.

"You're going to discover the truth."

# CHAPTER TWENTY-THREE

Two days pass. Dragon's alright after the first day, but his doctors insisted he shouldn't leave the hospital wing until they're sure he's clean of infections. Amara still needed medical attention, but Shirez made it clear to me that if she wasn't alright within the next twenty-four hours, she'd just escape from the hospital.

Luckily, there was no need. Eighteen hours later, Amara's doctors released her from the hospital. I haven't seen her since the rescue. I wasn't allowed to visit her in the hospital, something about mental stress. Despite hardly knowing her, I miss her in a way I can't quite describe. Maybe it's because I want to know her better. I need to know more.

A knock comes from the door to my new, comfortable quarters near the top center of the ship. At least that's what I'm told, it's easy to get lost in here. The room is bare, but at least the walls are painted white, making it look a little brighter inside. The thick blast proof glass is a bit dirty on the outside of my small window, but at least I can see the stars.

I open the door. "General," I say, bowing my head slightly to Shirez.

Shirez shakes his head. "Jaina, I've told you many times to call me Shirez. Titles make me feel old, and I'm not getting any younger."

"Yes, right. Sorry." I shoot him a small smile. "How is Dragon?"

"He's doing very well, much better than anyone could have hoped," he replies. "You do realize that he could have bled out aboard *The Odyssey*." Shirez pauses. "I don't expect my words to be welcome, but I want to thank you."

My face burns slightly, and I can't look at him anymore. "You have nothing to thank me for. I did what anyone would do in that situation."

"You did what only you could do," he replies softly, "and for that, I am forever in your debt."

His words terrify me more than I can bear. I want to argue, to disagree, but there's nothing I can say that can change the facts. Somehow I kind of healed Dragon, but it's not like I did a very good job. He's still been in the hospital for two days.

"Why did you come to see me?" I ask.

"Your mother wants to speak with you. She wants to explain some things."

My stomach churns slightly. I follow close behind Shirez to a small, cozy room decorated with two white couches across from each other, and a simple glass table between them.

When Shirez and I enter, Amara stands. "Shirez." She dips her head in acknowledgement. Her voice is sweet. "Thank you. Will you please give Jaina and I some time? I don't want to be disturbed."

Shirez bows respectively and leaves, closing the door behind him.

The woman who happens to be my mother is even more beautiful than when I first saw her. She's regal, like a queen. Her nose is thin and pointed, and her hair is long and a bit curly, but not too curly, like her hair can't decide whether or not it should be straight. I used to feel like it was unattractive on me, but on her it looks perfect. Maybe it's not so bad on me, either. She smiles, and it seems to light up to room. Even her slightly crooked teeth add to her beauty.

Amara is dressed in a black, kevlar corset with a maroon shirt beneath it, probably reinforced with Ryva spider silk. She's wearing black pants, probably bullet proof as well and combat boots that rise to her knees.

"Jaina, please have a seat." She sits on the couch then gestures to the seat next to her.

I do as she says.

"Jaina, there is so much I want to say. I don't know where to start," she begins, "but I want to say how sorry I am."

"What do you mean?" I ask, confused.

She looks down and shakes her head sadly. "When I was very young, much younger than you, my father was killed in front of me in an IA reconstruction camp. We were slaves to the Alliance. I swore to take revenge by destroying the savage system of government that murdered him. Every day since, I have fought for their downfall. The only way I could ever be whole again was if I brought justice to the IA. But then…" She smiles as tears well in her eyes. "Then I had you. Everything changed. When I fought, I no longer fought for vengeance. I fought for you. I worked toward creating a better world, a world I wanted you to grow up in, a beautiful world, without bloodshed, where Superior and Inferior were irrelevant. I failed."

"You didn't fail," I cut in. "You haven't won yet, but you didn't fail."

She looks into my eyes, a sad smirk on her lips. "But I have. I wanted a life for you, a life where you didn't have to fight, or experience war. I didn't want you to have a life in the Alliance. I wanted to raise you." A deep, agonizing breath escapes her throat, and finally, her tears fall onto her beautiful cheeks. "I- I was supposed to be your mother."

I wrap my arm around her shoulder. I'm trembling. "It's okay," I say as I wipe away my tears. "I know I'm not the person you wanted me to be, but-"

She stops me by placing a gentle hand on my shoulder, wiping her tears away. "You are more beautiful than I could have ever imagined, Jaina. You are strong and brave, but most importantly, you have a beautiful heart."

My breath quivers. "How do you know that? You've only known me for a short time."

"You lived with me for a year before they took you. Even then, you had the biggest heart. You were the light of my life. You always have been."

"What should I call you?" I ask.

Her deep blue eyes meet mine. "I won't ask you to call me *mother*," she starts. "You can call me Amara, if you like. Or...*Mira*."

"Mira?" I ask. "What does that mean?"

"It's the Kataran word for *mother*. It's the way my father referred to my mother when I was growing up."

"*Mira*," I say aloud. "I love it."

She smiles sadly. "Jaina, there is a lot more you must know. Shirez said Altair may have told you things, but there's a lot that even he doesn't know."

I raise an eyebrow. "Is that so?"

She nods. "Men like to think they know everything."

"That's true." I laugh softly. "Please, tell me everything."

Amara clears her throat and looks down at the floor before focusing back on me. "Have you heard of the prophecy?"

My stomach slowly bunches itself into a knot, but I nod. "Yes, but I don't know much."

"A long time ago, shortly after you were born, Shirez and I went to rally a people to bring them to the Resistance. These people were called the Dalivan."

"They see the future," I say, recalling what Dragon told me on *The Odyssey*. "So they created some prophecy. So what?"

"Jaina," Amara says gently, "I need you to listen, even if you don't believe it."

I nod, and swallow my fear.

"When we arrived, the Daliv leader greeted us. He said our arrival was foreseen. He said my daughter was part of a plan far greater than anyone could imagine, that she would save the universe from darkness."

I cock my head. "What made you believe him?"

"I didn't. Not at first. He said you would be a lost child, born of two words, that you'd grow up without a mother. That your only father would be the tyrant I had fought so long and hard to destroy. He said they'd turn you into a weapon, but once you saw the error in their ways, you would become the Light. Of course I didn't believe him, but I still acted out of fear.

To save you from that future, I kept you by my side at all times. It was dangerous, but even during battles, I made sure you were in a battleship not far from the fleet." Her voice begins to quiver, and she won't look at me. "In a siege against the Alliance, we attacked an IA base. We thought we had taken control, and the IAA surrendered. It was a ruse. Reinforcements came in and attacked us, killing almost everyone. A few survived, but we were taken prisoner. An assassin who had somehow learned of your location kidnapped you and turned you over to the Alliance leadership. In exchange for your life, I would go quietly to prison." She sighs deeply and meets my gaze. Her face looks so much older now, like she has lived through the pain of a thousand years in a single moment. "In trying to save you from the words of the Daliv, I fulfilled his prophecy."

Chills run through my body, and I feel frozen. "So..." I begin. "Everything in my life has been predetermined?"

She shakes her head. "We all have a choice in what we do, but we don't always have a say in the outcome. I thought that by keeping you closer to me, I was keeping you safe. I was wrong."

"Why does everyone think it's me? Just because the Dalivan think I'm the one doesn't mean I am. And born of two worlds? I'm not–"

"Your father," she cuts in, "was part of the Alliance. He was a very prominent and important man. You are born of two worlds."

"There could be others," I respond quickly.

"You're right. No one can know for sure whether or not you hold a place in this prophecy, but that is why I needed to speak to you. We must go to Daliv to find out if you truly are part of this."

A sigh escapes my lips as I lean back into the couch. Her eyes are fixed on me, and the pressure to answer is suddenly too great to ignore. "And if I'm not the Light, what do we do?"

"I return to the Resistance, and you may choose whatever you wish," she replies gently. "I pray this will be the outcome."

"And if I am?"

Amara runs her fingers through her long, dark hair. "Then you will have a responsibility to fulfill your role in their prophecy."

My hands tremble. "So I'll be forced to do as they command?"

Amara takes my hand and squeezes gently. "You are forced to do nothing. It will be your responsibility to be the Light, but if you choose to run from it, that is your decision to make. It isn't cowardice. And I will be happy for you as long as you are happy. It will all be your choice."

I take a deep breath and nod. "When do we leave?"

"If you are willing...immediately."

*Selene* is ready for transportation within the hour. All it needs is a bit more fuel, and we'll be ready to leave. It's smaller than *The Odyssey.* Amara instructed me to keep our departure quiet, so I haven't told anyone except for Liam, who's standing by my side. She said he could come.

"Are you sure you wanna do this?" he asks.

"I don't know. I just want to get it over with." My voice comes out tired and afraid.

Liam places a gentle hand on my shoulder. "I'll be with you the whole way, remember? You're not going to be alone."

"I know. It's just this whole prophecy thing freaks me out."

"I think it's kinda cool." His hand slides down my arm until he subtly lets go. "Do you know what you're going to do? Once they've decided if you're the Light or not?"

"Well, apparently if I'm the Light, it will be my responsibility to *save the universe from darkness.* We should just have everyone light candles," I spit out.

"I'm pretty sure it's a figure of speech," Liam replies in all seriousness.

"I was being sarcastic." I look at him, but he continues to stare forward at the ship. "Dragon said the Light is supposed to choose love and hope over hatred and fear or whatever. And this *Dark* does the opposite. But I've killed too many people. How does that make me worthy of such a title, even if I wanted it?"

"I think that simply because you see it as wrong, and don't want the title is exactly why it has to be you. This is a time of war, and yet you still show mercy to all those who oppose us. You care for the men who died defending the prison on Sol Veya. Why is that?" He asks.

"I-I don't know," I manage. "They're people too. They're blinded by money, or power, or loyalty, but they're still people. If we hadn't won the Trials, you could have been sent to guard that prison. So could Dragon and everyone we care about. It could've been us instead. But chance or fate or whatever it is ensured that things would happen differently. And that's not their fault."

Liam smiles as he looks at me, his eyes overflowing with...respect? "See? Who else could it be?" He turns back to the ship, admiring it as if it were some exotic princess. "Does your mother know I'm coming?"

"She does. Though, you might want to call her General until she tells you otherwise. Just as a respect thing."

He breathes out a laugh. "I'll keep that in mind. Is she okay? I mean sixteen years in prison can sorta mess with your head, especially if you're tortured."

"I really don't know. Shirez and I talked to her doctors while she was in the infirmary, and she has no signs of severe mental stress. It was all just physical."

"I've got a lot of respect for that woman," he says with a sigh. "I don't think I could've survived that."

"I had something worth living for," Amara's voice cuts in. She walks toward the two of us, smiling slightly. "Now that we've escaped, we can be properly introduced. Amara Indera." She reaches out her hand to Liam.

"Liam Rodan." He shakes her hand.

"And how did you and Jaina meet?" she asks, her gaze flickering between us.

"Well, um…" He takes an unsteady breath. "It's kind of complicated. We grew up together on Virana, at the Gifted School."

Amara flashes her slightly crooked teeth at Liam in a sweet grin. "It's a pleasure to meet you, Liam. I don't mean to rush, but we must be on our way. They're expecting us, I'm sure."

Without another word, she bows her head slightly, turns around and opens the ramp to *Selene*. Liam and I follow close behind. He closes the ramp behind us then we head into the cockpit. The two of us take seats behind her. Unlike *The Odyssey*, there's only room for three passengers.

"How far is Daliv?" I ask.

Amara turns to me as she operates the control panel. "Eight standard hours in a normal ship, but only four with *Selene*."

Liam looks at her curiously. "This is an IAA vessel. Extremely rare, almost royal class. How did you manage to steal this?"

Amara shakes her head. "I was a general for the IAA once. My troops gave me this ship, one of the fastest ever built."

"How did you work for them?" I ask, quite struck by the idea. "If you always wanted revenge, why would they let you be a general?"

"I was born in the IA. My mother died in childbirth so all I had was my father. We were Inferiors, the builders of the IA. When my father was killed...When my father was killed, I tried to escape the camp. I was caught every time and ended up in the camp prisons. I became well known to the guards. Your father was one of them." Amara lifts the ship into the air and exits the hangar. We drift out into space away from *The Justice* as she turns to Liam. "Are we charged to move into the hyperfield?"

He nods. "We're ready."

Amara presses a few more buttons and shoots us forward into the hyperfield. "You two should get your rest. If you stay with the Resistance even if you have nothing to do with the prophecy, the future

*Jessica K. McKendry*

will provide few chances to sleep. We'll be there soon."

I take that as a dismissal and head to the only bedroom in the ship. To my slight horror, there's only one bed. The room is tiny, but at least it's a big bed with three pillows.

I almost turn around and head back into the cockpit, but in all seriousness, I'm too exhausted to walk back there. I remove my boots and the warm white shirt I've worn for the past day and a half. I have a sleeveless, tight-fitting top on underneath. It's a bit revealing, but I can't get comfortable in a long sleeve shirt. Then again, if Liam is going to lie down in the same bed as me, I probably won't be comfortable at all anyhow. Without a second thought, I lie down on the bed, exhausted from the last three sleepless nights.

Liam enters the room and closes the door behind him.

Suddenly, I have to take deeper breaths, and for some reason, none of my muscles feel right.

He smirks at me. "Are you *sure* the universe isn't trying to tell us something?"

Placing my hand over my eyes, I groan. "I'm sure. Just suck it up and lie down."

Liam sits on the opposite side of the bed.

I take my hand off of my eyes and turn to look at him. "What are you doing?"

"What a strange way to change subjects," he mutters.

"What?"

He clears his throat. "'Your father was part of the IAA, and Liam are we ready to enter the hyperfield?' That wasn't weird at all," he says sarcastically.

"She told me earlier he was someone high ranking in the Alliance. I wonder if he's still alive."

Liam finds the light switch and turns it off. A soft nightlight comes on, giving the room a blueish glow. I lie still in the bed, afraid to move. Afraid to breathe. Afraid I'll move in a way that he'll see as sensual and he'll get the wrong idea.

Liam clears his throat. "Mind if I take off my shirt?"

I raise an eyebrow and cough out a laugh. "Go for it. This is awkward enough already."

His grin transforms into an amused smile as he takes off his shirt. I try not to watch, but before I can tell myself to look away, he's already done. He climbs under the covers after taking off his shoes.

The room falls silent, and I glance at Liam to find him watching me. "Can you like, not stare at me while I'm trying to sleep?" I ask.

"Sorry."

I close my eyes and take a deep breath. I feel my chest rising, and I remember how revealing my sleeveless shirt is. I need to stop everything, stop breathing, stop thinking.

I turn toward him and open my eyes. The moment I do, his snap closed.

"I saw that," I whisper.

Liam raises an eyebrow without opening his eyes. "I'm trying to sleep. Why are you staring at me in my sleep?"

I roll my eyes. "I'm not."

"Good. Let's go to sleep then."

I glare at him in case he opens his eyes, but he doesn't. So again, I slowly let my eyes close. The longer they're closed, the more paranoid I get until finally I have to open them again.

His eyes close instantly.

I laugh. "Liam, by the stars, stop!" I push his shoulder a little.

Eyes closed, he keeps smiling. "I didn't do anything, I swear! Stop imagining things, and let me sleep!"

I close my eyes once again and wait for the paranoia to return. This time, I feel a tickling sensation on my neck. My eyes shoot open as I sit up, grinning. "Stop it!"

He's a lot closer now, and he presses his index finger into the back of my ribs.

My muscles spasm as if comforting electricity flows through my whole body. I fall over in a very uncomfortable position, with my neck flung backward and my back twisted away from him. "This isn't fair!" I say giggling.

"I'm just poking you!" Liam cracks up almost more than I am. "How does that tickle?" He pokes me again, just below my shoulder blade.

When my whole body jolts into kicks, I uncontrollably swing my arms everywhere, trying desperately to get him to stop. "Mercy!" I cry. "Mercy, mercy, mercy!"

Finally, he stops. He collapses on the bed next to me, still laughing, and the sound makes me laugh more, too. After a minute, we're finally able to stop and breathe, but my smile doesn't fade.

"I'm sorry. I just needed to see your smile again." He smiles back at me.

I meet his gaze. "Thank you."

"Do you wanna go to sleep now?"

"I think we'll both need that."

I turn on my side so that my back is to him, and I finally let my eyes close. Surprisingly, I'm not uncomfortable. In fact, it feels good lying next to him. I listen to his breath slowing down, feel his muscles relaxing as he falls away from me into the realm of dreams. For the first time in three days, I'm able to drift off into the gentle darkness of my mind.

Sleep is sweet, and the horrific nightmares that usually appear don't come to me. My eyes flutter open slowly, and the room readjusts before me.

It's dark, and Liam isn't next to me anymore.

Even with the blanket wrapped tightly around me, I'm cold. I wish he would make me laugh and smile all over again. To take all the weight of the world off my shoulders.

The door opens, and Liam walks into the room. He has his shirt on again. He doesn't turn on the lights, and instead, he just gazes at me.

"How much longer?" I ask. "How long did we sleep?"

He smiles gently. "We have about ten minutes, maybe a bit longer. We're about to enter the atmosphere. Did you rest well?"

I nod sleepily. "I did, surprisingly. Did you?"

"Nah." He moves closer to me. "I was mostly staring at you."

I laugh and glance to the wall behind him, feeling a little too awkward to meet his gaze just yet. Liam laughs too, and gently touches my bare arm. Somehow I'm trembling. Not obviously, I hope. I almost shiver, but I feel warm at the same time. I swallow hard and meet his eyes. His handsome smile nearly makes me lose the strength to stand.

"You know that whatever happens out there, I'll always be by your side, right?" He asks seriously. His hand moves a little farther up my arm, onto my shoulder.

I nod, warmth coursing through me. "Of course," I manage in a murmur.

Liam looks down into my eyes. He's so close. My hand reaches around his waist, I'm not even sure how. I'm not in control of my own body, but I like it.

His arms wrap around me too, and our foreheads touch, our eyes close. I feel his breath on my lips, and I realize I'm not the only one trembling. Reaching my other hand into his soft hair, I want to cry. Why does this feel so right?

"What are we doing?" he whispers. His words brush against my mouth as he speaks.

"I don't know," I reply, just as soft. "But I like this." His lips close around mine, and everything feels perfect. I lean into him as I draw him closer to me. There's no space left between us, and still I try to pull him closer. He squeezes me so tightly in his arms. My heart is pounding furiously, I hear his breath, fast and warm against my cheeks. Our lips part only to reconnect again and again, by the stars I don't want this to ever end.

I feel myself falling, but I don't care. He pushes me against the wall and I wrap my arms around his neck. I'm still not close enough. I realize how much I love his lips, soft, warm, and comforting despite the severity, almost violence of our kisses. And I don't give a damn about this prophecy, about the Resistance or the Alliance, as long as I have him in my life, I know everything will be okay.

Liam holds me tighter in his arms, like letting go would destroy us. And maybe it would.

His lips follow the line of my jaw and down to my neck. My whole body tingles, and suddenly there are tears in my eyes, falling down my cheeks.

He stops. "What's wrong?"

"I'm so afraid."

Liam gently pulls away and looks down at me. He's breathless, and I can tell by his face that he'd much rather continue our session than talk, but he doesn't try to kiss me again. I wish he would. His eyes betrays all the kindness and goodness in the world. In that single look, I see how much he truly cares for me.

He holds me close a moment and brushes a strand of hair out of my eyes. I realize my hands are trembling still. "Whatever happens, you have me. You have your mom, you have Shirez, and…and you also have Dragon."

My face is wet with tears.

Liam brings me in, but instead of kissing me, he just holds me.

"Thank you," I breathe.

He squeezes a bit tighter. "No. Thank you for that amazing, sexy kiss."

I choke out a laugh. He kisses me on the forehead.

The lights turn on by themselves, and the floor jolts slightly beneath us. We're landing.

"You're gonna be okay. Oh, and don't forget your shirt. Here." He grabs my shirt off the bed and hands it to me.

I put it on quickly then dry my tears. "You'll come with me, right?"

"To the ends of the earth."

I open the door. We head out into the cockpit as my mother finalizes the landing sequence.

When we touch down, Amara shuts down the ship and stands to face us. "Did you rest well?"

"Really well," I reply.

She touches my shoulder. "Are you ready to discover who you are?"

I take a deep, shaky breath. "I'm ready."

"Let's get this over with," Liam says.

Amara nods for us to follow behind her. Liam and I move together. She opens the ramp, and we make our way down onto a stony pathway. The air is fresh, earthy. Beautiful golden flowers flourish in the reddish gravel. Liam taps me gently on the arm and points ahead.

Beyond my mother, a temple is carved into the base of two mountains. It's all the same color as the rusty gravel, except bright yellow, orange, and green painted areas brighten the place. Statues are carved into higher areas of the mountains, and the closer we get to the base, I see that the eyes, mouths, and parts of the arms or legs of the statues are tiny openings. In those openings, small figures sway back and forth in yellow robes. Atop each mountain, there is a shiny sort of disk, but I can't make out what it is from this far away.

"We have been waiting for you," a deep, wise voice says.

Many villagers in yellow robes stand before us. How long have they been there? Why didn't I see them before?

The small, bald man in front has golden-brown skin that seems to shimmer slightly in the sunlight. His face is wrinkled, yet his dark, sapphire eyes betray a youthfulness I cannot possibly understand. His bright yellow robes are rimmed with a deep red. The skin on his arms is much less wrinkled and tattooed with beautiful, intricate designs. In the middle of his forehead, there is the smallest tattoo of all–a seemingly perfect circle. Inside are two oversimplified fish-like shapes. One is right side up, the other upside down. The first has a black circle for an eye. The second has a black body, and the circular eye has no color. The design captivates me, and I struggle to look away as he approaches. His presence is the most comforting I have ever known.

My mother gets down on one knee, and Liam and I follow suit.

"Daliv Yuna," she says respectfully then stands. "This is my daughter."

"I can see the resemblance," Daliv Yuna replies. "I am happy to see you are free. Come with me, and we will discuss matters privately."

My mother inhales sharply, as if she's going to say more, but she sighs, and we follow him.

He takes us to the temple. The floors are some sort of jade, more brilliantly green than the jungle trees on Virana. None of us speak as we trail behind him through the simple halls. Finally, we reach a room with three other Daliv people. Two are women, and one seems to be much younger, with only a few wrinkles in her golden-brown skin. The tattoos on her arms look more colorful. Both of the women are bald, too.

Daliv Yuna faces us as the doors behind us close, seemingly on their own.

"We are the four most advanced Daliv," Daliv Yuna says. "We have all seen the same vision, as have many other Dalivan before our time."

Amara nods and takes my hand. "Masters, your prophecy about my daughter was correct. In trying to save her, I damned her to live amongst enemies without a mother. Your words are the reason I tried so hard to protect her."

The younger Dalivan woman nods, smiling sadly. "Your futures are always in motion. You will often meet your destiny as you try to run from it."

Amara squeezes my hand tighter. "It would've helped to know that beforehand." There's a slight harshness in her voice.

The older woman cocks her head, her expression emotionless. "We do not always see the path you take toward your future. We only see the outcome."

Amara's hand is sweating, and I can tell she's nervous. I squeeze back gently, hoping she finds comfort. "We have come to see if the second half of your prophecy is true," she says. "We want to know if she is the Light that you speak of."

Daliv Yuna's eyes rest on me. He seems peaceful, like he has discovered the secret to eternal happiness. Maybe he has. "That is only up to her."

I release my mother's hand and step forward, kneeling before Daliv Yuna. "With all due respect, if your prophecy is correct, it seems I have no choice in whether or not I am part of it."

"Rise, my child," Daliv Yuna says in the sweetest voice. "It is true that you have no choice in being the embodiment of the Light, but if you do not accept the Light into your soul, if you choose to reject who you are, you may run as free as you can be living in a lie."

I stand but keep my eyes down. "If I am the Light, what is my destiny?"

"Ah." Daliv Yuna sighs. "That is the trouble. We cannot show you your destiny until you have accepted the Light into your soul. We know what the Light is meant to do, but every choice you make will affect what is to come. Do you understand, child?"

I glance back to Liam and my mother. Both look onward with love in their eyes.

"What is my destiny when you see me now?" I ask.

"You are undecided, child," Master Yuna replies gently. "At the moment of choice, there is no visible future. No one can create a future for you but yourself. It is true that we can see the future, but we cannot make the future happen. That is up to you."

"A few days ago," I start nervously, "my friend was dying in my arms. I placed my fingers on his wound, and warmth and light flooded my soul. When I opened my eyes, he was healing. He would have bled out aboard the ship, but he survived because...because of whatever happened."

Daliv Yuna grunts gently. "For a moment, your kindness overpowered the denial of who you are, and so you were able to give him life."

"If I accept that I am the Light, will I be able to save more people? I will not hurt anyone with my power, so if I am destined to do some terrible deed, I will refuse that fate. I will run from it with all my heart." My voice trembles with emotion. "I will only accept if I can save more people, if I am not destined to hurt anyone else."

Daliv Yuna turns to look at his fellow Dalivan. The other three nod slowly to him.

Daliv Yuna smiles. "It seems you just did."

For a moment, I can't breathe. "Wh-What do you mean?"

"You have accepted the Light into your soul," the younger Dalivan woman says. "You are now the embodiment of the Light. You are hope, kindness, and love."

I can't feel my heartbeat. Maybe it has stopped altogether. Or maybe it's racing too fast. "I'm the Light? Just like that?"

Master Yuna nods. "Your destiny awaits." He closes his eyes, inhaling slowly, and then opens them. "I apologize, Amara Indera. Only the Light and Liam Rodan may be present."

The hairs on my arms stand on end. Liam was never introduced.

My mother steps forward and puts her hand on my shoulder. "I'll be right outside the door. Be brave." She exits the room, and the large, wooden door closes softly behind her.

"Why am I allowed to be here?" Liam asks as he moves to stand by my side.

Daliv Yuna blinks at him. "It has been foreseen. Now we will reveal your destiny."

Liam looks at me nervously, and I meet his gaze with faith. I have to have faith.

Daliv Yuna steps in line with his three fellow Dalivan. They join hands and sink to their knees. Their eyes close, and their heads bow down so they face the ground.

The room is silent for a momentary eternity.

Then in unison, their necks snap backward, forcing them to face the ceiling. Their eyelids open all at once, and a white light shines from their eyes. Their necks are bent unnaturally, but together, they speak.

*"Two worlds will come forth and converge
When tyranny and Shadow come to reign,*

*The child, lost, will find their way,*
*From the ashes, Light will rise again.*

*The Dark will choose his worthy one,*
*Acceptance must be within their soul,*
*For Light and Dark long to converge,*
*As every half yearns to be whole.*

*Upon the Mountain of Shadows,*
*The tyrant will fall victim to the price.*
*One pure of heart, and soul of Light,*
*Will make the final sacrifice.*

*And in the Land of Night and Day,*
*The Shadow will recall Initial Sin,*
*The Dark will cross into the Light,*
*And Ona's final battle will begin."*

The Dalivan relax, and their heads face the ground once more. When they look up at us, their eyes are back to their normal color, and they do not move or speak in unison.

Daliv Yuna stands, walks up to me slowly, and takes my hand in his. "Lost child of the Light, nail this prophecy into your mind. You must never write it down, for it may fall into the wrong hands as it had centuries ago. Promise me."

I nod quickly, but I cannot speak.

"My child, your destiny requires the deepest love and the greatest sacrifice. You will bring hope to those who have none. This is your future." Daliv Yuna squeezes my hand in his. "Jaina Indera, henceforth, you are the healer. The defender. The giver of love, kindness and hope."

In the mess of fear, I remember Liam's words. *Being fearless is just having no fear. There is nothing noble about that. Bravery is being afraid and still facing your fears because that's what's right.*

And in his words, I find courage.

Daliv Yuna bows his head. "Today, you have become the Light."

"No." I smile. "Today, I realize I always have been."

## END OF BOOK TWO

# ACKNOWLEDGEMENTS

I really want to thank my mom, for reading all the drafts of this book and supporting me through everything I had to get through to finish this. I also have to thank my dad. Even though he didn't think I'd ever finish this book, he kept me inspired and determined during the whole process. Another huge thanks goes to Nicole Zoltack, my trusted and wonderful editor, for helping me fix all my crazy errors!

Thanks to Alyssa McKendry, Ryan McKendry, and Lara Klaber for being so awesome and helping me edit. Also huge thanks to my beagle, Rory, for being so cute and cuddling next to me all the time when I write.

Thanks to all the people in my life who make life so incredibly interesting, I love you all very much (you know who you are).

I also want to thank all my family, friends, and fans who have been so supportive and excited for this book to come out, I'm sorry it's a couple years late!